Praise for *The* ◁ P9-DWH-123

"[May Alcott's] adventures illuminate the world of intrepid female artists in the late 1800s, a milieu too little appreciated today. *The Other Alcott* comes alive in its development of the relationship between Louisa and May."

—*The New York Times Sunday Book Review*

"Hooper is especially good at depicting the complicated blend of devotion and jealousy so common among siblings. . . . A lively, entertaining read."

—Stephanie Garber, *New York Times* bestselling author of *Caraval* and *Legendary*

"A fascinating concept, and just the way to kick off your celebration of the 150th anniversary of the publication of *Little Women*."

—Historical Novel Society

"This title is not to be missed by the classic's many fans, who will want to get an insider's look at the real people who inspired the March family."

—*Library Journal*

"If you loved *Little Women* (or even if you didn't), this engaging take on the real-life relationship between the Alcott sisters will fascinate and inspire. More than ever, we need books like this— in celebration of a woman overlooked by history, one whose story helps shed light on our own contemporary search for love, identity, and meaning."

—Tara Conklin, *New York Times* bestselling author of *The House Girl*

LEARNING TO SEE

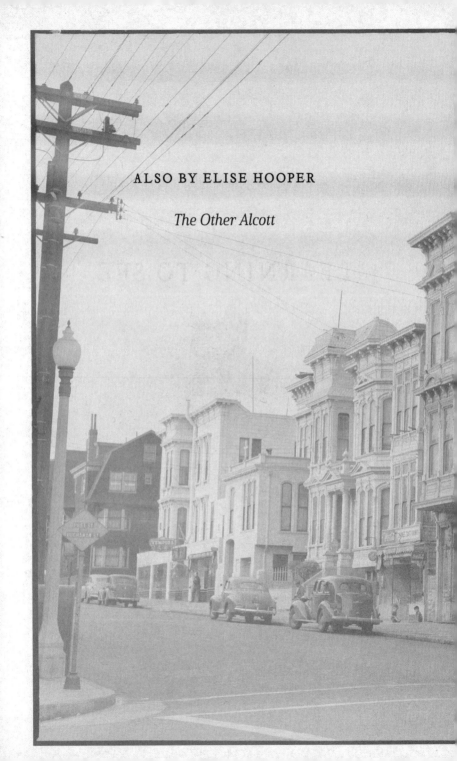

ALSO BY ELISE HOOPER

The Other Alcott

LEARNING
to
SEE

A Novel of Dorothea Lange,
the Woman Who
Revealed the Real America

Elise Hooper

WILLIAM MORROW
An Imprint of HarperCollinsPublishers

For Kate and Cookie.
I love you both.

P.S.™ is a trademark of HarperCollins Publishers.

HarperCollins books may be purchased for educational, business, or sales promotional use. For information, please email the Special Markets Department at SPsales@harpercollins.com.

FIRST EDITION

Designed by Diahann Sturge

Title page photo and chapter opener art © National Archives Catalogue

Library of Congress Cataloging-in-Publication Data has been applied for.

ISBN 978-0-06-268653-4

19 20 21 22 23 LSC 10 9 8 7 6 5 4 3 2 1

A NOTE FROM THE AUTHOR

Not many people's "real" lives translate perfectly into a dramatic arc that's ready for a novel. Events must sometimes be compressed, characters must be combined or omitted, dialogue imagined—all of this is the work of the novelist. Even a life as remarkable as Dorothea Lange's needed some reworking to create a clear emotional journey, so I must point out that *Learning to See* is fiction inspired by the life of Dorothea Lange. Through careful research, I assembled a time line of her life and steeped myself in her motivations, fears, and dreams, and deepened my understanding of the historical period and the people who touched her life. In the end, I stayed true to the basic contours of the historical record but allowed my imagination to create a story about love, art, and an indomitable spirit.

April 1964
Berkeley, California

CHAPTER 1

The envelope arrives on one of my good days. From my spot in the kitchen I hear the mailman's footsteps on the front walk and the click of the mail drop's lid, but then the phone rings, distracting me. When I lift the shiny black receiver to my ear, the coolness of it against my skin almost makes me shiver.

From across the phone lines, Imogen's unmistakable gravelly voice rasps, "I'm coming over to see you in an hour but can only stay for twenty-five minutes. From your house, I'll catch the bus over to Telegraph Hill."

"How about sometime next week instead? We're leaving for Steep Ravine later this afternoon. The house is a mess."

A pause. "Mess? Your house is always neat as a pin—I don't believe you for a minute. Are you unwell? Just yesterday when I was downtown, I saw that husband of yours. He couldn't bring himself to say your ulcers have been acting up again, but he hemmed and hawed enough that I know something's up."

"Oh, pish. I'm going great guns." This is a lie, but I don't have it in me to say anything more. "It's just that we're leaving once everyone returns from the store."

"All right. But I'm coming to see you when you're back in town. Take a look at your calendar. Go on, right now: pick a day so you don't forget about me."

Though her pestering usually makes me bristle, I soften. Through the years—developing our careers, beginning marriages, raising children, making ends meet, and ending marriages—our friendship has persisted. Honestly, its endurance amazes me sometimes. Friendship has none of the trappings of marriage—no ceremonies, no certificates, no children to keep it glued together—but it's this very precariousness that makes it so special. I've come to believe the test of a friendship lies in its ability to withstand bruises and wounds yet still persevere for no other reward than the comfort and joy each person finds in the other. "For heaven's sake, how could I ever forget about you?"

"Good question. Now if only the darned photo editor at *Vanity Fair* felt the same way." She raises her voice in breathy imitation, "'Oh, Miss Cunningham, I'm terribly sorry I forgot to return your call. We've been tied up in meetings all day.'" She snorts. "I'm in my eighties, and *I've* got a better memory than these whippersnappers. I tell you, these office girls, all they think about is the fella they're going out with that evening, what color they're going to paint their nails, how they're going to get their hair done next. Why, when we were their age, we were much harder workers, don't you think? We didn't take a damned thing for granted."

I nod my head in agreement, chuckling. "True, but I wouldn't wish what we went through on these kids. Plus, it probably wouldn't have killed us to have gotten our hair done every once in a while."

She lets out a squawk, spluttering about "wasting money."

"All right, all right. When I'm back, I'll call you and we'll figure out a day to visit. I can pick you up so you don't have to take the bus."

"But I like taking the bus. You wouldn't believe all of the interesting people on it."

"Interesting? God help us. But fine, the bus it is. I'm looking forward to seeing you."

"Sheesh, you sure sound it."

We both laugh before saying goodbye, and we're as good as new. Lord knows we've gotten used to each other's prickles over the years. Highs and lows and then some, but I consider myself lucky enough to have been blessed with two great friendships, both very different from the other, but each grand in its own way. Whenever anyone points out that I'm being difficult, I think of the loyalty of these two women; it's all the evidence I need to know that there must be *something* redeeming about me.

I scoop up two cans of sliced peaches off the counter, treats for the grandchildren, and place them into a wooden crate lying on the counter. When I straighten, a pain sears through my stomach, causing me to gasp and bend over. Poor health has plagued me for twenty years now, but this is something new. Something foreboding. Something that makes me think this is the real thing. The thing that could finally win. From my huddled-over position, I survey my kitchen, looking for items that still need packing, but everything is precisely where it should be. My teak bowls from Thailand catch the light and glow next to the sink. The white countertops gleam, nary a crumb in sight. I catch sight of my black leather camera bag next to the crate and sigh, closing my eyes. Imogen's right. We did work all of the time. And while it was wonderful, heady, and stimulating, all of our earnest conversations about craft, the constant yearning to find the right shot, the sense of accomplishment when the negative revealed exactly what I hoped, and sometimes even more—all of that work came with a price.

The pain in my stomach recedes like a tide pulling back and I straighten. The mail. I nearly forgot about it. Holding on to the kitchen wall, just to steady myself, I make my way to the front hall, bend over, and pick up the pile of flyers, bills, and magazines scattered under the mail drop. Within the mess, a bright white envelope stands out from the rest. Its paper, still crisp and stiff, speaks of heft, substance. I study the return address:

The Museum of Modern Art
11 West 53rd Street
New York, NY 10019

The black font, simple and elegant, makes my breath catch. Holy smokes. I return to the kitchen holding the envelope in front of me and open a drawer to find my letter knife lying where it should be. Pausing for a moment, I swallow before tearing a slit across the top to lift out the letter within.

After I read it once, I read it several more times, letting the words sink in. My hand lowers to my side, the paper rattling in my quivering fingers. Sucking in a deep breath, I fold the letter back into the envelope before nudging it into the pocket of the merino heather-gray cardigan sweater I like to wear when we go to the beach. Though there's still a list of things to be done before we leave, all thoughts of packing have scattered from my mind. As if in a trance, I walk out the kitchen door and through the backyard to reach my studio. I let myself in and sink onto one of the director chairs pulled up to my work counter. Through the nearby open window, there's a creaking sound of the oak trees swaying in the breeze. Otherwise, silence abounds. I'm suspended in a weird space of inaction, a paralyzing inability to think.

I lean over to open a drawer and retrieve a file. *California, 1936.* Black-and-white photographs spill out across my worktable. Faces of men, women, and children. All as dry, dingy, and cracked as the land in the background. I glance at the other folder tabs. *New Mexico, 1935. Texas, 1938. Arkansas, 1938. Arizona, 1940.* I've visited so many states, taken thousands of photographs. They gave a face to the masses struggling to make ends meet. They started conversations. Few would argue that my work wasn't important and useful. And while I don't regret my choices, I'm saddened that I've hurt people dear to me. Can I find peace with the sacrifices I made?

Within several minutes, the high pitch of young voices trills from the house. Everyone is back from the store. A spell has been broken. I rise, touching my hand to my pocket to feel the envelope. I push it down deeper into my sweater and walk toward the house.

May 1918
San Francisco, California

CHAPTER 2

Fronsie hustled toward me, a troubled look on her face, but I looked away. I just needed one more blessed minute to get a little coffee into my system, to start my brain moving. Leaning back in my seat, I took a long sip, breathing in the bitter, smoky aroma with satisfaction. It didn't taste particularly good, but it would do. If nothing else, it tasted better than the mud we'd been choking down in the dining car aboard the Southern Pacific for the last few weeks.

"Dorrie," Fronsie whispered, having circled our table to come up behind me and tug on my shoulder. "Dorrie!"

I lowered the white enamelware cup on the red-checked cafeteria tablecloth and turned to look up at her pretty face, normally pale and smooth as the inside of a cockleshell, but now pinched in concern.

"What?"

The way she looked down at the floor made me realize she was not about to complain about the runny scrambled eggs or the toast that tasted like pine shingles.

"It's our money." Her lower jaw slid back and forth, as if trying to dislodge something stuck in a molar. Her lip began to quiver. "My wallet. It's gone. Our money is gone."

"Our money . . ." I repeated. My hands clutched the edge of the table as I pushed out my chair and struggled to my feet. "What?"

"Someone must have picked my pockets as we ate," she said, her voice high and fast.

I looked away, searching the crowd surrounding us, but nothing appeared amiss in the room. Women sat in clusters around circular tables, their heads bent over plates of eggs, toast, and bacon. Given the early hour, the hum of conversation was still subdued. The scent of Ivory Flakes and rosewater wafted off all the freshly scrubbed faces. Nothing appeared amiss.

"I'm so sorry, I'm so, so sorry. I don't know how . . ." Fronsie mumbled, wringing her hands together as she spoke.

I looked into her big blue eyes—those eyes that could stop men and prompt them to offer us directions, martinis, rib eye steaks, whatever we wanted, now welled with tears as she grabbed her stomach, gasping, "I think I'm gonna be sick."

Without a word, I pushed her toward the door behind us to drag her outside. No wonder we were easy targets for a pickpocket, I realized, given our proximity to the entrance of the cafeteria. In and out—that's all it took for someone to make quick work of our savings. I rubbed circles on her back as she retched against the brick exterior of the building. With one hand still on Fron, I dug into my purse with the other and counted three dollar bills along with some loose change in my wallet. Three measly dollars. What rotten luck. I inhaled, trying to block out the sound of poor Fron's misery.

"I think that's it," she said, straightening and wiping her mouth with a cambric handkerchief she pulled from her pocket. "Oh Dorrie. Our boat . . ."

We both looked down the street in the direction of the Bay. All our hard work . . . $570. Gone. I stepped forward to the edge of the sidewalk, blinking in the bright sunshine. Since our arrival the previous night, everyone had been telling us May tended to be foggy. But the sky, clear as a promise, glowed cerulean blue overhead, and the smell of sawdust hung in the air, along with the tart sting of new paint. Across the street, men in dungaree overalls swarmed a construction site, causing a caterwaul of hammering and sawing. San Francisco was a city on the make.

From behind me, Fronsie moaned, "What should we do now?"

My gaze landed on a clump of bougainvillea spilling down the whitewashed side of the stucco building next to the cafeteria. The pink flowers gleamed brighter than any billboard advertising the merits of California, as if saying, *Look at us. We found a crack in this wall, took root, and now we're thriving.* I smiled. Even the name of this place was exotic. Like a flower. *Camellia. Gardenia. California.* I whispered the word again— *California*—letting the syllables glide around on my tongue. It had a far better ring to it than *Hoboken, Harlem, Hackensack,* or any of the places from back home.

I wheeled around to face Fron. "What about staying here? We could get jobs. See what happens." My words surprised me as they came out of my mouth, and for a flitting moment, I wanted to stuff them back inside.

"See what happens?" Fron repeated, her expression incredulous.

"Things could be worse," I stammered. "What if this had happened in Yuma?"

"You're serious."

"I am."

"But what about our plans? All of our efforts to go off on a grand adventure. You're not sore we won't be celebrating your birthday aboard a ship to Hawaii?"

I stepped back to where she leaned against the brick wall, twisting her handkerchief, and rested my back next to hers. True, we would no longer be setting sail for Honolulu on Thursday. We would no longer be departing America for foreign ports, for our grand tour around the world. The last year of working long days, of forgoing pleasures for the sake of saving our money—all of that disappeared with some vamp with sticky fingers. And yes, regret stung inside my chest, but I pushed it away. All I knew was that I could not go back home. I reached for Fron's hand. "This place could offer us a fresh start. I'll ring in my twenty-third birthday here."

"Well, it's not what I pictured, but I suppose we can give it a go." She tented her palm over her eyes and craned her head toward the Financial District. From across the street, a man noticed us, stopped his hammer in midair, and whistled. I glowered at him, but Fron, smoothing her hair, smiled and said, "At least the fellas here are handsome."

"Right. Now let's hoof it back to our rooms and figure out a plan."

"What would I do without you? You're right, things could be worse," she said, before wrapping her arm around my shoulders and starting to sing Marion Harris's song "I Ain't Got Nobody Much," gazing at her reflection in the store windows we passed.

> Now I ain't got nobody, and nobody cares for me!
> That's why I'm sad and lonely,
> Won't somebody come and take a chance with me?

Her voice sounded clear and lovely. We *were* both lucky to have each other. Fron was the grease to my wheels. Whenever I had an idea, I could count on her to set things into motion. Years ago, I had snuck out of the front door of Wadleigh High School for Girls and been brought up short to find Fron leaning against a lamppost across the street from the huge building where we were both supposed to be parked in a geometry class.

"Hey, took you long enough," she had said.

I looked around. Was she talking to me?

"Yeah, you. I've been waiting for you."

"For me? Why?" Girls like her weren't usually interested in girls like me. "What do you want?"

"I've seen you cutting class."

"So?"

She grinned. "I want in. You seem interesting," she said, matter-of-factly handing me a roll of Life Savers. I peeled one from the top and popped it into my mouth, clicking the candy against my teeth while watching her out of the corner of my eye as I considered this development. A breeze blew down the sidewalk, causing bits of trash to swirl in a small tempest. Gusts sent scraps of paper flying into the air, only to collide with my black-wool-stockinged shins and cling to them. I stood stork-like, trying to push the paper off my left leg with my right foot while attempting to maintain a sliver of nonchalance. Through all of this, somehow Fronsie's blond waves remained unmoved, smooth and glossy; her long, slender legs stayed free of stray garbage. She exuded perfection and control. She could have whatever she wanted and for some reason she chose me. But I never asked why again. From that day on, we were inseparable.

As we walked toward San Francisco's YWCA, a young fella slowed as he neared us, wolfish, appraising Fron's willowy figure. She was looking in the other direction at a store window filled with calculating machines and typewriters so he gave me a saucy wink instead. By any standards, Fron was the looker whereas I was short with bobbed brown hair and a withered right foot, but still, I had nerve, which we were going to need, judging by the three lonely dollar bills in my wallet. I smiled tightly, pressed myself closer to Fron, and sped up our pace, despite my limp.

WE ARRIVED AT the YWCA and pushed through the front door into the parlor, where we found Mrs. Weber, the house matron, account book in hand, scowling. "Vat brings you girls back so soon? You have your ship tickets already?" Her tone was surly, her German accent more pronounced than before, each syllable clipped. When we took our rooms the day prior, she had done little to hide her skepticism of our plan to travel around the world. "Da last thing I need is a pair of angry fathers or husbands spitting nails and making a scene in here over der missing girls." Only by adding a little extra money to our nightly rate as "insurance" had we convinced her that we weren't runaways.

Fronsie smiled sweetly, but started blinking her eyes as though she might begin weeping. Leave it to her to pull out a bit of theater. I held back a grin as she spoke in a quivering voice, "Oh, Mrs. Weber, why, we've just had the most dreadful turn of events. We've been robbed!"

"Robbed?" the older woman repeated, looking us up and down with narrowed eyes.

"Yes, at the cafeteria you recommended. But have no fear, we are fine and plan to remain here in San Francisco. I mean, one bad apple can't ruin this whole place for us, right?" The downward set of Mrs. Weber's mouth made it clear she believed bad apples to be in abundance, but Fron kept up her prattle. "The only thing is, we have very little money now and need permanent quarters. Someplace affordable *but* safe and befitting two respectable young women."

"Vithout letters of assurances from your families, no one in der right mind will take you two in. At least, not da type of establishment you vant." She folded her arms across her chest, tucking the ledger against her bosom.

"Well, the good news is that Dorothea and I are very employable. I worked at Western Union in New York City and was employee of the month back in February. I have a letter of introduction and the boss promised me a job in any of its offices around the world should I ever want one. I'm going to visit the office here later today to inquire about resuming my employment."

Mrs. Weber grunted and turned to me. "Vat about you?" she asked, making a point of eyeing my right foot dubiously.

I felt my face flush and shoulders tighten, but Fron took my hand firmly in hers and leaned in to speak conspiratorially. "Dorothea is very talented. She's trained as a professional photographer, so it's just a matter of time before she owns a successful studio here in the city. Just think: you'll be able to say you knew her! What luck for you." She straightened up, looking as if she hadn't a care in the world. "Now, where do you recommend we look for longer-term rooms? With your high standards, I have no doubt you'll steer us in the right direction."

Fron's friendly voice took the edge off my resentment, but it still simmered as I watched Mrs. Weber nod as she put down her ledger on a side table. She scribbled on a corner of paper, ripped it off her book, and handed it to Fron. "See dat you two have new rooms by tomorrow." She shook her head at us. "And my girl is scrubbing at da front stairs, so don't go making a mess of her work. Take da back stairs up."

Fron nudged me past her and we walked through the door into the kitchen and its stink of onions and liver. My stomach turned at the sight of a platter of raw brats lying on the counter, glistening in their fleshy casings. We climbed the stairwell until we reached our room on the second floor. I sat on the edge of the bed, fingering the thin seersucker quilt as Fron shut the door behind her and leaned against it, a bemused smile on her face. "I thought you were going to blow a fuse on that old battle-ax."

I shook my head. My gaze dropped to my feet. I flinched at the sight of my practical black boots next to Fron's stylish heeled Keds. My withered right lower leg looked pathetic. I hated that it gave people a chance to doubt me.

She dropped to the bed beside me. "Pay no attention to her."

"Thanks, but we better hightail it to Western Union and see about a job for you. At least one of us needs to be employed by the end of the day."

Fron nodded and reached into her purse. "At least I've still got these," she said, holding out her sterling silver cigarette case toward me. I slid one out with a grateful nod. Tucking it into the side of my mouth and using both hands and a whole lot of elbow grease, I jimmied the one small window between our twin beds open while she fished around for her lighter. The satisfaction of lighting up underneath the handwritten ABSOLUTELY NO SMOKING sign posted next to the window made me grin. We sat on the sill, alternating turns exhaling out the window.

"So, what kind of a job are you going to get?" Her voice had a careful edge to it that belied the casualness with which she asked the question.

From the alley below, doors slammed and men called to each other in languages I didn't recognize, no doubt preparing midday meals for the handful of restaurants in the area. The yeasty smell of freshly baked rye bread made my mouth water. "Not sure. I don't want to work as an assistant to a portrait photographer anymore. I've done that already. Twice." I took a deep drag, absorbing the feeling of smoke burning down my throat, the fine line between pain and pleasure.

Wham! Our door banged open. There stood Mrs. Weber, hands on hips, face purple with anger. "I knew I smelt smoke!"

"Say now," Fron began to protest. "You can't just barge—"

"Out! Both of you. Right dis *instant*! Dis city almost burned down once, you fools!" She raised both her fists toward us, trembling in fury. The pale face of the kitchen girl gaped at us over Mrs. Weber's hulking shoulder.

Fron and I looked at each other, aghast. Tossing the butts from the window, we scrambled to our feet. Fron said, "You can't—"

"Out!" Mrs. Weber bellowed again. She picked up Fron's suitcase and tossed it into the hallway, where it landed with a clatter. Silk stockings and a couple of shirtwaists spilled across the hardwood floor. We grabbed at our remaining items scattered around the room. A hairbrush, Fronsie's shower cap, my slippers. Tossing everything in my suitcase still at the foot of my bed, we scurried past Mrs. Weber, pausing only to shovel Fronsie's possessions back into her suitcase and snap it closed. We fled down the stairs and out onto the street, cringing as the heavy oak door slammed at our backs.

Shaken, I turned to Fron, knowing my face looked every bit as white as hers. "Well, I guess I can't be picky about my next job."

In the distance, church bells clanged for a noon Mass. The day was getting away from us. Fron fell to her knees, unclasped her suitcase, and riffled past a herringbone wool skirt and a felt cloche until she pulled out an envelope and held it to her cheek. "Oh, thank goodness, I still have my Western Union letter." The relief stamped across her face morphed into horror as she patted her pockets. "But oh no! Where's the boarding-house list?"

We both looked back toward the closed doors of the YWCA. No doubt the scrap of paper lay fluttering around on the stairs like a feather fallen from a bird in flight, but there was no chance either of us would knock on that door again. Not if we wanted to live another day. What now? Evening would arrive before we knew it. Where would we spend the night? My heart thudded in my ears. *No, no, no, this isn't the way our adventure ends.* I tried to quell the panic rising in my chest. *Think, one step at a time.* Then I reached for Fron's shoulders and looked into her red-rimmed eyes. "This isn't your fault. No more tears. Let's go to Western Union and get you a job."

I stood, pulling her up with me and slapping the dust off her skirt as she ran the backs of her hands across her cheeks. I hated to see her look blue. This was *my* fault. Fron, beautiful Fron, she could have been back in New York City choosing a handsome beau from a long line of suitors if she hadn't left it all behind. She could have married any of the dapper bankers or lawyers who'd come knocking—and there were so many of them, all their knocking had practically chipped the paint off her parents' front door—but Fron was a gal who never failed to surprise me. She had it all: good looks, smarts, and a sparkling personality. But rather than taking the easy road to settling down, she claimed she wanted some adventure first. Well, I was dishing that up for her in spades.

"Jeepers creepers, why is everything in this city uphill?" Fron huffed as we pushed ourselves up the street after asking a store clerk where we could find the city's Western Union office.

"But the fellas are mighty handsome here, remember?" I asked, forcing a laugh. Fron joined me, her laughter real. She could move from anxiety to confidence with an ease I admired. "So, when we get to the office, I'll wait outside with our suitcases while you go sweet talk your way into a new job."

"You're not coming in too?"

I smiled at her. "I know what you'll do, and you'll be swell. March on in there and act like you own the place. We don't want them to catch a glimpse of our luggage and see how desperate we are, do we?"

Fron shrugged. "I suppose not. Okay, I'll do it."

"Atta girl," I said, pushing up my sleeves and switching my suitcase to the other hand. The early afternoon sun beat down on my back, making a steady trickle of sweat drip down my spine. My head throbbed from the clanging of the street traffic, yet we continued to trudge along. We had to catch a break soon. Didn't we?

CHAPTER 3

True to form, Fronsie landed a job at Western Union without even breaking a sweat. She emerged from the shop's doorway, a triumphant grin on her face. I knew exactly what had happened: while leaning onto the counter, gazing up at the saps behind it, she had held out her arm, dangling her letter of reference from the New York office, her long, pale fingers cradling her chin. The manager's mouth would have fallen open, as he wished it was his hand caressing her cheek. She probably topped the whole thing off with a winsome smile and batting her lashes. The girl could always be counted on for an impressive show.

"I know I've told you this a million times, but your talents are wasted," I said, glancing back at the shop, expecting to see all of the men's noses pressed to the glass. "Why aren't you onstage?"

"Oh heavens, you know I want nothing of the sort. I'm just a simple girl." She flipped a penny into the air and caught it with the same hand. "Just want to find and marry the man of my dreams and settle down."

"Well, at this rate, you sure are going to break a bunch of hearts on your way to the chapel." My stomach growled. Breakfast had been ages ago and supper hour neared. "How 'bout we find a bite to eat before we figure out where to look for a lodging house?"

Fron snapped her fingers. "For once, I'm a step ahead of you. I told the boys at Western Union I was looking for new digs and one of 'em has a sweetheart who lives in a good place. He gave me the address." She slipped a strip of paper from her breast pocket with exaggerated ceremony.

"Quick thinking." I reached for the paper, but she held it aloft.

"You know, it wouldn't kill you to add a little sugar to your own act."

"What?"

"I'm just saying, you're so determined to get what you want. Your headstrong ways worked in New York, but you may need to sweeten things up a little out here." Her smile never faltered, but she fiddled with her pearl earring, a nervous tic if I ever saw one. "Maybe we should go back to Western Union and get something to hold you over until your game becomes clearer."

I pressed my lips together before speaking, my voice firm. "I'm going to open my own portrait studio." But even as I said it, I doubted myself. How was I going to pull this off? The only

San Franciscan I knew, Mrs. Weber, had just thrown me to the curb. With no knowledge of this city, no contacts, how was I going to make things happen?

"But . . ." She stopped next to a store window and whistled. "That outfit is the cat's meow." My gaze followed her pointing finger and landed upon a shop mannequin modeling an emerald-green hobble skirt made of silk with a matching batwing chiffon blouse.

"Don't try to distract me," I grumbled, but momentarily blinded by the sun's glare on the window's glass, an idea flickered through me. "Wait a minute, let's go in."

"Now you're talking!"

I pulled on the brass door handle to enter and stepped onto a marble floor with Fron trailing me. The din of Market Street's streetcars banging along their tracks receded as I took in the rows of pastel walking suits and silk evening gowns.

"Welcome to Eaton's. May I help you find something?" A young woman with dark hair styled into perfect marcel waves appeared before us.

"May I look at your business directory?"

Her carefully arched eyebrows knit together. "Our business directory?"

"I'm looking for a store that specializes in photography service and supplies."

The woman smiled. "Hon, you don't need a directory for that. I'll tell you where to go: Marsh's, farther that way on Market." Her crimson lacquered fingernails fluttered toward the door. "Head outside, turn left, and you can't miss it. It's where everyone goes for cameras and film."

I thanked her, pried Fronsie away from caressing an oyster-colored linen suit, and steered us out of the store. Though every ounce of me wanted to head straight to Marsh's, I knew we needed to find lodging before it got much later. We bought a couple of apples from a corner grocery and headed toward the address Fron had written down at Western Union. Biting into the crisp skin and hearing the crack of the fruit's flesh brought tears to my eyes. Lord, I was hungry. I paused midway up a steep block to catch my breath and nibble my way around the fruit's core.

"I almost swallowed mine whole." Fron giggled. "So, the address should be right . . . *here.*" She pointed to the brass numbers tacked to the wooden doorframe of a narrow brick building. We rang the bell and a scowling dark-haired woman came to the door. While Fronsie spoke, her Western Union letter pushed out in front of her chest like a parade flag, the boardinghouse matron frowned. "Sorry, no rooms available," she said, pushing the door shut right on our noses.

Fron spluttered in indignation, but it was too late. The lock clicked inside.

"Well, let's try another place," I said, guiding her elbow in my hand and leading her down the steps back to the sidewalk.

"What other place?"

I sighed. My stomach let out a low moan. If anything, the apple seemed to have awakened my belly to how hungry I felt. "There's got to be something else around here. Keep a lookout for any signs advertising rooms to let."

We made inquiries at four more lodging houses. Each time we were told no. Unused to being refused, Fron tightened. Her shoulders worked their way up to her ears and her tone became high-pitched, a little more frantic with each attempt. "Why on earth is this happening?" she gasped to me as a fifth door closed upon us.

Violet light filled the evening air though the streets still bustled with people as if it were midday. Despite the late hour, the city crackled with energy. Nighttime would be upon us soon. I had seen the way each rooming mother gave my gimpy leg the side-eye. I knew what they were thinking: *If she's damaged on the outside, imagine what's wrong with her inside.*

"Come on, we will find something. We have to," I said over my shoulder to where Fron stood wilting like a daisy in need of water.

A white placard dangled off a nail toward the end of the block. I rapped on the door. A small woman opened it, her hair covered in a paisley-patterned scarf. Fron opened her mouth to speak, but I cut her off. "We've just arrived from New York and are interested in your room." No theatrics, no flirting, we just needed a place to sleep. As I spoke, the scent of oregano and garlic seeped past me, thick enough that I could have wrapped my hands around it. I gasped and almost lost my balance as I leaned into the delicious aroma. The woman caught my arm.

"New York?" she asked.

I nodded.

She said, "My two sisters live in East Harlem. You're far from home." With a pitying pat on my shoulder, she gestured toward the back of the house. We staggered in, our suitcases clunking against our kneecaps, past the grim crucifixes dotting the hallway, past the peeling wallpaper and into a poorly lit kitchen. Moments later, our chins only inches from the rims of our plates, Fron and I bent over steaming homemade spaghetti noodles swimming in thick red sauce. Our new boarding matron explained the terms of our room while we shoveled the food into our mouths faster than you could say *grazie*. She wore a severe expression, but as she scooped more food onto our plates, satisfaction danced in her dark eyes.

THAT NIGHT I dreamed of being tied up in a dark place. I attempted to cry out to Mother, but only a gasp emerged. Father? Where was he? Bound into place, I felt intense heat flame inside my skin; I bucked and writhed, trying to escape my capture. I awakened, my nightgown and sheets drenched in sweat, and sat up gasping, throwing off the sheets clumped around my arms, legs, and ankles.

Across the room, Fronsie lay sleeping on her back in the other twin bed, her breathing steady, her long limbs graceful in their effortless sprawl. I could practically reach out to touch her pale shoulder, given the floor space between us was scarcely larger than a bath mat. I raised the window shade to let the glare of moonlight fill the space around us. Pushing away strands of my hair plastered to my damp cheeks and forehead, I placed my palm on my chest. Beneath my skin, my heart beat with the fervor of a hurricane. I stared at the cracks in the plaster wall beside me, breathing hard. *One, two, three.* By counting the lines rooting up to where the wall met the ceiling, I steadied myself.

That dream hadn't visited in months, maybe years. But even though I was almost twenty-three, it still possessed the power to transport me back to my terrified seven-year-old self, trapped in the feverish ravings of my sickroom and my bout with polio.

I wriggled my misshapen foot out from the sheets, staring at how the light fell upon the spaces between my rigid toes, the way my foot curved inward. I could travel anywhere in the world but this would remain with me. This was the part of home that I could not flee. I'd trained myself to walk in a way that disguised my limp and could wear trousers that covered the awkward bend of my lower leg, but I was stuck with that foot, no matter how hard I worked to hide it. I pulled off my sweaty nightgown, tossed it on the floor beside me, and stretched out my arms and legs against the scratchiness of the pilled white sheets. I yanked down the window shade, curled back into bed, and closed my eyes, listening to the mournful lowing of foghorns coming from the Bay.

CHAPTER 4

The following day I met Fronsie during her lunch break so we could stroll over to Marsh's to see about a job for me. We paused on the sidewalk to check my reflection in a store's window. Rows of straw boaters, bowlers, and wool fedoras floated beyond my face as I surveyed my appearance. I frowned.

"Here, let me help." Fron angled my chin toward her and grazed my lips with a small metal cylinder.

I pulled back. "What are you doing?"

She grinned and winked. "Look at this," she said, showing me the cylinder and sliding her index finger up and down the side of it to push a small nub of what appeared to be dark red lip rouge into view. "It's called a lip-stick. Fancy, do you think?"

I wrinkled my nose. "Too fancy for me."

She sighed theatrically and pouted, tucking the cylinder

back into her purse. "Fine, but at least let me do this," she said, reaching forward to pinch my cheeks.

"Ouch."

"You have great cheekbones."

"They're not cheekbones. I think it's baby fat. My face is too round."

She rolled her eyes. "You're a knockout."

We faced each other for a moment without saying anything before she nodded at me. I took a deep breath and turned toward the store. We entered to see a display of steamer trunks of varying sizes piled upon one another. Racks of film and frames lined the wall at the rear of the store. Behind the back counter stood a man with a dour expression and thinning, dark hair plastered over the pale dome of his head. A weak chin and severe underbite accentuated his long nose. He reminded me of the large rats I'd seen back at the wharves in Hoboken, boldly scuttling across the shipping pallets in broad daylight.

I walked over to the counter. "Excuse me, but are you hiring?"

He appraised me up and down, pausing on my trousered legs. "Looks like you might be cut out for a different type of place. Perhaps a hardware shop?" He reached into a bin of envelopes and flipped through them in search of something. When I didn't move, he added, "Do you know anything about photography?"

I stepped close to the counter and rested my palm on it decisively. "In New York, I worked in the studio of Arnold Genthe."

"Huh, the same Genthe who used to run a portrait studio here on Nob Hill?"

I nodded, making sure to keep my face unexpressive, aware that looking eager would give this man too much power. "I know how to develop from negatives, make prints, retouch, and mount."

"What's your name?"

I hesitated, struck by unexpected inspiration. "Lange. Dorothea Lange." Behind me, Fronsie shifted but I kept my eyes locked on the man, hoping she would stay silent. She did.

"Well, we're busy here and my last girl just quit. Pay's ten dollars a week."

I'd made fifteen a week for Genthe and twelve at Kazanjian's but couldn't let this opportunity slip by. I needed it. Swallowing back the tinge of pride that made me want to negotiate, I nodded. "Shall I come tomorrow?"

He bobbed his chin at me. "You're a feisty little thing, aren't ya?"

"I'm new in town, just trying to get settled."

"All on your own?"

"No, I'm here with a friend." I pointed to Fronsie, who was wandering around the racks of frames. "We were on a trip around the world, but have decided to stay." I said this, eager to show off our independence, but as he looked back and forth between us with a sly grin, I got the feeling I shouldn't have revealed so much.

"Doors open at nine. Come fifteen minutes early through the employee door in the back. You'll see it off the alley. Tell 'em Dwayne Keeler hired you and your name's on the list."

I nodded. Walking away, I felt his gaze crawling over me. I slowed my pace, holding my head high, but his voice called out again.

"Hey, what's with the limp? You gimpy? We're busy here, everyone's gotta pull their own weight."

I stopped, silently cursing my foot, and hesitated before looking back over my shoulder at him. "I dropped a suitcase on my toe yesterday."

He cocked his head but nodded before giving a slow lick to his index finger, watching me as he did so. The gesture prompted the hairs on the back of my neck to rise, but I said nothing more. I nodded to Fronsie, and we retraced our steps through the store and exited without saying a word. It wasn't until we reached the end of the block that I said, "So, now we both have jobs."

She dipped her head soberly, confirming my uneasiness that my position at Marsh's felt uncertain, my new supervisor untrustworthy. "Why did you say your last name was Lange?"

I sighed and looked down the slope of Market Street toward the Bay, glimmering in the distance. Our move to California offered a fresh start, a new life. Here, my father didn't abandon me. Instead I was abandoning him. The only way to free myself from those memories was to keep moving forward. "It's my mother's maiden name. No more Nutzhorn. I'll never be known as Dorothea Nutzhorn again."

CHAPTER 5

It didn't take long for me to figure out where I stood with Dwayne Keeler.

But first, I delighted in the metallic smell of developer and fixer that wafted toward me when I approached the photography counter on my first day at Marsh's. During my trip westward with Fron, I had imagined photographs of the scenery we passed. When we got on a train in New Orleans, I framed the beautiful women preening on the French Quarter's cast-iron balconies; the slash of Texas's endless brown horizon; the jagged lines of New Mexico's red mesas; the crosses of the saguaro cacti in Arizona—I imagined composing all of these images from the airless stifle of a second-class train compartment. But now at Marsh's, surrounded by film and other photography supplies, I ran my index finger along the handmade

Japanese photo paper, testing the texture and comparing the surfaces. I studied the images that customers turned in, relishing in the unexpected scenes that appeared within stacks of photographs.

In the darkroom, I learned about my new home by inspecting the ghostly images of the city that darkened into sharp lines and inky shadows as they floated in developer. I felt omniscient. I could see everyone and everything. From the blank fog of white photography paper, images of the city's beaches and parks emerged, yet the landscapes were often devoid of people. In San Francisco there was the sense of space, rugged terrain, and open land not yet hemmed in with people, even though paradoxically another common theme of these photos was development. Judging by the number of ribbon-cutting ceremonies I sifted through, the city had been growing and building since earthquake and fire had leveled it a little over a decade earlier. I was also astounded by the number of automobiles that appeared in photos. Roadsters, sedans, coupes, and phaetons—the drying line in the darkroom almost resembled a Ford catalog. It seemed everyone in California spent their leisure time driving, and when they weren't driving, they were posing for pictures in front of their automobiles.

Yet the magic of the darkroom became something worrisome whenever Dwayne Keeler hovered nearby. For the first few days we worked side by side unspeaking, but his silence carried a weight, a warning. In the dark, I felt him watching me as I pushed photo paper into the developer to let it ripple in the gentle waves. When I'd pull the paper out, each drip echoing in the pan became an ominous sound, like the steady rhythm of a ticking clock, and although I wasn't sure what the countdown was for, I sensed Keeler biding his time for something.

I didn't have long to wait.

On my fifth day at Marsh's, I was in the darkroom enlarging a print. I bent over to find a new carton of photographic paper underneath the worktable. When I straightened, Keeler lunged behind me, unyielding, in a way that forced me to slither upward between him and the tight space of the counter. He pressed into my back and whispered, "You're still limping. There was no suitcase accident. You a cripple?"

It was his use of the word *cripple* that made me freeze, squeeze my eyes shut, and stay silent. It brought all earlier humiliations roaring back: Mother's insistence that I hide my foot; tight expressions on my neighbors' faces whenever I appeared on the sidewalk; the whispers of my classmates. Back home I had been evidence of contagion. Since then I'd masked my limp, but San Francisco's hills were taking some getting used to. The climb to the new rooms I shared with Fron at the top of a four-story walk-up made me weary. I'd become less careful than usual. My gut sank as I realized there was an insistent hardness pushing against my backside. I steeled myself. I was trapped and Keeler knew it.

He shifted his head so he was breathing rapidly into my ear, a hot, damp breath that made me shudder with revulsion, but fighting every instinct, I stayed immobile and stared straight into the darkness, my knees clenched together. My trousers couldn't be yanked up easily like a skirt, but nausea burned in my throat. His hands groped around the front of my pants while he rubbed against me. Finally, when I sensed him weakening, I pushed back from the counter, sent him stumbling, and dashed toward the door.

Outside of the darkroom, I gasped and reeled past the counter toward where the suitcases stood, gleaming in rows like soldiers at attention. I leaned my palm against the solidity of a heavy steamer trunk to steady my legs. The brightness outside the store beckoned me. I could walk outside and never see Dwayne Keeler again. But then I took a deep breath. Though I could still feel his hardness and his pathetic contortions against my back, I was still in one piece. I rolled my head side to side, feeling the tendons of my neck and shoulders stretch. I made a decision. *There's no chance I'm letting him run me out of here.*

"Excuse me, you all right?" A man appeared and he studied me, eyebrows arched in concern. "You're white as a sheet." I blinked and nodded, shrinking back. "Sure you're okay?"

He wore a worried expression but nodded in an attempt to cue me into agreeing with him. His kindness brought me back to solid again. My shoulders loosened and my voice sounded normal when I said, "I'm . . . fine, thank you for asking."

"Good, because I'm not the fellow you want in a crisis. I get scared at ghost stories and faint at the sight of blood."

I surprised myself by laughing weakly.

"My wife is definitely the one we want around here if there's a crisis. She can set broken arms, make up a plaster for hornet stings, and stitch up a wound. She's much more helpful than I am."

"Is she a nurse?"

"God no, she's a photographer. In fact I'm here to pick up an order for her. My name's Roi Partridge."

Talking business brought everything back into focus. We walked to the counter, where I pulled a file box toward me to find his order. Sure enough, there was a manila envelope with his name. I held it in front of me, peeking inside to confirm the contents. "Right, I remember these. Your wife's photos are top-notch."

"Oh, are they?" He folded his arms across his chest, amused. "What's so good about them?"

"Well, I like the informality of how her subjects are posed." Since Keeler still hadn't emerged from the back, I opened the envelope and a handful of photos tumbled out onto the counter. I studied an image of two seated young boys, both wearing alert, amused expressions as they looked into the camera. Light from an adjacent window poured across the two bodies, creating a rectangle of illumination underneath their legs and arms. The lighting was beautiful, and his wife captured the spontaneity of their expressions and postures so naturally. I was charmed by the way neither boy seemed aware of the photographer, how they appeared engrossed in their own discoveries. Everything that happened moments ago in the darkroom faded away when I looked at the photos.

"Any mother would love to have these. Are these boys the reason your wife's so good with crisis?"

"Yep." Roi chuckled. His bushy light brown hair threaded with gray made him look disheveled and playful. "You're not the usual gum chewer they keep around here, huh?"

"Nope, guess not."

"You take an unusual interest in the work."

I swept the photos back into a pile to push into the envelope. In the time we had been chatting, a sense of daring had replaced how rattled I'd felt after fleeing the darkroom. It was time to focus on what came next. "I'm a photographer too. Just arrived from New York." Saying the words aloud made me feel like a new woman. I pushed myself off from the counter and stood a little straighter.

"New York City?"

I nodded.

"That so? What makes a bright young thing like you decide to head west to parts unknown?"

"I needed a change of scenery."

With that, he threw back his head and laughed, long and deep, before saying, "Don't we all?"

I introduced myself as Dorothea Lange, and he explained that he did lithography work for an ad agency over on Sansome Street and was creating some billboards for Marsh's. As Roi told me this, Keeler came out of the darkroom. My expression must have darkened because Roi looked at him carefully, as if studying a glass plate negative for cracks.

"Keeler, you finally have someone here who actually knows about photography."

My boss nodded, feigning disinterest as he pored through customer photos, but from the way he glued himself to the counter just a few feet away from us, he was listening to our every word.

"I've got an appointment in Mr. Marsh's office upstairs to show him some mock-ups of the billboards so I should get going, but I'm going to tell him what a fine hire you've made, how Miss Lange here is a real professional." At this compliment, I couldn't help but smile at Roi. He continued, "And, Miss Lange, you need to come to dinner to meet my wife. How about this Thursday evening—"

I accepted before he finished speaking.

After Roi sauntered off with a cheerful goodbye, I looked over to see Keeler's face puckered in annoyance, but he said nothing. He kept his distance from me, but I knew it was just a matter of time before the old lecher pulled some other funny business. I needed to get out of that place. Fast.

THREE EVENINGS LATER I slid off the black leather seat of Roi Partridge's Model T and stepped out onto the sidewalk in front of his bungalow in Oakland. Before opening the latch on the front gate, I undid the buttons on my cream-colored wool cardigan. On the ferry boat, about halfway across the Bay, it had become about twenty degrees warmer. We had emerged from the tendrils of low fog, and San Francisco vanished behind its cloudy layers like something from a fairy tale.

I walked up the front pathway and a shadow appeared behind the screen door. "You must be Dorothea Lange," a woman's voice said.

I laughed. "The one and only."

She stepped outside, studying me as I walked up the stairs. "I'm Imogen Cunningham." It hadn't occurred to me that she would not have the same last name as her husband; I looked at her anew. She appeared to be about ten years older than me. Though she was plain as a penny and rather long faced, her gray eyes were sharp and bright, taking in every detail of me as I crossed the threshold into the house. Three naked toddlers crawled into the room and swarmed upon her, anchoring her to the spot by the door. I tucked my right foot behind my left, hoping to avoid close scrutiny. "These are our three sons. Gryffyd, Rondal, and Padraic. Lucky me, I have early crawlers."

I laughed. "Can you tell all them apart?"

"Barely. But see here, Gryffyd is almost three." She nodded to the boy worming his way across the plank floor as he stalked a spider crawling along in front of him. Deep in concentration, the boy held a small glass aloft over the poor creature. The two babies leaned against their mother's legs watching their brother, and she gestured at them. "This pair, Rondal and Padraic, will be one in the fall. All right, off of me now. Everyone outside."

Roi scooped up the babies, a tangle of glowing suntanned arms and legs, and headed toward a screen door at the back of the room.

"We can eat in the backyard, but the food's still in here. Come and help me carry it outside."

I followed her into the kitchen and picked up a milk-glass bowl filled with chicken salad. She led me out back, where we placed the dishes onto a round table set under an arbor of wisteria. Conical bunches of the lavender-colored flowers hung overhead, filling the air with their sweet fragrance. Though it was cooler out of the sun, I took off my cardigan and placed it on the back of a folding chair as I sat. This family charmed me. The idea of a husband and wife, both artists, seemed very bohemian.

She sat down across from me. "I'm glad to meet a new photographer in the area. Roi said you practically leapt across the counter with enthusiasm when he met you."

"I liked your photos, that's for sure. I'm not one for posing and draping, but it's not easy to get such natural shots of children at that age."

"Not unless you stick them in starched Sunday finery and bribe them with sweets. Then, sometimes, you might have a chance."

"Sometimes."

Across the yard, Roi played with the three boys on the grass.

Imogen served me a helping of chicken salad. "So, how did you get into photography?"

I looked away, self-conscious about my informal training. On the drive to the house after picking me up at the ferry terminal, Roi had told me all about his wife's background. She had studied at the University of Washington to better understand the chemistry behind photography, then traveled to Germany to study on an art scholarship from her sorority before returning to Seattle to open a photography studio. Before marrying Roi, she'd already had her work featured in several shows. Imogen was the real thing: an artist. How could I explain my own patchy background? How could I make skipping classes in high school to wander from Central Park down to the Bowery to watch people sound impressive?

Wiggling my finger upon the bowl of my spoon, I watched the handle tap against the tablecloth like a Morse code telegraph key. "Honestly, it was a bit of a whim. I decided I wanted to become a portrait photographer because I've always been interested in people," I hedged. "My uncles were lithographers, so there were already some craftsmen in the family. Everyone told me I had an eye for beauty. My mother viewed this as an unfortunate quality and thought me too much of a day-dreamer, but my grandmother encouraged my interest in fine things. So, I got myself a position as an assistant in Arnold Genthe's studio in New York and in a couple of other portrait studios before going to Columbia." I glossed over the fact that I had never graduated from college. "And now here I am. I've been too busy at Marsh's to create any of my own photos. I'm eager to get back at it, though."

Imogen tugged at her earlobe and grimaced. "I know what that's like. When I was cooped up here with the boys, I realized I was in danger of losing my marbles. So, I started photographing what was around me—the boys, the garden—and now I feel sane. Or at least saner."

"May I see what you've been working on?"

She studied me for a moment, glancing at my untouched plate before turning to her family still playing on the grass. "Roi, can you keep the bees away from the food?"

He grunted his assent. As we rose to walk indoors, she muttered, "I hope you weren't hungry. That wild pack will eat the whole spread while we're inside."

ON A TABLE in the corner of her living room, Imogen's photos lay in careful rows. Seeing them made a hunger rise up in me. How I longed to feel my camera in my hands again! Her work mostly consisted of photos of the boys, both inside the house and out in the garden. In her pictures, they played. For the most part, they ignored the camera, but sometimes they looked into it with clear eyes as if looking directly at their mother, not a machine. She captured their bodies, beautiful shapes within small spaces of light, and their expressions, content, curious, and full of mischief.

"They look like children."

She raised her eyebrows at me.

"I mean you have a real record here of who these boys are. When they've grown up, you'll look at these and hear them calling to each other, smell the grass on them."

Imogen looked back at the table. "You should come with me to next week's Camera Club meeting. It's in the city. You could meet with other photographers and have access to a darkroom. Who knows, maybe you'll be able to find a way out of Marsh's to do something else. I assume you want to get out of there?"

I nodded so vigorously I almost made myself dizzy.

"Of course. You're a woman who won't settle for filing negatives for long. San Francisco is just the place for you."

CHAPTER 6

A week later, I greeted Imogen outside the Ferry Building so we could walk to my first Camera Club meeting together. She pulled her boiled-wool jacket around her shoulders with one hand, a black leather folder clutched in the other. "Didn't you bring some work?" she asked, gesturing at my empty hands.

I swallowed. "I don't have anything recent."

She raised her eyebrows but said nothing. I wanted to kick myself for being unprepared.

We arrived at a nondescript building a block south of Market Street. Once inside, a few men gathered around the coffeepot greeted Imogen. When she introduced them to me, they nodded with interest. "Have you already hung your work?" one man with reddish hair asked, pointing to the far wall where photographs tiled the walls.

Imogen nodded. "I'm about to. Remember how last time we talked about cropping images close to abstract them? I've been experimenting with that idea. Here, let me show you." She started opening her portfolio to pull out images of maple leaves and succulents. "See? No fancy lens, no etching stylus." The plants took up the full frame, leaving no room for negative space. Cropped close to defy how the eye views an object, only part of each leaf was visible. The abstraction was modern and intriguing. The other photographers, mostly men, pushed past me to see. I tapped my toe and looked around the room. Who could I talk to? Who looked intriguing? Most important, who could get me out of Marsh's?

A few feet away stood a slim woman surrounded by another cluster of men. One of them scowled at her and said, "You went down to Portsmouth Square today? Are you nuts?"

Unfazed, she folded her arms across her chest. "Give me a break, I was wearing a face mask—there was nothing to be afraid of. I wanted some photos of the open courts and the pro- ceedings against Tom White. I needed to hear what the police were going to say."

A different man blew cigarette smoke out of the side of his mouth. "That case is a bust. The kid's guilty as sin."

She let out a short, amazed laugh. "Are you pullin' my leg? The case is no dud; he's been set up. The police are lying through their teeth. I've read their report. It's a load of bunk. Everyone knows it."

"It's dangerous down there. Doesn't the *News* have a fella they can send to cover it?"

At this, the woman's eyes hardened; she lowered her chin

as if steeling herself to run at the man. "Do you think it's dangerous because of the epidemic or because there are Negros there?"

"Aww, hell, Connie, don't get all hot under the collar. I don't mean to cross you, I'd just hate to see something bad happen, that's all." The man put out his hand and she paused before accepting it. With peace established, the cluster broke apart, everyone veering off in different directions, but I followed the woman to a table covered with back issues of *Camera Work*. She looked at me, and without waiting for introductions, waved a magazine in the air. "Have you seen this? I swear, Stieglitz is a genius."

I reached for the magazine. She handed it to me, pointing to a few abstract photos of Paul Strand's. In one, my eye was arrested by a stark white picket fence running along the foreground of a landscape shot. I shook my head. "I haven't seen these, but I just arrived from New York and have visited Stieglitz's gallery bunches of times."

"Really?" She extended her hand. "I'm Connie Kanaga. You're new here, huh?"

"Dorothea Lange." I pushed my hand out toward her, bobbing my chin to the men who'd just been circling her. "You sure told them off."

"They don't mean to sound like such grandmas but that blasted Spanish flu has everyone on edge. So, you're fresh from New York," she said, taking my hand and grinning. Her eyes were dark and wide-set, her complexion as clear and smooth as white marble. "And you're a photographer?"

I nodded. "I've taken a spot at the photography counter at

Marsh's while I get settled." I knotted my hands in the pockets of my trousers, but tried to keep my voice upbeat. "I met Imogen's husband, Roi, there."

Connie turned her head to find Imogen on the other side of the room, a determined expression on her face, hands gesturing at the photos on the wall. "Ahh, Imogen, she's a real pistol. Boy, she could talk technique all day long. She just lives and breathes talking craft. Bet my editor wishes I took more of an interest in that stuff," she said with a laugh, pausing to light a cigarette. "You know anything about newspaper work?"

"No, my background's in portrait photography. I'm looking to open my own studio. Figured working at Marsh's might lead to some connections."

"Huh." She surveyed the room and leaned in closer to me, lowering her voice. "Tell you what: there are some fellas here loaded with money. They're more dealers than actual photographers. Find them and convince 'em why they should invest in you. Could be your ticket." She bobbed her head toward a handsome blond man in a tan jacket. "See that one? He's got his fingers in all kinds of galleries in the city. Get close to him and who knows what could happen?" As we watched, the man grinned at the group he was talking to and clapped one fellow on the back. "But be careful what you offer in exchange."

When I got home that night, I found Fron lying belly-down across her bed, reading *McCall's* and waving her fingers in the air to dry her nail lacquer. If I needed to show up at the next Camera Club meeting with a portfolio of portrait work, surely her pretty face would increase the odds of me finding sponsorship. We spent the next couple weeks composing shots of her.

I developed them at Marsh's first thing in the mornings when business was slow. With Roi popping in frequently to visit, Keeler gave me a wide berth, though almost every day I found his cigarette butts floating in the developer pan I used. Like tea leaves at the bottom of a cup, they served as a message: it was just a matter of time before he tried more funny business.

By the time of the next Camera Club meeting, I was ready. I even let Fron work some beauty magic on me. With my hair waved and my lips colored in a pretty shade of raspberry red, and armed with a black leather portfolio filled with portraits of my gorgeous friend, I felt invincible.

That evening I sought out a couple of agents, lit their cigarettes, and reeled off my spiel, enticing them one portrait at a time. Since a keen sense of cultural inferiority nagged at the Westerners, I exploited my New York roots. I emphasized my Columbia photography classes and time spent with Genthe. The men agreed to meet for some dinners to discuss my plan more. All the while, I remembered Connie's warning and made sure to arrive early at these meetings to slip the maître d' some cash along with my request for a busy, well-lit center table and instructions for a signal I'd give so a taxicab would arrive for me exactly when our dinner ended. The last thing I wanted was to be stuck in a dark, out-of-the-way booth or receive offers for walks or rides home and be left vulnerable to advances I could do little to stop.

A few times I arranged for Fronsie to meet me outside the restaurant at an appointed time to escort me home. One evening I stepped out to find her waiting for me in a steady drizzle. "I suppose this matronly getup comes in handy during weather like this," she huffed, pulling her kerchief tighter around her hair.

"For Pete's sake, if they got a load of you, all of my work to avoid this trouble would be out the window in a second."

"But you'd have your funding faster than you can say '*cheese*.' All of this thinking ahead is a lot of work." Fron looked at me with a sly smile. "Say, why don't you just marry one of them and get the money that way?" When I rolled my eyes at her, she laughed and pulled me close. "Oh no, not you, Miss Lange, not you."

All of my planning paid off. I secured investment offers and managed to seal the deal. From there, I made the necessary arrangements. Fronsie and I found studio space on Sutter Street in the ritzy neighborhood of Nob Hill, two blocks away from the bustle of Union Square, and next door to a newly opened Elizabeth Arden salon. The whole operation was pricey, but if there was one thing that Genthe taught me, it was *Charge top dollar for your services and never apologize; people will respect you for it.* I crossed my fingers and hoped he was right.

DURING HER FIRST visit to my new studio, Imogen shook her head as she marched past the fountain in the courtyard and through the French doors to enter the reception area. Eying the stamped-tin ceiling, she trailed a finger along the carved whorls on the fireplace's mahogany mantel while making her way across the room. A shaft of sunlight stippled the Turkish carpet on the floor. She looked out of one of the tall windows before turning and asking, "Goodness, how did you pull this together so quickly?"

"The San Francisco Camera Club."

"I've been a member for years but have nothing like this."

I pulled open the curtain to let in more light. The fact was that Imogen and I spent our time at Camera Club differently. While she bickered with members over camera settings and composition, I'd been sniffing out opportunities. Imogen saw herself as an artist, I held no such illusions: I was a business-woman with a valuable craft. "I made sure to meet a couple of fellas who could sponsor me."

"But this place must cost a fortune."

"Don't fret, the terms are generous," I assured her, leading the way to the red velvet couch where I planned to start all of my client meetings. "I can do this."

Back in New York, I'd learned proof-making and retouching techniques, but what I had really learned was how to run a shop. By answering phones, booking appointments, and watching Genthe operate his studio, I learned how to select clients and pose them in flattering ways, how to hire staff and price my work, and most important, how to encourage my clients to refer their friends to me.

She ran her palms over the couch. Her frown faded into admiration. "It's lovely."

"Thank you," I said, turning to a barrel-shaped container sitting atop a wooden table next to us. Its brass surface gleamed. "And look at this."

"My goodness, what is it?"

"Fronsie found this at a fusty antiques shop over on Post Street. It's a samovar—to be used for serving tea. The seller assured us it's Russian, but who knows? I can get to know my customers over cups of tea and cakes from the bakery down the street. I want to make portraits that feel natural and intimate. Earning my clients' trust is important for that." I knew that with the right atmosphere, one that was comfortable and beautiful, I could build a business because women, often mothers, tended to be the primary clients of a portrait photographer.

She shook her head. Her teeth were long with gaps between them, and she possessed an unfortunate habit of sucking on them sometimes when she brooded. "Well, this all looks good. Do you have a darkroom?"

I pointed to a door that led to the downstairs basement. It was cramped but fit my equipment and had narrow windows for ventilation. "It's a vast improvement over my last darkroom in New Jersey. There, I worked in a chicken coop."

Imogen smiled, probably thinking I was speaking figuratively. I was not. In Hoboken, an unused chicken coop had sat in our backyard, and no one minded when I converted it into a darkroom. I wouldn't miss its low ceiling, walls of exposed nails, and the sharp lingering stench of ammonia.

"Well done. This place is no chicken coop, that's for sure. Now you just need to fill it with clients."

With the studio set up, my investors introduced me to members of San Francisco society. I developed a dependable roster of women who sought me out to photograph them and their children over the course of the next year. The gap between photographer and sitter turned out to be an easy one for me to breach because I found I had more in common with my clients than I would have imagined. These women, wives of the wealthy men who owned the city's newspapers, department stores, and law offices, were young and progressive, interested in art, culture, and politics. They'd arrive at my studio lugging garment bags filled with gauzy dresses and satin purses stuffed with dangly diamond earrings, emerald necklaces, and ruby stickpins. The women would spill their treasures across my red velvet couch and ask me what to wear. I'd move the gowns aside and steer them toward several dove-gray plain silk tunics I kept ironed in a closet. The most successful portraits, I assured them, were not meant to serve as evidence of their success. Those types of photographs were too old-fashioned, too much like portraits from the Renaissance of Italian noblewomen bedecked in all of their finery. No, instead I wanted to show them something new: a soft focus on the subtle laughter behind their eyes, the graceful curve of their shoulders, the tender way they held their children to their breasts. I wanted to show simple beauty, love, and individual character. Although sometimes they initially resisted, set on showing the trappings of their accomplishments, soon customers flocked to me for the naturalism that I promised. From there, it didn't take long before my customers were visiting at all hours, not necessarily seeking my services but to talk, to confide in me. They believed I saw them as individuals, not merely as prizes. And they were right, I did. It was a mutual respect. Even though these women were practically swimming in cash, they admired my independence and delighted in my singular vision of them as forward-thinking and artistic. I'd become a self-made woman.

In the evenings, my clients and artist friends would arrive at my studio. We'd roll up the carpet, put records on the Victrola, and set about to dancing, mad about Wilbur Sweatman's Original Jazz Band. We must have listened to "Kansas City Blues" so many times that the shellac almost wore off the record. Ah-yee, a lovely Chinese girl Fronsie hired to be my receptionist, would weave through the crowd serving slices of pound cake on a silver tray.

One night, with revelry well under way, I stood by the front door, watching everyone dance, and smoked a cigarette.

Connie Kanaga sidled up to me and held out a mason jar filled with a clear liquid. "Want some?"

"What is it?"

"Who cares?" She slugged it back and shivered before giving a little shimmy along to the saxophone blasting away on the Victrola. "Whew, it's pretty potent."

Memories of Grandmutter's stony stare and the insults she would growl after several glasses of brandy prompted me to wave off Connie's outstretched offering.

She leaned in closer so I could hear her over the music. "Guess what? I was doing some portraits today for Mrs. Hearst and she offered me a job at her husband's paper."

"Really? Did you take it?"

"Hell, no! I don't like Hearst's politics one bit. I can't work for him."

"So, the *San Francisco Daily News* is treating you well?"

She shrugged. "Well enough." She stepped back and patted down her black curly hair while looking around the room. We both leaned against the wall and I handed her my cigarette for a drag. Exhaling, she said, "Everything's pretty good right now. I've got a little portrait work when I want it and I've started spending Sundays with Louise Dahl. You know her? She's been at a few Camera Club meetings. Anyway, we wander around Russian Hill and take photos of whatever strikes our fancy. I'm allowing myself one day a week to experiment with whatever I want. You should join us sometime."

I blew out a long stream of smoke. Brown splotches from developer fluid stained my fingers holding the cigarette, evidence of my long days. Spending eighteen, maybe twenty hours at my studio had become a daily standard. "I can't. I'm too busy."

"It's amazing what you've built here, but you should give yourself some time to play around, find beautiful things. My work gets pretty stale if I just do the same stuff all the time. And portrait work, well, you know, you're always working with clients, trying to meet their expectations. It can get a little confining, right? Sometimes you've got to connect with that artist inside you again."

I almost snorted aloud. *Stale?* Work was anything but stale. A short article had run in the *San Francisco Examiner* a month earlier declaring me the most sought-after portrait photographer in the city. Since then, Ah-yee could barely keep up with all of the scheduling requests flooding the studio. Connie was probably making peanuts at the newspaper, so taking time off to connect with some sort of inner artist wasn't much of a trade-off, but it all sounded like something I could ill afford. I was making money hand over fist.

"Suit yourself. But you never know where you'll find inspiration."

I nodded, feigning agreement. But when I turned to snuff out my cigarette in an abandoned glass, my hand trembled. When was the last time I'd felt truly inspired?

LATER THAT EVENING, long after everyone had departed, I sat downstairs in the basement developing some work. As I rinsed fixer from one of the images, I heard *tap, tap, tap* overhead, but it wasn't the normal sound of a woman's high heels on the floor of my reception room. *Tap, tap, tap.* My hands hovered over the rinse bath in front of me. I looked toward the ceiling into the darkness. I tugged the paper out of the water, stood, and clipped it to the drying line behind me, still straining to hear the strange sound overhead as I scurried to climb the stairs. I pushed the door open only to find my reception and studio areas empty. I circled through the rooms, studying the floors as if expecting to see animal tracks. Finding nothing, I stepped outside into the courtyard and blinked my eyes to adjust to the darkness, listening to the sound of water burbling in the fountain while I pondered what I'd heard moments earlier.

"Dorrie?"

Startled, I jumped. Roi materialized near the art gallery next door.

"Sorry, didn't mean to scare you."

"Were you just in my studio?"

"What?" He looked confused. "No, I just dropped off some prints at a nearby gallery and thought I'd come by to see you."

I shivered and folded my arms across my chest, making some silver bangles I'd taken to wearing clatter as they slid up my arm. "Huh, the strangest thing just happened while I was working downstairs. There was an odd tapping sound, like someone walking across the floor, but on peg legs or something. Anyway, by the time I got upstairs to investigate, no one was there."

Roi drew nearer, looking around the courtyard. "Ha, bet

that was Maynard Dixon in his cowboy boots. I'm surprised I didn't pass him on my way here."

I blinked, trying to place everything I knew about Maynard Dixon, one of the city's celebrated artists. His prints and paintings were everywhere. From *Sunset Magazine* to Jack London novels to Standard Oil ads, all kinds of outfits hired him for his illustrations. He was known for his depictions of the American West of everyone's imagination. Noble Indians, rugged cowboys, galloping stallions, all of that. According to rumors, he'd stopped doing ad work to focus on his paintings, big canvases with cumulus clouds hovering over mesas and mountains and craggy landscapes glowing in bold colors. He had real vision and distinct artistry. I'd seen the man once at a gallery opening on Post Street but kept my distance, intimidated by the way his light blue eyes roved the crowd intently, belying the boredom his tall, droopy stance implied. "Why in the world would Maynard Dixon come to see me?"

Roi chuckled. "I can think of a few reasons." He shook his head. "Oh boy, Imogen will give you an earful about him."

He continued to tell me about some of the work he was doing at the agency, but I barely heard a word. All I could think about was Maynard Dixon and the way the tanned skin at his throat glowed when he threw back his head for a deep laugh, the kind of laugh that made me smile even though I hadn't heard the joke. Something awakened inside me that I hadn't even known was sleeping. Would he come back? I hoped so.

CHAPTER 7

The next afternoon, I was reviewing several invoices when Imogen stopped by my studio. She studied some of my recent portraits tacked up to my board and glanced at the clock on Ah-yee's desk. "You've forgotten about the Camera Club meeting tonight, haven't you?"

"Oh horsefeathers, I did. I'm afraid I can't go," I mumbled, running my index finger down the following day's list of appointments. I smacked my palm against my forehead. "Good grief, I meant to grab something for Sophie's birthday tomorrow. She's coming in to have her portrait done."

"You're giving her a gift?"

"Well sure, we've become friends over the last year."

Imogen sniffed before walking over to the samovar to fix

herself some tea. As a little liquid spilled from her cup to the floor, she let out a string of curses. Ah-yee swooped in with a rag to soak up the small puddle while Imogen moved aside, shifting from foot to foot. "You're always too busy for Camera Club these days."

It was true. I hadn't been to a meeting in months. Business was keeping me hopping. And furthermore, I didn't enjoy the meetings. I could tell my commercial success put off some of the men who had been working for a long time. They viewed me as a hack. After all, what did I know? I was just taking pictures for rich people. All of their talk about artistic philosophy and technique made me feel inferior and bored me to tears. The people who I liked from the group, Connie and a few of the fellows who had initially invested in me, often visited my studio, so there didn't seem to be a need for me to go to Camera Club anymore. "I've been tied up lately."

"These days it seems you're a businesswoman more than anything else."

Despite her criticism, I didn't want to see her go. She could be tetchy, but I knew if I was patient, we could have an enjoyable afternoon together. "Do you want to stick around? I can make more tea, turn on the Victrola?"

Surprised, her expression softened. She reached out to let her fingers graze my cheek. "I don't mean to be such a wet blanket. Keep doing what you want to do, but I should go."

We smiled at each other. She patted my shoulder and said, "If I get there and that Ansel Adams is yammering on about Yosemite, I'm likely to go plum crazy. Really, it's all he can talk about."

"You can always come back here."

"Thank you, I just might. You're a dear," she said, pulling her portfolio off the floor and waving goodbye.

LATER THAT EVENING, Ah-yee wished me a good night as she gathered her handbag. She paused, framed in the wide doorway of the reception room, and giggled at the sight of me, sitting on the floor of my studio surrounded by photos. I called goodbye before turning my attention back to the pile of prints I was organizing into stacks around me. *Good, bad,* and *maybe* piles. The *bad* pile grew frustratingly high. Perhaps an hour passed before I heard *tap, tap, tap* coming from the courtyard in front of my studio. The front door opened, revealing a tall, lanky man with a silver-handled cane wearing black cowboy boots, a black ten-gallon hat, and a black cape—*a black cape*! Who on earth would wear such a thing? Maynard Dixon, that's who. On anyone else, his getup would have looked downright crazy, but somehow he pulled it off. It must have been his confidence: the way he hung his thumbs on his belt, how he draped himself against the doorjamb, the crooked grin that spread across his face as he held my gaze.

"Evenin'. I'm Maynard Dixon."

I said nothing but raised my eyebrows. He scratched his chin before saying, "You Dorothea Lange?"

"I am."

"You're not an easy lady to find."

"I'm always here. Maybe your tracking skills need work."

"That so?"

"I heard you stopped by for a visit last night." I made my

voice cool, as if celebrated male painters visited my studio every day. "I was downstairs, working in my darkroom."

He nodded slowly, left his post by the door, and circled around the reception area before pausing in front of the Russian samovar. "What in the devil's this contraption?"

"It's for serving tea. Want some?"

He cocked his head from side to side, taking it in, and gave a low chuckle. "I'm not much of a tea kinda fella. Got anything stronger?"

"There's probably something with a little more firepower in the sideboard over there."

When he saw me starting to rise, he raised a hand. "Stay put, I didn't mean to interrupt you from working. Want something to drink?"

"No, thanks, but please help yourself."

At my refusal, he stopped and glanced at me before veering away from Ah-yee's desk to enter my studio and appraise the portraits spread around me. He dropped to the ground and leaned against the wall with long, slender legs stretched out in front of him, ankles crossed. He picked up a few of my photos and studied them.

"Are you interested in having your portrait taken?" I asked.

He raised his gaze from my work, his eyes glittering with mischief. "Nope."

"So, this is a social call?"

"Something like that," he said. Though it was November, the skin of his face still glowed with color from the sun. White crinkle lines etched around his eyes, giving him a weathered finish. "Do you always grill visitors like this?"

"Not always," I said, my heart hammering in my chest. We held each other's gazes straight on for a moment, before he waved back at the entry.

"Doesn't seem safe to leave your door unlocked with you in here all by yourself."

I considered his point. "Until you showed up, it's never been a problem."

With that, he leaned back his head and let out a deep rumble of laughter. His eyes closed, and his long dark mustache bobbed as his narrow chest heaved up and down. I laughed along with him. I wished my camera was within reach to capture the unself-conscious expression of pleasure dawning across his face, across his whole body. As he reached the end of his laughter, still smiling, he sighed with satisfaction and slapped his thigh. "Guess I had that coming," he said, rising to his feet with the same fluid ease I imagined he could mount a horse or slide down beside a campfire.

Still seated on the ground, I tucked some hair behind my ear, flustered at the disappointment I felt as he took a few steps toward the door. He paused and turned back to me.

"I reckon you're gonna start locking that door now?"

I pretended to give thoughtful consideration to his question before shaking my head. "Nope."

"Atta girl." He grinned, winked, tipped his cowboy hat at me, and was gone.

MUCH TO MY relief, the following day was filled with portrait sessions, one after another, giving me little time to dwell on Maynard Dixon's visit. Friends started arriving as evening fell. Our usual routine commenced: the carpet was rolled back, someone put a record on the Victrola, and Ah-yee appeared with a tray of little powdered lemon cakes. All evening, I couldn't keep my eyes off the door, but Maynard's tall, lean silhouette never appeared. Annoyance seeped through me. *Why did I get my hopes up?*

Around nine o'clock, Fronsie and her handsome new beau, Jack, arrived. Her eyes glimmered with a spark. Something was up. We'd barely been talking for a minute before she thrust her pale hand out at me. "Look!" she said. On her finger, a diamond ring dazzled, catching the streetlights from the window, the rays refracting onto my shirt as I admired it. "I'm going to be Mrs. Stockton." Jack looked pleased as punch as she nuzzled into his shoulder.

"Isn't that ducky?" If my voice sounded flat, the loud music covered it up and the darkness shadowed the stunned expression I knew to be written all over my face.

Fron turned to the group and prattled on about how Jack had surprised her earlier that evening with a proposal. While everyone leaned in to admire her ring, I edged backward until I was against the wall. Had it even been a full month since she'd told me about going to a dance hall one evening after work and meeting a handsome fella who told funny jokes? Since then, stories of him peppered our recent conversations, but I must not have been paying attention. She had gotten serious about him and I'd missed it. Work had been consuming me. I waved my hands around to clear the cigarette smoke clouding the air and watched as they leaned into each other to kiss. The crowd cheered. Tears blurred my vision. After all of this time, she was going to leave me.

Someone turned the music louder and people started dancing.

"Hey, pal, you all right?" Jack came to lean against the wall beside me. I nodded. He looked back at Fronsie, who was dancing with a friend, and wonder widened his kind, dark eyes as he drank her in. "Can't believe I found such a swell girl. I promise I'll take good care of her."

At that, tears spilled from my eyes, but I brushed them away. Without looking at me, he held out his handkerchief. "Sometimes smoke makes my eyes water too."

I chuckled, taking it gratefully, and said, "She's lucky to have you."

TUCKED IN OUR little side-by-side twin beds later that night, Fronsie sighed. "I think it was my destiny to meet Jack."

"Really?"

She propped her cheek on her palm and looked at me. Her fair hair gleamed silver in the moonlight reflecting through the crack between our Swiss dot curtains. "Oh, absolutely, he is the *one*."

I raised my eyebrows, both intrigued and skeptical. Bunching the pillow up under my head, I gazed back at her. "You've had a line of beaus behind you like ants trailing a piece of cherry pie for as long as I can remember. Do you honestly think there's just one man out there for you?"

"Oh yes, I just know it in my gut. It sounds corny, but everything about Jack feels right." When I remained quiet, she asked, "Don't you think there's someone out there just for you?"

I made a noncommittal sound, glad for the dark as I pondered this idea. The thought of one person out there for me felt terrifying. It was too specific. Too limiting. What if we failed to cross paths? What if something happened to that *one*?

"Oh, there's someone out there for you. I know it." Fronsie rolled onto her back and stared at the ceiling as if her sense of resolution settled everything.

I tipped away from her and squeezed my eyes shut. Destiny didn't sit well with me. I hated to think anything about my future was fixed. The idea of a master plan lurking beyond my control, beyond my reach, alarmed me. I wanted to be able to change. I wanted options, a measure of control. But at the same time, I wanted mystery. Was that too much to ask? Life needed to stay interesting and keep me on my toes or otherwise what was the point?

CHAPTER 8

About a week later, after the room cleared from another one of my parties, I sent Ah-yee home. I wanted to have the studio to myself for a bit. Ever since Fron had announced her engagement, I'd felt out of sorts. Looping around the reception area picking up stray cigarette butts and straggling jars of liquor, I stooped over for an abandoned pocket watch and straightened to find Maynard standing in front of me.

"Goodness," I said, raising my hand to my heart. "You frightened me."

"Did I? You don't seem like one who frightens easily." He reached for an abandoned highball glass. Half moons of rose-colored lipstick stained the rim. He placed it on a tray resting on my velvet couch. "So, you had a party and didn't invite me, huh?"

"You don't seem like one who waits for invitations."

Chuckling, he turned to the Victrola, flipped through the records, placed one upon the turntable, wound the crank, and let it start playing. He extended a hand out to me. "Let's dance."

"Sorry, I can't . . . I don't dance." I looked away as if searching for more debris.

"I find that tough to believe. Come on."

He reached for me, took my hand in his, and slid his other hand along the small of my back. I averted my gaze from his, but gently he pulled me closer until my head was almost resting against his chest. From the Victrola, Charles Harrison's voice crooned "I'm Always Chasing Rainbows," and I found myself leaning into Maynard and his smell of smoke and dried leaves. We swayed. In his embrace, I loosened like a flower blooming in the warmth of indoors. With my head only reaching his chest, my limbs short and his long, we didn't fit together easily, but somehow I nestled against him. His breath warmed my scalp. Could he feel my heart pounding? He hummed along to the music, seemingly without a care in the world, so I exhaled, trying to follow his lead. The sharp edges of his callouses scratched against my palm as he shifted and tightened his grip on me. Slowly we circled the room, unspeaking, sinking deeper and deeper into each other. The music seemed to fill my body and it felt like I was drifting gracefully in his arms. Was this what Fron felt when she was with Jack? In all of my fervor for work, maybe I'd been overlooking something important. Just when I reached a point of hoping our dance would never end, a scratching sound filled the room. The record had ended. We stayed in place, pressed against each other for a moment longer before separating.

"Hey, kid, you done for the night?" Up close, the dazzle of blue eyes against his straight dark hair left me breathless. He certainly wasn't handsome in the traditional sense. He was bull-legged and too skinny, his nose too long, but there was a ruggedness, an energy that produced a sizzle inside me. My vision seemed to blur a bit when I got up close. Not trusting myself to speak, I simply nodded before stepping back and pretending to frown at the overflowing ashtrays surrounding us.

As if reading my mind, he said, "Your girl can straighten things up in the morning. Come on." And with that, it was all I could do to grab my sweater off a peg by the door as he propelled me out of the room.

I gave him my address and we stepped out onto Powell Street, my hand in his. While in my studio, I had been confident and in control, but as soon as we passed the shuttered clock repair store at the end of the block, I felt awkward and slow. He said nothing about my limp and seemed happy to lope along, swinging his arms to and fro, appraising the surrounding darkened storefronts from top to bottom. Letting out a low whistle and grasping my shoulder while nodding his chin upward, he said, "Look at that." Above, a full moon, luminous as a pearl, hung over the edge of the buildings' roofline, huge and low. "Rare sight in the city. Usually I've got to be out in wide-open country with big sky to catch a moonrise like that."

"Full moons bring out all shades of crazy," I said, quoting Mother without thinking.

He looked over at me with a quizzical expression. "What does a girl like you know about crazy?"

"My mother was a social worker in New York when I was a girl. I often accompanied her on rounds during the evenings. Full moons reliably brought out tragedies of all shapes and sizes—fistfights, drunken accidents, sometimes even murder and suicide."

"Jesus, and you saw these things?"

"No, not firsthand, but my mother would have to go see the families of the bereaved and abandoned."

"She worked, huh? How modern. Bet that's where you get your spitfire, from her."

I lowered my eyes to the sidewalk. I'd made it sound frightening and reckless, me trekking through the Bowery with Mother, but really, my younger brother, Martin, and I had been forced to tag along because who else was going to watch over us at night while she worked? Once Father left, she had to work; first as a librarian, and then as a social worker. And although the social work hadn't been suitable for children, it fascinated me. I'd wanted to see people, all sorts of people, and how they really lived. This interest was the same thing that propelled me to skip classes during my high school years to wander through the city's Lower East Side. I never feared the drunks zigzagging along the filthy sidewalks, the slatternly women lurking in doorways, the big eyes peering through dingy, lower windowpanes of crowded tenement buildings. I shook my head, thinking of my customers all tied up in strings of pricey pearls. My life was so different now. That girl who had wandered the Lower East Side almost felt lost to me. Perhaps it was for the best.

After a minute or so of walking in silence, Maynard cleared his throat and asked, "Where do you like to eat around here?"

"I've discovered a few good spots on Grant over in China-town. You ever go there?"

"Nah, if I can't pronounce the joint's name, I'm not trying it."

"You're missing out. There are some wonderful places, cheap and delicious."

"No chance I'm eatin' frog legs."

"Oh, dry up, we don't eat frog legs," I said, shaking my head at his teasing. "Where do you go?"

"I've always been a regular at Coppa's, but he has to keep shutting down, thanks to our boys in blue, so I'm in the market for a new spot. I'm more of a North Beach type of fella, though, not Chinatown, although the siren call of the Barbary Coast sometimes lures me in." He waggled his eyebrows for comic effect.

A cable car clattered by defying all sense of gravity as its boxy frame rose up the hill. When we turned the corner onto Clay Street, a cold, damp wind hit us straight on, making May-nard nudge closer to me.

"Do you live on your own?" he asked.

"I will soon. I've been living with a friend of mine from back home, but she's getting married in a couple of weeks." Just saying the words aloud made my stomach flip. I was going to miss Fronsie terribly.

"What are you doing tomorrow evening?" he asked.

"My, my, look at you planning ahead." I laughed, turning to study his profile. The long straight nose, high cheekbones, hooded eyes.

"I had no idea you were such a hostess. Figure I better snag an appointment in the narrow gaps in your schedule."

"Well, unfortunately, I'm tied up. It's my roommate's engagement party."

"How 'bout I go with you?"

His question, delivered effortlessly, took me a moment to register. I stopped walking, certain I'd misheard him. "You want to go to Fronsie's party with me?"

"I do." He narrowed his eyes in challenge. "That is, if you don't have a fella lined up already."

It probably should have embarrassed me to admit I'd planned to go alone, but the bustle of the last few months had left me too busy to concern myself with appearances. My thoughts scattered. I simply stared at him. I'd never met anyone so forward, so bold. An expression of amusement settled upon his face as he saw my confusion.

"I suppose so," I murmured slowly.

"Well, if that's not an enthusiastic invitation, what is?" He stopped to give me a small bow, laughter dancing in his eyes. "Fine, I accept." He pulled me close again to continue walking. "But the thing is, if this is an engagement party, I need a present. Do you have a few minutes? Let's run down to my studio and pick out a painting."

"But . . ." I spluttered, still puzzling over how he wrangled an invitation out of me so easily, "I'm already bringing her a crystal vase from Gump's. I'm happy to add your name to the card."

He snorted. "I've never given anyone anything from Gump's in my life and don't plan to start now."

"What's wrong with Gump's?"

"Everything's wrong with it. Let's give your New Jersey girl a taste of the real West."

I was prepared to say that a painting was too much, too generous, but in the reflection of the moon and streetlights, hurt flinched in his eyes and I changed tack. "Your work is beautiful. If anything, it should be saved as a wedding present."

A sly grin slid across his face. "So now you can't get enough of me and I'm invited to the wedding? Miss Lange, you're one smooth operator."

Flustered, I opened my mouth but nothing came out. He laughed.

"All right, all right, I can see you're overcome with excitement. Let's get you home. I'll pick out a painting on my own."

We resumed course to my apartment, tucked close together. Excitement tingled at my fingertips as I gave him the details for the following evening. When we arrived at the door to my building, he studied the brick exterior. Dark windows faced out at us blankly. With my heart in my throat, I stepped forward, unlocked the building's entry gate, and pushed it open, my hip propping the door. I turned to him, but he glanced up and down the block and again at my building before smiling in a surprisingly sad, forlorn way. "Kid, I'm looking forward to seeing you tomorrow evening. I'll be here at seven. And remember: no vases."

I nodded, leaning forward slightly, lowering my lashes, ready for whatever came next, scarcely able to breathe. But nothing happened. He turned and sauntered toward downtown. Confounded, I watched as he retreated into the darkness. He raised a hand without looking back and kept moving. Stepping into the dark recess of the vestibule, I let the door close with a heavy thud, taking satisfaction in the sharp sound disturbing the silence of the street.

I sunk onto the second step of the stairwell, glaring at my right foot. Why had I allowed myself to get my hopes up? Moments earlier my stomach had been aflutter with excitement. Now it simply hurt. I lowered my head and pushed my palm into my brow. Maynard Dixon was older, established, and distinguished in his handsome, rangy looks and forthright manner. Everyone knew him. He was a *real* artist, a painter who commanded attention. And what was I? How could I have possibly thought that he possessed anything more than a passing curiosity in me? I was a fool.

It made sense why Fronsie had found such a becoming bridegroom. Somehow she glowed with respectability. She knew which fork went with which course. She knew how to keep moths away from precious garments. She knew the exact phrasing of what to write on a consolation card. But I'd never received this type of instruction from my mother, never had that type of family. When Fron had met Imogen's boys, she hadn't missed a beat and sat down to play jacks with them, whereas I barely could remember their names. It was easy to picture her with a family of her own, yet all of that felt beyond my reach. I massaged my temples.

A memory of Father flashed through me. In my mind's eye, he ambled down the sidewalk away from our house, hands in his pockets, kicking at clumps of dry leaves as if playing with a ball, never glancing back once. If he had, he would have seen

my twelve-year-old face pressed to the window, breath fog-
ging the glass. That had been the last time I'd ever seen him.
How could he have just left like that?

Years before he took off, he had hoisted me onto his shoulders one evening to watch a performance of *A Midsummer's
Night Dream* in the park down the street from our house. During the scene when Hermia and Helena squabble, as his body
heaved with laughter, I'd wobbled upon his shoulders but
hadn't felt unsafe. Not for a moment. He'd held my shins
close to his chest, his hands warm and big, his grip secure but
gentle. How was I supposed to reconcile this memory at the
park with the fact that he left several years later without any
warning? Without even looking back? Had it been my sickness
that drove him away? He'd been a handsome man, vigorous
and charming, playing tennis with friends every week and
doling out Tootsie Rolls to the neighborhood children. Had he
been ashamed at the way my leg never recovered? Whenever
Mother nagged at me to walk straighter to hide that limp, he'd
pressed his lips together sternly and turned away. I must have
embarrassed him.

After he left, my family rarely sat down for meals together.
Mother had long workdays in the city. Grandmutter found
complaints in the way that Martin and I talked too loudly together, left our toys dangerously underfoot, never did well in
school. Any sense of security evaporated. One day I'd had legs
that worked perfectly; the next day, I didn't. One day I'd had
a father; the next day, I didn't. Was this how life was to work
for me?

But then I remembered how Maynard pulled me close to

dance; his whistling as we walked up Nob Hill; his insistence that he take me to tomorrow's party. If I told Fronsie about his abrupt departure, she would have told me I was overthinking it. In her mind, all of his teasing and gentle gestures would have outweighed our awkward parting. And really, his behavior at the end had been gentlemanly. He had done nothing unseemly. I nodded to myself. I had to stop worrying that everything could be taken away. I needed to believe in this man.

CHAPTER 9

Three days later from a position across the street, I watched the entrance to the building housing Maynard's studio and gathered my nerve. His behavior during the evening of Fronsie's engagement party, two nights earlier, had left me baffled. It had been a dizzying ride of an encounter with him that swung from shared jokes and heady embraces to stony goodbyes. *What was happening?* I stared at the towering fortress of concrete in front of me, contemplating what to say to him.

As soon as Maynard had arrived at our apartment to escort Fronsie and me to the Pacific Heights home of her soon-to-be in-laws, he barely paused to let us get a word in edgewise, so quick was his conversation. While Fron curiously eyed the large rectangular package wrapped in brown paper tucked under his arm, he carried on about a description of recent shenanigans at the Bohemian Club. Our audience for his story-telling increased once we arrived at the party. We were soon surrounded by an assortment of guests. Bay Rum, brilliantine, and lily-of-the-valley powder rose with the heat from every-one's bodies. Dressed to the nines in evening jackets and pastel silk drop-waist chemise dresses edged in seed pearls, the group leaned in, eager for his next anecdote.

Our host, Mrs. Stockton, Fron's future mother-in-law, normally an austere-faced society matron, transformed into a giddy debutante when Maynard stood next to her. Look-ing out the huge bay windows running along one wall of the house's dining room, we admired the view of the Marina Dis-trict below us, and fainter in the distance, the Marin Head-lands.

"I should set up a canvas here and do some painting—what a view," said Maynard.

"Mr. Dixon, you're more than welcome to use our home for your art anytime." She eyed his black Stetson as if it were a dash of whipped cream on top of a dessert she was considering spiriting away to the pantry to gobble down in secret. "Per-haps you have a new collection in mind?"

"That's kind of you but I'm not a city fella. There's not an ounce of San Francisco blood running through these veins. My family's a bunch of ol' Confederates from Virginia. My grandfather decided to light out for the West after fighting for the Rebs and settled in what's called the Alabama Colony, outside of Fresno in the San Joaquin Valley. That wide-open landscape marks all my work."

"So, your family was in ranching?" Mrs. Stockton asked.

Judging by the glow in her cheeks, no doubt acres and acres of green, fertile farmland flooded her imagination.

"Ha, wouldn't that be grand? My father served as an attorney but never seemed to have much work." Maynard paused and gave her a sly wink. "You know most disputes out that way tend to get settled with six-shooters. Yet somehow he managed to meet a lovely young gal on a trip into the city here and sweet talked her into marrying him."

"My, my, how adventurous."

"Indeed, my mother was a force to be reckoned with."

"And what did she think of Fresno?"

"Not much, but she was determined to bring some culture out to the hinterlands." He paused to smile as a nostalgic expression, almost dreamy, flitted across his face. "When I think back to my childhood, I hear her voice. She read to me all the time. *Ivanhoe, A Tale of Two Cities, Robinson Crusoe*—that was the stuff of my boyhood. You see, I had bad lungs—asthma. Pardon my French, but I was the poor little sonofabitch stuck inside hangin' onto his mama's apron strings. No vaquero work for me. Instead I lost myself in the world of books."

"Is that when you started drawing and painting?"

He nodded. "I also write poetry, but never much liked going to school, so by 'bout sixteen years old, I was off on my own, determined to devote my life to writing and painting the Old West." As the eyes of everyone widened in awe, I marveled at his ability to enthrall men and women alike. Maynard Dixon certainly knew how to make an asthmatic childhood sound romantic. What a card.

He turned to Fronsie. "What do you say, Miss Ahlstrom,

would you like to open up what we brought for you?" At his use of *we*, everyone's gaze slid over me, interest and envy shining in their eyes. I moved closer to his side, savoring the attention.

When Fronsie lifted the painting from its wrapping, a canvas showing an expansive sky over a jagged line of purple mountains, there was a sharp intake of breath as everyone in the room leaned in to admire his work.

"Say, you outdid yourself, Mr. Dixon," Fron said, her smile as wide as I'd ever seen it. She threw her arms around him, thanking him enthusiastically, and although Maynard brushed off her compliments, his grin widened and his face flushed slightly. "Now come on, everyone, let's celebrate!" she said.

Furniture and rugs had been cleared out of the Stockton's drawing room ahead of time. A six-man band assembled around the grand piano, where couples started dancing to "Tiger Drag." I peered into the mass of bodies: whirling, swinging, and shimmying, arms and legs flailing, occasional slivers of skin gleaming in the darkness. A bare shoulder, forearm, a splay of fingers. Maynard stood beside me. When he draped his arm around me, all thoughts of the dancers vanished. I could feel heat across every inch of his arm running along my bare shoulders. It wasn't until the piano player started a new song, slower this time, that he pulled me into a corner. As the vocalist sang out "Let Me Call You Sweetheart," I settled into his arms. I could sense people smiling and whispering as they watched us. With my eyes closed, my cheek resting against his shoulder, his fingers rubbed circles on my lower back, each so electrifying, sparks flashed throughout my body. We stayed close together even when the next song started, faster and louder, until bodies bumped into us and we were forced to separate, smiling at each other, giddy in the darkness.

Later, the three of us, Maynard, Fronsie, and I, took a cab home. As our driver barreled down Sacramento Street toward the dip of Van Ness and then flew up Nob Hill, we laughed and sang silly nonsense songs. The energy of the party still coursed through our bloodstreams like the effervescence of champagne. We unloaded outside of our apartment, and Maynard walked us to the door after paying the driver. "Ladies, it's been an honor to escort you two beauties to tonight's gala. Fronsie, your fella Jack is one damned lucky man. The lads of this city will suffer a great blow when you become Mrs. Stockton." He bent over at the waist to give an elaborate bow while brandishing his cowboy hat toward us. "But now I must bid you both *adios*."

"What? Don't you want to come up for a nightcap?" Fron protested. "Our rooming house matron is deaf and won't hear a thing. Why do you think we picked this place?"

"Sorry, kiddo, not tonight," he said. Stepping away from us on the sidewalk, he called out:

> I love the rugged contour of your strength
> That points the sky with pinnacles of steel;
> Your jaunty men make confident with health,—
> Their care-free swagger and their careless jokes;
> The laughing pretty girls upon your streets,
> Keen-eyed and heedless of the dusty winds.

We watched as he finished his lines, turned, and sauntered away, whistling.

"So, he really is a poet," Fron murmured. "Well, I wasn't quite ready to say goodbye to him yet, and I certainly can't imagine that you were either." She hiccupped and looked at me queerly for a moment before shrugging and humming as she entered the building ahead of me. When we reached our rooms, she threw herself onto a small chair in the living room. "Boy, that Maynard, he really charmed the pants off everyone."

I looked away, unclipping my earrings, bracing myself against the question I knew was coming—*but now, why in the world isn't he up here charming the pants off you?*—but after a brief silence, she uncoiled the long string of pearls from around her neck. "Who knew my in-laws could throw such a bender?"

I nodded in relief, dropping to our mohair sofa as she began a running commentary on the party. My earlier sense of anticipation and excitement faded. A shaky sense of disquiet settled over me. When we had danced, he had tapped his fingers up and down my lower back to the rhythm of the piano, making me giggle and push into him to stop. He'd acted so happy to have me near, to claim me as his own. So why had he just left so abruptly again? Why did our evenings always end so oddly?

I was still pondering that same question two days later as I stood within spitting distance of his studio. Exactly what game was this man playing?

"Aww, for Pete's sake. Enough is enough," I said aloud, eliciting a startled glance from a woman carrying a handful of shopping bags.

I pushed my pocketbook onto my shoulder and snaked through the traffic to reach his building. According to a list next to the front door, Maynard's studio was on the second floor. I stepped around several empty wine bottles flanking the entrance, opened the heavy black door, climbed a flight of stairs, and searched the numbers along the long, musty hallway. I found Maynard's studio. A horseshoe nailed into place above the door marked the spot. I knocked. He called out to enter, so I went inside to find him sitting at a table with Roi playing cards.

"Dorothea!" Roi scrambled to his feet.

"Welcome to the Monkey Block," said Maynard, pulling out a chair for me. I raised my eyebrows and he added, "That's what we call this delightful place."

"Delightful, huh? If you say so." I waved at them both to sit. "You boys working hard?"

Maynard spun his chair around. Straddling it, he ashed his cigarette into a small earthenware pot. Paintbrushes littered their game of poker. Striped Mexican saddle blankets in crimson, gold, green, and turquoise covered a couch under the windows along a wall. Piles of finished paintings filled the studio. They leaned against chairs, a table, the walls, anything stationary. A shadowbox of arrowheads and a bleached cow skull hung on the wall over his desk. I pointed to an arrangement of circular frames on the opposite wall. Feathers of different sizes and colors hung from them. "What are those?"

"You don't know what a dream catcher is? Kid, I need to get you out of the city." His eyes brightened.

I moved toward a shelf, pretending to admire a cluster of

several baskets and three ceramic coiled pots while I hid a smile. *He wanted to take me places.*

"You like those? They're Hopi, a tribe of Indians in Arizona," Maynard explained, pointing at the row of pots.

I nodded and looked at the two men sitting at the table. "So, what kinda trouble are you both cooking up?"

"We're about to get started on a project together. A mural for the agency Roi works for. And hey, he and Imogen are having a party this Thursday. You free?"

"Well, it's not exactly a party," Roi said, scratching his scalp, looking back and forth at us.

"You always say that but then half of Oakland shows up." Maynard lifted his cigarette, took a long drag, and exhaled a smoke ring before nodding his chin at me. "So, what do you think? Should we go?"

"It's really nothing. You may not want . . ." Roi's voice trailed off. He shifted his weight from side to side.

Maynard gave him an amused shake of his head and looked back to me. "Well?"

My throat tightened over his earlier use of *we*. It was so confident, said with such ease. I'd been wearing anxiety around my shoulders like a stole for the last couple of days, but it dropped as his familiar scent of leaves and bark wafted toward me on the smoke from his cigarette. I reached for one he'd left perched on the rim on his ashtray, picked it up, and took a drag, only to find the dry mixture tasted like kindling and left me choking.

Maynard laughed and patted my back as I spluttered. "Easy

there, that's not a Lucky, it's kinnikinnick, a special blend that
the Indians smoke."

"A blend of what? Woodpile?" I asked, picking pieces of to-
bacco off my tongue.

"Something like that. Now how about that party?"

I coughed a final time. "I suppose so."

Maynard wrapped an arm around my shoulder and shook
his head in mock sorrow. "She supposes so. I tell you, this gal
plays hard to get." He leaned close and reached out to trace a
finger tenderly along my cheek, before straightening and saying, "Okay, kid, now I've gotta get some work done. I'm going
to be swamped all week to hit the agency's deadline, but I'll
swing by your studio on Thursday afternoon so we can head
to the ferry together."

Before turning toward the door, I paused, wanting to talk
to Maynard alone for a moment, but the men were already
sketching on a large sheet of paper hanging on the wall. I let
myself out and stood in the building's hallway, annoyed I
hadn't managed to speak my mind. Then I raised my hand to
where he had just touched my cheek. Maynard had been eager
to see me, keen to invite me to a party. He wanted to take me
on a trip. He was charming, funny, a little bit reckless. Could
he be the one for me? What was I so worried about?

That night I dreamed I was running across a field. Nimble
and limber, exhilaration filled me as I ran faster and faster,
the long grass beneath me growing blurrier and blurrier. I ran
for no other reason than the joy of freedom. I awoke with a
start, my feet still wheeling under the blankets. I grew still

and then rubbed at the tears stinging my eyes. That damn dream again. I'd been having it on and off for years. I hated it. I hated remembering I once had two perfect feet and legs, only to awaken and realize my imperfections.

FOUR NIGHTS LATER, we arrived at Roi and Imogen's to find the small bungalow stuffed with people, many of whom I'd met before at other parties. As Maynard guided me into the front room, I saw Imogen carrying a tray of drinks in from the kitchen. At the sight of the two of us, her mouth pressed into a thin line. Ansel Adams, a photographer friend of Imogen's, clapped Maynard on the back, and I lost sight of her as Anne Brigman, another photographer I'd gotten to know through Camera Club meetings, closed in on me for a merry embrace. I stood in a small circle talking to Anne and some others, when I felt a tug on my elbow. I turned to find Imogen glaring at me. "Dorothea, I need to speak with you outside."

Warily, I excused myself and followed her to the dark back-yard. The white flicker of moth wings danced around us like snowflakes. I shivered in the damp evening air. Inside the house someone—probably Ansel Adams—started banging away on the piano. Loud voices and laughter spilled from the doorway behind us. "How do the boys sleep through all this?" I asked.

She waved off my question and turned to me. Her pale face glowed light blue in the darkness, as if underwater. "Roi says you and Maynard are thick as thieves all of a sudden."

I shrugged, annoyed to be dragged outside for a scolding. Inside, people started singing. "Ansel's such a show-off on the piano," I said, rolling my eyes.

"Well, what's going on with you two?"

"Ansel and me?"

"No, you and Maynard."

"Search me. Nothing, really."

She let out an exasperated chuff of air. "He's trouble. First of all, he's old enough to be your father."

I winced at the mention of my father.

She noticed my reaction and continued, louder and faster, "He's forty-five! What are you now: twenty-three, twenty-four? Why, he's got about twenty years on you."

Twenty years? I hadn't realized he was that much older but feigned nonchalance. "It's nothing."

"Is that really what you think? What do you know about him? Has he told you about Lillian?"

"Lillian?" I repeated, my heart hammering in my chest.

"Yes, his first wife, Lillian. Did he tell you about her? How they fought? How they drank like fish? Had affairs? How she's been *institutionalized*?" A faint thread of spittle landed on Imogen's chin. With every question, her voice became more strident and agitated. "How about Constance? Has he mentioned abandoning his ten-year-old daughter in a boarding school all the way across the country?"

Imogen may as well have punched me in the gut. I raised my hands to cover my eyes. Her voice softened. "He hasn't told you any of this?"

I took a deep breath, trying to steady the shaking that had started in my knees but was now working its way upward to my voice. "No."

"I'm sorry," she said in a low tone, looking at the ground.

"Are you?"

Her face snapped up in confusion. "Of course I am. I'm angry he's led you on."

"It doesn't seem like you're angry. In fact, it feels like this is awfully satisfying for you."

"What on earth do you mean?"

Blood roared in my ears as I glared at her, and I could feel my entire body trembling. "You're always giving me a rough time about running a business instead of . . ." I paused. What exactly *did* Imogen think I should be doing? "You have no respect for my work."

She stepped forward, raising her hand. "Stop right there. I respect what you do. It's just that I worry about you. You're so driven to make money that you're not taking enough chances to cultivate your talent. And now you've taken up with Maynard? It's all a distraction from the art you could be producing. Come to Camera Club more. Be a part of the community of artists that we're building."

"Ugh, I'm sick of talking about Camera Club. I'm working like a madwoman to build something of my own. And now you're giving me grief about the one bit of fun I've allowed myself?"

She spread her hands in surrender. "Fine. You're right, I've overstepped. But be careful. He will bring heartbreak."

I spun back toward the house, trying to stave off the tears stinging my eyes, and flung open the back door, keeping my gaze trained to the ground as I pushed my way back into the party. Maynard's laugh rose over the din, so I followed it to the front porch, where he stood outside, smoking with a circle of men. The group fell silent as I clattered into their midst. "Maynard, I'm leaving."

I expected him to try to convince me to stay, but he said nothing. His smile faded. A seriousness settled into his eyes. Keeping his gaze on me, he said, "Hey, Ansel, can you give us a lift to the ferry?"

Ansel agreed and led us down to his black motorcar parked along the street, gleaming in the reflected lights from the house's windows. The three of us climbed inside. As we sped along the quiet streets, Ansel rattled on about a recent trip down to Yosemite, but Maynard, sitting next to him in the front seat, only grunted occasional replies. When we arrived at the ferry terminal, I threw open the door and hopped out before anyone could say anything. I headed straight for the ticket window gleaming brightly in the darkness. The car roared away behind me but I didn't look back. Instead I purchased my entry and hustled aboard, pushing my right foot forward with each step despite its aching. I needed to get as far away from Maynard as possible. I reached the bow of the boat and stopped. Fog obscured San Francisco's bright lights, but I knew they were out there ahead of us. While breathing in the brackish salt air, I leaned against the railing over the inky dark water and felt the rumble of the boat's engine deep below me. I wished I'd never laid eyes on Maynard Dixon.

Meeting him had changed everything. Ever since he'd first strolled into my studio I'd felt undone. I'd hungered for him and suspended the guardedness I'd been holding close to my chest for years. But now with Imogen's revelations, it felt as though all of my hopes had sunk deep underwater, fathoms away. All of Maynard's charisma, his attention, it was an illusion. How had I allowed myself to believe that a man like him felt anything genuine for someone like me?

A voice from behind me interrupted my thoughts. "What did Imogen tell you?"

I refused to look back. I folded my shoulders inward as if I could protect my heart from him. "Enough."

A heavy sigh. "I'm sorry."

"Sorry? You're sorry?" I turned to face him. "I've been so confused trying to make sense of you and now I learn about—" My voice broke, and I swung back toward the water. There was no chance I'd let him see how badly he'd hurt me. I'd wanted—no—I had *needed* to believe in him. Swaying back and forth with the boat's lumbering movement, I refused to look at him again. The city drew near, its lights glimmering. I sighed, hollowed out and empty with disappointment. I'd been so desperate to think he was the one for me.

When the boat bumped into its slip, I turned. Maynard lingered a few feet away watching me. I looked away quickly, but he said, "Let me walk you home."

I gave a brief nod. We plodded through downtown and up Nob Hill, side by side, saying nothing. When we reached the final block and my apartment loomed in the distance, he stopped. I kept walking, but he grabbed my arm and said, "Listen, I'm sorry. I should have said something earlier, but I just couldn't bring myself to disrupt what was happening between us."

I laughed bitterly. "It's obvious now that nothing was happening."

"Nothing? How can you say that?"

I pulled my sleeve out of his grip. "Yes. You have a wife, a daughter. What have I been? A diversion?"

"For Chrissake, Dorrie. It's been nothing like that. First of all, that marriage is over. And from the moment I first saw you sitting on the floor of your studio, you're all I've been able to think about." He stepped closer, scrutinizing my face. "Your green eyes. Your mysterious smile. Your discipline. Jesus, you work more than anyone I've ever met. And you don't give a rat's ass about what anyone thinks of you. You have your own way of doing things and everyone else can be damned."

He looked at me for a response, but I felt frozen, trying to make heads or tails out of what he was saying. I mumbled, "That's got to be the first time a man's ever used the words *rat's ass* in an apology."

"See? Just like that." He pointed at me, grinning, and looked around as if we were surrounded by an audience. "You never give an inch." He kept talking, continuing his apology, but then stopped and pushed his cowboy hat back momentarily to rub his forehead. He looked both dazed and sad. Gone was the showmanship from Fronsie's engagement party. Gone was the cowboy who had grabbed me to his chest to dance in my studio. Without quite knowing what I was doing, I reached out and took his hands in mine. I raised them to my cheeks, still cool from the damp of the ferry ride. Without a word, I pressed my head into his firm chest. He cupped my chin in his fingers and tilted my face to kiss me. With his mouth upon mine, desire filled me. A cold wind raced along the block, its teeth nipping at us, but it did nothing to chill my craving for him. Yet he pulled himself off me. We both tottered the final few steps to my building. Once we reached the door, I knotted my fingers into his and didn't let go. Tugging him inside the stairwell, we crept up each step breathlessly. Exhilaration flashed through every nerve of my body. Face flushed, hair tangled, I knew if I passed a mirror, I wouldn't recognize the reckless woman possessing me.

In my dark tiny sitting room, our footsteps echoed. It was still early and Fronsie was out somewhere with Jack and wouldn't be home for a couple more hours. I led Maynard straight through to the small bedroom I shared with Fron. My heady sense of daring wavered a little at the sight of the two twin beds, each lining opposite sides of the room primly, chenille bedspreads smoothed over hard mattresses. Before I lost my nerve, I faced away from him, slid my jacket off, and offered my back so he could unbutton my dress. Instead he placed his hands on my shoulders and gently turned me. With his hands on both sides of my face, he looked, *really looked*, into my eyes—I swear, he looked right into me. My brain couldn't string words together, my lungs couldn't fill, my stomach felt full of fireworks. All movement stopped and we stared at each other. He lowered me onto the edge of the bed. Kneeling, he removed my shoes. A flash of panic came over me—my practical black Mary Janes. Surely they'd knock some sense into him; he'd stop this and leave me forever. My wretched foot ruined everything!

But he didn't pull away.

His face hovered mere inches from my mangled right foot. I tried to wriggle out of his grip, but before I could protest, he had it tenderly in his grasp and bent to kiss it. And then, my foot was on fire. He continued to kiss along my ankle and up the inside of my withered calf. My whole body quivered. He rubbed gently up my leg to the inside of my thigh. The floor seemed to be collapsing and it felt like I was falling, falling, falling. But I wasn't, not really. With his hand still between my legs, I was exactly where I wanted to be. A lump rose in my throat, my eyes stung with tears of joy, of relief . . . of everything. What had I been worried about? He slid up to the bed beside me and kissed my neck. It tickled and I laughed. While we lowered our heads to my pillow, every fear I'd ever had slid away.

CHAPTER 10

Two months later, Maynard and I spent a few days in a rustic cabin, once part of a miner's camp, nestled on a ridge near Sonoma. Those February nights were chilly. Mornings started crisp, but then the sun would emerge. Clearings warmed, the woods remained cool. A short hike downhill took us to a feeder river where Maynard caught trout for our dinners. If we headed uphill, a panoramic view rumpled with hills and valleys opened below us. It was there, on that hillside, that Maynard spent most of his time sketching landscape studies as I wandered, looking for interesting shapes and textures to photograph. Towering redwoods, abandoned mining shacks, the reticulated veins in wild cabbages—I photographed it all. More than anything, I loved coming upon Maynard perched on a fallen tree trunk, one of his smokes in hand, intent on his sketchpad, his head occasionally bobbing up to take in the vista. Somehow he'd reduce everything he saw to its most elemental shapes, to angular, simple expressions of space. Eventually he'd drop his sketchbook to tackle me in the long grass, eager to nibble on the tops of my ears where the sun had burned them as pink as raspberries, my fair skin the curse of my German blood.

After the first night of sleeping in the cabin, fusty and thick with the smell of old smoke and damp wood, we abandoned the rickety metal cots, nestled our bedrolls together outside, and lay on our backs to stare at the stars. Our breath sent vapors drifting overhead. Tangled under the covers, our bodies heated our nest. While he pointed to constellations and told me how the Hopi believed there were nine universes, I stroked his forehead and traced the line of his jaw. My hands wandered farther down under the blankets, and eventually I climbed astride him to block his view of the sky. The groaning of nearby trees swaying in the wind, the scraping of dry leaves, the crackling of small animal paws around us, all made the surrounding wildness infinitely more romantic. It felt as though we were the only two people left on earth and that suited us just fine.

Tempting as it was to stay hidden from the world, I had portrait appointments booked back in San Francisco. We finally pried ourselves away from our encampment to return to the city. On our way down the hill to the road where we had prearranged to be picked up by a farmer in his truck, Maynard announced that his daughter, Constance, was staying with his great-aunt Esther in Sausalito while on a holiday break from her boarding school. Since our ferry back would leave from there, he suggested we visit her. I agreed, guilt threading its way through my conscience. Why had Maynard not visited the child earlier during her break?

After being delivered to the ferry dock in Sausalito, we heaved our packs over our shoulders and plodded several blocks lined with gingerbread-trimmed Victorians until we reached a white picket fence encircling a small cottage. Colorful phlox and foxglove surrounded the place. Our knocks on the front door were answered by a smiling older woman who greeted Maynard fondly and welcomed us inside. On a needle-pointed chair in the parlor, a young girl sat picking at invisible pieces of lint on her plaid skirt. Her expression remained sullen despite Maynard's enthusiastic greeting. Her limbs stayed wooden as he embraced her. The glow of our trip faded as I stood before Constance. Through expressionless eyes, she took in the bandanna covering my wild hair, the scuffs on my brown leather boots. Our hostess brought out tea. Constance, hands clenched in her lap, spine rigid, remained unmoved by Maynard's attempts at charm.

"So, your father says you're in fifth grade," I finally ventured.

"Sixth."

Maynard gave me an apologetic widening of his eyes and I nodded. "I see. What's your favorite subject in school?"

Without answering, she gave me a long look.

"Now, Consie," Maynard said, briskly wading into the conversation. "Dorothea is a portrait photographer. It's about time I get a new picture of you. She could do it. What do you say?"

Her granite-colored eyes didn't so much as blink. She said nothing. By that point, I felt so eager to escape the girl's resentment, I was practically ready to dive into the Bay and swim back home. Why wait for the ferry? When the clock on the doily-covered end table clanged at the hour and Aunt Esther announced our boat would be arriving shortly, I almost leapt out of my seat to run for the door.

The older woman escorted us outside, merrily describing how busy the afternoon boats could be, but Constance remained in her seat. On the porch, Aunt Esther whispered, "I'm sorry, the girl seems tired. I think she woke up too early this morning."

Maynard shrugged. "Adults are boring. I'm not surprised she seemed a little distracted."

Distracted? I wanted to protest, but one look at Maynard's hopeful expression and I held my tongue.

As we said our goodbyes, I looked past Aunt Esther and saw Constance's face peeking around the edge of a lace curtain. I gave a small wave, but she stared right through me.

By the time we arrived back at my studio on Sutter, my head was throbbing as though it intended to crack open. Maynard helped me lie down on the velvet sofa. He then handed me a glass filled with honey-colored liquid.

"Drink this," he commanded, lifting the tumbler to my lips.

My nostrils flared at the medicinal smell of alcohol, but I didn't protest. My throat ached as the liquid worked its way down. He lifted my feet and sat down on the chair, resting my heels on his lap.

I groaned. "Maynard, she hated me."

He pushed off his cowboy hat, tossed it to the floor, and rubbed his hands through his black hair. "Kid, she doesn't hate you, she doesn't even know you. I'm the one she's not so thrilled about, but I mean to make things right with her."

I closed my eyes and exhaled slowly, letting the warmth of the alcohol seep up from my belly to untie the knots in my neck. Without the lights on, marine shadows of the late afternoon swam along the walls. Noise from the street outside sounded distant, almost as if we were in a small underwater cavern.

He ran his hand up the inside of my leg and rested it on my thigh, its pressure a reminder of all that had been right in Sonoma. "Hey, I have some great ideas for a couple of new canvases. That trip to the cabin was exactly what I needed." His hands continued to travel upward, and I couldn't help myself from arching toward him. "I know what can cure that headache," he said, laughing.

"What if someone comes in?" I whispered as Maynard climbed on top of me.

He winked. "Stop thinking about everything."

"I never stop thinking."

"I know, it's one of the things I like about you."

"What else do you like about me?"

"Stop talking and let me show you."

Despite the tightness in my chest about Constance, I pulled him toward me and wrapped my legs around his waist, ready for the world beyond that room to fall away.

CHAPTER 11

Wedding Announcement—March 21, 1920

Miss Dorothea Lange, aged 24, portrait photographer, married Maynard Dixon, renowned painter, in a small ceremony with Mrs. Florence "Fronsie" Ahlstrom Stockton serving as matron of honor and Roi Partridge as the best man. The bride hails from New York and graduated from the art school of Columbia University while the groom . . .

Aboard the train, I leaned into the sunlight coming through the window to scan through the newspaper's wedding announcement for the millionth time but it still didn't feel real. Mother had written a short telegram: *I wish you all the best.* In it, I heard all that was unspoken between us: *I hope you picked well, better than I did.* I glanced over at Maynard dozing beside me and felt a tickle of excitement in my chest. *Of course I did.* It was a relief when Mother hadn't come out for the ceremony, citing the long distance as too much. My old life was better left behind.

With the clipping folded between my fingers, I thought back to when Maynard proposed. We had lain sprawled on one of his Navajo blankets on the floor of his studio, our limbs braided together. He had surprised me by asking, "What do you say we make this official, kid?"

"What are you talking about?"

"I'm talking about getting hitched."

I rolled over onto my stomach and rested my chin on my palm. "Your track record isn't so good."

"It will be different between us."

"Gee, thanks, that's the oldest line in the book."

"Ha, that's what I love about you: you're such a romantic. Well, what do you say? I'd like to make an honest woman out of you."

I smiled. An honest woman was easier said than done. But still, this felt right. "I suppose if you're willing to roll the dice again, I'm game."

"Thatta girl," Maynard said before pressing his lips to mine. "Should I write to your father to ask for permission?"

"My, my, aren't you feeling traditional?"

"I'm not sure you'd call anything we just did traditional," he said, winking. "But really, should I write him?"

I straightened up to look for my blouse in the tangle of

clothes nested around us. Dust motes held suspended in the late-afternoon sunshine flooding through the windows. All felt surprisingly peaceful in the Monkey Block.

"He's dead."

"Sorry, I'd no idea. You never mention your family."

"It's nothing, it was a long time ago. I barely remember him." I slid my blouse over my shoulders and turned away to button it, closing my eyes briefly. In truth, I had no idea where my father was, but suspected he was alive somewhere, rarely thinking of me, my mother, or my brother.

The train lurched, derailing my memories. I glanced at the wedding announcement a final time. I'd send it to my mother, along with a letter in which I'd made no apology for changing my name from Nutzhorn to Lange. My ears burned to think of the description of me graduating from Columbia, but it had come out so easily when the reporter called. And really, who cared about a few old details when my success in San Francisco was indisputable? Mother was hardly someone to quibble over the truth of anyone's past.

I pocketed the wedding announcement and glanced out the window at the scenery drifting by in a blur of tall brown grasses, red rocks, and the jagged lines of far-off mountains. Arizona. For our honeymoon, we were finally going to roam the land that Maynard loved. He sat next to me, still asleep, his head leaned back, mouth opened slightly. He was a terrible passenger, impatient and incapable of entertaining himself. He claimed reading or sketching on trains gave him headaches so he'd nagged me about playing cards as soon as we left the station in San Francisco. Hearts, poker, gin. We played them all until I insisted he deal himself a hand of solitaire. He barely made it past creating the tableau before he leaned his head back and nodded off. Finally, quiet in our compartment.

My stomach growled, but I was reluctant to awaken him. Instead I leaned forward and took a biscuit tin of crackers from my satchel. At the thought of food, my mind turned to the kitchen in our new little bungalow back in the city. It had taken Imogen a while to get over her grudge against us marrying, but she'd come around. She could never stay mad at me for long. Before the wedding, she helped me paint the kitchen of the new place where Maynard and I would live upon our return. While we covered the walls a cheerful yellow, she said, "Do you know why I don't drive?"

"Because you don't know how?"

"I didn't grow up in the city like you, I could have learned."

"Because you like being difficult?"

"Ha, I suppose that's part of it. Since I don't drive, Roi's forced to stick around and help me."

I stared at her blankly.

She shook her head with impatience. "Make sure you don't end up doing everything for Maynard. These men only think of themselves. When I was pregnant with the twins, Roi disappeared from our place in Seattle to go to Carmel on a sketching expedition. He said he'd be gone for a few weeks but was gone for four months. Well, I was having none of it, so I closed my studio and moved to San Francisco with Gryffyd. Roi was none too pleased by my impulsiveness, but what could he do? I was practically bursting with two more of his sons. He buckled down and took a job with an ad agency. So, what I'm saying is don't make his life too easy. Don't neglect your work to do everything for him."

I hated to be told what to do but nodded, pretending to agree. The truth was that I wanted to do everything. In my experience, tenacity was the key to success. It had taken me this far in life. The same ethos could apply to my marriage, couldn't it? Since meeting Maynard, I could see his confidence growing after the ruinous ending of his first marriage. He was healthy. His color looked better. He stopped drinking. He was painting all day and into the evenings and kept talking about how inspired he was. All because of me. After this trip, our new lives together would begin. There was no chance our marriage would resemble his first. I'd nurture Maynard instead of competing with him and punishing him as Lillian had. By all accounts, she'd been a talented artist, but a miserable one, drowning in depression and alcohol. I was nothing like that. There would be no competition between us. This marriage would be different. Better. Certainly better than what I'd grown up seeing with my own parents.

WE ARRIVED IN Kayenta, Arizona, near the border of Utah, and our host, John Wetherill, a friend of Maynard's, met us at the station to drive us to our destination, a nearby Navajo reservation. Our first few days were spent examining the terrain, so different from everything I'd ever known: wide sweeps of empty desert, soaring sky, endless clouds. It felt timeless, nothing like the city. The simple geometry of the landscape's lines and bold shouts of color left me awed. During each sunrise and sunset, under a sky bruised with purples and rippling with flames, the desert was reborn. The air thrummed with possibility. It gave me a sense of the mysticism I imagined sailors felt when surrounded by the ocean: a sacred unification with nature. We were small and large at the same time, both diminished and empowered. And Maynard's transformation astonished me. The misplaced energy, the restlessness, the twitchiness—it vanished. He appeared calm and ignored everything except for the land. For hours, he would sit on a camp stool, sketching with pastels and watercolors while I wandered nearby, taking photos and collecting stones and small plants. I'd never seen him so focused and peaceful.

Eventually John brought us to an old trading post. The men explored the wash outside the squat sandstone building while I wandered the interior, inspecting the baskets dotting the walls, shelves of Hopi pottery, barrels of horse tack, and bowls of colorful glass beads. From a case of silver jewelry, I took out a big, clunky silver Navajo bangle and slid it onto my narrow wrist. Pleased with how it bent and distorted colors and shapes on its shiny surface, I raised my arm and studied it. From over my shoulder, Maynard appeared. "What do you say, want a trinket as a reminder of this trip?"

My enthusiastic response was all he needed to hear. After he purchased the bangle, we left the post and drove through the Painted Desert. While John and Maynard talked quietly in the front, I rested my forearm along the rim of the car's open window and watched as settlements passed, sometimes no more than a gas station and a few lonesome outbuildings. The day's heat and the land's constancy lulled me into a state of drowsiness until we approached a sign that read, TUBA CITY

INDIAN SCHOOL. I craned my head around to take a closer look, but we had passed it. "Wait," I called out to John, "I'd like to see that." They turned to me, confused. I pointed to the road behind us. "Let's go see that school."

John looked puzzled. "I don't think the landscape around there has any particularly interesting features."

"I don't care about the landscape. I'd like to see the students."

In the front seat, Maynard lit a cigarette and the woodsy smell of the kinnikinnick smoke wafted over me. "There are Indian kids? I'd like to see it too."

John's shoulders rose and the cords of his neck tightened, but he said nothing and pulled a U-turn on the empty road, heading back toward the Indian school. After about a half hour, we arrived at a three-story Federal-style brick building. We all climbed out and stood, stretching our limbs and brushing dust off our laps. "I'll go in and see if we can get a tour," John said.

Maynard leaned against the car and studied our surroundings. The property consisted of the large rectangular schoolhouse, a rickety water tower listing to one side behind it, and a scattering of several more buildings. A pale sky drained of color pressed down on the loneliness of it all. It seemed like the last place a parent would choose to send their child.

After a few minutes, John emerged from the double doors of the main building and walked toward us, a young man at his side. "Apparently we're too late to visit any classrooms today, but we can view the students singing hymns before they head to work."

"The students work?" I asked, looking back and forth at John and the young man beside him.

"Yes," said the man. Muscular and compact, he stood ram-rod straight and wore his hair cropped close to his head. He pointed to the smaller buildings flanking us. "This boarding school is entirely self-sufficient. There's a bakery, a laundry, and woodshop. The boys spend half their days in lessons and half working and cleaning."

"How productive." Maynard let out a rueful laugh. "Sounds like the army: drills in the morning, chores in the afternoon."

"This school is administered jointly by the Bureau of Indian Affairs and the U.S. Army," the man said, ignoring Maynard's sardonic smile. "I'm Lieutenant George Beasley."

Before anyone could say anything more, two rows of children emerged from the school and marched down the steps to create several lines. Once in formation, they faced the last man to exit the building, the headmaster. The boys wore uniforms of black knee socks, dark gray short pants, and jackets buttoned up the front. A small army. Three rows of grimly set brown faces stared at the man as he marched down the lines inspecting the appearance of each child. I heard him murmur something to one boy who bent over and yanked up his sagging socks. The headmaster then scolded a different boy for missing a button on a jacket.

The rumble of an engine in the distance made all faces turn. A lone motorcar chugged along the road toward us, trailing a cloud of dust behind it. Once parked, a man in a suit emerged from the driver's seat. He opened one of the backseat doors and pulled out a bundle drooping from his arms. As I looked harder, the bundle became a young boy. Beside me, Maynard stiffened. Tussled and squirming, the boy wriggled out of the man's arms and began to run, his little legs appearing to move as if on pistons, kicking up dust. The man took several large steps, scooped up the little lad, and tucked him under his elbow.

"Excuse me," said Beasley, leaving us to stride over to the new arrivals. While the three rows of boys began singing hymns, he consulted with the man from the car over the writhing boy.

> *Turn your eyes upon Jesus,*
> *Look full in His wonderful face,*
> *And the things of earth will grow strangely dim,*
> *In the light of His glory and grace.*

Suddenly a keening pierced the flat melody coming from the boys in the school yard. I spun around to locate its source and realized the newly arrived child was wailing. Without looking at the boy, the driver of the car cuffed him soundly on the ear with his free hand. The howling stopped, the singing continued.

"What the hell?" Maynard said, beginning to walk toward the threesome at the car, but John stopped him with a tug on the upper arm.

"Don't get involved," John muttered.

"Get involved with what? What's happening?" I said.

John looked away toward Beasley, who was hurrying back toward us, eyeing Maynard warily. Behind him, the other man dragged the young boy toward the doors of the school. Meanwhile, all of the other students lowered their eyes and stared at the ground in front of them. A hum seemed to fill the space around us, an angry buzz like a swarm of invisible bees. It made me breathless, dizzy. Beasley pulled a handkerchief from his pocket to mop at his brow when he reached us.

"What's with the kid?" Maynard asked, his eyes cold.

"A new student. Arrivals can be"—he licked his lips and the smell of Juicy Fruit chewing gum reached me—"tricky."

"Where are his parents?" I asked.

Beasley shrugged. "An official from the Bureau of Indian Affairs brought him. I think he was found somewhere on the reservation."

"He was found somewhere? But what about his parents?" I persisted, despite the tightening of Beasley's jaw. "*Where* are the child's parents?"

"We give these boys a better shot at life. We clean them up, educate them, teach them to work. We're taking care of these boys in ways that their families cannot. The government is doing these children an enormous favor. We're breaking the cycle of neglect that's endemic within this population."

"So, it's a 'kill the Indian, save the man' type of thing?" Maynard said, his voice a low growl.

Beasley nodded briskly, ignoring Maynard's glare. He ran his fingers down the line of buttons on his military uniform, checking to be sure they were all fastened. "These boys are extremely fortunate. Who knows what would become of them if we didn't help?" It wasn't a question. We were meant to know exactly what would become of them. Alcohol addiction. Poverty. Tuberculosis. He droned on, describing the importance of rules and the daily routine for the students: no traditional Indian activities; no speaking Navajo; no tribal clothes. I stepped backward and drifted closer to the children, but they didn't even look at me. The headmaster continued to prowl along the rows of boys, his expression stern. A limp rendition of "To God Be the Glory" rose from the pack without any inflection, any enthusiasm. Behind one boy, the headmaster stopped, his lip curled. He rapped the child across his calves with a short riding staff. I glanced back at Maynard. Two red circles glowed high on his cheekbones.

"Let's go," said John, steering Maynard toward the car.

I followed them with Beasley, who folded his handkerchief into a square and tucked it into his back pocket as he walked alongside Maynard and John. "Would you like a tour of the bakery? The laundry? Watch the boys at work? You'll see how smoothly operations run here."

"We've seen enough," Maynard said, reaching for my arm. While John cranked the engine, I turned, resting my foot on the running board, to scan the children, looking for sadness, curiosity, hope, or even anger, but there was nothing. Just dark, ancient, unblinking eyes. Three rows of them. Surrendered. The fight in them long extinguished.

We drove off. Both men sat in front, looking straight ahead at the ribbon of road unspooling in front of us. How could we drive away from all of those children? I shifted my legs, peeling them, hot and damp under my linen trousers, off the black leather of the backseat. I felt sick and helpless. I'd always found school boring, but had never witnessed such systemic cruelty. And it was run by the government. Wasn't this an institution to be trusted? The fact that those boys were at school under such dubious circumstances appalled me, but what could be done?

Our drive back was quiet. I kept waiting for Maynard to say something, to question what we had seen, but he remained silent. When he opened the door for me back at our post, he kept his eyes to the dusty ground. Later that evening, his back slumped as he sat at the dinner table. The creases next to his eyes appeared deeper. He simply looked sad.

In our rooms several hours later, I slipped off the Navajo bangle and put it in a velvet jewelry bag deep in my luggage, out of sight. If Maynard noticed, he said nothing.

We spent the next few days visiting Monument Valley and the Mesa Verde cliff dwellings. I wanted to talk about Tuba City but didn't know where to start. When I suggested we visit a nearby Indian village, Maynard shook off the request, his eyes never meeting mine. He stopped including Indians in his compositions. Those boys at Tuba City Indian School had flattened him. They ran contrary to everything he wanted to believe about the timelessness of the desert, his beloved Old West. The Indians in his paintings had always been noble and proud, steeped in mystique and beauty. At his core, Maynard was a romantic. Oppression and neglect were not themes he was equipped to depict. Their blight upon modern society was not something he could bring himself to explore. It all represented too much heartbreak for him to handle.

We stayed in Arizona for another week. Maynard focused his energy on sketching the landscape, the sweeping acreage of dusty flatness, the mountains, and the sky wide open over it all. He retained his earlier sense of calm, but sorrow had crept in. I saw it in the darker colors that suffused his skies, the savage angularity of his compositions. I tried my hand at capturing the desert with my camera, but my heart wasn't in it. At the same time, the idea of returning home left me conflicted. The thought of going back to those society portraits gave me a sense of unease. All of those wealthy families—many whom were now friends—documenting their success, it was all so predictable. But what was the alternative? Seeing the Tuba City Indian School troubled me, but what could I do about it? What power did I have?

CHAPTER 12

We arrived back in San Francisco eager to immerse ourselves in our usual routines, work, and social circles. While we had been gone, Ah-yee had booked appointments so my calendar was busier than ever. Wanting to push what we'd witnessed at Tuba City from my mind, I stashed the jewelry bag with my silver bangle into the deep recesses of my top dresser drawer. I wanted it out of sight.

After a day at my studio, I'd arrive home to make a late dinner for Maynard and me. We'd dine with candles and a flowered cloth spread over our tiny kitchen table. If the evening was warm, we'd move the arrangement outside to eat, our laughter bouncing off the flagstone paver stones and walls of our cottage. Sometimes after we'd finish our dinner, I'd undo my blouse, lingering button by button, while Maynard watched from across the table. I'd tease my sleeves off my shoulders languorously. He'd pull me from my seat. Sometimes we would only make it a few steps from the table before collapsing to the floor, pulling off each other's clothes. Sometimes we'd make it to our bedroom. Either way, I'd awaken in the morning and find our crusty dinner dishes still set on the table, but I didn't mind. This was how I'd pictured married life. We were in love and nothing seemed to weigh upon us. We could go away for unexpected trips to Marin County to camp on the beach; we could eat dinner naked at midnight; we could stay in bed until two in the afternoon on a Sunday; we could arrive unexpectedly in each other's studio, forgo work, and make love. We could do anything.

Since I was in charge of my studio, I could set my own schedule and so, for several years, Maynard and I would escape the city together and explore his favorite parts of California and the Southwest. One evening, after we had returned from another trip to Arizona, Maynard arrived home to find me preparing dinner. I smiled and handed him a plate of chicken thighs, broiled potatoes, and a fruit salad. He practically jittered with energy as he tucked into the meal. "I'm almost done with the sketches from Arizona, but the series isn't yet complete. I need more material to fill it out, so I want to go to New Mexico for a sketching trip," he said, before forking a hunk of chicken into his mouth.

"New Mexico? Did you sell those canvases you painted when we got home from Arizona?"

He nodded while chewing. "Bender came by to take them." Albert Bender, a wealthy art collector, had been a patron of both of us and served sometimes as an agent to Maynard. "He suggested I'm getting close to being ready for some shows in the Midwest and the East, but I need some more paintings before I start trying to put anything together. The city's grating on my nerves. The noise, the crowds. It will be good to return to some open country. I'm going to leave next week, and I need to go alone. I'll get more done."

Alone? I sat back in surprise. Everything . . . his current work was indisputable. But still, it hurt me not to be included. I tried to remain objective. Perhaps he was more productive without me. And I couldn't very well clear my schedule with such little notice. Maybe going by himself did make more sense. "How long will you be gone?"

"Three weeks. Not a day longer."

At that point, I had no reason to doubt him.

Alone, I found more hours to work each day. With no other responsibilities, I experimented with photographing clients outside of my studio, sometimes at their homes or landmarks throughout the city, such as the Palace of Fine Arts or Baker Beach. I wanted to capture people where they felt most comfortable, locations that represented something important about them as individuals. As a result, San Francisco began to feel like my own.

But then three weeks passed. No Maynard.

A month.

Then two more weeks.

No Maynard.

I sat at our kitchen table inspecting the calendar, my dinner growing cold beside me. When was the last meal we had shared? He had now been gone for more than twice the amount of time he had promised. No word arrived in the form of a letter, postcard, or telegram. Where in God's name was he? All of my familiar old panic returned. What had I done wrong? What if he didn't want to return? What if he'd met someone else? He had such a way with women, such charm, such insouciance. I squeezed my eyes shut against unbidden images of him dancing with someone else, embracing her, running his fingers down her spine. My appetite vanished but I picked at the pink marbled slab of ham, lifted a piece to my mouth, and forced myself to chew, even as queasiness tightened my throat. Starving myself would not bring him home any sooner.

And then one evening, as I returned from my studio and walked up the brick pathway, past the red geraniums, nasturtiums, and marigolds, a familiar smell of burning bark floated toward me. I rounded the corner. There sat Maynard, examining me through the smoke of his cigarette, his familiar grin as lopsided as ever.

"Evenin', ma'am, aren't you a sight for sore eyes?" He rose, slapping dust off his dungaree-clad legs. "Did you miss me?" he asked, having crossed the empty space between us to pull me into him.

"Where have you been?" I pushed him away.

He raised his arms in surrender and said, "Time got away from me, but it was a great trip. You should see all of my sketches."

"You said you'd be gone for three weeks, but it's been two months!"

"Were you worried about me?" His voice was low as he reached out to knit his fingers through mine with one hand while snaking the other around my waist and trying to lift my shirt.

"You can't just march in here and expect me to . . . to . . ." I said, trying to wrench away as he leaned into my neck and started kissing my earlobe.

"Relax, I'm back." His breath in my ear was hot and gave me shivers. My resolve wavered. "Don't give me such a hard time. I thought you'd be happy to hear I have so much new material. This new collection is going to knock everyone sideways. I need this, baby. I need a successful show."

His wheedling left me confused. Didn't I want him to be successful? For a moment, I hung limp in his arms, but then I stiffened and pulled out of reach, placing my shaking hands on my hips. "Just don't feed me a bunch of lines. If you're going to be gone for longer, tell me. I pictured you lying broken at the bottom of an abandoned mine shaft somewhere." I kept the visions of him dancing with another woman to myself.

Sheepish, he hung his head. "Sorry. I just lost track of time."

Lost track of time, my foot. I remembered Imogen's warning. Balling my fists into my pockets, I was irritated by both his glib attitude and at that part of myself that was relieved he was back and pleased to see me.

WITH MAYNARD HOME, his stories and jokes filled the cottage, but by fall, I could sense he was restless again. No matter how much I humored him by cooking his favorite meals and spend-

ing evenings down in North Beach listening to music and visiting with friends, Maynard acted itchy. He complained about
all of the streetcars and automobiles. He bemoaned all of the
new buildings crowding out the natural light. I could tell it
was just a matter of time before he announced a new trip. But
in October, I had my own announcement to make.

CHAPTER 13

I gave birth to Daniel Rhodes Dixon in the cottage on May 15, 1925. He emerged into this world as a squalling, ornery little scrap. With his tiny, flailing limbs so fragile, I held him with caution. Maynard, on the other hand, scooped him right up and folded him into the crook of his elbow. "A son," he crowed. "Now don't be intimidated. Treat him just like a puppy and he'll be fine. Look at how strong those paws are already." He marveled as Dan's tiny fingers grasped onto Maynard's hands and didn't let go.

I wanted to point out that puppies were fuzzy, acted silly, and then slept all of the time, whereas the creature in Maynard's arm was slippery, mottled in color, restless, and angry, judging by his constant wailing. At my breast, the baby refused to nurse easily. It was as if he could sniff out the fact that I'd been worried about his arrival from the outset. All this time with Maynard, I'd tracked my monthly cycles, holding him off during the times I considered unsafe. It frightened me to realize I'd miscalculated at some point. The betrayal of my own body shocked me. Everything had changed.

About a week after Dan was born, Imogen visited. She took one look at me and plucked the baby from my arms, announcing she was taking him for a walk. I collapsed into bed and fell into a deep sleep, only to dream about running. I dreamed I was running across a beach. The slapping sound of my soles hitting the hard, damp sand became faster and faster. I flew across the beach before awakening with a gasp. Why did I have to torture myself by dreaming about running? The front of my shirt was soaked with milk dripping from my breasts.

Imogen appeared, Dan in her arms. "Hush now, everything's all right," she said gently, handing the baby to me. I ripped my shirt open and placed him to my breast, wincing as I did so, but then relief swept over me as he began to nurse. The burning pressure in my body abated, my heart slowed. I leaned back onto the pillows and closed my eyes.

After a few deep inhalations, the smell of roasting meat reached my nose. "Imogen?" I whispered, not wanting to disturb the baby. "What are you up to?"

She reappeared in my bedroom doorway holding a bowl with steam rising from it. "Meat loaf's in the oven. I took the baby to the store to get some groceries. Your cupboards were bare. What in the world have you been living on?"

I shrugged, unable to remember the last thing I'd eaten.

She came closer, sat on the edge of the bed, and reached

forward to push some hair out of my face. "You must take better care of yourself. The baby and I stopped by Maynard's studio. He said this little fellow isn't nursing well. You need to remain strong. Now open up," she said, lifting a spoon toward me. Confused, I stared at her. "I've made a split-pea soup and am determined to get some of it in you, so open up."

Without protest, I let her spoon some of the soup into my mouth. Bits of carrot, onion, peas, and the smell of ham. My friend's kindness made tears course down my face.

"I know you're in bad shape if you're actually letting me help you," she said.

At some point, I closed my eyes and fell back asleep, sated.

When I awoke again, the bedroom was bathed in deep shadows, but I could see light peeking around the cracks of the closed door. My head felt as if it was filled with sand, but I lurched out of bed and crossed the room. The brightness of the kitchen left me shading my eyes. Imogen guided me to a chair and placed a plate of meat loaf in front of me. Without standing on ceremony, I pulled it toward me and dug into the mashed potatoes on the side. So great was my hunger, I barely stopped to breathe.

"Has Fronsie come by to see you?"

"She just had another baby. A girl. Two weeks ago," I managed to say in between bites.

Imogen held on to the back of the chair, a hand resting on my shoulder, and watched me devour the food on my plate. "I'm going to leave when Maynard returns, but I've filled up your cupboards and icebox with food. I'll return in three days to check on you."

The idea of being left home alone with Dan made me light-headed. The food in my mouth turned to leather. I swallowed a lump of it. "Please, please don't leave."

"Now, now," Imogen said, sliding into a chair beside me. "You'll be fine. Make sure you continue to get some rest. Sleep when the baby is sleeping and you must keep eating to keep up your strength."

"But what am I going to do? He cries all the time." By now, I was blubbering in a way that frightened me.

"Take it one day at a time. Don't get ahead of yourself," she said, her hand on my shoulder. She took a look at my plate. "You did a good job on supper. Let's get you back to bed for some sleep. I'll bring in the baby to feed when he's ready."

I pulled myself up and leaned on Imogen. Though she was small and slight, she bolstered me with surprising strength. "I just feel so heavy—"

"Shhhh, you will figure this out," she said, leading me back to my bed, but I kept crying, tripping over my right foot awkwardly until she laid me down and arranged the blankets around my shoulders. Concern wrinkled her eyes and mouth. At that moment, I would have given anything for her to have climbed into bed beside me and held me. Instead she sat next to me and took my hand in hers. With her by my side, I drifted off to sleep.

I SURVIVED THE next three days. Maynard surprised me by coming home from his studio several times a day to check on me and the baby. Each time he arrived at our door, I'd melt into his shoulder, inhaling the sharp smell of turpentine. We'd plunk down on stools on the porch. While Maynard held the baby, I'd listen to him tell me about what he was working on and who'd stopped by his studio that day. I'd roll my neck, rub at the small of my back, all while trying to absorb the sunshine beaming down on me over the stucco wall next to us. It felt as though I'd been shrunk and dropped into a glass jar. Though I could see everything around me, colors were not quite right, sounds were muffled, my depth perception was off, and everything seemed distant. I wanted to crack the glass that encased me and escape, but I was so exhausted. I could scarcely lift my arms from my sides to hold the baby.

Imogen visited every few days for several weeks, each time bringing food. Several clients arrived bearing flowers and more food. Seeing their faces awakened something inside me. My senses seemed to sharpen.

One morning I awoke and realized the baby had slept for five hours in a row. I brewed coffee in the kitchen. My hands did my brain's bidding without the slight delay that had been unnerving me since Dan's birth. I picked him up, felt the soft fuzz of his downy head against my cheek, and sank into a chair. Under my palm resting on his back, I could feel his little heart beating with the persistence of a hummingbird's wings. He fit so marvelously against my chest and shoulder, his legs pulled up underneath him, curled like a fiddlehead fern. The smell of powder, his warmth, the threads of blue veins rooting underneath the velvet of his skin—he was mine.

Imogen visited the following day, saw me nursing, and said, "You look better."

"I am. Thank you for all of your help. I'm not sure what I

would have done without you." I removed Dan from my breast and lifted him to my shoulder, patting his back. "I've been thinking about getting back to my studio."

"Already?"

"Yes, Elke Minor stopped by with those lovely flowers." I pointed to a cut-crystal vase of irises in the middle of the table. "She asked when I planned to be back in the studio and it got me thinking."

"Elke is one of your clients?"

I nodded.

"Figures she didn't bring something useful. No food or clothes?" Imogen said with a sniff. "It's easy for her to think about getting back into routines—your clients probably hire baby nurses for all of their children."

I ignored Imogen's grumbling and leaned my cheek against the side of Dan's head. He grew heavy. "I've been thinking that maybe I can bring him to the studio and still get work done. Ah-yee is the oldest of six, so she knows her way around children. I could offer to pay her a little more," I whispered. Without waking the baby, I rose and walked into our bedroom. Sliding him off my shoulder, I placed him on his belly in the middle of our bed. His tiny hands balled under his chin and his knees curled into his chest as though he were a snail pulling into its shell. Before returning to the kitchen, I slid down next to him, breathing in his milky scent and tracing the whorls of dark hair feathering his skull. His vulnerability made my throat thicken. All curled up, he was barely longer than the length of my forearm. The stir of feelings he brought up in me left me breathless. With a sigh, I returned to the kitchen, stretching out my arms and shoulders while taking my seat across from Imogen once more. "Thank you again for all of your help. What would I have done without you?"

She nodded. "When are you planning to go back?"

I glanced over my shoulder at the bedroom door. "As soon as I can. We could use the money. Maynard's work is selling, but it's inconsistent."

"You won't be able to do as much as you once did."

"We'll see."

"Maynard should go back to advertising work. It's steady income. Once the boys arrived, Roi took that teaching job at Mills."

I stood and moved to the sink to wash dishes. "Maynard's painting is going all right. He's got loads of material from his last few trips. Bender's been telling him he could put together a couple of shows in the Midwest. Maybe the East Coast too. He seems very determined and optimistic."

"Advertising work could provide some steady income."

With my back to her, I grimaced. Maynard would never forgive me if I asked him to take a job like that. He'd done that kind of work in the past and sworn it off. No, he needed to be free to continue painting. I turned and leaned my back against the sink to face Imogen. "Dan's a good baby and sleeping for longer stretches. I miss my camera. I can do this." And I truly believed I could.

April 1964
Steep Ravine, California

CHAPTER 14

The skunky smell of saltwater floats toward me as I pick my way down the sandy beach, careful of the pain lurking in my side, ready to pounce and bite if I provoke it.

"Grandma," Nathaniel calls, rushing up the beach toward me, churning up a small sandstorm in his wake. His cheeks puff in and out with exertion, but as he reaches me, he slows, his movements suddenly deliberate and controlled. He places something onto my outstretched hand with the same type of care I imagine he'd use with a sacred artifact. A small blue robin's egg, shattered along one side and empty, rests on the meat of my palm.

"My, now that's an unexpected find down here."

"I know, I know! How did it end up on the beach? Where's the chick?"

I shake my head, all the while watching his pale green eyes, the color of sea glass, widen with the wonderment of possibilities. After offering a couple of ideas for how the egg landed down here, he darts off again, eager for more discoveries. Though he's gone, I can still see his afterburn image in front of me. His expression of delight. The little gaps in his smile and the streaks of sand tracing along his sun-bronzed cheekbones.

Sudden coolness crosses over me. I shiver and look up to see the sun blocked momentarily by a cloud. I glance at my wristwatch. Dan and Mia are due to arrive in a few hours to help us pack and head home. I lift my arm to shade my eyes against the glare of the sun off the wet sand. On the hillside above, the cabin, all angles and worn shingles, clings to the ridge like a barnacle. Below it, farther down the beach away from me, the grandchildren knot over something at the waterline, probably a jellyfish or some marine oddity. When I drop my hand back to my side, the corner of the MoMA envelope inside my pocket nudges at my palm. Four days have passed since it arrived. I keep the letter close but have said nothing about it to anyone. I'm still making sense of it.

I consider calling out that it's time to clean off, brush hair and teeth, and pack bags, but then what? We'll just sit in the main room looking out the window wistfully to the ocean below. No, it's foolish to disturb the children. Here, away from the city, they need to lose themselves in the beauty of the wide-open sea, the wind, and worlds that exist under every rock along the beach. There will be plenty of time for tidying when they get home. When we're here, I try to let them set our schedule. Time at the beach is for letting the children bask in fresh air and freedom.

Nathaniel bounds back toward me, something new in his hand. "Another find! This shell is all brown and crusty on one side, but when you flip it over, look at the beautiful evening sky on the smooth part inside."

I follow his instructions. Sure enough, a pale blue twilight color glows where his finger points. "You're getting very good at seeing things, *really* seeing them."

"I've been practicing."

"Good. It takes a lot of practice to see things as they are, not as you want them to be."

"Did you practice seeing when you were my age?"

"Oh dear, I'm still practicing. Every day."

He nods with satisfaction and then pushes his head toward me to reveal a seaweed crown atop his blond hair. "Look"—he says—"I'm a Neptune."

I admire his handiwork, enjoying the unexpected change of direction in our conversation. "Here, you can be whatever you want."

He considers this. "What's a bonapart?"

"A bonapart?" I squint, trying to make sense of this question.

"Yes, Dad says when you're here, you're not the bonapart you are at home."

Realization lodges in my chest with a thud. *Bonaparte.* Napoleon Bonaparte. After years of warfare, Dan and I have finally arrived at a fragile truce, but still, he holds much against me. Anger, resentment, betrayal. It's all in the riptide below the surface. "I believe he's referring to a famous French emperor."

"Emperor?"

"It's a fancy word for 'king.'" My knowledge of aristocratic titles is a bit uncertain, but he doesn't press me.

"So, your castle is back at home?"

"Right. When I'm here"—I pause and look at the waves pushing onto the shore—"I don't have to run a kingdom. I can...relax."

Somehow my feeble explanation satisfies him. Or maybe he sees through my charade. Children are good at that. Either way, he looks out to sea and says hesitantly, "Mom and Dad will be here soon, won't they?"

I nod, dropping my hand into my pocket, and hold the letter between my fingers. It no longer crackles. It seems to be loosening, becoming a part of me. The salt air is softening the paper. Maybe it holds the answer, the way to bridge the gap between Dan and me. "Yes, in a bit. Have you missed them?"

He wrinkles his nose. "No, being here is my favorite place in the world." Gratitude floods me and I reach for his shoulder to squeeze, but he wriggles from under my touch. "Why do you and Dad have so many disagreements?"

I take a deep breath. "Well, I suppose we disagree on some choices we've both made. Sometimes we hurt each other, but we're learning to move beyond the past."

His eyebrows, frosted white with dried saltwater, rise as he studies me with a dubious expression. "Like what kind of choices?"

I pull back and forth at the camera strap around my neck while considering his question. Where do I start with my answer?

September 1925
San Francisco, California

CHAPTER 15

I don't have a single photo of me with Dan as a baby. Not a single one. In many, Maynard holds him, but there are none of the two of us together. Imogen photographed me once around this time. In the photo, I'm smiling mischievously and looking out of the frame as if laughing at a joke, but I'm alone. My eyes crinkle with a smile that spreads to every corner of my face, so my happiness must have been real, but I don't remember feeling that way when Dan was an infant. All I remember is bone-crushing exhaustion. I spent my days caring for him while cramming in studio appointments, cooking meals, scrubbing the grit and cobwebs out of our cramped little cottage, washing endless piles of clothing and house linens, wringing them dry, and putting them away, only to begin the whole routine again the following day.

Somehow the portraits I took during that era of my life show none of this. Elegant young women finger strings of pearls as they stare off into the middle distance while leaning against blank walls; well-clad fathers sit next to sons, ambition practically crackling off the paper; proud mothers preen over their plump, well-scrubbed children. A dreamy, soft focus gave all my subjects a look of perfection and peace. I edited flaws. Everyone's best angle showed. The monochromatic palette removed any dissonance between colors that didn't match. Everyone looked lovely and whole, present and thoughtful. My portraits satisfied my clients, and of course, that pleased me, yet an undertow of unease pulled at me.

One afternoon while rummaging through my dresser for a clean bandanna to cover my hair, a green velvet pouch caught between my fingers. I lifted it from the drawer and peeked inside to find my old silver bangle from my trip to Arizona with Maynard after we married and wriggled it onto my wrist. I remembered his expression of glee as he handed me the gift and placed it around my freckled wrist. Its heft felt satisfying, substantial. But then I thought of the Tuba City Indian School. It all came back. The empty faces. The wailing of the newly arrived boy. My feeling of helplessness. I shuddered, pulling the bangle off my wrist, and returned it to the pouch, pushing it to the rear of the drawer.

I backed away from my dresser, but could still feel the bangle's presence and all of the emotions it dredged up. Almost six years had passed since our trip to Tuba City Indian School. Was I the same woman who had fled that awful place? I had become so busy, too desperate to keep up with work, to think about what I was doing, to think about where I was going with my life. I took pride in making my clients satisfied, but I was running myself ragged. Why? What did all of my hours of toil add up to? Did my work matter? If I quit, sure, my clients would miss me for a bit, but they could find someone else who could make them look beautiful and intelligent. What was I running from? From the kitchen, Dan squalled. I went to him, unable to think past his cries.

ONE AFTERNOON, I stood at the worktable in my studio when the sound of giggling startled me. Fronsie leaned against the open doorway, her arm around Ah-yee. Clad in a pale blue suit-styled jacket and skirt, she smiled and winked. "Yoo-hoo, remember lil' old me? Jack's mother has taken the girls for the day so I thought I'd pop by for a visit. Ah-yee says you have a break in your schedule, so I'm going to drag you out for a bite to eat while she watches Dan. You're working too much."

I didn't protest as she pulled me out of the studio and down the street to a café, where we enjoyed a civilized hour of catching up over coffee and pastries. When the bill came, she smiled and swiped it from the waiter's hands. "I still have a few minutes of freedom. Let's go see Maynard. It's been ages since I've seen him." Off we went to the Monkey Block.

When we sashayed into his studio, he dropped his brushes and slapped his knee in delight. "Holy cats, aren't I the lucky bastard? Mrs. Stockton! To what do I owe this honor?" While she embraced him and demanded a showing of his latest work, I wandered from wall to wall soaking in his paintings of big stretches of Sonoran Desert, hot with golden hues and burning reds, the compositions often sweeping and a bit savage. Over the last couple of years, Maynard had left for several more sketching trips throughout the Southwest—Utah, New Mexico, Arizona. Each time he came home brimming with ideas that prompted him to disappear to the Monkey Block. And here it was, all that he had been creating: big skies you wanted to fall into. Some bold cerulean blue, some paler with pearly dawn lighting. Dark blues and rich purples lurked in the shadows of mesas. The paintings made goose bumps prickle my flesh. I exhaled and shook my head in admiration. This was nature down to its most basic lines and telling colors. Maynard's genius radiated from every canvas.

Fronsie accepted a light from Maynard, inhaled, and exhaled with a contented sigh in front of one of his larger canvases. "I could just sit here all day staring at these."

"Let's hope you're not alone. I'm heading east at the end of the month to tour with this collection. I need some big sales."

I tucked my arm around Fronsie's and beamed with pride. "The critics in Los Angeles love it all. Bender's been getting flooded with inquiries from Chicago and New York."

"I can see why. Aren't you two just the cat's meow?" Fronsie exclaimed, pulling Maynard to the other side of her so the three of us stared at a canvas filled with Utah's boxy mesas. "And to think I'm in the company of two of San Francisco's most successful artists."

I glanced at Maynard as he turned to tease Fronsie about buying one of his pieces. Was I an artist? I wouldn't have classified my portraits as *art,* but they were certainly doing well. I had a craft that my clients appreciated. So, Fron was right, wasn't she? I reached for her cig and took a long drag. I needed to stop overthinking everything. Maynard's work would sell like hotcakes on the East Coast. It sure seemed like we had the world by the tail.

AFTER SPENDING A month in New York, Maynard traveled home and came straight to my studio from the train station, his clothes wrinkled, face sullen. Sidling over to my appointment book, he picked up Dan and stood at Ah-yee's desk, tracing a finger down the long row of clients I had booked for the week. Tightness settled around his eyes when I asked him about the trip.

"I forgot how miserable the East Coast is," he grumbled. "Macbeth Galleries only sold a couple of my paintings. They're a bunch of goddamn lemmings back there. It's all Nancy-boy designers with only an eye on Stieglitz and all of his *isms*. Cubism, expressionism, surrealism, modernism . . . it's bullshit. No one wants anything different. I'm done with that dog-and-pony show."

My back tensed, but I kept my voice steady. "Did you get to see Consie?"

Maynard's frown deepened. "Yes, she's happy where she is with Lillian's family nearby and wants nothing to do with me."

This wasn't how things were supposed to go. "Well," I said, forcing a bright note into my voice, "Bender came by the other day to ask when you'd be back. The Biltmore's interested in a commission. Some murals, I think."

He nodded, somewhat mollified, but his frustration didn't dissipate. He started disappearing for hours without explanation. When he did come home, he was distracted and short with me. I told myself this moodiness was just a phase. A dark period. All artists went through it.

One evening he came home insisting I accompany him to a party in Oakland at Willard Van Dyke's studio. "All you do is work," he grumbled as I handed him a plate of stew. He stuffed a forkful of roasted carrots into his mouth.

Wounded, I stepped back, tucking my hair under the scarf I wore around my head. Several evenings ago, the cloying scent of Shalimar had drifted over our bed after he came home late, disheveled and drunk, his eyes blurry from the smoke at Coppa's. His teeth had been stained a dingy grayish-purple hue from red wine. I never wore Shalimar. I'd wrinkled my nose but said nothing though the memory niggled at me like a painful hangnail. Perhaps he was right. It seemed I needed to cut loose and keep him company before he found somebody else who would.

Out of the corner of my eye, I spotted a frayed spot developing on the knee of my trousers. I glanced at my reflection in the dark window. Had I brushed my hair at all that day? When was the last time I'd sat back with a cigarette, listened to music, and watched people dance? It was true, I was working almost all the time.

"Fine. Let's go."

Surprised, he stopped chewing. "Really? You'll come?"

"I'll call Ah-yee to watch Dan and get ready while you eat."

A FINE RAIN shimmered in the air as we approached the old barn Anne Brigman had converted into a studio. When she decided to move to Southern California a couple of years earlier, she gave the space to Willard Van Dyke. The barn was built around several trees. Their boughs poked through the ceiling. A pale blue shower curtain hung at a crooked angle in an attempt to try to keep the rain out. Judging by the raucous sounds already roaring from the party, I estimated everyone to be several drinks deep into Willard's famous five-star punch.

The party annoyed me from the moment I walked in. A rumba pulsed from the Victrola in the corner. The room was packed. I'd only taken a couple of steps into the scrum when someone spilled a cup of sangria on my sleeve. Dismayed, I looked at the dark red stain spreading over my arm, ruining the shirt. No one apologized.

Conversation was impossible over the music. Maybe it was just as well. What did I have to say? *I've been crazed keeping up with my clients and washing diapers and scraping off dirty dishes?* I tried to imagine how Ansel Adams would respond to that and almost laughed. While everyone clustered around Maynard, I wandered through the crowd and found Imogen, feeling grateful as she pulled me into a knot of conversation. Ed Weston stood next to her, pontificating on his favorite topic: the soul of photography. That he wore a batik turban made it difficult for me to take him seriously. His lover, Sonya, her wide-set dark eyes half closed, leaned against his shoulder, clapping along to the music, but her timing was off. It took all my willpower not to hold her hands together for a moment to get her on beat with the music. She opened her eyes fully and took me in. "Well, look who's here. You've managed to pry yourself away from all of your fancy-pants clients in Pacific Heights for a night?"

The rest of the circle laughed and I smiled along, but reconsidered giving her a good smack under the guise of helping her get on tempo.

"Now, now," chided Imogen, "I'd say Dorothea's the hardest-working woman in San Francisco."

"Sure, sure, gotta keep up with market demands," said Ed, giving me a brief once-over. "I heard Maynard's trip east was a bust. Those heels should have more respect for us out here." His gaze circled the crowd as heads nodded along to his tirade. Imogen held my hand tightly but she couldn't resist weighing in. I sighed and looked around as they griped about Stieglitz's control over the East Coast's art market.

My head ached, my lower back throbbed. How much time had passed? An hour? Two hours? How was it possible to feel so alone in such a packed crowd? I needed to go home to relieve Ah-yee. I looked around for Maynard, but couldn't find him anywhere. When I started asking people if they'd seen him, they averted their eyes, mumbled responses, and laughed nervously. Everyone appeared to step out of my way.

I found Ansel outside playing horseshoes with Willard.

"Have either of you seen Maynard?" I asked.

They both continued staring at their target, deep in concentration, horseshoes in hand, and shook their heads.

"It's gotten late. I've got to get home to my baby." My voice sounded shrill, but I didn't care. Suddenly, I hated everyone.

Ansel gave a wild toss to his horseshoe and howled when it curved far to the right, away from the target. "Dammit, I'm terrible at this blasted game." He swayed, eyes unfocused. "I need to hightail it back to the city too. Come on, Dorrie, you can hitch a ride home with me. Maynard can make his own way back."

"Are you too tight to drive?" I asked.

"Nah, I did my usual trick of swilling olive oil to coat my gut before I started drinking."

"You ass, that only helps with tomorrow's hangover," Willard said, elbowing him in the side.

"Shut up, I'm fine." Ansel pulled his car keys from his pocket and held them up, nodding at me. The thinning hair atop his head stuck out in all directions. He looked anything but fine, but I felt desperate to get away from there.

My face burned as I gathered my purse and linen jacket and met him at the front door to leave. Where the hell was my husband? Was relief stamped across everyone's faces as I said goodbye? I couldn't tell. On the walk to the car, I was thankful for the darkness, for it hid my eyes filling with tears. Ansel's tireless energy usually exhausted me, but on that night, I was also grateful for his boundless stamina. Always a big talker, he nattered on from the moment he revved the engine and squealed the tires away from the curb at Willard's to when he pulled alongside the gate in front of our cottage and I spilled out. When I ducked down next to the passenger window to thank him, he gave me a smile filled with pity. My shame, a molten heat shifting and swirling inside me during our drive, solidified into anger like a rock lodged underneath my rib cage.

All night long sleep eluded me. Maynard never came home. At one point, I went into Dan's room and sat next to his crib, trying to calm my nerves by watching the rhythmic rise and fall of his chest. He slept with arms outstretched above his head in a pose of complete surrender. How had we produced this perfect little creation? When gray light appeared in the window and Dan awoke, I fed him oatmeal before placing him in his buggy outside the door of the kitchen. I knew exactly where I needed to go. Down the sidewalk we went, the buggy's wheels creaking along the concrete, my calves and thighs burning from exertion as we rushed downhill toward Cow Hollow. Fatigue weighted my eyes and the pale glare of morning left me dazed, but exercise stirred my blood, made the cogs of my brain start turning.

I am a fool. Maynard was running around with other women and barely covering his tracks. How long had this been going on? My hands were cold on the handle of the buggy, my knuckles white. By the time I reached Fronsie's door, nothing but fury fueled me.

She blinked in surprise when she opened the door. "Well, I expected the milkman, but you're a much better arrival. Want some breakfast?" I shook my head. Just seeing this woman, my dear friend after all of these years, almost brought me to tears. She nodded and ushered me through her house, past the kitchen table still set with the remains of breakfast, to the grassy backyard where her two daughters sat in front of three shallow tin baking pans filled with water. I plunked Dan down with the girls and watched the toddlers dip their chubby fingers in the water and splutter with enjoyment. An intense expression of concentration settled on the face of Fronsie's four-year-old daughter, Louise. She picked up a measuring cup, filled it with water, then poured it into another measuring cup. Water spilled over the sides, but she seemed not to mind. Jack poked his head out the kitchen door.

"Fron . . ." He blinked when he saw me. "Oh, Dorothea," he said, reaching to the loose end of the necktie draped over his shoulder to arrange himself. He lifted his wrist to look at his watch. "Sorry, am I running late?"

"No, it's early. Sorry to show up like this," I said, rubbing at my eyes. The smell of coffee drifted out from the open kitchen door. Without thinking, I took a gusty inhalation.

"Want some?" Fronsie said, gesturing back at the house.

I smiled weakly as she turned to go back into the kitchen.

When she rejoined me outside after a quiet conference with Jack, I accepted the outstretched coffee gratefully. The mug burned my palms, but in a good way. My stiff fingers wrapped around it, happy to absorb the heat. I felt her waiting for me to say something, but I blew on the surface of my drink, watching the liquid ripple, before saying, "Maynard's having an affair. Maybe more than one. It could be a dozen. I don't even know."

Fron smoothed down her apron and glanced at me. "Does he know you're onto him?"

"At this point, how could he not? I went to a party with him last night and he vanished and never came home. It's like he wants me to know."

"You look exhausted."

"I didn't sleep a wink." My voice shook, my head felt fuzzy, and bile rose in my throat. Without a word, I pushed my coffee mug toward Fron and ran inside to the washroom.

I leaned over the toilet, retching. Once finished, I stood and dabbed at my mouth with some bath tissue. My wan face stared out at me from the gilt-edged mirror. Red-rimmed eyes, my complexion the color of dirty bed linens—I knew what this meant all too well. I did some counting on my fingers before opening up the washroom door and trailing my palm along the wall to steady myself as I headed back outside. Taking a deep breath, I stepped down onto the flagstone patio and resumed my spot next to Fronsie, still watching the children.

She raised her eyebrows. "You all right?"

"I'm pregnant again," I answered.

Fron raised her eyebrows.

I pulled a bobby pin out of my hair and stabbed it into a new spot, wincing as the metal hit my scalp. "This marriage will not be a failure. I need to get my husband back. I've got to fight for this, Fron."

"Of course you do," she replied, a sad smile on her face. "You never give up on anything."

MAYNARD ARRIVED HOME later that evening to find his favorite dinner, pork chops and baked beans, waiting for him on the table. A sheepish look slid over his face as he took a seat. "Bender sold three of my canvases today," he said, eyeing me for any sign he was in the doghouse.

I smiled and congratulated him as I took a seat across from him. I knew about the sold paintings already. Earlier at Fron's, I'd cleaned myself up and left Dan with her so I could make several house calls to three of my favorite, most trustworthy clients. Each woman had assured me she had a blank space on

LEARNING TO SEE   135

her wall that would look much better with one of Maynard's paintings on it. From my spot across the table, I studied him. Bags hung under his dark eyes, his cheeks looked thin, his color sallow. I thought back to the lanky, golden-skinned man who built us a blazing fire and then recited poetry to me at our little miner's camp in Sonoma. This was the same man, I reminded myself. I couldn't allow myself to be weak and give up on him. From the other room, Dan chortled to himself. I placed a hand on my belly while reaching for Maynard's with the other. When I told him about the new baby, he squeezed his eyes closed for a moment.

"Dor, you know my pops died in an asylum."

Confused, I shook my head.

He nodded. "Yep, cracked right up. Who knows why?" He shook his head, staring off at a spot on the wall. "But I'm not going to be that man. I haven't done right by Consie, but I'll be a better father to our children. I promise." He placed his hand atop mine upon my belly. I exhaled and squeezed his hands.

OUR SECOND SON arrived on a morning in June made gloomy with drizzle. When I called Maynard in Arizona, where he was working on a mural commission, he gave a loud *whoop* into the phone and suggested the baby be named John Good-news Dixon. I agreed. *Good news* was exactly what we needed. I tucked my new rosy baby under my chin and smiled. We were getting a fresh start.

CHAPTER 16

Good news was short-lived in 1929. A few months after John's first birthday, the stock market crashed. New York City, where it all began, felt very far away from the diapers, bills, appointments, and making of meals that marked my days. Sure, the newspapers blared headlines with big, bold type describing how millions of dollars were lost, but we all thought it was limited to the East Coast. And really, how do millions of dollars simply disappear? The whole thing defied any sort of logic. At first. But then little things started creeping into our daily lives, making it all more real. Clients began canceling portrait appointments. Not many initially. Most were the type of people who could withstand some economic uncertainty. But requests for Maynard's art dried up overnight. Galleries called off exhibits; museum curators decided not to acquire new work; builders backed out of new projects left and right; and most of his mural commissions were abandoned. Little did we know that of the hundred canvases he would paint over the next several years, only a few would sell.

Maynard tried to recalibrate his expectations. He entered a competition to paint a mural for the San Francisco Stock Exchange Building and then headed to the Tehachapi Mountains to paint for several months, leaving me to hold down the fort with two small children. When he returned, he was outraged to learn that his friend Ralph Stackpole had awarded the commission to Diego Rivera, the renowned Mexican muralist.

"Rivera's a goddamned Communist, for Chrissake," Maynard fumed as he stormed around the living room of our new, larger house down the hill from our old bungalow. "And he's mocked our financial institutions. Why in the world would they give the commission to him?"

"Seems to me you've done your own fair share of criticizing the city's 'money boys' over the years." I shook my head in annoyance, thinking of all the times Maynard complained about my clients. "Maybe you shouldn't have gotten so hot under the collar and quit the Bohemian Club. You'd still be sitting tight with that crowd."

He glared at me. "A man's got to hold to his principles."

"True, but a man's got to be willing to own up to the cost of sticking to those principles."

He snorted. "Those fat cats talk a big game about being good Americans. Well, if they were such good Americans, they wouldn't have given the damned job to a foreigner."

"A travesty," I said, my indignation tepid.

"Don't you even care? He stands to make four thousand dollars from this mural."

Four thousand dollars. Maynard sure knew how to get my attention. I couldn't even allow myself to think about how we could use that money. Suddenly John weighed a thousand pounds in my arms. He had a tooth coming in and had kept me up much of the night crying and fussing. I'd brought the boys to Fronsie's in the morning before hurrying to a couple of portrait appointments. Now a throbbing headache, made sharper by Maynard's anger, twitched behind my eyes. Dan came running through the room wielding a stick, pretending it was a gun.

"Pow!" he yelled, taking aim with his stick at a line of glass bottles on the windowsill and pretending to shoot. *"Pow, pow, pow, pow!"* He spun around and the backside of his stick knocked a stack of books off a chair onto the floor. The loud thud startled John. He began to wail.

Maynard stopped his circling the room and bent down, his knees cracking. He looked Dan in the eye. "Hey, pard, slow down in here. You gotta be more careful." He took the stick from Dan, inspected it, and raised it to his eye as if looking through a scope. "Is this the business end of this rifle?"

"Yes, sir," Dan said, nodding, a smile dawning across his small face.

"This is a fine weapon you got here. If you go outside and set up some targets, I'll come out to join you for a few shots." He looked over at me and winked. "I might pretend one of them is Stackpole; the damned phony wouldn't know great art if it came up and bit him in the ankle."

I nodded, rubbing at John's back, trying to quiet him. It

felt like grains of sand lined the insides of my eyelids, and a twinge of nausea clung to me from the lack of sleep.

"You know the worst part about it all? The biggest insult is that I'm going to have to see Rivera every goddamned day while he's here because Stackpole's loaning him his studio down the hall from me." Maynard sighed and scanned the back window to watch Dan in the yard. As he started to walk out of the room, he turned. "Every time I have to take a piss, I'll have to pass that goddamned Mexican."

With Maynard out of the room, it felt like a storm had passed. The air became lighter. John drooped, asleep in my arms. I rocked him back and forth, thinking about Rivera. Even with the big flap over the Stock Exchange commission, everyone seemed in agreement that he was one of the finest artists in the world. Maybe having him in the studio next door to Maynard's wouldn't be such a bad thing.

RIVERA AND HIS young bride, a shy woman named Frida Kahlo, arrived in the city to begin his commission. Like bees drawn to a picnic, San Francisco society swarmed the couple with invitations, all eager to fete the famous painter.

Maynard came home one evening after spending his day at the studio and threw our front door open with such venom that the doorknob gashed a hole in the wall. "I knew it. He's a know-it-all," he huffed. "He must have wasted an hour of my time telling me that California's got everything an artist needs to make it and we don't have any excuses for mediocrity. As if I don't know that. Hell, that's what I've been saying for the last twenty years." He threw his black Stetson at the wall and tugged his fingers through his hair, then sighed and shook his head. "I don't even know how he hauls his fat ass up those narrow stairs."

A week later, we received an invitation to have dinner with Rivera and his wife at Ben and Betsy Blumberg's, a family I'd long done portrait work for. Fronsie was busy so we found ourselves without anyone available to watch the boys. I called Betsy and explained the jam we were in.

"Bring them," she said. "The boys can join our girls upstairs with the nanny. The more the merrier."

I accepted her generous offer. How nice it would be to have a nanny. Especially one who viewed adding two more children to her charge as a *merry* turn of events.

We arrived early to the party. A maid took our coats and Betsy, slim and elegant in a bias-cut Vionnet dress, ushered us upstairs to a spacious high-ceilinged apartment she called the nursery. The slump in everyone's fortunes seemed not to extend to the Blumbergs. The nanny, a young uniformed Scottish girl with lustrous russet hair, greeted us with a warm hello. Dan took one look at her sparkling, citrine-colored eyes and wordlessly pushed himself onto her lap, handing her a book to read without taking his eyes from her face.

When we made it down to the party, Maynard elbowed our host. "Your girl up there has a brogue stiff enough to hang a flag on. How do you understand a thing that comes out of her mouth?"

"I don't. I leave it all to Betsy," said Ben, looking bemused.

"Ahhh, must be nice to be a captain of industry," Maynard said. I flinched with embarrassment, but Ben chuckled and they drifted toward the large doorway to the next room. A group of men spilled out, guffawing at a joke someone had told. A few faces were recognizable. Albert Bender, Ralph Stackpole, and a few other artists I knew from the Monkey Block stood with martini glasses in hand. "Look who's arrived: it's Mr. San Francisco himself," Bender exclaimed. Maynard grumbled a response, but his expression brightened when someone gave him a Scotch.

I settled onto one of the damask couches in the drawing room to catch up with a few of the wives, some of whom were clients of mine. We all tugged out cigarette cases and lit up as we awaited the grand arrival of Rivera. People spoke to each other without listening, all eyes darting toward the foyer.

An hour after the dinner was scheduled to start, Rivera had still not arrived. My stomach growled as I stubbed out what felt like my fifteenth cigarette in a silver ashtray of Betsy's. A commotion at the door caused everyone to swivel their heads. In walked Rivera, but I couldn't take my gaze off the delicate, tawny-skinned woman in a colorful floor-length Mexican-style skirt and blouse standing at his side. Three ropes of turquoise beads encircled the woman's throat. Black braids, thick as Dan's forearms, wrapped around her head, making her look like an exotic Mexican princess. Embroidered flowers encircled the hem of the skirt and danced around her bodice. While voices rose in excitement and introductions were made, we all crossed the foyer to the dining room. She moved in a way that was all too familiar to me. I watched her cross the marble floor, her long skirt pulling to the right with each step to reveal a slight limp.

Though Rivera was huge, corpulent, really, and the shape

of an anvil, he glided through the crowd with surprising grace on incongruously spindly legs. He reminded me of the wild cattle, shaggy and thick, we'd seen in Arizona years ago, creatures capable of crossing narrow plank bridges spanning irrigation streams with nary a stumble.

Betsy, eager to get the dinner under way, seated everyone. Maynard and Rivera landed at the far end of the long table, but the painter's wife sat only one seat away from me. I studied her as the first course of jellied tomato cream bouillon was served. She sat upright as if balancing a stack of books on her head and nodded politely along with the conversation. She picked at her crown roast of lamb but didn't appear to eat much. Though she maintained a smile throughout the entire meal, I detected a sadness in the way she watched her husband out of the corner of her eye. After the final course of individual raspberry mousse cakes was served, we all stood. I inched over and introduced myself.

"Ah, I've met your husband at his studio," she said, her accent thick, her voice melodious and husky. "He showed me some of your photographs. Your portraits are beautiful."

"Thank you. How are you enjoying San Francisco?" The banality of my small talk horrified me, but I found myself tongue-tied by her exotic beauty.

"I have not seen much yet. Like my husband, I am an artist and have been busy at work on my own painting."

I nodded, admiring her confidence. "Your skirt is extraordinary."

She looked down at the bright crimson fabric around her

waist. A stripe of orange ran below the crimson and then a cream-colored panel constituted the final portion of the skirt. When she raised her face to me, she smiled. Her big doe-like eyes sparkled. "Thank you. It's native Tehuana dress that the women of Oaxaca wear." I must have looked blank because she added, "That's a part of the country down in the south, on the Pacific side."

"The vivid colors . . ." Mesmerized, I leaned forward and touched her turquoise-colored blouse.

She laughed. "How interesting that color attracts you since your work is black-and-white."

I made a face and nodded in agreement. "I'm always drawn to color."

"So this is the photographer," a voice boomed from behind me. I turned to see Diego Rivera swaggering toward us. Up close, his teeth had gaps and were rather yellow, his nose bulbous. I couldn't reconcile his ugliness next to the beauty of his wife. "Tell me," he said, tilting his head to one side as he observed me. "Have you ever tried Mexican chocolate?"

"Chocolate?"

"Yes, Mexican chocolate," he repeated. He reached out his hand to take mine in his. "It's the best. Spicy and dark. You must come to my studio and try some. Sometimes we melt it and drink it. Tomorrow, you must come. Once you've tried it, you will not even know how to describe the flavor. It's like . . . well, when have you ever felt an ecstasy you wished could last forever?"

I felt my face go hot. He grinned.

"Yes, this is why you must try it." With my hand still in his, he started walking and I followed him several steps. "And bring me your photographs, please."

"You would like to see my work?"

"Yes, when you come tomorrow." He laughed as he spoke, amused at my confusion, but he reached out to smooth down my hair along the side of my head, his palm lingering on the back of my neck. He drew me closer.

I smiled, noting the dark hair that appeared at his throat above where his cream-colored linen shirt was buttoned. His cheeks, dark and soft, reminded me of clay and the impulse to touch his face came over me. Next to elegant Frida, it was impossible not to feel plain, but under Rivera's admiring gaze, I knew my green eyes sparkled, my figure enticed. I felt beguiling. Was this Rivera's magic? That his ugliness made women feel beautiful? Emboldened, I said, "Perhaps we can make a trade. A few of my photos for a few of your sketches. Some souvenirs."

"I like this idea, yes." Still holding my hand, his smile appeared incandescent.

Frida came toward us, a curious glint in her eye, and she slipped my other hand in hers, stretching me between the two of them. "Tomorrow," she purred. "I shall give you one of my long skirts. A gift. We're about the same height. Let's see what a little color does for you."

Almost breathless, I thanked her, slipping my hands from their grasps, and turned to find Betsy behind me, the familiarity of her a welcome refuge from the giddiness brought over me by Diego and Frida. "Dorothea," she said, "I just sent word upstairs for the nanny to bring down your boys."

We began our goodbyes. The nanny appeared, John asleep in her arms, Dan by her side rubbing his eyes. Maynard bent over to scoop up Dan but straightened quickly, rubbing at his nose. "What the hell? He smells like a Portuguese whorehouse!" As if a wasps' nest had been thrown onto the foyer's marble floor, everyone stepped back in shock, no doubt wondering what exactly Maynard did with his time when he wasn't painting.

The nanny hurried to say, "I tried to clean him up best I could, but when he used the toilet, he got into a bottle of scent . . ." Her explanation tapered off in the silence that had overcome the room.

Urgent choking erupted from someone. Everyone turned to look for the sound, and there stood Frida, coughing and laughing, tears streaming down her face as she shook her head and raised a hand to her forehead in mock surrender. "Señor Dixon," she managed to say between fits of laughter, "you have the most wicked sense of humor."

Her heavily accented pronunciation of *wicked* and the way she was now leaning on Rivera to hold her up started a ripple of laughter through the crowd. Maynard shook his head in amusement as he picked up Dan. I slid John into my arms. We took our leave of the party. On my way past Frida, I looked at her and gave a small nod. She returned the gesture so subtly that no one noticed our exchange, but a bond had been forged.

The next day when I went to visit the Riveras in the Monkey Block, Frida handed me a bundle wrapped in white tissue paper. "Open this before you try any of Diego's chocolate."

I opened the paper to find a long turquoise skirt decorated

with embroidered flowers at the bottom. The blouse was a pale yellow with delicate pin tucks along the bodice. I let the skirt unfold and fall to the ground and held it in front of the trousers I was wearing. Frida studied me and nodded. "I thought perhaps a darker color might feel more natural. You like the length?"

Overcome by the beauty of the garments, I said, "They're glorious."

Without taking her eyes from my face, she asked, "You cover up your leg too?"

"Yes, polio. I was seven."

"I was also seven. My right foot was damaged as well."

We were silent in the face of such coincidence, but then she went on to tell me of a horrible trolley car accident that had left her severely injured several years earlier. Plagued by pain that confined her to bed for long stretches of time, she began to paint. Eventually doctors discovered three of her vertebrae had never healed and insisted she wear a back brace. Raising her blouse, she gave me a glimpse of the leather bands and iron bars wrapped around her waist.

"That looks terribly uncomfortable," I said.

"And yet still he loves me," she mused, nodding her chin toward Diego moving around in the adjacent room. "Through all of this."

For the duration of her stay in San Francisco, Frida and I continued to spend time together. News that Diego had begun a very public affair with Helen Wills Moody, the tennis champion, raced through our social circles, but we never spoke of it. Frida started painting in my studio, some days arriving pale and stiff-faced. She blamed back pain, but it could have been heartbreak too. Citing her health as the reason, she stopped going to social events and art shows. We worked in companionable silence for hours together, focused, comfortable, and productive. Sometimes Maynard dropped in to pace back and forth in front of the velvet couch. He would slow his steps near my opened appointment book, his gaze flinty as it traveled the list of clients booked for the week. Once when he left after mumbling something about an errand, Frida said, "He's envious you still have work."

"But business is slow. I had to let my assistant go."

She shrugged. "Still, men like to be the providers."

I knew she was right. What would keep Maynard from getting restless? When Frida and Diego pulled up stakes and returned to Mexico several weeks later, I decided our family needed a change of scenery too. I knew just the place.

CHAPTER 17

I found a used Model T listed in the newspaper and bought it from a fellow in greasy coveralls on Valencia Street. Since I'd never learned to drive, Fronsie accompanied me to provide some pointers. She sat in the passenger seat, arms folded tightly across her chest, a worried expression pinching her pretty face.

"Good heavens, don't you have any faith in me?" I asked.

"How in the world do you two plan to get to Taos in this rig?"

"We're smart, we'll figure it out."

Fronsie's skeptical expression told me exactly what she thought about our intelligence, but I brushed off her doubts. Four days later, Maynard, the boys, and I headed south on 101 bound for Taos, a town Maynard had long spoken about visiting. He'd been offered studio space by his friend Mabel Dodge

Luhan, the wealthy heiress, and we took her up on the offer. A couple of hours south of the city in the Santa Cruz Mountains, I discovered that Maynard, who insisted on driving, possessed an unfortunate tendency to look out his window, inspecting the landscape, instead of keeping his eyes on the road. After taking a bend a little too casually, the rear tires spat gravel. I could contain myself no longer. "God help us! Maynard, let me drive so you can take in the scenery all you want."

"Dammit, woman, stop talking."

I glanced back at the boys, both dozing, and spoke through gritted teeth. "If we end up in a ditch . . ."

"If I hit a ditch, I'm sending your side into it hardest."

I pursed my lips together and looked away, annoyed with his dark humor, but even more annoyed with myself for getting him started. I must have nodded off because the next thing I knew the automobile was tumbling, bumping down-hill. A squealing sound filled the air. My head struck against the window. Stars danced across my vision. The sound of the boys shrieking rang in my ears. We jolted to a stop. Thrown against the dashboard, I heard a muffled sound of crying. "John? Dan?" I pushed myself upright, dizzy and dazed. "John? Dan?" I called again, louder.

Though my forehead throbbed, panic filled me with deter-mination. I crawled over my seat and into the back. Dan's little red shirt lay crumpled below me so I reached down and peeled him off the floor of the motorcar, my heart in my throat. Under-neath him lay John, motionless. Fear choked the breath out of me. I pulled their faces toward me and inspected them closely, running my hands up and down their limbs. Both whimpered as they pushed their little heads into my shoulders. I let out a ragged breath. "Are you all right? Does anything hurt?" They both continued to weep, but I found nothing amiss as I patted them down. Saying a silent prayer of thanks, I rocked back and forth with them and peered into the front seat.

"Dorrie? Dorothea . . ." Maynard moaned.

"Hush, don't scare the boys," I whispered to him, leaning forward to see what had happened. He was still seated in front of the steering wheel, yet his wrist dangled at an unnatural angle. "Hold on, let me settle these two and I'll come around to check on you." While Maynard continued to groan, I wiped the tears from the boys' faces, pulled two butterscotch candies from my pocket, and handed one to each before going around to the front of the car to open Maynard's door. It appeared we had run off the road, dodged a copse of trees, and skidded down a short embankment. Remarkably, the car appeared undamaged. I opened the driver's side door and peered in to assess Maynard.

"Honest, I wasn't trying to kill you. I'm sorry I said that earlier," he moaned through clenched teeth.

"I know, I know." I pulled him forward and inspected his face. A goose egg, shiny and purple, already bulged by his left temple. When I tried to ease his sleeve up to look at his arm, he scrunched his eyes closed and growled. "Hold on, your wrist doesn't look right," I said.

He let out a string of oaths. I glanced back at the boys, but they were sucking away at their candies and sorting tubes of oil paint that had scattered over the backseat from Maynard's paint box.

I bit my lip. "Well, what do you want me to do? I can drive us out of here, but we should find a doctor in San Jose."

He cursed some more. "Nah, I don't want to pay for a damn doctor. Just splint it."

I stared at him. Who did he take me for—Florence Nightingale? I noticed he was still talking through clenched teeth, color drained from his face. "What's wrong with your mouth?" I asked.

"My jaw is killing me. It took a wallop as we went down the embankment."

I debated returning to San Francisco as I looked around the wreckage of our belongings strewn throughout the car. A long wooden spoon had landed on the floor of the backseat. I reached for it and then pulled the belt off the jacket I was wearing. With the spoon and belt in one hand, I bent over to feel around under the driver's seat. Sure enough, my fingers came upon a smooth cool glass surface. I gave Maynard a long look and pulled out a bottle of whiskey, still remarkably in one piece.

He took it from my outstretched hand with a sheepish expression but didn't hesitate to lift it to his lips for a few good long slugs. I let him drink—he was going to need all of the fortification he could get. After he'd drained half the bottle, I took a deep breath and seized his arm, pushing it against the handle of the wooden spoon, straightening it as best I could as I wrapped it with my jacket belt. As he yelled, I inspected my makeshift splint. It would have to do the trick.

"Oh, stop your grumbling," I admonished, pushing him

along the front seat to the passenger's side. He closed his eyes. His head lolled against the side of the car while I put the lid back on the bottle, now significantly emptier, and tucked it back underneath the driver's seat. Before settling behind the wheel, I circled the automobile. The wheels looked fine. Only one headlight was cracked.

Taking a deep breath, I climbed into the driver's seat to assess the three pedals on the floor of the car. I turned to check on the boys. Both looked back at me wide-eyed, but I gave them a wink. "Come on, I can do this," I muttered, concentrating on the steps Fronsie had demonstrated back in San Francisco. Once I had the hand brake lever in neutral, I pushed the clutch into a low gear and the car began rolling forward. I pushed down on the throttle and gave a holler. We made a slow curve, gaining momentum, before I jerked the wheel back toward the hill and we clambered up the embankment, the engine revving with a worrying groan. As the car stopped shaking once we hit the asphalt of the road, I exhaled.

The boys cheered.

Maynard snored.

"Victory!" I crowed, though I kept my eyes firmly directed to the road ahead.

I DROVE FOR four more days, Maynard sauced the entire time. By the time we arrived in Taos, the whole lower half of his face had swelled and a purplish bruise resembling a storm cloud from one of his paintings enveloped the left side of his face. Mabel Dodge Luhan set us up with a small adobe casita on the outskirts of Rancho de Taos, a picturesque village about four

miles south of the main city of Taos. The town's doctor visited us and pronounced Maynard's wrist and jaw broken. My
irritation over his injuries was offset by the doctor's compliments on my improvised splinting, but any satisfaction over
my nursing skills vanished when I realized what a demanding
patient Maynard would prove to be. Dirty jokes, endless cold
compresses and glasses of water, and games of poker became
the order of each day.

Along with playing nurse, it fell to me to settle us into our
new home. The stark lines of the stucco exterior, the bundles
of red chilies dangling from the walls, the crimson, green,
and gold wool blanket hanging off the side of the adobe—it all
charmed me, but the reality of our primitive conditions soon
wore thin. Without any running water or electricity, my days
became filled with maintaining a cooking fire, sweeping the
dirt-packed floors, and hauling water from the outside well by
the front door.

Beyond our new home was wide-open space, bare of any
real trees beyond a few stunted cottonwood groves dotting the
landscape. Now three and six, the boys found it to be heaven.
A neighbor, a Mexican man missing a front tooth who barely
spoke a lick of English, brought a small pony over to us. It
hardly took a week before the boys were riding the creature
around the property like two vaqueros.

After several weeks, Maynard was able to leave bed. The
first thing he did was head into town to outfit his new studio
with supplies. He returned home later that afternoon describing the market square that consisted of a post office, two sa-
loons, and a one-eyed, three-legged mutt who guarded the

village's one general store with impressive ferocity. For Maynard and the boys, our new home offered endless opportunity for adventure. For me, it was one chore after another, but as Dan and John came in for meals with high color on their faces and Maynard started to stand a little taller, I told myself it was all worth it. The children grew at an astonishing rate. It seemed they ate three times their body weight several times a day.

Every morning when I was pumping water at the well in front of the casita, a car drove by with a solitary figure inside, the same time every morning, seven days a week. Never once did he glance over at me in curiosity. One morning, as I placed a bowl of scrambled eggs on the table for breakfast, I mentioned him to Maynard.

"Oh, that's Paul Strand."

Hmmm, another photographer from New York. Years earlier, I'd seen a show of Strand's at Stieglitz's gallery in Manhattan but never met him in person.

"He's got a studio down the street from me. Pretty uppity, never talks to anyone."

I pulled a pan sizzling with frying bacon off the cookstove and forked a few strips onto each boy's plate. It felt like all I did was prepare meals. Wiping my greasy hands on a dish towel and watching them eat, my chest tightened. I tried to imagine what it would be like to walk out the door, drive to a studio, and work for the day, without making any food for anyone, fetching water, sweeping, or laundering clothes. I turned to the tub for washing dishes and tried to push any thoughts of photography from my mind. But that night, as I finished putting the plates away on the shelf, I found myself gazing out the window and studying the skeletal outline of a bare cottonwood in the dusky twilight. I could practically feel the heft of a camera in my hands, the smoothness of its metal against my fingers, and the pressure on my brow as I looked into the viewfinder. As I stood thinking, John came to me and nudged his head into my hip. A handful of small golden leaves gleamed on his head like a crown. My hand lingered on his shoulder while I admired the contrast of gold in his dark hair. Then I brushed them away. "Are you ready for bed?"

I took his muffled snufflings as affirmation and squatted down to cup his chin with my hand. "Did you polish your teeth?"

"Dan says it will wash away the taste of your apple pie if I do."

"That may be the case, but you must clean them anyway."

His face crumpled in disappointment so I took one of his hands in my own. Tiny dark arcs of dirt appeared above the pink of his nailbeds, remnants from a long day of outside play. "Come now, time to get ready for bed." Despite dragging his feet, he followed me. After I had tucked him into his cot, I returned to the window and looked out into the darkness. I wasn't sure how much longer I could last without my camera.

WINTER NEARED, ITS winds howling along the flats surrounding our chilly adobe. Money was running low. Maynard and I agreed it was best to return to San Francisco. My portrait business could pay our bills. I knew Maynard and the boys were disappointed to leave, but I could scarcely wait to have the steering wheel in my hands and head back. At the outskirts of the city, ominous signs greeted us. The boys huddled close to the windows, looking at rows of ramshackle hovels and lean-tos constructed from wooden boards, tarps, strips of canvas, shingles, abandoned signs, and sections of fencing. Anything that could be salvaged and used as a building material lined the edge of the highway. Occasional stumps of stovepipes spewed black plumes of smoke into the air above the huts.

"Please, darlings, don't press your noses against the glass. You'll leave tracks all over it when you do that," I said.

"But, Mama, look at all those people camping. I've never seen tents like those before," said Dan.

I glanced over at Maynard glowering at the road, the brim of his cowboy hat pulled low. We neared a wizened man sitting by the shoulder of the highway on an overturned pail. He stared at the passing motorcars. Behind him, a cloth covering the opening of a nearby culvert fluttered in the wind, the only sign of movement. This was not the same place we had left.

CHAPTER 18

The city was quiet. It took me a while to figure it out but then I realized the motorcar traffic had lessened. Unable to afford gasoline, people walked everywhere. And the constant building projects that once choked the city's streets had dwindled. Gone was the sound of hammers and saws, and now idle men peppered the streets, arms folded, leaning against the walls of buildings watching people pass. Younger boys clustered at street corners, offering newspapers, shoeshines, rags, sometimes boiled peanuts. I always tried to drop a nickel into one of the chipped mugs they clutched in their grubby hands but waved off whatever they were peddling. I wanted nothing in return, just a little peace of mind that maybe they'd find something to eat that day.

One of the first things I did when we got back to the city

was join Imogen for a Camera Club meeting. With Maynard struggling to find any sort of paying work, I needed to keep a handle on my business. The Camera Club's numbers appeared to have thinned, but people still turned out. Some members had stopped driving in from surrounding areas, but Willard and several others still took the ferry across from Oakland. I missed Connie Kanaga; she had left for New York City a few months prior.

Unsurprisingly, word in the crowd was that there was little work to be had. I came away from the meeting feeling low and guilty. I was in better shape than most. I still had clients, but how much longer would that last? Imogen and I remained quiet on the way home, each immersed in our worries.

We entered my kitchen and found Roi, Maynard, and both Imogen's and my boys gathered around a cutting board with a block of sharp cheddar in the center of the kitchen table. A tin of crackers lay on its side. Several apple cores, brown and lank, were tossed next to the sink alongside a stack of dirty plates.

"Hmmm, what's been happening here?" asked Imogen, taking in the two empty wine bottles between Maynard's and Roi's elbows. "Everyone was pleased to welcome Dorothea back into the fold."

"Oh yes, everyone's always happy to see Dorothea," Maynard slurred. "Why, there's been a line of her clients out the front door since we got home. Hardest worker in town. I wager if she was a man, she'd be a captain of industry by now, lording over us all. It's a shame all of that ambition is wasted in a woman."

I closed my eyes, my lungs constricting. So, this was how he was going to be tonight. I swallowed and looked to Roi and Imogen. Roi appeared to be fishing his finger about in his glass for a piece of cork or something, but Imogen glowered at Maynard.

"But such is her lot in life that she's married to you instead," she said. "It's lucky there are still people around here with money to spend, right?"

"I'm tired of 'em all feathering their nests off our work."

"Sounds like you're oversimplifying things a bit."

"Right." Maynard thumped his glass down and a splash of wine sloshed over the side, spreading onto the table like a bloodstain. "All my clients have flown the coop. Bunch of rich assholes."

"Stop it," I told him, glancing at the boys and grabbing a dish towel to clean up the mess. "No one likes it when you get going on this."

"I'm just sayin' what everyone's thinking."

"Quit feeling sorry for yourself," I said.

"Oh, you're a fine one, aren't you?" Maynard looked at me, eyes piercing over the rim of his glass. "Cold as Christian charity."

"The way I see it, you can either sit around and feel sorry for yourself or get to work. When times get tough, some people head down to Coppa's to drown their sorrows, while real men get to work. I've always thought of you as a real man, Maynard."

"Your wife is right," Imogen said. "You're enough of a poker player to know you've got to play the hand you're dealt, no complaints."

"Imogen, mind your own potatoes," Roi snapped.

She sniffed and clapped her hands, urging the boys to rise. As she bent over to pull a sweater over Padraic's small shoulders, Maynard slouched in his seat and dropped his head on his arms crossed on the table. The spark that had always lit him up from within appeared to have guttered. On her way out the door, Imogen took my hand and squeezed it before I led Dan and John away for bed.

I CONTINUED TO work but my appointments became fewer and fewer. Whole days passed without any portrait sessions, so I filled the time with developing and filing negatives. When I did book a client, I struggled with occupying the boys. For a while, Fronsie helped me by having them play at her house with her daughters. Then one day she announced they were leaving for New Jersey to be closer to her family. Jack's parents had both died the previous year. The Wall Street crash had been too much strain on his father and he had dropped dead of a heart attack one afternoon in his office. Jack's mother had followed soon after. No one spoke of what exactly happened to her, but I gathered from Fronsie that several bottles of pills had been involved. It wasn't an unusual story. Times were tough and grim endings were all too easy to spot in the *Chronicle*'s obituaries. The prospect of Fron's departure devastated me.

I went to visit the day before they left and Fron offered me a seat on a packing crate while handing me a teacup filled with something that was not tea.

"What's this?" I asked.

"I'm using up the last of our sherry. Come on now, you're joining me for one today. Otherwise I don't think I can get through this." She threw her drink back and then blew out her cheeks. "I can't believe I'm leaving."

"I hate to see you go. You've always been my proof that happy endings exist," I said before taking a measured sip of my drink, my eyes watering as my throat burned.

"Not sure how much of a happy ending this is," said Fronsie, frowning. "And besides, don't let yourself think you don't deserve happiness."

I nodded, raising the gilt rim of the Limoges teacup to my lips to hide my frown. People did not always get what they deserved. My right foot was proof of that. Those young faces at Tuba City Indian School also came to mind. And what about all of the men out of work whom I passed every day lining Sacramento Street? Surely there were plenty not getting what they deserved.

Fron interrupted my thoughts. "How's work?"

"We're certainly not buttering our bacon these days. I seem to have about one appointment for every three that I used to book." While we never went to bed with empty stomachs, our kitchen cupboards were closer to empty than I cared to admit. For dinner, I often fried slices of stale bread soaked in bacon grease, condensed milk, and an egg or two. My income barely covered the rent on our house and two studios. I'd been toying with the idea of newspaper work, but what would I do with the boys? At seven and four, they were too young to be left alone, and school only absorbed a fraction of Dan's day. Without any family around, who could watch them? I couldn't afford to pay anyone. I picked up Fronsie's carton of cigs and tapped one out to light.

"What about Maynard?"

"He was denied the mural commission on the Coit Tower project. There are rumors of some other commissions, but I don't even remember the last painting he sold."

Fronsie let out a low whistle and lit a cigarette. We both watched the smoke drift toward the ceiling in lazy spirals. "Is he being difficult?"

I nodded. Ever since we had returned from Taos, we fought, fought, fought. About everything. Money, disciplining the boys, his late nights, my clients—but our arguments always circled back to money. I was scraping by; he was making nothing and resented me for supporting us.

To make the situation even worse, he was pickling himself every night in North Beach's gin joints. The rare times he was home, the boys watched him. The way he climbed the stairs, sometimes stumbling, how he lifted a glass to his mouth, sometimes spilling. I knew how to watch people too. It was the same way I watched Grandmutter after she'd gotten into her bottle of brandy.

Fronsie tapped her fingers on the crate to get my attention. "Listen, you've got to look out for you and the boys now."

I shook my head past the fuzzy sherry haze enveloping me. "What do you mean?"

She shrugged, pouring another drink, and kept her eyes on the cup. "I'm worried about you. He almost killed you on that drive to Taos."

I sighed, remembering the letter I'd written to Fronsie after we'd arrived in New Mexico. My complaints about the car accident had been fresh and full of indignation. Sure, Maynard could be boorish, but was he really dangerous? Even at his lowest moments, he'd never raised a hand to me or the boys and that was more than many wives could say. And what was I supposed to do? Leave him? Where would that land us? I'd had front-row seats to divorces during my parents' split and Mother's tenure as a social worker. I knew how it worked. On what grounds could I sue for divorce? I had no evidence of anything that would hold up in court and no judge would ever grant the children to me. And if that wasn't enough to discourage me from doing anything rash, I knew firsthand how the stigma of having divorced parents felt; I refused to put that on my boys.

"Dorrie, you know, you could come with us." Fronsie leaned toward me, nodding as she spoke, the force of her idea making her voice faster. "You could leave him. We could all drive back home together. You'd have your mother to help with the boys. Think of how much better it could be." Her eyes widened and she reached for my hands. "Think of it!"

Oh, how I longed to say yes. For a moment, all I wanted to do was nod my head and let Fronsie and Jack sweep me and the boys back to New Jersey. But then the cold metallic truth of it all clanged through me: I couldn't retreat to all that I'd been wanting to escape for almost as long as I could remember. I couldn't leave Maynard. I refused to have my boys grow up without a father. I pulled Fronsie close and rested my chin on her shoulder. Breathing in the tang of rosemary that clung to her hair, I wept for all that we were losing by separating. My dearest friend. Fron had been my home ever since arriving in California. Even twenty years after that first conversation outside of Wadleigh High School for Girls, our friendship still amazed me. How could I move forward without her?

CHAPTER 19

I walked to the bank heavy with dread. When the cashier showed me the receipt with our paltry balance, the numbers blurred before my eyes. I took the slip of paper and hurried past the marble columns at the entry, pulling my coat close against the cold rain spitting outside from the low gray sky. I stepped down the wet, slick stone steps carefully to the sidewalk. The last thing I needed was to slip and break my leg or hip and be unable to work. How would we eat then? Maynard had just gotten an ad job to make some posters but it would only cover his rent at the Monkey Block. What about the rent on our house that was due in two weeks? I pressed my fingers to my temples and stopped under the awning of a small grocery. My stomach growled at the rows of canned food in the window. I pulled a pencil out of my bag to tally up my client appointments scheduled for the rest of the month. Would there be enough work? A sharp tug at my sleeve made me look down. A young boy's face peered up at me.

"Hey, lady, want a paper? Lindbergh just paid a fifty-thousand-dollar ransom but his baby's still missing!"

I stared at him uncomprehendingly. Long dark eyelashes framed his brown eyes. Those eyelashes would have been a mother's pride and joy. But where was this kid's mother? His clothes hung on him, dirty and ragged. Holes gaped at the toes of his cracked brown leather boots. My breath caught in my chest and my heart battered against my ribs. Despite the cold, sweat beaded on my forehead. "Where do you live?" I managed to ask.

He took a step away from me. "You want a paper or not?"

"Here." I thrust two quarters toward him. "Take these to your mother."

His gaze locked on my fingers holding the coins. Without saying anything, he swiped the money and ran. The drab color of his ragged clothes made him disappear into the gloom of the city block within moments. I walked toward the Monkey Block, worrying a stray piece of yarn from my sweater with chapped fingers. Dan and John would not end up like that.

IN MAYNARD'S STUDIO, I showed him the numbers. I'd been arranging and rearranging them on the pencil-smudged bank receipt, trying to see something promising, but there was no escaping the truth: we were flat broke. "I can't figure out how we can keep going like this."

The wood of Maynard's desk chair creaked as he dropped

onto it. He raised his hand to his mouth and doubled over in a hacking, barking cough that sounded painful. When he was done, he looked at me. Pouches of violet-colored skin hung under his eyes. He rubbed his cracked lips together. "What do you suggest?" he croaked.

My legs quivered as I sat down on a stool across from him. I didn't want to say what I'd been rehearsing in my head for the last few days since visiting Fronsie, but I didn't see any other way out of this. I took a deep breath. "We need to separate for a bit. Get rid of the house. Live in our studios. We need to figure out how to make this marriage work." As the words left my mouth, there was no turning back. I folded my arms across my chest to keep my hands from shaking.

"Split up?"

"We can't even sit down for a meal without ripping each other apart. Have you noticed how John flinches every time our voices rise? How can we keep going like this?"

"And what about the boys? I'm not failing those two." His eyes sparked with anger, but a hint of resignation cracked in his voice. "I suppose you want to take 'em?"

"There's an agency on Gough that will foster children out temporarily."

Maynard stared at me, for once, speechless.

"I have to work. Fostering them out is the only way."

"Foster them out? What does that even mean?"

"They'll live with a family who can care for them while we cannot. It will get them out of the city. Keep them safe." It came out as a whisper. Judging by Maynard's shock, my expression must have revealed how terrified I felt.

"Jesus. For how long?"

"Until we can figure out how to live together again."

"But, Dorrie, there's no telling how long this downturn will last. This could be life now."

Although I'd told myself I wouldn't cry, tears started down my face. "There's no other way. I've tried and tried to think of something."

"Jesus."

"Is that all you can say?"

"Well, what do you want me to say? How about I'm furious that I can't keep my family together? That I can't even earn a dime anymore?" He pushed over a pile of canvases that rested against his desk. A cloud of dust arose from the clatter. He dropped his head into one of his palms. "I've seen those kids at the Sisters of Mercy. They look like little ghosts," he whispered.

I'd walked past the cold limestone façade of the nearby orphanage and seen it packed with children whose families were dead or unable to care for them. "I know. The boys cannot end up there," I said, swallowing back the sick feeling that came over me when I thought about the place.

Maynard nodded.

We were both silent. My head ached. I hadn't slept since I'd started thinking about separating. Each night I lay in bed, wide awake, trying to piece a plan together for how to get us through this, but Maynard was right. There was no telling what the future would bring. And while I hated the idea of giving up the boys with every ounce of my being, I couldn't figure out another way to survive. I needed to keep them off the streets. Though Maynard was a lousy husband, he'd always been good with the boys. If only he could shore himself up, he could come back and we could resume our relationship as a family. That was my hope and I'd cling to it with everything I had.

Maynard interrupted my thoughts by jumping to his feet and pacing the small room, his hands waving through the air with each step. "What's wrong with this country in which a man can't take care of his own family?"

I didn't know what to say.

TWO WEEKS LATER, Maynard and I drove the boys onto the ferry to Sausalito and then disembarked and headed through the Marin Headlands to the small town of San Anselmo. Down a winding road lined with redwoods, we drove, everyone silent. Maynard's knuckles glowed white on the steering wheel. He hadn't looked at me since the four of us had climbed into the car back in the city. From the backseat came the occasional sniffle. Each whimper broke my heart. My teeth dug into the sides of my mouth in an effort to keep my own tears at bay. Even with the coppery taste of blood, I kept my jaw tight.

"Mama, can we come home next weekend?" Dan asked.

I stretched my stiff face into a smile and turned to face the boys, trying to sound cheerful. "We will come to see you here next Sunday. We can go for a hike and enjoy a picnic."

"But what about home?"

"There's so much to explore here." I talked about games we could play and tried to sound like I believed my enthusiastic babble. Maynard coughed to get my attention, and I turned to the window, inspecting the numbers on the cluster of mailboxes that came into view with the bend in the road. "Slow down, I think one of these might be it." I checked the address on the letter we had received from the placement agency. Number 214 was the second mailbox on the left. "Turn here," I said, pointing down a dirt driveway. A modest white shingled house sat at the end of the drive, surrounded by flower beds filled with lilies the color of butter. Blue-and-white-checked curtains hung in the front windows. An older man and woman stepped outside onto the small front porch to greet us.

Under the awkwardness of knowing we were being scrutinized, Maynard and I exited the car and opened the back doors to retrieve the boys. John came out willingly but hid behind Maynard, while Dan folded his thin little arms across his chest and stared straight ahead, ignoring my whispered entreaties to get out of the car.

In a trembling, thin voice, he said loudly enough that all could hear, "I'm not going *anywhere*."

"Daniel Rhodes Dixon, please don't make this any harder. You're going to have loads of good adventures here, I can tell." My own feigned cheerfulness sickened me.

Dan bent over and buried his face into his knees. Maynard nudged me aside, leaned over, and spoke low. "Son, get out of the car right now."

With exaggerated slowness, Dan, his lower lip jutting out, climbed from the car and stood beside it.

"Well, good morning," said Mr. Tinley as he and his wife joined us to make introductions.

"I've already baked a pie using apples from our orchard. We can have it later with our supper," said the older woman, smiling. "Our boys loved apple pie when they were young," she added to Maynard and me.

In her letter, Mrs. Tinley had explained she was looking forward to having boys again in the house since theirs had grown up and left. I studied the sturdy-looking couple. He smelled of peppermint oil and wore a neatly pressed light blue buttoned-down shirt and dark brown pants with suspenders. Metal-rimmed spectacles perched on the bridge of his nose, giving him a curious, scholarly air. Next to him, his wife wore a pale pink cotton striped dress. Her graying hair was gathered into a low bun and her broad face looked grandmotherly and comforting. At Mrs. Tinley's invitation, we all walked to the porch and took seats while she poured glasses of lemonade from a sweating pitcher. When Mr. Tinley offered to show Maynard and the boys around the barn, she beckoned me into the house. Inside, the kitchen glowed with tidiness. She showed me the bedroom the boys would share. Two Jenny Lind twin beds lined the walls with a braided rug lying between them. I pictured the boys sleeping in there, their small limbs twisted in surrender under the light blue bedspreads, and must have looked stricken, because she patted my shoulder.

"Now, now, I'm sure this is difficult for you, but we'll take good care of them."

Unable to reply, I nodded, turned away, and went down the stairs to await Maynard and the boys on the porch.

I barely even remember saying our goodbyes, but I can picture the boys watching us drive off. John cried out. Whatever he said was lost in the rumble of our motorcar, because Maynard didn't stop. Unlike me, he never looked back. As their little figures faded in the distance, a throbbing began in my temples. I remembered my own father sauntering down the front walk of our house in Hoboken before he vanished forever. *This is not the same thing*, I told myself. He had left and broken my heart. Digging my right fingernails into my left palm, I gritted my teeth. Unlike him, I had no other choice.

THAT NIGHT I dreamed of running. Two perfect feet led me down a dirt path toward the beach. When I reached the sand, its warmth traveled up through me and I felt my pace quicken. I ran and ran. I awoke alone in my studio and let myself cry since no one could hear my tears.

CHAPTER 20

Alone in my studio, the days stretched before me with few client names penciled into my appointment book. Without the boys and Maynard, I felt adrift and unmoored. I needed to stay focused on work and hoped my routines would save me. On the bulletin board, where I tacked my best recent portraits, thoughtful and dreamy faces gazed past me. Over the years, I'd created a roster of clients who respected craft and appreciated beauty. These were good people. Yet something was missing. I had reached a point where these portraits weren't enough. It wasn't just an issue of money—although I needed that too—I needed to find something more substantial. Something to lose myself in. I needed work that would consume me, distract me from everything I had lost.

I stood in front of the window. Fog blanketed the city,

low and heavy. Without quite knowing what I planned to do, I pulled on my navy wool peacoat and shoved some scrap newspaper down my sleeves to steel myself against the cold. I grabbed my Graflex and walked downstairs to the curb below my window. From the Bay, a damp, bracing wind screamed up the street, blasting me as I clumped along the sidewalk. My eyes teared and I shivered, feeling stripped but alert. A gnarled hand reached out from the shadow of a doorway, clutching a tin cup. I dropped a nickel in and kept walking. Block after block, more and more of these men appeared though they tried to be invisible. They squatted alongside stairwells, leaned against the sides of buildings, and slept, curled up on the sidewalk, silent as a forest.

I found myself in the area near the waterfront known as the White Angel Jungle. Here, the suppertime crowd awaited entry to the nearby soup kitchen set up in a junk lot. Longshoremen, railroad men, carpenters, lumberjacks, truck drivers—all out of work and hungry. The line of men unspooled down the block. They hunched in dark coats and flannel shirts with broken-brimmed caps pulled low.

I edged closer to them, examining their expressions, expecting to be told to go away, but no one even noticed me. They murmured to each other, heads close together. Most gazed right through me, dispirited, sunk deep within their thoughts. I raised my camera hesitantly, lifting the range finder to my brow. I focused and then peered through the viewfinder and snapped a frame. The click of the shutter sounded like a gunshot to my ears. I raised my head, looking around, but still, no one even glanced at me. I'd been holding my breath, but exhaled and took more photos of men crouching on their heels, studying the sidewalk as if there were a message emblazoned upon it about what to do next. By the time the White Angel soup kitchen opened and the men filed inside, I'd used an entire film pack.

Despite the misery surrounding me, my heart galloped. Pacing the nearby streets had taken my mind off the cold. Every time I snapped a shot, exhilaration filled me. There was something about being invisible and seeing everyone and everything that made me feel more alive than ever. When I used all of the film I'd brought, I hurried back to my studio to develop the images. My fingers had swollen from the damp cold and my right foot now throbbed, but I barely registered the discomfort. In my darkroom, I thawed and developed the film.

One image in particular caught my attention. In the developer pan, a mass of men in charcoal-colored wool coats, fedoras, and caps took form. Back at the White Angel Jungle, I had climbed onto the back rim of a parked truck to get a few shots looking down upon the vagrants. The angle had given me the most depth. I'd focused on one man facing toward my camera. He leaned against a rickety wooden barricade, clasping his tin cup between his hands, deep in thought. His head bowed enough so his eyes weren't visible, but the gray stubble of his beard showed the grim set of his jaw. The light captured his beat-up fedora missing its band, and the whiteness of his hands. Something about how his shoulders bunched toward his ears, the resignation in his hands, the dejected tilt of his chin—his posture said everything about helplessness and grief. After I rinsed all of the images and clipped them on my drying line, I took the photo of the man down and pinned it to the board with my most successful portraits. This photo was trying to tell me something.

THE NEXT DAY Imogen dropped by. Earlier in the morning, I'd visited a client's house in Pacific Heights for a portrait sitting. The photographs still hung drying on the line. Imogen walked along the images, nodding her head in approval, but it wasn't until she saw my photo of the man in the White Angel bread-line that she cocked her head in interest.

"What's this?"

"A candid I took yesterday."

"Where?"

"Down by the Embarcadero. The White Angel Jungle."

"You went down there all on your own?"

"Well, I didn't have any appointments and thought I'd get outside of my studio to see what was happening."

"What are you going to do with it?"

"I have no idea. But there's something about being out there, photographing real people, struggling people. I don't know, but someone needs to witness what's happening." I'd been wrestling with this idea since my trip to the waterfront. Could there be power in seeing people and then recording what I saw? My camera could document everything. Unlike what a writer or a painter chooses to include in their compositions, my camera recorded all of the details objectively. Or was it truly objective if I was the one controlling it? Maybe it was as close to truth as I could hope for. And truth was what was needed. The grief on the streets outside of my studio door felt real; it needed to be seen and felt by more people, people who were in a position to do something to help. I still wasn't sure what would come from these images, but I needed to have faith that my ideas would take shape as I continued to experiment.

Imogen pulled out her portfolio to withdraw several portraits. "Ansel's criticizing the lighting in my recent work. I know he's taking a dig at my matte-surfaced platinum paper. I'm so tired of that know-it-all greenhorn."

I held up a print of a woman, in which Imogen had both a close-up of the woman's face and an image of her standing with her arms out. The double image gave a dreamy quality to the portrait. But who cared about such a refinement of technique while the world was going to hell in a handbasket? There was no immediacy or urgency in her work. It felt like a luxury. "I see what you're doing. It's"—I cast around for something—"interesting."

Imogen pulled her lips together at my response, before stepping back and looking me up and down. "You look thin."

"I've been busy." I sighed, dropping onto a stool to rub a hand across my eyes.

"I just came from Maynard's. He looks awful too."

Leave it to Imogen not to mince words.

"What are you two doing?" she asked.

My cheeks stung as though she had slapped me across the face. "If you've come here to make me feel bad, don't bother. Don't you think I feel badly enough on my own?" My heart began to thump like mad. It was all easy enough for her to criticize. Roi had a steady teaching job, her boys had gotten old enough to watch after themselves, but what in God's name was I supposed to do? Every time I passed the little lads down by the ferry terminal trying to sell cigars, I felt a cold sweat break over me as I pictured Dan and John left to fend for themselves. My time with them on the weekends made me hungry to see them more, but paying work was harder and harder to secure. "Someone in this family needs to make money. I've done what I had to."

Imogen frowned. "It just breaks my heart."

"Well, thank you for stopping by to let me know how heartbreaking my life is for you."

She must have seen the fury spinning in my eyes. She lowered her voice. "Listen, I'm sorry. I'm not your enemy, Dorothea. I came here to talk about art, but clearly you're in no mood for this. Use your anger. Get out of here. Go find more photos like that one," she said, pointing at the man in the breadline. "That's the best work I've seen from anyone in ages."

"Oh my God." I choked out a strangled sound, half laugh, half sob, and leaned in to hug her. "You're right." I grabbed my jacket and the Graflex and hurried past her toward the door.

I HOPPED ON the first streetcar to stop and headed west toward the flats of the avenues. A salty smell of the ocean and a cold iron dampness crept into me. Near Land's End, I exited the streetcar. The sky darkened and occasional raindrops splattered against my face. Knotty branches of cypress trees cut across the path as I pushed my way toward the ocean, closer to the steady crash of rollers hitting the beach below. I didn't know why I was drawn to the ocean, except that almost thirteen years ago I'd been stranded on this shore, broke, and far away from all that I knew. But Fron and I adapted and built new lives. Now I was lost again. Had the time come to adapt and rebuild once more?

Raindrops the size of dogwood blossoms hit me, cold water stung my back through my jacket. All at once, the sky opened, the rain fell in torrents. I held on to a young cypress and pulled myself under its branches, but they provided little shelter. Thrusting my camera between my back and the trunk of the tree and holding it in place by the small of my back, I raised my arms and hands to protect my face as rain lashed down upon me. My skin puckered and rose in surprised goose pimples. I held on to that cypress with all I had. The tempo of drumming rain intensified. Rain became hail. Balls of ice the size of small buttons pelted my scalp and shoulders. Hail shifted back to rain. The ground below my feet churned with water. A deafening roar filled the air. The earth trembled below, shaking and rattling me. And then, as quickly as the storm started, it ended. The rain stopped. Clouds scuttled past. Plastered to the tree, I wiped water from my face and looked around. What had just happened?

About ten yards ahead, the path broke off into jagged nothingness. I reached behind me to pull my camera from its hiding place. It was completely dry. I inched closer to where the path broke off and peered over the edge. The cliff had collapsed and slid down to the ocean below. My legs started shaking. If I had made it a few steps farther, I would have been standing on the spot that had dropped into the chopping waters of the Pacific. Stripped of everything but the fact that I was alive, I looked around with wonder.

Why hide in my studio when I could see what was happening in the world firsthand? I had to take some risks. I had to answer the itch inside me that demanded scratching. I wasn't Imogen; playing with technique didn't absorb me. I wasn't Ed Weston; abstracting plants and seashells wasn't my forte. I wasn't Ansel; landscapes didn't speak to me. I was a photographer of people—men, women, and children who worked, suffered, rested, and loved. Now I understood what that photo of the man in the White Angel breadline was trying to tell me. I lived for the moment when time slowed, when I could capture an expression or gesture that communicated everything. I needed more of those moments. If I was going to give up my family, every second needed to count. The sacrifice had to be worth something bigger than me.

CHAPTER 21

I took to the streets again. A new energy thrummed through me ever since the landslide at Land's End. Over the summer, newspaper headlines had been dominated by one man's name: Franklin Delano Roosevelt. He had captured the Democratic Party's nomination at its convention and no one could stop talking about him. Newsreels showed a toothy smile, balding head, and awkward gait that I recognized: polio. While the country shouted that Hoover's time was over, this man, FDR, rose on a tide of hope. Although I had never been one for politics, I began to hope for him too, this man for whom I felt a deep and surprising kinship.

On weekends Maynard and I visited the boys. When I didn't have weekday portrait appointments that fall and winter, I roamed the streets. I found men filed into lines, heads bowed, and spines slumped. They curled into balls on the side-walks trying to sleep. San Francisco, once gleaming and full of promise, had become crowded with despair. From my studio window, vagabonds shuffled along the street.

One morning I made my way down Market Street, Graflex in hand. I found myself outside of the cafeteria where Fronsie and I had been pickpocketed almost fifteen years earlier. It was still a cafeteria. I pushed through the front door and found myself surrounded by women, their heads bowed over bowls of steaming barley soup. The red-checked tablecloths had been replaced by plain oilcloth the color of potato skins. The room had the hush of a library. No one raised her head to ac-knowledge my arrival. I slipped toward a table and took a seat to study the crowd. Next to me, a woman gave a polite nod and lowered her eyes as she sipped coffee. Her pale celery-green cardigan looked faded and she wore a hat style from several seasons ago, but her hair was combed, her clothes clean. It was her silk stockings that caught my attention. Dozens of neat re-pair seams ran along her legs like scars. Her meticulous effort to maintain appearances nearly broke my heart.

I introduced myself, explaining I was a photographer. "Would you mind if I take some photos of you?"

"Photos?" the woman asked, raising a roughened, chapped hand to her cheek as if to block me.

"I don't need to capture your face."

She bit her lip and cast an anxious glance around the room.

"Here, you can photograph me," said the woman next to her, taking a deep drag on her cigarette and exhaling. She raised her hands to the sides of her face and looked toward the ceiling with a wide-eyed expression. "This is my best Marlene Dietrich."

The three of us giggled. She looked just like Dietrich on the promotional posters for *Shanghai Express* that had plastered the city a year earlier.

"Perfect," I said, snapping a shot of her. It wasn't the composition I wanted, but it allowed me to take out my camera. As the women settled back into their coffees, nodding at me, still with faint smiles on their faces, I took several frames of the first woman's painstakingly mended stockings. Those repairs told a story. After a few more minutes of chatting, I rose from my seat and was on my way.

I started visiting the hobo jungles scattered around South of Market. Everywhere I looked, suffering abounded. One morning I came across a man sitting on a wooden crate, his face hidden as he rested his head on his forearms, an overturned wheelbarrow next to him. Overturned—wasn't that how we all felt? I photographed the scene and moved along.

Maynard stopped by my studio one evening shortly after I'd visited the women's cafeteria. He shook his head at my new images of the downtrodden. "Those places are unsafe."

"They're fine. All people want is help."

"How are you helping?"

"I'm not sure."

He grunted. "That's something I never thought I'd hear from you. You're always sure about everything."

I continued filing portrait receipts instead of answering. He kept on talking, complaining about how Hoover was hiding in his bunker in Washington, D.C., but his question echoed in my mind: *How was I helping?* I still had no idea. I hadn't tried selling any of these photos to the city's newspapers. I'd never created work before simply for creation's sake. In the past, everything had led to a paycheck. But now, with an absence of readily available work, I felt free to take some chances. Something was shifting in my work and in me.

Maynard rapped on my worktable. "Hey, did you hear Imogen, Ed, Willard, and Ansel have started a new photography group?"

"Yes, Imogen's mentioned it."

"She didn't invite you to join?"

I shook my head and his face grew stormy. He slammed his hand on my desk, rattling the surface. "Dammit, Dorothea, you're every bit as good as them. Why the hell aren't you in this group? You know, they're going to exhibit together. Your work should be included."

I sighed. "Honestly, I don't have time for a new group. And I don't want to sit around and talk about art." I meant it. At first, I'd felt a prickle of indignation when Imogen mentioned it but didn't extend an invitation for me to join, but this new group disdained the hazy, slightly out of focus photographs that constituted the majority of my commercial portrait work and demanded what they called "straight" photography. No soft lens, no textured papers, no etching stylus. They were all caught up in arguing about art and photography's possibilities and limitations, but I didn't have time for debate. I didn't want to explain myself to anyone.

Maynard coughed. "You know what I may do? I'm going to get a photograph of my ass and send it to 'em. That's what I think of their stupid new group." While he continued to rant, I swabbed at the lens of my Graflex to clean it until he said, "Hey, you don't even care, do you?"

I looked up to see Maynard studying me expectantly.

"What?" I asked.

"You don't even care about f/64, do you?"

"f/64?"

He let out an impatient groan. "That's what they're calling themselves."

"Oh. I get it, the camera setting—right."

Maynard laughed and draped himself on the edge of my desk, crossing his denim-clad legs at the ankles. "It's so pretentious. Bunch of sycophants."

His indignation on my behalf warmed me and I smiled at him. Though he kept laughing, his eyes grew sad as they met my own. God, how I loved his blue eyes and how they reminded me of the sky. An odd silence settled over us as we took each other in. The quiet of the studio amplified the fact that we were alone without the boys. I wanted to say something about them, but if I said their names, I knew I would weep and not be able to stop. He might have felt the same because without a word, he stood, tipped his hat, and walked out.

DESPITE MAYNARD'S WARNINGS to stay out of unsafe areas, I felt pulled to explore the unrest percolating throughout the city that spring. Labor activists called for strikes. I ventured into the streets to see the city's May Day demonstrations firsthand. Depicting the taut energy of the protesting crowds proved to be tricky. I had imagined compositions showing anger and frustration but instead settled for unimaginative, expected shots: fat, surly policeman and picket signs. Though my Rolleiflex was more compact and better for action shots than my Graflex, its bulk around my neck, compounded with my limp, made me slow and vulnerable, but I kept at it, impressed by the energy of the activists.

Several of my friends had joined the Socialist Party, a few others dabbled in Communist groups, and many from the Camera Club joined the Artists and Writers Union. I started attending various leftist meetings but didn't commit to anything. Maynard avoided getting involved in any form of political expression. He viewed these allegiances as substituting one form of authority for another. A year later, when the WPA, a New Deal program designed to encourage public art, sent him to the Boulder Dam in southern Nevada to sketch and paint scenes from the massive construction site, he came back disillusioned, saying darkly, "The desert will get the last laugh." Appalled by the dangerous working conditions, he was also angered to have received only $450 for what he considered to be several thousand dollars' worth of art. I urged him to join me on the streets. In May, we took to the waterfront when longshoremen went on strike in San Francisco. Soon the strike spread up and down the West Coast, and truck drivers and warehouse workers also stopped working in solidarity. The port, normally a hive of activity, became silent. Maynard and I traveled the docks, him with his sketchbook, me with my camera.

One morning when I stopped by his studio so he could join me on my walk to the docks, a new painting rested on his easel. In it, men trudged along a dark city alley, eyes on the ground. "This is new."

"Yeah. I've been avoiding what's happening out there for too long. I just can't make arty paintings anymore, something's gotta be human here." He stood beside me, scratching his chin. "Where's this all leading?"

I shivered. No one knew what lay ahead.

ON A COOL July morning, I heard the masses of people along the Embarcadero before I saw them. Maynard had stayed in his studio to paint so I went alone. When I reached the crowd, a tinge of anxiety crept up my spine. I photographed the faces surrounding me, contorted in angry grimaces. The mood of the crowd had shifted. A new restlessness simmered, its pace quickening like a slow river hitting a narrower, faster section of rapids. The noise of grumbling voices became louder. A man's voice on a megaphone echoed across the crowd, but I couldn't make out the words. People closed in on me, jostling and pushing. A loud explosion reverberated somewhere by Market Street behind me. Gunshots. Screams pierced the air. Hectic movement overcame the crowd. With my camera equipment hanging heavy on my shoulders and around my neck, I stumbled but managed to stay on my feet. A cold terror seized me. If I fell, what then? Would I be trampled and crushed? I pictured Dan and John. My breath became ragged. With my right foot, I couldn't run. Folding my arms across my camera at my chest, I ducked my head to compact myself. More shots rang out in the distance. A fist collided with my forehead but glanced off, its aim uncertain. I gasped and kept moving. People started to run. Gaps opened in the crowd. I shoved my way off the Embarcadero and huddled in an alley. Bent over, resting my trembling hands on my knees, I struggled to breathe through the fear coursing through me. My fingers traced a goose egg above my eyebrow. Within ten minutes, I had made it back to my studio. I pulled off my equipment and lay on the wood floor, exhausted and frightened, but also exhilarated.

THE NEXT MORNING'S newspapers called it Bloody Thursday. Two men had been killed, scores injured. I printed out my photographs and spread them around me on the floor of my studio. They weren't very good, but it was a start.

I crawled over to my cot and reached underneath it for a wooden box I kept stashed out of view. Once located, I lifted the lid and dug around inside. Mashed underneath some old sweaters lay a small velvet bag. Inside, darkened by tarnish, was the old silver Navajo bangle Maynard had purchased for me almost fifteen years earlier during our honeymoon, the same day we'd visited the Indian Boarding School. Slipping the bangle back on my wrist, I studied my photographs of Bloody Thursday. Though not great, they felt risky, worthwhile. They were proof I had been there and survived. They made my heart hammer, pricks of sweat break out under my arms. This discomfort, this fear—I was creating something interesting. I was no longer the woman who had fled the Tuba City Indian School in a panic.

I was no longer helpless. I finally felt awake.

April 1964
Steep Ravine, California

CHAPTER 22

Dan and his wife, Mia, arrive just as the children and I are packing the groceries. Nathaniel wraps his arms around his mother the way a pea vine clings to a gate. Eager to show off the latest treasure trove of beach finds, the other children pull their mother across the room to the door that leads to the beach. Nathaniel follows in their wake like a piece of flotsam, leaving Dan and me behind, alone. He asks me about the weekend and I recite our activities: beach walks, blueberry pancakes for breakfast, several hands of rummy. "Nathaniel was eager for me to read his *Henry and the Clubhouse* aloud. All the kids seemed to enjoy it."

Dan nods, a faraway expression clouding his face. What books did he enjoy as a child? I wish I could remember, but can come up with nothing and feel guilty. I hate that guilt is always a close companion when I'm with Dan. A moment of silence hovers between us, and then I blurt out, "I need to go to Washington, D.C. Will you travel with me?"

"Washington?" He fiddles with a button on his shirt, a wariness in his voice. "What's this about?"

"I need to see my work from the war."

"It's a long trip. Are you sure you're up for it? Can't you get permission to have the photos sent to you?"

"I want to see my Manzanar photos. All of my work from 1942." It's the one year that's missing a file back in my studio.

Dan gives me a wary look. "The impounded ones?"

"Yes." I consider explaining more, describing this new pain that won't leave me alone or telling him about the MoMA letter, but say nothing. He paces toward the window and looks out at the beach below before pushing his thick black-framed glasses up his nose. He tugs his earlobe. Through all of this, he avoids looking at me. An anxious insularity has descended over him. "Where's Paul?" he asks.

"He's repairing a cracked step on the beach stairs. He should be up shortly."

"Why won't he go with you to Washington?"

"Because I haven't asked him. I'm asking you."

He looks away from the window and examines my expression, clearly surprised. In many ways, so am I. Without thinking about it, my fingers slide down my cardigan and I realize my other hand rests on the envelope in my pocket. Without saying more, I hold my breath, awaiting his answer.

July 1934
Oakland, California

CHAPTER 23

I stepped back from my print of *Street Meeting, San Francisco* and smiled. It was the last one I needed to hang. Willard moved beside me and surveyed the line of my photos.

"Well done, Dorothea. This show will get people talking."

"I hope so," I said dubiously. Would people really come to this exhibit? Who would look at photos of a labor strike? The laborers? Newspapermen? Other photographers? When I asked Willard this question, he brushed me off, assuring me there would be an audience for my street photography, but I wasn't so sure. Yet even if no one came, the experience of taking them had changed me.

But people did go to the show. One morning, after finishing a portrait session in my studio, the phone rang. I answered it and a man introduced himself to me as Paul Taylor, an economics professor at the University of California at Berkeley.

"I saw your work at Van Dyke's studio," he said.

I smiled to myself. *So, that's who's going to the show—professors.* Well, it could have been worse.

"I've got an article coming out in *Survey Graphic* and I wondered if I could use two or three of your photos to accompany the piece?"

"Is there any payment involved?"

"Yes. It won't be much," he sounded apologetic, "but it's something." He went on to give the contact information for his editor in New York, who would be able to tell me how to get paid. I hung up the receiver after giving permission and unwound the phone cord from my finger. The payment didn't have to be much. What was important was that *someone would pay for these.*

Several weeks later I received another call, this time from Willard. He invited me to go on a photography expedition. Dr. Taylor, the same Paul Taylor who had called me about the *Survey Graphic* article, had invited Willard to assemble a group of photographers to visit a self-help cooperative at a sawmill in Oroville.

"Isn't Taylor an economist?" I asked. "Why does he need photos?"

"He says he believes in using them to add some humanity to his academic writing. I imagine it's all pretty dry."

Intrigued, I agreed to go and found myself driving out to Oroville a week later. Though California didn't enjoy the same type of season changes I'd grown up with in the Northeast, a burnished golden glow suffused the landscape. The light, the leaves, even the burned-out grass covering the foothills looked luminous. I snuck glimpses of Paul Taylor sitting in the passenger seat beside me: tall, clean-shaven, brown hair combed along a perfectly straight part. In beige pants, a pressed white oxford shirt, jacket, but no tie, he was dressed as if planning to lecture a group of undergraduate students later that afternoon. The only sign he wasn't heading to campus was his brown leather work boots, but even they gleamed with polish.

We drove several hours to reach the sawmill. Upon arrival, we split off to work. I pulled my Rolleiflex from my camera bag and drifted inside the sawmill's main room to scope out the workers. Given that the only light came from the open doors and the gaping cracks between the wooden board siding, interior photography would be impossible, but I lingered, listening to the men complain about the lack of oil for their machinery and the need for parts to arrive from Oakland. No one noticed me.

I moved back outside and photographed a group unloading timber from a beat-up truck. I focused my camera on the determined expressions, dirty dungarees, and bent backs of the men. The whole endeavor felt futile, but they gave no sign of being discouraged.

Beyond the truck, Dr. Taylor emerged from the building where he had been interviewing workers. I gave a quick nod, turned, and hurried over to a lean-to constructed under a canvas sheet strung between the pine trees. A man worked small pieces of scrap wood through a lathe, careful to make every last piece into something that could be sold. His hands were blackened with grease and his overalls looked as though they'd never made the acquaintance of a washboard, but his concentration and graceful fingers never faltered. I photographed him from several angles, careful not to interrupt, before continuing my tour of the camp. Around a corner, I found a woman standing in front of a laundry line. Dingy linens hung behind her. In her meaty forearms that could have snapped me in two, she held a tiny, pink-faced baby and cooed at it with unexpected tenderness. Captivated, I photographed them.

ON THE DRIVE back to Berkeley, Imogen was my sole passenger. I hadn't seen much of her in recent months. After a few minutes, I turned to ask her a question, but she was asleep. Using one hand, I draped my jacket over the front of her as a blanket. On the distant horizon, dark clouds appeared. What had looked golden on the way to Oroville now just looked plain dreary. My thoughts drifted to Dan and John. During our last visit, John had scampered ahead of me on long, lean legs while we were hiking in the Marin Headlands. His hair, lightened in the sun, no longer curled in ringlets close to his ears, but flopped in thick hanks over his eyes. He was growing and changing. God, I missed them. I tightened my hands on the steering wheel and forced myself to think about work, how Dr. Taylor had interviewed people at the sawmill. He asked simple questions and jotted down the answers in a small black notebook. *How long have you been working here? Where did you come from? Who did you come here with?* The exchanges had been conversational. He had been unassuming, easy to speak with. I'm not sure what I had expected from this trip, but I felt wrung out by the quiet earnestness and hope in the workers' eyes. And then there was everything I was trying to avoid thinking about. I sighed.

As we passed signs for Albany, Imogen stirred and rubbed at her face. "Sorry, I didn't mean to fall asleep on you."

"Don't worry, Sleeping Beauty, I've rather enjoyed the silence. It's not every day that I get a few minutes to think."

"Thinking, huh? Careful where that leads," she said gruffly.

I turned off the highway and drove east on University Avenue through the manufacturing district, passing under the Berkeley sign at San Pablo Avenue. Dusk cloaked the street in a violet haze. With electric bulbs behind the G and A on a GARAGE sign burned out, only RAGE glowed.

Imogen watched a Key System streetcar with only a handful of passengers glide the opposite direction toward the Bay. "I stopped by Willard's and saw your strike photos. They're powerful. We've got a new f/64 exhibit coming up. Maybe you should exhibit with us."

"We can see if the timing is right. But you don't need to invite me. Honestly, there are no hurt feelings."

"I'm glad. Listen, I've been meaning to talk with you." She cleared her throat and shifted to look out the window, away from me. "Roi's divorced me."

I gasped. "When did this happen?"

"I went to New York last April without saying anything to him before I left."

"You snuck away?"

"I had to. He was opposed to me going, so I left and mailed

him a letter from Chicago saying I needed to test out some of my new work beyond California. When I returned, he'd gotten a divorce in Reno."

I shook my head. "What did you do in New York?"

"I met with *Vanity Fair* and they offered me some new projects." Wind from the open window blew her thin, graying hair back from her face and she glanced over at me. "You know, I went to Stieglitz's gallery too."

"You did?"

"All the fellas are always complaining about him, how judgmental he is. So, I just walked in there and asked to photograph him." She giggled. "I didn't even have my camera on me, but he let me use his. When I got home, I sent him the images. He wrote back to say he liked my portraits."

"Really?" I was still shaking my head, both impressed and amazed by her audacity.

"Yes, but he also pointed out that he always looks good in portraits." We both started laughing. "Can you believe that?"

"The nerve!"

"I know." Our laughter tapered off and we were quiet for a moment. "Oh, I suppose I should have seen it coming. All those years I focused on raising the boys . . ." Her voice trailed off before she folded her thin arms across her black blouse. "I thought once they were older, I could step deeper into my work. I organized f/64, put together shows, got offers from magazines to publish my work. I thought he'd be proud of me after seeing how long I'd been patient. When we first met, I owned my own studio. I always assumed he understood I'd return to it once the boys didn't need so much of my time."

"And now he resents your successes."

"I suppose so."

We turned onto her street and I stopped the car in front of her bungalow. Neither of us moved to get out. Though cool evening air seeped in through the open windows, the car still radiated warmth. I pushed my shoulders back into the seat to stretch my lower back, cramped after the long drive. Imogen, while never a beauty queen, looked especially drawn and defeated.

From the open windows along the homes lining the street came the scrape of cutlery, the clatter of dinner dishes. She raised her bony wrist to check her watch. "I'd better get inside to feed those boys. They've probably chewed right through the cupboards by now. They're like locusts." She gave a wry laugh.

I tried to picture what Dan and John were doing at the Tinley's and swallowed past a lump in my throat.

We climbed out of the car and removed her bags from the backseat. With her camera bag resting on her shoulder, she straightened and faced me, but her expression was lost deep in the shadows of the late hour. In a voice layered with disappointment and fatigue, she thanked me, and I pulled her toward me. Wrapped in my arms, her narrow back trembled under my fingers. I could trace the bones of her spine under the thin layer of her cotton blouse. For all of her bluster, she felt like a cluster of twigs. I squeezed her before letting go. "Chin up, dear friend, if there's anyone who can pull through something like this, it's you. Please let me know if I can help somehow."

She gave a half smile and waved as she walked toward her house.

Back in my car, I sat for a moment before pressing the starter button. Imogen had always been so confident and measured in her life. To think of her secret mission to New York left me stunned. The end of Imogen and Roi upset everything I had always taken for granted. Hard times were forcing us all to change: our homes, our jobs, our families. Being broke compelled us to adapt to new circumstances, but I could feel deeper changes inside myself too. I was becoming someone new. Did anyone else see it?

DR. TAYLOR ARRANGED to show our Oroville work at Willard's gallery on Brockhurst. When I brought him my photos, I held my breath as he looked at them.

"You moved around the camp effortlessly," he said, before glancing at my right foot and reddening. "I mean, you didn't seem worried at all about those . . . rough types."

"I know my way around them." I hesitated for a moment, wanting to ask something that had nagged at me ever since the trip. "Do you think it will work? The cooperative . . . will it help?"

"It's hard to say. There are a lot of forces working against those people. The state's resources—its land, water, workers—they're all being manipulated in ways that regular people can't control. Or at least can't control yet. But that's what we're trying to do. We need to teach everyone how the system is failing by showing the effects on the people who have the most to lose." As he spoke, he pushed up his sleeves.

I pointed to a row of photos already hung on the wall. "Are those yours?"

"They are."

"I didn't realize you were taking pictures too."

"Well, I only took a few. Some are from other site visits. Obviously, I'm no artist."

I pointed to one of Imogen's photos. "She's a real artist. See how the composition works so nicely here? I like how the man's off-center in front of that door. It's visually pleasing. The light's good. Why, he's even labeled with that sign right next to him. She's done everything right in that photo."

He tilted his head to study it. "Yes, but she set up her camera in front of that door and waited for ages for someone to come into her shot. I watched you. You didn't wait for shots. You followed people, studying them closely. You got the details that tell a story. Like in this one." He pointed at a photo of mine with three children looking into the camera. "Sure, at first this looks like some kids playing, but then you look closer and you realize those two boys are watching after that little girl, the toddler. Where are the parents? They're off working or looking for work and leaving all three young children to fend for themselves. Probably all day. It's sad but what else can they do?" His jaw tightened while he continued to stare at the photo. He was angry on behalf of these people. But then he looked back up at me, almost shyly. "I don't know who will come to this exhibit, but I'm trying to figure out a way to show the human side, the human cost to this problem. Economists love numbers, and I can write a report that's filled with statistics, but I think the number crunchers and the policy makers sometimes resist facing people as human beings. Statistics make it so the numbers can be manipulated any way they want, so they don't have to think about the humans who comprise those statistics. But if I can get them to associate numbers with human beings . . . now that would be something else."

Our conversation paused and we both looked at each other, uncertain how to proceed. I turned to the wall of photographs, anything to look away from Dr. Taylor studying me soberly.

"You have a knack for capturing what I'm trying to communicate," he said.

I took a few steps closer to the wall of photos. "I like how this work makes me feel useful."

He moved forward so we were side by side. "Would you be interested in doing more?"

"I have a portrait studio over in San Francisco."

"I understand, but you're good at this. You have an eye for seeing people and you can use it to help them. Do you want to do more?" He looked at me, waiting for a definitive answer.

As our gaze met, I realized he saw me in an entirely different way than others saw me, and how I saw myself. For so long, I'd been viewed by everyone as a society portrait photographer. No one saw me as an artist. I was a businesswoman with a trade. Success had limited me from seeing myself any other way. But this man saw something else in me. He saw me as an artist, a storyteller. Even though it went against every logical calculation in my head, I took a deep breath and said, "Yes."

CHAPTER 24

D r. Taylor was as good as his word. It didn't take long for him to call me. SERA, the State Emergency Relief Administration, hired him to investigate the sudden influx of people arriving in the state in search of work. After he explained the project to me, there was a brief pause over the phone before he said, "They couldn't understand why I needed a photographer, so you're budgeted as a typist."

It was my turn to pause. "My typing is terrible."

"You won't be typing. I just needed a way to work you into the budget. Don't worry, you'll be taking photos of migrant farmworkers."

"All right, but just so you know, I've never been to a farm and barely know a mule from a tractor."

He laughed. "I'll be there to help."

I hung up the phone and smiled. This man—Dr. Taylor—
his interest in people and how they lived and worked, fascinated me. The logistics of the new project meant I'd be heading
into interior California. I needed to move the boys from the
Tinleys' in Marin County. It was too time-consuming to continue heading back and forth from north of the city by ferry-
boat. Two massive bridge projects were under way for the
city: one crossed the mouth of San Francisco Bay from north
to south; the other would span east to west to connect the city
with Oakland. But with neither bridge set to open for a couple
more years, it made sense to house the boys in the East Bay
since that was the direction I seemed to be traveling most.
I found a new family in El Cerrito who could board them.
When I said goodbye to Dan and John in their new home, I
pulled each one close, breathing in the smells of grass and
little boy sweat that clung to them. I brushed at my eyes and
slid into the car. Unable to look back at them, I shifted the car
into gear and drove away.

The next morning, I arrived in Berkeley at Dr. Taylor's house
at sunrise to drive south toward Nipomo in San Luis Obispo
County. He introduced me to Tom Vasey, one of Mr. Taylor's
graduate students; Rosa Valdez, our Spanish-speaking transla-
tor; Ed Rowell, a reporter for the *San Francisco Chronicle*; and
Irving Wood, from the state's Division of Rural Rehabilitation.
I couldn't picture how this crowd with fancy titles was going to
descend upon a migrant camp without disrupting things but
I trusted that Dr. Taylor knew what he was doing.

Because Mrs. Taylor needed the family vehicle, I drove us
all in my station wagon. In an earlier planning phone call,

Dr. Taylor mentioned he wanted maps for the report, so I suggested Maynard for the job and he was to meet us down south in a few days. Before we climbed in, Dr. Taylor said, "Now, Dorothea, just get a lay of the land. If you don't get any pictures today, that's fine. I want you to get a sense of what we're working with." Vasey and Wood exchanged glances and I imagined they thought it was pure foolishness to bring along a portrait photographer. I vowed to prove them all wrong.

After several hours, we turned off the highway and drove down a long, narrow dirt road, following hand-drawn signs directing us to the work camp. My stomach rumbled with hunger. The sun was well up in the sky, giving the air a dusty, dry feel, and the land around us was filled with nondescript scrub brush. Intermittent pieces of garbage along the side of the road indicated the first sign of the camp. It was as if Hansel and Gretel had left a trail of old, busted-up tires, splintered boards, broken bottles, and filthy rags to guide us. Maybe there was a reason SERA never had budgeted for a photographer before. Maybe the migrants would be hostile toward having their photos taken. I chewed my lip. What lay ahead?

Within minutes we arrived at a cluster of tents and slowed to a stop, cutting the engine. The smell of burnt cooking oil hung in the air. The men conferred while I leaned my head out the window, eyeing the shacks constructed of canvas tarps, collapsed cardboard boxes, dried brush, and sheets of corrugated metal. Outside one, a thin woman in a faded calico dress set a plate on an overturned crate serving as a table. Four children swarmed from the recesses of the tent and began digging into the pan with their bare hands. I couldn't tell what

she served them, but the kids inhaled whatever it was, pushing the food into their mouths with both hands. The young
mother watched with a dull expression.

From the front seat, Dr. Taylor spoke to me. "You and Ed
can start investigating while I conduct some interviews. Just
do the best you can."

"Sure, Dr. Taylor, I'll just bring one camera."

"That should be fine. And please, call me Paul."

I nodded and smiled and decided to bring the Rolleiflex
since it would be lighter and less conspicuous than the Graflex. We got out of the car and Paul approached an old man who
had come out of his raggedy tent to watch us. Taking off his
hat, he said, "Good morning, sir. Know where we can get some
gas around here?"

"There's a small town 'bout three miles down the road.
Reckon you'll find a gas station there."

"Thank you." Paul nodded and looked around. "How long
you folks been here?"

The man creased the visor of his cap and lifted it to scratch
his scalp as he looked around. "'Bout six weeks."

"What kind of work are you finding?"

"Well, there's folks pickin' peas a couple miles yonder." The
old man poked his index fingers past a copse of trees, all with
splintered nubs marking where bottom branches used to be
before being taken away for kindling.

The old man wore grubby overalls and a faded plaid shirt.
Gray stubble bristled his hollowed cheeks. When was the last
time he'd eaten anything more than a can of beans? Next to
him stood a stack of crates filled with dented pots and pans.

Paul's gaze never left the man's face, but he raised the small black notebook he carried at his side and began jotting down notes as the man continued to speak.

"He's good, huh?" Ed whispered next to me, nodding his chin toward Paul. "He never makes people feel like they're being interviewed. You'd be amazed what kinds of things they tell him." He pointed toward a cluster of tents. "Well, what do you say? Should we look around?"

I nodded. We wended down a narrow path in between rows of tents and brush shelters, stepping over empty flour sacks, a pile of potato peelings, and soggy, faded piles of moldering newspaper scraps. In front of us, a trio of small children appeared, blocking our way.

"Hello," I said to the largest one, a girl who sported a lopsided bobbed haircut. She stared back at me.

"Who you?" asked a little boy at her side. He appeared to be about five years old and wore denim overalls without any shirt underneath, despite a cold breeze clipping the air.

"My name's Dorothea Lange." I considered saying more, but didn't have to because the little shaver cut back in.

"Name's Tommy. This here's Hildy." The young boy pointed to a toddler who ambled around the corner of a tarp-sided tent. "That's Bert, my baby brother." The youngest sucked his thumb and stared at us. I tried not to think about how dirty his little hands were. Flies hovered around the baby, landing on sores that ran up his scrawny forearms, but he didn't bother to wave them away. Tommy stepped closer to us and uncrossed his wiry arms from his chest. With his eyes on my camera, he pointed to it and asked, "What's that?"

As I explained how I used the camera to take photos of people, I felt stricken by how the children's collarbones protruded from their clothes and the sores clustered around the edges of their mouths.

"Tommy, how old are you?"

"Almost eight. Reckon you wanna take our picture?"

"I'd be happy to."

Hildy smiled and wrapped an arm around Tom while pulling Bert against her hip. Her calico dress practically begged to be handed down to a smaller girl, straining as it did across her knobby shoulders. She was missing several teeth. Those that remained were gray. After I took a couple of photos, the children offered to show us around the camp. We followed them. Soon a gaggle of pale-faced children trailed us as we plodded deeper into the camp. The tents thinned. Piles of food scraps attracted flies. An unbearable stench filled the air.

"Tommy, where are the privies?" Ed asked, wrinkling his nose.

"Well, no one really uses 'em anymore because they got so full. Now people just go wherever."

I didn't dare inspect the murky sludge squelching below my shoes. "Tommy, what do you say you introduce us to your mother?"

"Sure, lady."

To my relief, we returned to the tents. Our pace slowed as we approached a tent with a roof made from thatched long dried grasses and corrugated metal siding. A woman appeared in front, pushing lank light brown hair out of her face.

"Ma, this lady here's takin' pictures," Hildy said.

The woman said nothing, her expression wary. She took in my limp as I neared. Her guarded expression softened and she nodded at me.

"I'm Dorothea Lange and this is Ed Rowell."

"Esther Crawley."

I could see a large bucket of water next to the front door of the tent.

"May I have a glass of water?"

"'Course. Set yerself down." She pointed to a crude bench constructed out of rough boards, and I lowered myself onto it while Ed stood next to me.

I nodded to Mrs. Crawley. "You've got a fine set of children here. I've got two boys of my own. They sure keep me on my toes."

She chuckled, handing me a jar with water. I lifted it to show my appreciation for her hospitality, but having no idea where the water had come from, I only dampened my lips with it.

I thought about how Paul approached people and cleared my throat. "How long have you all been here?"

"Three weeks, I reckon. We were down south 'round Barstow 'fore that, but nuthin' to be found in them parts."

"What kind of work's around here?"

"Mostly pea-pickin'."

"And there's enough of it for all of you?"

"Not really. My husband's been workin' off and on, but ain't been nuthin' for me now fixin' on a week." She pointed at my camera. "What's with that?"

"I'm taking photos for the State Emergency Relief Administration. It wants to know what's happening down here so the government can figure out how to help folks who need it."

"Well, if you gotta job to do, go right 'head."

I rose from my bench and backed up to take a wide shot of the tent before moving around. I tried to notice everything: the neatly stacked dishes by the shelter's entrance, the limp laundry hanging on a line, the oil cans scattered next to the cooking fire pit. After a few minutes, Ed and I took our leave and headed off to find Paul. He was still talking to the same old-timer, who nodded at me by way of greeting. I took that as a signal and took a few photographs of him. After a bit longer, Paul rose and shook hands with the man.

ONCE WE WERE back on the road, the encampment disappearing behind an outcropping of junipers, Paul got right down to business. "Tom, did you get a count on how many tents were there?"

Tom looked at the map he had sketched in his notebook. "Twenty-eight."

"How many people do you think were inhabiting that camp?"

"I'm not sure how many were off working. There were more kids than I expected, though. Babies too."

Paul frowned. "Rosa, did you talk to anyone?"

"I talked to one family from Arkansas, but didn't see any families from Mexico."

Paul nodded but sounded puzzled. "Neither did I. Dorothea, were you able to get any photos?"

I nodded, but before I could say anything, Ed jumped in. "She was a natural out there. She's got a real knack for talking with the women and children."

I felt my cheeks warm.

"When do you think you'll be able to have them developed?" Paul asked.

"As soon as we return."

He turned the car off the dusty road and onto the highway. We stopped at several more camps, each as dismal as the first. By late afternoon, I'd eaten some crackers but was ravenous. We hadn't stopped for a single meal all day. Low grumbles emanated from everyone's stomachs. When we arrived in San Luis Obispo, folks practically fell out of the car, eager for a closer look at a menu posted in a window advertising a $1.95 rib-eye dinner. We were each on a daily stipend of four dollars. The idea of spending so much money on a fancy dinner when we'd spent the day among people who could barely get a pan of cornbread out to their families left me cold. In the thickening dusk, I could make out a sign for a diner farther down the street.

"If you don't mind, I'm heading over there," I said, sliding my camera bag higher onto my arm.

Paul frowned. "Don't you want to eat?"

"I do, but honestly, I just can't stomach eating at a place like that after all I've seen today. I'll meet you all back here in a bit." I gave a polite nod and walked toward the diner. After a moment, the sound of footsteps echoed behind me, and I glanced over my shoulder. Paul fell into step next to me, grinning sheepishly. I nodded, surprised at how pleased I felt to find him beside me. "Tomorrow morning we should get some food to take with us in the cars. You've got to figure in some time to feed everyone in between stops at the camps," I said. I was overstepping, but Paul nodded, unfazed by my directness.

"You're right, sorry, I sometimes forget."

The ease with which he apologized surprised me and I looked away at the shuttered storefronts we were passing. "It's all right. It's obvious you've got other things on your mind. I'll remind you in the morning." I looked over at him, expecting to see annoyance, but he smiled.

By the time we arrived at the diner, the rest of the group followed behind. We entered and slid into a couple of booths to order plates of mashed potatoes, roasted carrots, and stew for sixty-five cents. As I pierced a carrot with my fork, I tried to picture one of the nearby fields. Where had this carrot come from? Who picked it? I'd never wondered about these things before. My appetite sputtered, but I continued eating, not wanting anyone's labor to go to waste. Throughout the meal, I could feel Paul studying me. Every time I caught his eye, he gave me a small smile, his dark eyes warm and kind.

CHAPTER 25

Afetr several days of driving along the fields of San Luis Obispo County, the group met up with another vehicle of state officials and some headed back to San Francisco. Only Paul and I pressed on. We headed farther south to the Coachella Valley, where Tom Vasey and Irving Wood planned to meet us again the following week with Maynard. When Paul and I stopped at an auto court in Santa Maria for the night, I walked down the street to a pharmacy to purchase a small notebook so I could write down what I was photographing, where we went, and my expenses. When I spoke with lettuce pickers outside of Indio, I wrote that they made fourteen cents for picking a crate and could make seventy cents a day if things went well. They were permitted to sleep in between the rows of plants at night for sixty cents. It didn't take a mathematician to see how this was going to work out.

I also began to note what people were saying. Their words captured their situation better than anything I could dream up. When one grizzled old man leaning up against his broken-down jalopy said, "This life is simplicity, boiled down. Seems like God's forsaken us back in Arkansas," I nodded, repeating his words to myself until I got back to the car and wrote them. I started developing my photographs in the bathtubs of the auto courts and the old cabins where we stayed. Grimy, grim faces peered out of my images, daring me to look away.

Irving, Tom, and Maynard met us at a camp outside of Blythe. Maynard's face froze as he took in the squalor surrounding us. He remained silent as we walked through the camp. Even though it was just after six o'clock and the sun was on the wane, the temperature still hovered around the mid-nineties. Beads of sweat rolled down my back, even though I was standing still, not even lifting a finger. At one point, an old truck belched its way into the snaggle of tents. A couple of men and four boys slid off the empty truck bed, their faces weary, their clothes filthy from a long day working in a nearby field. Two of the boys appeared to be about ten years old, the others couldn't have been more than thirteen. After the group trudged past us, Maynard let out a low whistle. "What the hell kind of country are we living in? Those young boys have been out there in the sun all day working?" He shook his head as he spoke.

"I guess I'd better get my camera. There's still enough light to get some work done."

As I brushed by him on my way to the car, he reached out and held on to my arm. "When we get back, let's get Dan and John. That money I made from the murals for the Department of the Interior and the money from this report should see us through the next several months."

The sun had ignited two red splotches on his cheeks, but he was still pale, even with the flush of the day's heat. He swallowed, twitching the rough, loose skin of his neck, and pushed back his cowboy hat to rub away some sweat. His hair, once jet black and thick, now hung stringy and gray.

I nodded. He let go of my arm and turned the other direction to cough. At sixty years old, his health was worsening. I went to the car to retrieve my camera and, hidden from view, I bent down, closed my eyes, and rested my forehead against the hot black leather of the seat, wincing at the sound of Maynard's hacking cough. The thought of our boys working all day in a field in this heat made me sick to my stomach, but unlike Maynard, I didn't yearn to race home. Instead, I wanted to do more. Of course I longed to hold my boys in my arms, but how could I turn my back and return to San Francisco and resume my portrait business after photographing scabby-kneed children poking reeds into a muddy culvert looking for critters to eat? I needed to help these people if I could. As soon as this thought flickered through my mind, guilt washed over me. What kind of a mother didn't put her children above everything else? What was wrong with me? Without looking backward, I hurried toward the tents, pushing thoughts of Maynard and the boys away.

THAT NIGHT AS we turned off the lamp in our musty auto court room and settled upon the lumpy mattress, Maynard pressed himself to my side and caressed my shoulder. I rolled over to look at him, trying to make out the outline of his face next to mine, but his expression was lost in the shadows. He eased me onto my back and settled on top of me, his bony hips pushing against me. His fingers combed through my hair and held my head in place while his dark eyes searched my face as if he was preparing to ask a question. Instead he placed his lips atop mine and ran his hands down to my ribs. Relieved not to speak, I arched to meet him and sighed as he pushed into me.

Afterward, I pulled the sheet over my breasts and stared into the darkness. Next to me, Maynard's breathing steadied into sleep, but I was awake, my mind restless. A shaft of brightness from the bare electric bulb outside our doorway lit a sliver through the curtains, creating a stripe of light on the wall next to me. I reached out to pick at a chip of flaking oatmeal-colored paint, thinking of Paul in the room next door. Was he asleep? The plaster wall felt flimsy underneath the pressure of my fingers, as if I could peel a hole right through it and see him looking back at me. I pulled my hand back and tucked it under the thin sheet. My cheeks burned to think of him so nearby. I hoped he hadn't heard me with Maynard.

Was Paul lonesome? All of these nights in different rooms, day after day immersed in the dreariness of the migrant camps—did it wear on him? I squeezed my eyes shut as if it would stop my questions. Why was I thinking about Paul? He wasn't thinking about me.

With Maynard snoring beside me, I climbed out of bed and knelt at one of the smeary windows to pull back the curtain and see a line of parked automobiles outside. A battered red truck loomed in front of me, a NO RIDERS sign stuck to the windshield. I lifted my eyes from the line of vehicles to look at the stars gleaming overhead. How many times had I seen Orion and the Big Dipper over Maynard's shoulders as he lay atop me, our bodies entwined under the night sky? We once had such passion. Now we were stuck in this little fleabag, making love resignedly under a water-stained ceiling. What had happened to us?

I searched the northern corner of the inky night sky, thinking of Dan and John sleeping in someone else's house. I pictured the dark fringe of Dan's eyelashes resting on his soft cheeks as he slept, how John tended to sleep with his limbs sprawled wide like the arms of a starfish. When I thought about them, a void cracked open inside me. I missed everything about them, the feeling of their smooth, warm hands in my own and the gritty smell they carried on their skin after a long day of playing outdoors. But they were safe and healthy while so many others were not. Out here, in the fields and on the streets, not only was I earning a paycheck, but I felt useful. Maybe our work could lead to some help for these migrants. Was this grandiose? Could some photographs make that much of a difference? Paul seemed to think so. Maybe I could help families who were not as fortunate as us. I had to try.

We wrote and assembled the report back in my studio in San Francisco, Paul on his typewriter, me curating photos, Maynard creating pen and ink maps. I obtained heavy cardboard to make covers, waxed them to look professional, and used a wire spiral binding for the pages to reveal the crisis we had seen unfolding firsthand.

"Gosh, fifty-seven photos are in here." I needed both hands to lift the report from the table. "Think it's too much?"

Paul shook his head. "No, they make this problem real. Don't you think, Maynard?"

Maynard nodded without any of his usual wisecracks, his eyes trained on the finished report resting on the table. "I won't lie, I've been dubious of the government's help," he said, pulling on the corner of his mustache. "But I sure hope this damned thing works."

His words raised goose bumps on my arms. In all the years I'd known him, he'd never been one to throw around the word *hope* before. The three of us nodded in silence. But how could a pile of paper change any of the misery we'd seen?

LATER THAT WEEK, Paul telephoned my studio to tell me about his meeting with the SERA officials. He described how the director of the agency tore five pages of my photographs out of the report and handed them around the group as he read my captions aloud.

"Wait, they ruined my binding?" I bristled. "It cost me an extra three dollars to make it that way."

"That's not the point."

"Easy for you to say. I messed up my fingers on that darned binding."

"Listen to me: SERA's allocated two hundred thousand dollars to build twenty camps for migrant workers in California."

My breath stopped. I slid my back down the wall until I was sitting cross-legged on the floor.

"Dorothea? You still there?"

"I'm here."

"It was amazing. I've never seen government types get so riled up. It was all because of your photos. They made the difference. *You* made the difference."

I laughed to cover up the tears seeping from the corners of my eyes. Paul continued talking, outlining our next project, but I only smiled, not hearing a word of what he said. For now, I just wanted to close my eyes and enjoy the sense of joy spreading through me.

CHAPTER 26

Our next assignment was in the Imperial Valley, a hot and dry stretch of land in Southern California, patched with fields. When Paul told me to pack for a three-week trip, I almost balked. How could I be gone for so long? I rarely went for more than five days without spending time with Dan and John. I visited Maynard in his studio to plan for my absence and found him sitting on a stool staring at a canvas resting on the ground in front of him. Piles of papers cluttered the tables in the room. The air was tart with the smell of linseed oil and turpentine, but also still and warm like a rarely visited attic. As I crossed the room, I picked up a small Hopi pot and blew on it, raising my eyebrows at him as a cloud of dust spread through the hazy air. The studio's usual sense of energy and vibrancy seemed extinguished. "Ever heard of a feather duster?"

"I've been busy, woman," he growled.

I picked up a painted board from a small table and studied the brown expanses surrounding a woman standing next to a tarp tent and parked car. "Is this from your trip to San Joaquin Valley last month?"

Maynard grunted a sound of assent. "Yep, part of my *Forgotten Man* series," he said. "So, I'm assuming you're here to tell me that you're leaving for somewhere?"

I told him about the assignment with Paul.

"How long will you be gone?"

"Almost a month."

"And you've got everything you need."

I started to answer, to list off all of the things I was packing—film, tripods, my cameras, tools, notebooks—but he interrupted me. "I wasn't asking for a packing list. It wasn't a question. I simply observed that you always seem to have everything you need."

"Well, I spend a lot of time planning."

"Have you ever wondered if you spend all that time planning so you don't think about what you're leaving behind?"

I opened my mouth to speak, but nothing emerged. What *was* I leaving behind? I hated leaving the boys, but what about my marriage? I once felt such passion for the man in front of me, but now could barely summon anything other than concern for him. He had once radiated such charm and virility, creativity and humor. The old man slumped in front of me was a mere shell of that character.

He coughed. "Bender came by with a commission for me and said he's got a client who's willing to rent his house on

Vallejo for cheap. I told him I'll use money from the new project and take it. When you get back, we can all move in. Together at last." Even as he spoke about what we had both hoped would happen—our being reunited under one roof—he didn't look me in the eye. What could I say? He noted my silence and rose, thrusting his hand out to me. "Well, have a safe trip, pard."

I stared at the orange and yellow paint streaking his hand before placing my hand in his. This was the state of our relationship: a handshake.

"Tell the lil' fellas I'll head over to see 'em one of these weekends while you're gone."

I nodded, suddenly desperate to get out of that room, that building, away from the shadowy figures in his new paintings, away from the feeling of failure I got when I looked at him. I swallowed back tears, let go of his hand, and fled.

PAUL AND I left Berkeley in my station wagon. He drove so I could lean out the window and take photos. Dust-covered jalopies carrying oil cans, battered suitcases, and washtubs lined the highways wherever we went. It looked like people were wearing their homes inside out. Tables, trunks, sideboards, bedding, even a goat in a pen—all could be seen strapped to the sides of the old jalopies. Sometimes the wheels of the vehicles were barely visible underneath all the rakes and shovels tied to the sideboards.

Our days on the road started early, when the air was cool and we'd find people working in the fields. Then, as the day heated up, we'd knock off for a few hours, eat, review our notes, and plan our travel routes. When we weren't hanging around a greasy spoon overlooking a stretch of highway, we spent hours in the car together, sometimes talking, sometimes watching the miles tick past in silence.

Paul's upbringing on a small farm in Iowa gave him a passion for protecting the individual farmer, whom he viewed as under siege by the rise of big business, especially in California. With his Midwestern wholesomeness and professorial air, he was an unlikely rebel, but his determination to defend the underdog workers appealed to me. Listening to him made me feel smarter and worldlier. I devoured everything he told me.

When we arrived at a site, I'd take several establishing shots from the roof of the car to show the field or encampment. One early evening when the sun still blazed overhead, I bent over to pass Paul the camera and put my hand on the ridge of the car's roof to climb down from my perch. Pain seared through me as the metal rim of the roof rack, heated from the sun, burned my palm. I pulled away, crying out, and lost my footing. With the Graflex still clutched in my hands, I crashed off the side of the car, straight into Paul's arms. He caught me easily. In the grip of his large hands, I felt safe. He didn't release my waist right away but looked down at me.

I let out a nervous laugh. "Just what we need, a photographer with a broken leg."

"Are you hurt?"

The burning of my palm turned my stomach, but I swallowed past it. "No, just clumsy, but then again, that's nothing new."

"You're not clumsy at all. You always look quite graceful weaving through the fields," he said, lowering me to the ground.

Nothing on the camera appeared damaged, but he checked the lens and the pleats of the bellows before handing it back to me.

I could feel my face reddening beyond what the heat called for. With the camera hanging around my neck, I ducked and wiped my sweaty palms down my denim trousers, shuddering as my burned hand stung. Despite the pain or maybe because of my light-headedness resulting from it, an unexpected desire to reach for Paul and place his hands back on my waist overcame me. I held back the urge and escaped into the fields.

A FEW DAYS later, we stopped in Yuma, a dusty pile of buildings at the border where Mexico meets California and Arizona. At a gas station, I stepped out of our car to stretch my legs. A truck, rusty and dented, pulled in behind us. Three men hung off the back and clambered down when the rig stopped. A scrim of red dirt covered the truck's faded green paint. One of the men, sucking on a piece of straw, circled it, checking the tires. When he saw me, he tipped his cap.

"Where you from?" I asked.

"Oklahoma. Got blowed out."

"Blown out?"

"Yes, ma'am. Ain't you heard 'bout the storm?"

"No."

With one foot balanced on the back bumper, he took the hay out of his mouth, now soggy at the end, and eyed me. "Ev'things blowed off in the wind and made the sky's dark as night all the time. Nothin' there now. Reckon them banks are havin' a field day, forclosin' on everythin', sellin' it all off. Mark my words, the day of the small fella's gone." As he finished speaking, the bumper under his foot lurched to life. Diesel exhaust bellowed out of the tailpipe.

"Where are you heading now?"

He shrugged, pulling himself onto the back of the truck to find a spot within the lumpy tarps.

The truck became smaller and smaller as it huffed its way into the distance. I leaned into the window of our car. Paul was consulting a map. "Have you heard anything about a dust storm?" I recounted my conversation with the man from Oklahoma.

"Hmmm. Yuma's usually an entry for Mexican migrants. I'll check my notes, but I think 1933 is when I first started noticing an uptick in white migrants in California." He looked behind us in the direction of Arizona. "Hold on a sec," he said, swinging open his car door and getting out to approach one of the filling attendants. "Excuse me, think you can keep a tally of people coming through here? I want to know where they're coming from."

The attendant, a young boy I figured to be about fifteen, scrutinized Paul with a dubious expression. "How am I supposed to know where they're from?"

"Check their license plates. Or just ask them and keep a list. If I'm not back later today, I'll return tomorrow and want to see that list." He handed the kid a one-dollar bill.

The boy's eyes widened as he took in the money, a smile spreading across his freckled face. "Sure, mister."

Paul pulled a pencil from his breast pocket and jotted a few more things down on the piece of paper, instructing the boy to collect as much information as he could from the people who stopped. We returned the next day. Paul ran a finger down the crinkled piece of paper the boy gave him. Kansas, Oklahoma, Texas, Arkansas—people were arriving from states in the middle of the country, all looking for work. "If this list is any indication of even a fraction of the people arriving, this spells trouble. The state's not ready for this."

From Yuma, we headed north, stopping in migrant encampments along the way. Outside of Bakersfield, we pulled off the highway to check on a dirty Model T stranded at the side of the road. Inside the automobile sat a weary couple, both hollow-eyed.

"Need some help?" Paul asked.

They looked back and forth at us with blank expressions. I stepped forward, thinking the woman might be more likely to speak with another woman. "Where you from?"

"Texas Panhandle," she whispered, eyes red-rimmed. The rabbit fur collar on her wool coat hinted at better days.

"We got family comin' 'long to help us," her husband said, his light gray eyes faded within the dusty creases of his face. "Been ditched and stalled here for a bit. Now we're stranded."

While Paul continued to talk with them, telling them who we were, I held up my camera. The husband nodded, so I stepped back to take some photos. After a few minutes, we took our leave and settled back into the station wagon. I pulled out my notebook and wrote down the words I'd been repeating silently: *ditched, stalled, stranded.*

"More people from the middle of the country," Paul said with a sigh, before pressing the clutch and turning on the ignition.

We returned home. After I spent a few days hidden in my development room, we reviewed the photos from our trip. I said, "I think there's a different story than we expected unfolding in front of us."

"What story is that?"

I shifted in my seat, tucking my right foot underneath my bottom so I could be higher to see the photos better. He waited. I swallowed, amazed that he took my opinions so seriously. After all, he was the expert on labor migration. "Well, I'm not sure," I confessed. "I thought we were telling a story about migratory labor, up from Mexico, but that's not what we're seeing, is it? Not with all of these people arriving from the middle of the country."

Paul nodded, resting his chin on his hand as he took in my work. The photos showed a migrant encampment in a Bakersfield dump. Parked jalopies sagged under layers upon layers of bedding, frying pans, and wooden water buckets. Bony children leaned against the muddy tires, glaring toward the camera.

"It's a present-day westward migration." I reached for a photo of a canvas-topped truck, placed it in front of him, and tapped on it. "See? The new covered wagon."

He folded his hands across his chest. "Dorrie, I think you're onto something."

I startled at his use of my nickname. He'd never called me that before. When he realized I was staring at him, he flushed, pulled three photos in front of him, and studied them. Though I resumed sifting through the photos, all I could think about was the unexpected comfort I took in him calling me *Dorrie*. I smiled to myself and snuck another peek at Paul. I was starting to wonder about the story between us.

CHAPTER 27

Our next trip was to the Sacramento Valley. One afternoon, after I walked through the gate of a peach orchard where I'd been photographing several families at work, I found Paul leaning against the hood of the car, bent over his notes. He glanced at me, his frown vanishing, and grinned. "I thought I'd never get you out of there."

"Sorry, I got drawn into following the children. Good Lord, the malnutrition, the flies. One mother told me she just buried her child because of tonsillitis. Tonsillitis!"

Paul nodded and straightened. He pried his glasses from his face, placed them down on his notebook and, blinking in the sunshine, he stretched his hands skyward. His face looked different without his glasses. Vulnerable. Younger. The undersides of his wrists faced me, appearing above the cuffs of his shirt. Pale and soft. Without thinking, I reached for his hand and placed it on my cheek. My gaze met his, though my heart pounded. Around us, the heat of the day silenced the usual sounds of the fields. No birds, no running water, no voices. Just the low drone of insects, yet even that seemed muted. It was just us. He caressed my cheek and along my neck until he reached my shoulder. Then he pulled me into his chest and kissed me. My white cotton shirt clung to my back, damp with perspiration, but I didn't care. We were stuck together, and I liked it, the breathless feeling of our lips together, his chest and arms tight around me. Paul felt solid, like a force. In his arms, I felt protected and shielded. Safe. I wanted to stay here, despite the itchy smell of dust and heat clinging to us, yet I stepped away. "Let's go somewhere."

He nodded, desire filling his eyes. Without speaking, we loaded my equipment into the trunk and slid into the front seat side by side. He shifted the vehicle into first gear. We rolled down the road. Streaks of white shot through the pale blue of the afternoon sky. I rolled down the window, exhaling as the wind blew strands of my hair out of my face. With my other hand, I ran my palm up his arm to his shoulder. He reached for it and kissed each of my knuckles, his eyes still on the road. He lowered our entwined hands to his thigh. I stared at them.

Nothing felt surprising anymore.

This wasn't the flash of attraction I'd experienced with Maynard. It was less of a shock of electricity, more like the pull of gravity, timeless and predestined. There was a steadfastness, a sturdiness to Paul that was new to me, certainly nothing like what I'd encountered before. I bit my lip. Maynard. For as long as I could remember, our relationship had been precarious. Maybe that had been the beauty of it. He'd always felt dangerous and surprising to me, an unpredictable force in my otherwise orderly existence. But the thing that had once burned incandescent between us had grown cool and dull. God, I'd been so young when I met him, so eager to be loved.

I glanced at Paul's face. Rumors circulated about his wife, Katherine. People whispered about her beliefs in open marriage, her involvement in multiple affairs. I'd caught glimpses of her here and there around Berkeley. Blond hair, pastel-colored dresses with peplum waists, handbags that matched her shoes. The rumors were hard to believe, but at the same time, Paul had given off an air of loneliness ever since I first met him.

We arrived in the empty parking lot of an auto court. He turned off the ignition. An intensity hung in the air around us despite the outward calm of the scene. Though we stared straight ahead at the stucco exterior of the building, we may as well have been standing at the edge of a bridge, contemplating jumping. I think I swung my door open first, but Paul stopped me by grabbing my arm.

"I'm getting one room."

"Yes." As soon as the words left my lips, I knew I'd made a choice from which there would be no return.

I STARTED CALLING him Pablo. The nickname made us both giggle. He often spoke Spanish in the fields; the language sounded musical and romantic. For the next few days, whenever I called him this, he flushed. I'd hit the right spot, and he enjoyed all that the insinuation implied. Our trip was nearing its end. With San Francisco about one hundred and fifty miles away, we would be home the following evening. Over the course of the summer, everything had changed.

We drove north toward the city. Paul said, "I've been thinking."

I turned my face to the steady line of empty horizon to my right and stared out the window. I did not want to think.

"I'm prepared to ask Katherine for a divorce."

There it was. The word I had been dreading. *Divorce.* I swallowed. "Already?"

"Why not? Nothing's going to change. I don't want to be apart from you any longer."

Though the station wagon motored forward, I felt like I was sinking. I closed my eyes.

"Come on, look at me. You know this is the right thing to do."

I moaned. "Is it? God, it feels right to us, but you have Katherine, I've got Maynard. For crying out loud, we've got five children between us. Do you think they'll think this is the right thing? I've seen the heartbreak that results from"—I couldn't even say *divorce* aloud—"this kind of thing firsthand."

He downshifted, our speed slowed, and the car rolled to the side of the road. The air was motionless and heavy between us. "Maybe not at first, but they'll come to understand," he said.

"I don't know."

"About us?"

"What am I going to do about Maynard?"

"You two have been living separately for the last three years."

"I know, but I feel responsible for him."

"He'll be fine."

I raked my hands over my face. "Will he? He's sixty. He's ill."

"He's a survivor."

But I didn't want Maynard just to survive. He was so talented. "He could have been such a success if he had been more ambitious. I never pushed him as I should have."

Paul rested both hands atop the steering wheel and sighed. "Sometimes we can't fix the people around us, no matter how much we try."

He was wearing short sleeves and stretched his arm out to me. Cords of muscle ran under his skin and flexed as he reached for me. I shimmied along the seat and rested against him, leaning my head onto his shoulder. I didn't have to fix a damn thing about Paul. What a relief. There were too many other things to fix in life. "I dread this whole business, but I'll talk to Maynard when I get home."

"What about your portrait business?"

I pulled my head off him. "What do you mean?"

"I'm going to Washington, D.C., next week and plan to get you a government job. A new division's getting started, and I think I can have you hired as a staff photographer." He looked over at me. "I should bring a couple of your prints to show them. Maybe some of your shots from Nipomo."

I stared at the windshield. Splotches dotted the glass: dead bugs, dust, grime. I shuddered. "You think I should close my portrait studio?" I repeated. A trickle of sweat ran down my spine.

"Well, sure, don't you? It really hasn't been open for ages. You'd just be making it official."

"But I supported my family for years with that business."

He reached over and caressed the back of my neck. "We will support our families together now. I'll help."

I nodded but closed my eyes. Even though I hadn't made any portrait appointments in months, the idea of giving notice to all of my clients to tell them that I was closing down permanently made me feel as though I were made of concrete. All those times Maynard received a rejection notice from a gallery, each time he came home tight, each time I smelled perfume on his collar, I knew I had the means to independence if I ever needed it. I hated to give that up, yet was there another choice? I glanced at Paul and softened. Since meeting him, I was a new woman. I'd never imagined finding such a partnership, a true meeting of the minds. Our timing was terrible, but if I'd learned one thing so far it was that life could be unpredictable and full of heartbreak. When beautiful moments present themselves, you have to seize them. Though I had no doubt in my mind that Paul was worth seizing, I feared what I'd be dropping as I grasped onto him. Only so many things can fit in the palms of one person.

CHAPTER 28

With me at the wheel, Maynard and I drove out to El Cerrito to retrieve the boys together. We were both quiet. We'd moved into our new rental house that morning. It hadn't taken long since we didn't have much anymore. I'd left most of my things in my studio and suspected Maynard had done the same. Though it looked as if everything was returning to normal, nothing was normal. I put down a box in the small attic bedroom and turned to find Maynard watching me. I should have explained what was happening with Paul, but I couldn't bring myself to say anything. Not yet. I wanted one day of the four of us together—one day—before I smashed it to smithereens.

We drove over a crest in the East Bay's rolling hills to see the boys waiting by the mailbox in the distance. As we neared and started waving, they jumped up and down. John leapt into the air with the graceful athleticism that young children possess. Dan moved more awkwardly. His gangly arms and legs wheeled outward, flapping in unabashed delight. He wore glasses now and sunlight glinted off the lenses in blinding bursts. Despite the heaviness in my heart, I couldn't help but laugh as I stopped the car. John yanked open my door. Both boys tumbled on top of us, wriggling and yelling. Excited chatter continued for the ride home and into dinner. From across the table, I tried to catch Maynard's eye, but he avoided my gaze.

"Pops, remember when you taught my class at school?" Dan asked during the middle of our meal.

"Ha, I didn't teach. No teacher would be fool enough to put me in charge. Why, if it was up to me, I'd have set everyone loose and taught 'em all how to shoot a rifle. You know, something useful."

John looked back and forth at Maynard and Dan, narrowing his eyes to determine if they were pulling his leg. "What do you mean? Pops went to school with you?"

"One day, he just showed up. Boy, oh boy, were the kids impressed with his cowboy hat."

"Pretty sure no one else's father at that prissy school wore a cowboy hat. Those old stiffs were a bunch of pencil pushers," agreed Maynard, grinning, before forking some baked beans into his mouth and chewing noisily.

"As I recall, many of those so-called pencil pushers bought a number of your paintings," I pointed out.

"I never said they didn't have taste," said Maynard through a mouth full of food. He swallowed and winked at the boys.

"Pops did a bunch of sketches on the board of cowboys and Indians, and then all the kids begged him to draw their portraits. And he did." Dan's eyes were distant as he looked past us at a spot on the kitchen wall, smiling, before looking at Maynard again. "That was the best day of school ever. I think about it all the time."

Maynard's smile weakened. He tugged the napkin tucked into his collar off and folded it into quarters, not looking at any of us as he did so. His chair made a scraping sound as he pushed back from the table, stood, and reached over to muss Dan's hair. "That was a good day, son. The best." He glanced at me with a stony expression and left the room. A moment later, the front door slammed. Both boys lowered their eyes to their plates and continued to eat without talking. Though food remained on my plate, I pushed it away and rose. "Who wants dessert? I made chocolate pudding."

They yelled with glee and scrambled to clear their plates. I spooned out two bowls of pudding, set them on the table in front of the boys, and went back to the counter, where I folded my arms across my chest and watched them eat. They spoke of going down to the wharf the following day to fish, excitement high and sweet in their voices. At that moment, all I wanted was to wrap my arms around their bodies and scoop them close to my breast to protect them from everything that was about to happen.

I WENT TO bed alone, but something woke me in the middle of the night. Maynard had come home and now lay snoring beside me. I rose, wrapped my bare body in the worn kimono I'd bought in Chinatown years earlier, and crept downstairs. The kitchen door squeaked as I opened it to slip outside. On the steps, with my knees pulled into my chin, the sky was clear, except for low-lying clouds scuttling across the night sky like fish swimming in black water, obscuring stars as they moved. The sense of being alone felt luxurious. It gave me time to think.

Overhead, the stars appeared to rearrange themselves with a speed that left my head reeling. All of the pieces of my life—my family, my home, my work—were spinning. Things were changing. My work with Paul felt important and useful, and I awaited word from him with an intensity that frightened me. I wanted this new job he spoke of. Most of all I needed him, yet at the same time, I dreaded the moment everything would shift. All these years I'd kept myself going using only my own momentum. From my own childhood, I'd learned it best not to rely on anyone. At forty years old, I was about to change all of that and it terrified me.

THE NEXT MORNING while the boys were outside playing, I cornered Maynard as he finished shaving in the bathroom. "We need to talk," I said.

He bobbed his head in agreement, toweled off the remaining patches of shaving cream, and followed me into our room, where he dropped onto the bed, folded his hands behind his head, crossed his ankles, and gave me a taciturn stare. I dropped next to him and sighed.

"Maynard, this is over. We both know it."

A quick flash of anguish appeared across his face, but he closed his eyes, shutting me out of his pain. His Adam's apple bobbed. "So that's it?" he asked, opening his eyes.

"I'm afraid so."

His long fingers pulled at his mustache. "We had a good run."

"We did."

"I've been thinking. If everything hadn't come crashing down around us, do you think we could have made it?"

I thought back to our camping trips over the years, to Utah, to Lake Tahoe. Sleeping under the stars. Building sweat lodges and fishing. The freedom of all of us swimming in mountain lakes. Those were the golden times and while it tempted me to focus on them, the dark times remained all too close. "I don't know. There are so many ways to change history and wonder, *What if?*"

"I guess. It just feels like we're marionettes, our strings being yanked by forces we can't see. I hate it." His voice lacked the bitterness it once had. Instead all I heard was resignation.

"I don't think that's it at all. We've got to pull through this somehow. We've got to keep trying, help more people."

A fly buzzed nearby, bumping against the windowpane over and over again. Maynard watched it a moment, before saying, "You're taking up with Paul?"

My finger followed the neat stitches of white thread on the quilt. "Yes."

"Well, we've been dealt a tough hand, but you worked awful hard at keeping us together. Harder than you should have, I suppose. I've been a lousy husband."

I pivoted to lie down beside him, my arms behind my head too, my elbow grazing his. An overwhelming sense of exhaustion pushed down on me. "You were my first love."

From where I lay beside him, I heard him suck in his breath. "Do you regret it?"

"No." And I meant it. "With you, I grew up."

He was quiet a moment. "What about the boys?"

"Paul and I'll take them. Between the two of us, we'll be earning enough. We're going to move over near campus. They'll be close and you can see them when you're able."

"Paul's a good man. I sure wish it didn't have to end like this, but he'll be steady." We were silent until Maynard rolled to his side to cough and then rose and shuffled toward the door. He turned to me. "You tell the boys." And then he left. His footsteps echoed in the hallway as he retreated downstairs.

Maybe his parting words should have angered me, but I accepted them as my penance. Although I dreaded it, I would tell the boys and be forthright. My mother hid the dissolution of her marriage for too long. The uncertainty had confused my brother and me terribly. I would be direct and not hide a thing from Dan and John. Just thinking about breaking the news to them made me cringe. But this was my decision; I would take responsibility for it.

Still on the bed, I stretched out my hand to rest upon the warm imprint where Maynard's body had lain. He reminded me of our first house, the bungalow on Nob Hill. At first I'd poured so much enthusiasm into making it just right. Then frustrations began with when the paint started flaking, pipes clanked, the windows rattled in their frames, and the ceiling plaster cracked.

We were too busy to maintain the house and eventually outgrew it and needed to move. Yet I still felt fondness for that tiny place, how it represented my new adult life. That was Maynard to me now. Was I supposed to cry? It saddened me to see the door close on that part of my life, but at the same time, relief trickled through me drip by drip.

CHAPTER 29

I longed for Paul's return from Washington. Everything felt too unsettled with him gone.

I was in my studio cropping some images when a knock at the door made me jump. When I opened it, there he stood in the cramped hallway littered with dusty packing boxes from the milliner's studio next door.

I threw my arms around his broad shoulders and tilted my head to kiss him, but he turned away, looking up and down the hallway before nudging me into my studio and closing the creaky door behind us. Once we were alone, his serious demeanor cracked into a smile. "I was able to return home a few days earlier than expected. Did you get a call from Stryker?"

"Yes." I released my arms from Paul's neck and sat down on the windowsill, still trying to gather my thoughts about my conversation with the man. Three days earlier, I'd been about to walk out the door to the grocery store when the telephone's shrill ring made me freeze, my hand on the doorknob. I lifted the receiver and said, "Lange."

After a slight pause, a man's voice cut into the static of the line and he introduced himself as Mr. Stryker, from the U.S. government's resettlement agency. "Dr. Taylor came in for a meeting yesterday and introduced me to the mighty fine photography you're doing in California. I'm calling to offer you a job as a paid photographer on my staff."

Though I'd been hoping to receive this offer, my legs started shaking. I wrapped the phone cord around my index finger while questions raced through my mind.

"Miss Lange, are you there?"

"Yes, yes, I'm here. I—"

Without waiting for me to go on, Mr. Stryker cut back in to explain the terms of my employment. "The rest of the photographers are here in Washington, but I'd like you to remain in the West. I've looked over a couple of your reports. The work is splendid and represents what I'm anxious to have more of. I'll have a Mr. Hewes call you with the particulars, but in broad strokes, this is the job. What do you say?"

It felt like I hadn't breathed the entire time he spoke. I inhaled. "Yes."

"Good, good. I want you to continue visiting migrant camps. Look for the significant details. See what's happening out there. What does it look like, feel like? What exactly is the human condition? Can you do that?"

I nodded. "Yes, that's what I've been doing."

"Swell," he replied. Voices buzzed in the background, speaking to him, distracting him. "All right then, Hewes will be in touch. I'll have a letter your way soon, outlining your first assignment."

"Yes, sir."

He said something more, something about welcoming me, but I could hear that our conversation no longer held his interest. We said goodbye. I placed the phone back on its cradle and stared at it, my hands empty at my sides. After twenty years of setting the direction of my own work, I would now be answering to someone else.

Even several days after the call, a pit of lead weighed in my stomach. "Yes," I repeated to Paul. "I spoke with Stryker and he offered me the job."

"Good, he was very impressed with you. Some of the other photographers came in to look at your work while I was there. Everyone was interested." He looked at me eagerly as he told me this. I nodded. Concern grew on his face. "You told him yes, didn't you?"

"I did."

Relief eased his tense expression into a grin, yet a deep crease between his eyes hinted at trouble. "I think we'll be heading back out to Marysville for the first assignment. We won't be working on the same project, but we can travel together, me doing what I need to for the Social Security Board, while you work for the RA."

I asked him a few questions about how his own meetings had gone in Washington, and as he answered, he began to pace around the room, his arms crossed in front of his chest. Each time he circled the room, I grew increasingly tense.

"Paul, please stop moving for a minute." When he froze, I said, "I've spoken to Maynard. He agreed to a divorce."

Paul blinked a few times, before taking a wrinkled handkerchief out of his pocket and rubbing it at his temples. His face looked gray as he pulled off his glasses and proceeded to polish the lenses. Outside, the tinny drone of a lemonade seller's music played in an endless loop. "I spoke with Katherine last night." He dropped to my stool, his face slack with exhaustion. "Do you have anything to drink?"

Paul never drank before five o'clock. I pulled out a half-full bottle of gin and two small glasses from a nearby cabinet, listening as he described how his wife had fallen completely apart upon the news. I poured him a glass and then poured myself one. Its sharp piney smell almost took off the hairs in my nostrils, but I closed my eyes and tossed it back.

He slugged back a shot too and said, "I've just come from checking her into the hospital."

My brain struggled to make sense of this. "The hospital?"

"It seemed like the safest thing for her. She spent the whole night raving. The doctors said she might be in for a couple of weeks." He paused. "She always claimed to never believe in a conventional marriage, yet it seems appearances meant more to her than I expected. She grew up in a very traditional family. I'm afraid she wasn't really as open-minded as she believed herself to be. Her reaction stunned me."

I certainly understood how hard it could be to let go of the past and nodded sadly. "Were the children there?"

"At first. But then when I saw how Katherine . . ." He shook his head. "I called my sister and she took them back to her house for the night. How did Dan and John react to the news?"

"I haven't said anything yet. I will."

He nodded. "It's almost done."

It was. My empty stomach roiled from the gin and for a moment I feared I might vomit. I placed my glass down on the floor and moved to sit on Paul's lap, bury my head in his neck. His shirt smelled musky and needed changing. He pulled me back and looked into my face, concentrating as if something were written in the whites of my eyes.

What?" I said.

"When I talked to Stryker, I didn't come right out with the fact that you and I are marrying," he confessed. "The government won't hire two people from the same family, much less a married couple, so I thought I'd keep it quiet. It will come out in time." Behind his glasses, dark circles ringed his eyes. Deep creases were carved into his forehead. Normally so solid and poised, he appeared leached of confidence.

"Of course." I pressed my lips to his. Although he hesitated at first, he pushed back and opened his mouth against my own.

What he didn't tell me that afternoon was that rumors were already circulating about our affair. Berkeley was a small community and news traveled fast from kitchen to kitchen, sidewalk to sidewalk, shop counter to shop counter. It seemed no one could picture him engaging in anything scandalous, although apparently, it was not such a leap for everyone to paint me as a husband stealer. When Berkeley's rumor mill sprang into action, it was my reputation that suffered. At the grocery store, women I knew turned and backed out of the aisle if they saw me coming. The secretary at the economics department at Berkeley never relayed any of my telephone messages to Paul. I told myself none of it mattered and steeled myself to disapproval. I was used to being on the outside.

ALTHOUGH MAYNARD ACCEPTED my request for a divorce without argument, Imogen didn't surrender anywhere as easily. I drove over to her house, and we sat on her front steps, cups of weak black tea balanced on our knees.

"You can't do this. You can't leave Maynard."

"You didn't want me to marry him. Now you won't let me leave him?"

She threw the tea from her cup into the rhododendron bush and jumped up from the step to stand over me. She blinked back tears of frustration. "I never thought you'd give up on him. What's he going to do now? For crying out loud, he's sick."

"He's a survivor." Paul's words came out as my own and I hoped they were true.

She glowered at me and placed her empty teacup on the step next to mine before dropping down beside me and resting her chin in her palm. "I'm so sorry, but I hope you won't regret this business with Paul Taylor."

Though there were many things I felt uncertain about, Paul was not one of them. I reached out to smooth back her hair, which had grayed almost overnight, it seemed. "You know all the times you've criticized my photography for being too commercial?"

"I've done no such thing."

I shook my head, unwilling to get drawn into arguing with her. "Well, anyway, when I'm photographing people in the fields and working with Paul, I know I'm doing the right thing. Every day I head out to work, I feel nervous and excited . . . and even a little scared. This work means something, it's making a difference."

She turned to look at me, sliding her toe back and forth across the paving stone of her front walk. We scowled at each other for a few beats and then she shrugged with resignation.

"It will all come at a terrible cost."

"I know."

"Do you?"

I let out an exasperated groan. "What do you want me to say?"

"Fine." She threw her hands in the air. "Have you told the boys?"

I bit my lip and shook my head, dropping my gaze to adjust the silver Navajo bangle on my wrist.

Her voice lowered. "That's the real kicker, isn't it?"

I said nothing so she slid closer and wrapped one of her slender, bird-like arms around my shoulders. We sat in silence. I looked at the chipping white paint on her front gate and remembered the girl who had stood there twenty years earlier, only a couple of dollars in her pocket, fresh off the train from the other side of the country and thinking she knew it all. But it wasn't regret that filled me. Through being humbled, I actually felt stronger. The world had expanded and shown me how much I had to learn, and it was this prospect that thrilled me. While I regretted hurting people close to me, I was working toward a larger purpose.

A COUPLE OF mornings later, Dan came running into our room while Maynard and I were dressing. He hopped on the bed and began bouncing. I tightened my belt and decided to come out with it all at once. "Dearest, your father and I will no longer be married, but it doesn't change the way we both feel about you. We both love you and your brother and you'll be able to see your father whenever you want." The creaking of the mattress springs quieted as he became motionless, his face solemn.

"I want to see him all the time," Dan said.

Maynard, Dan, and I all stared at one another.

"Of course you do," I said. "We all wish for that, but we're going to do things a little differently now."

John padded in. I repeated what I had said to Dan.

"The three of us will move in with Mr. Taylor and his three children."

"What about Pops?"

Maynard cleared his throat. "You know me, boys. I'm an old dog. No new tricks for me. I'll keep on doing the same thing I've always done. I'll stay here and paint."

"But he'll visit us often," I added.

With blank faces, the boys left our room to go outside and play. Maynard followed them out without meeting my gaze. I sat down on the edge of the bed, trying to interpret the weird silence that hung over the house. I told myself they would need time to make sense of it all.

When I tucked John into bed that night, he kept his little arms wrapped around my neck as I tried to stand. My back tightened, almost hurt, but I let him pull on me. I deserved the pain. I rested my cheek against his soft face and kissed him again. When he let go of me, I turned to Dan. Kneeling on the floor next to his bed, I smoothed his dark hair away from his forehead, tracing the freckles scattered across his pale face. Dark, liquid eyes looked up at me.

"You got what you wanted," he whispered.

My hand stopped sweeping at his bangs. "What do you mean?"

Instead of answering, he rolled away to face the wall. I bent down to kiss his earlobe, and he flinched. His shoulders curled in on themselves like a dried leaf. Closing my eyes against the prickling of tears, I rubbed circles on his back, feeling his knobby spine underneath my hand. No response. After several minutes, I pulled myself to my feet and walked out of the boys' bedroom. I latched the door behind me and rested my back against it, muffling a sob with my knuckle in my mouth.

CHAPTER 30

Before I knew it, I was caring for five children: my two boys, Paul's son, and his two daughters. Once she was released from the hospital, Katherine Taylor and Maynard skedaddled to Carson City to shack up together for several weeks. The whole thing felt desperate and I felt even worse about hurting them. When they returned, she announced she was moving to New York City to enroll in a degree program for clinical psychology. She left a week later. Although she'd return to the Bay Area in several years, the children never lived with her for extended periods of time again.

Maynard retreated to his studio in San Francisco to paint. And Paul, even when he was surrounded by the children, never quite seemed to register their presence. Somehow he was able to bow his head and read through reports even with clarinets playing and games of Double Dutch surrounding him. Whenever I tried to get his opinion on what to do with the children's education and care, he looked at me blankly. Anything to do with the children resided within the realm of motherhood; I was expected to know what to do.

Our first assignment for the government together was slated to begin in October, so I needed to figure out care for all five children immediately. I considered the Ojai Valley School for the older children, but its location near Santa Barbara made it difficult to figure out how we could all easily spend time together on the weekends or when Paul and I would be home in between assignments. While I made phone calls and wrote letters to secure a new situation for them, I began to unravel. Stomach pains plagued me. I bit my fingernails down to ragged messes. My head hurt all of the time.

I found us a new home that fall, a three-bedroom two-story house built out of redwoods on Berkeley's Virginia Street, near the university's campus. The rooms were cramped and tended to be dark, but the view of the school's elegant granite Campanile tower from the house's eastern windows appealed to me. I scrubbed the place within an inch of my life to prepare it for our new family.

Sometimes I'd put my dusting rag down and wander upstairs, drawn to the western-facing second-story windows. If the weather was right, I could make out the smudge of San Francisco across the Bay. I mourned leaving the city, though I said nothing about it to anyone. It never occurred to Paul that I might possess any second thoughts about leaving the city, becoming a faculty wife, and moving to a house in a quiet neighborhood. And I didn't, not really. But there were moments, especially when the children were all underfoot, when I'd sneak up to the window in our bedroom, look across the glittering Bay at the distant hills of San Francisco, and imagine myself in my old studio on Sutter.

MY FRIEND, EDYTHE Katten, stopped by one morning to visit our new house. She paced the sunken living room and admired the decorative stonework of the fireplace. "This is a Bernard Maybeck, right?"

I nodded.

"Hmm, I thought you'd get more space over here."

"I thought so too, but apparently not. We have only three bedrooms upstairs. The boys are all sharing a room, and the girls get the other."

"And you leave town soon? What are you doing with the children?"

I rubbed my temples. "I still don't know. I decided against boarding school because we'd only have a few weeks a year to gather as a family."

"Hmmm. What about a nanny? I suppose Kathy, Dan, and Ross are a bit old for that. What are their ages? I can barely keep track of this brood of yours now."

"I know, I can barely keep track either. Kathy is thirteen, Dan and Ross are both ten, John is seven, and Margot is six."

"Ouch, Kathy's thirteen? That's a bit of a challenge, isn't it? Well, we've had some lovely girls work for us. Hire one who's just arrived and has no family around so she won't have any distractions. Want the name of the agency I've used?"

I chewed the inside of my mouth. Edythe appeared immune to my distress and turned to admire a painting of Maynard's hanging on the wall. Her hair hung in perfectly smooth dark curtains down each side of her face. She wore a two-piece knitted wool suit similar to what all of the Hollywood actresses were sporting in the fashion magazines that Kathy pored over. From the looks of Edythe, you'd never know most people couldn't afford a fifty-cent dinner in San Francisco. Many of my former clients had cadres of cooks, nannies, drivers, and gardeners, but they were members of a different class. Even with wages falling, I couldn't bring myself to hire staff. I hated the idea of someone living in my house and managing it without me. It felt so upper-crust, so elite. When so many people were living hand to mouth, how could I justify such a luxury? And how could I expect a complete stranger to navigate the complications of melding our new family together without me to guide them?

"No, but thank you. I've just mailed a letter to a kind couple who own a rustic camp in the Sierras. I might send the boys there for some freedom and fresh air."

"That sounds marvelous! How rustic. Why, that's just the ticket to keep them busy and healthy. And the girls?"

"They might stay with Paul's aunt."

Edythe nodded and looked at me sympathetically. "It must be hard to send them away."

"It is."

She had no idea.

WHEN I LEFT the boys at the Gays' house, surrounded by acres of glacier-fed streams and tall pines, Dan wore a pinched expression. He turned without saying goodbye and marched past the flagpole and into the main house. John, seeing me stricken, reached around my waist to embrace me, but his need to comfort me felt a thousand times worse than Dan's coldness. Ross looked dazed, alone, and lost. He stood on one foot, the other raised to scuff at a mosquito bite behind his knee. When I embraced him before I left, he felt limp in my arms.

Kathy Taylor simmered with resentment of me and seemed spitefully happy when we told her that she and Margot would stay with Paul's aunt in Oakland until Thanksgiving. I drove them over there one afternoon. Margot sat in the front seat next to me while Kathy sat in the back, ignoring me. Tears coursed down Margot's face the entire time. At first, I tried to talk with her, but her responses were limited to sniffles. Silent, we watched the houses pass. Paul had confessed to me that he suspected Margot may not have been his because Katherine had taken up with a different professor around the time she discovered she was expecting the new baby. I considered it part of Paul's infinite goodness that he adored Margot despite questioning her paternity. She was a beautiful child. A headful of lovely golden ringlets gleamed around the apples of her cheeks and her caramel-colored eyes. When we pulled up to a pale-yellow cottage, I double-checked the address. This was the place.

"When will my father come back for me?"

Surprised to finally hear her little lilting voice, I smoothed down the flowered skirt on her frock and considered my response. "Your father is busy, but I'll be back for you. I promise."

From the back, Kathy snorted.

Margot's eyes glittered again with tears. I was tempted to embrace her, but something held me back. She needed to be strong on her own. She could survive this, just as I had. And as a result, she would be more resilient to life's inevitable disappointments. My early disappointments had become a source of my strength. I'd come to believe my discipline came from the independence required of me in my childhood. Looking at the unmarred rosy nobs of Margot's knees resting on the edge of the seat of the Ford, I wanted to tell her this but knew she wouldn't understand. Some things can only be learned through trial. Instead I reached for her hand and said, "Be strong."

After saying goodbye to the girls, I scurried down the front path, eager to get out from under the scrutiny of Paul's aunt. I clambered into the car and rolled down the window as I drove so the rush of air would dry my eyes. I made it three blocks before pulling to the curb and leaning my forehead against the steering wheel. A sharp pain in my side throbbed. Breathing deeply didn't help. Suddenly I was weeping, noisy, snuffling gasps, accompanied by hot tears that made the pain in my side worse. There in the car, with the soapy smell of Margot's shampoo still in the air, and the sound of my ragged sobbing, guilt swept over me.

Over the past few weeks, each time I had witnessed a woman tending to her children on the sidewalk or in a store, a little piece of me crumpled inside. The truth was that I enjoyed my work in the field. And when I wasn't in the field, photography was always on my mind, even when tending to my children.

Was that wrong? Selfish? Honestly, though, I couldn't imagine myself any other way. The prospect of not challenging myself creatively left me desolate, yet ambition felt like a curse. I was good at photography, competent and respected. Good in ways that I rarely felt as a mother. Just thinking these thoughts made me shudder. What kind of woman felt that way?

I lifted my head from the steering wheel and wiped the tears from my cheeks. Just as when I'd first taken the boys to the Tinleys in San Anselmo, I vowed to make this work serve a larger purpose. Refuge would have to be found in my photography.

WHEN PAUL AND I returned a month later, we rounded up the children and set out to celebrate Thanksgiving as a new family. He invited several colleagues to join us and though I hated to think of the extra work those guests would entail, their presence would be helpful to relieve the pressure of us all being together for the first time. I spent the week waxing the floors, shopping, preparing dishes in advance, and assembling a seating plan that would keep Maynard near the boys and away from Paul's aunt, who would not have been amused by his profane sense of humor.

On Thanksgiving Day, jammed with people, the house on Virginia Street felt ready to burst. At one point, little Margot and I were alone in the kitchen. I removed the giant, glistening turkey from the oven. Arms trembling under the weight, I raised it to the counter but misjudged the height. The pan jostled against the cabinet, sending the turkey sliding downward. It landed with a juicy *splat* on the floor. I stared at the bird splayed on the linoleum in horror. I wanted to scream in frustration, but then saw Margot gaping at me. Slowly, I lowered the pan to the floor, winked at her, and dragged the slippery creature back into the pan. "No one will ever know," I whispered to her. She giggled and the brightness of her smile made me believe this new family of ours would work.

DURING A BRIEF trip to New Mexico that December, I put on a new gabardine suit one morning. Paul and I drove to the town hall, parked next to a large outdoor Christmas tree decorated with electric lights, and a justice of the peace married us in a quiet civil service. We treated ourselves to a lunch of steaks and champagne. Then we headed to visit two migrant camps before driving back to Berkeley to join our family. This was to be our new life.

CHAPTER 31

Two years passed. During the fall of 1937, the *San Francisco News* published a week-long series of articles titled "The Harvest Gypsies" written by a young man by the name of John Steinbeck. The articles detailed the horrific conditions facing migrant workers in the Central Valley—the food shortages, the labor unrest, the unsanitary living conditions—all of it. Several of my photographs accompanied the series. Many local Californian officials, politicians, and police considered the reporting to be inflammatory. As a result, tensions arose between many of the state's resettlement camps and the surrounding communities. Because of "The Harvest Gypsies," my work reached a wider audience than ever. The RA office became flooded with requests for my photographs, but suddenly my work had become dangerous. At the urging of Paul and Stryker that I find some protection, I hired Imogen's son Rondal to be my assistant. A tall, strapping young man of twenty years with a blaze of red hair, he made for a reliable companion. More than security, I needed an assistant. Aside from trying to care for the five children Paul and I now shared, taking, developing, captioning, and filing photographs took up the bulk of my days. During the summer months, Paul and I left the children with his aunt and took longer trips to the South to study how sharecroppers lived and to the middle of the country where dust storms left the land desolate. Another year passed. My work became successful in a way that it never had been before. But still, I could not avoid trouble: Stryker fired me.

This wasn't the first time I'd received a pink slip. From the very beginning of my work with the government, problems arose. If I had a dime for every frustrated letter that Stryker and I exchanged over the course of our working relationship, I could have solved the country's economic woes in a heartbeat. Instead, I clashed with him on everything. We argued about my editing techniques, film development, where to archive my negatives, my cropping of images, and I could barely wring my promised salary of thirty dollars a week out of him. The work exhausted me, Stryker exhausted me, but at the same time, I felt challenged and awakened to the world in an exhilarating way. Nevertheless, the RA suffered from constant budget shortfalls, and though I'd been laid off before, each time Stryker assured me that he'd hire me back as soon as he was able.

But this time, after Steinbeck's articles came out, being

fired felt different. When I scanned the termination letter from
Stryker, he offered no assurances. I hurried from the kitchen
into my studio and stared at the row of "Harvest Gypsies" clip-
pings pinned to the wall. Because the government owned all
of my photographs, I had nothing to show for my last several
years of work. Stryker would need to grant me permission to
use any of my own photos in future projects. While I stared
into the sun's reflection off the glare of my worktable, contemplating my next move, the phone rang. I answered it, and the
secretary from the boys' school greeted me in a cautious tone.
Dan had disappeared.

I DON'T REMEMBER driving to the school, but I must have, because the next thing I knew, I was in front of the secretary's
desk, breathing in the cloying smell of discarded orange peels,
and sliding my silver bangle around my wrist while I waited
for the woman to get off the phone. She raised her index finger,
signaling me to wait, and made clucking sounds in response
to whoever was on the other end of the telephone line. When
she dropped the phone back in its cradle, I started to introduce
myself, but she cut me off.

"Daniel never arrived at school this morning."

"I . . . I have no idea where he could be. Could something
bad have happened to him?"

She gave me an exasperated look. "Unlikely. When
thirteen-year-old boys don't appear at school it tends to be
because they've discovered a more interesting diversion than
algebra and literature."

I shook my head. "Should I go to the police?"

"Goodness no. Usually students turn up when school lets out. He may arrive home and try to pull the wool over your eyes by pretending nothing happened."

"Won't he know you called me?"

She shrugged. "There's no telling what goes on in the mind of a teenaged boy."

I envied her calm expertise in this realm. "Are any of his friends also absent?"

"Who are his friends?" she asked, her head bowed over the attendance list on her desk, awaiting my answer.

I opened my mouth but then closed it. The truth was I didn't know any of the names of Dan's friends. I fingered the buttons on my coat, racking my brain for a name. Good Lord, did he have any friends? Chastened, I shook my head. "Don't bother. I'll go home and wait for him."

She cocked her head at me with a curious expression and assured me she'd call if he arrived at school.

I returned home and sat at my worktable stacked high with photographs waiting to be captioned, but I couldn't bring myself to start sifting through them. Instead, I leaned over my file cabinet to look for a recent photo of Dan. After several minutes of digging, I found what I wanted. I held up a photo of Maynard sitting with his new wife, Edie Hamlin, at our dining room table, one arm wrapped around his young, dark-haired, smiling bride, while the other draped along the backs of the boys. From his position on one side of his father, Dan gazed across Maynard's chest at the woman, his dark-rimmed glasses askew, hair mussed, a shy grin perking at the corners of his mouth. Two years after our divorce, Maynard had met Edie Hamlin, a fellow painter. Young, nurturing, and patient, she quickly fell for him. Far from scaring her off, his health problems and irascibility charmed her and they married shortly after meeting. This photo represented one of the few I had of Dan in which he looked happy.

I glanced back toward the "Harvest Gypsies." My walls displayed the faces of strangers, but I had to dig through my files to find pictures of my own children? I stared at Dan's image. Who was this child? Who were his friends? What did he like to do? A dizzying sense of uncertainty came over me. Did I even know my children anymore? When was the last time I'd asked the boys a question about who they had sat with at lunch or what they liked about baseball practice and listened to their answers? With a shaky hand, I propped up a few photos of Dan and John playing in the garden with Ross and Margot. I stared at the faces so intensely the images blurred and were no longer children, but shapes and varying shades of black and white.

DAN DID NOT arrive home when Kathy and Ross returned from the junior high school. There was still no sign of him an hour later when Margot and John returned from elementary school. When Paul returned from his office on campus, I told him the news.

He shook his head. "If he's not home in an hour, I'm going to look for him."

I nodded and continued to make dinner while helping Kathy with her geometry homework. Just as Margot started setting the table for dinner, Dan sauntered in. At the sight of him, the other children, sensing trouble, scattered.

"Where have you been?" I demanded.

He shrugged, a defiant set to his jaw.

"Your school called hours ago to say that you never arrived."

"So?"

"So?" I repeated, incredulous. "*So?* I've been worried about you all day."

He raised his eyebrows. "That's a first."

"What do you mean?" I glanced through the doorway of the living room toward Paul. He sat on his favorite brown leather chair, his head bent over a thick black binder of documents.

Again, Dan shrugged with practiced teenage nonchalance. "What's for dinner?"

"There will be no dinner for you," I snapped. "You're grounded for two weeks. Come home right after school. You're not to go anywhere on weekends."

With a bored expression, he opened a cupboard in search of food.

"Did you hear me? No dinner! Now go to your room." Ignoring me, he stretched his arms toward the ceiling as if rising from a long night's sleep. My hands tightened on the counter in front of me, my face growing hotter and hotter. "If you keep this routine up," I hissed, "I'll ground you for even longer."

"Go ahead," he said, his expression curling into an ugly contortion. "You're so busy, you'll never even notice or even remember since you've got so many other important things happening in your life." He brushed by me. "Stupid cow," he muttered. When he pulled away, we stared at each other for a moment, both stunned at the venom in his voice.

And then Paul was between us, clutching Dan's shirt in

both hands, pushing him toward the doorway where there was a step down to my studio. He pushed Dan off the edge and sent him sprawling onto his back. Dan's glasses flew off and bounced along the floor of the studio before coming to a halt, one lens cracked. Framed in the doorway, looming over Dan, Paul clenched and unclenched his fists, his shoulders heaving in anger. "You will never, *never* speak like that to your mother again. Do you understand?"

In the silence that followed, Dan, white-faced, looked up and nodded, his bottom lip trembling. I hurried past Paul to retrieve Dan's glasses. Astonished, I paused between my husband and son. Never before had I seen such force, such anger from Paul. He stepped back and walked away. I crouched next to Dan to hand him his glasses. "I'll take you to get these fixed tomorrow after school," I said, running a hand along the side of his head, smoothing down his hair.

He flinched under my touch and snatched the glasses from me while scrambling to his feet. His gaze spun around the room wildly and landed on one of the photos I'd placed on my desktop earlier in the day, a photo I'd taken on Mother's Day, years earlier. In the picture, Dan's small chubby fingers held a bouquet of lily of the valley he'd given to me. Pointing at it, he spat, "That photo is a lie."

I looked at the image, speechless with confusion.

"I brought you those flowers as a gift and you wouldn't take them. You made me hold them while you ran off to get your camera. And when you were done photographing them, you just tossed them onto the table. I never saw those flowers again, except in this picture."

"But I took the photo to remember the moment."

His eyes burned with resentment. "That's just a dumb photo of my hand, not me. We never had a moment." And with that, he fled the room. Seconds later, his feet pounded up the stairs to his bedroom.

I lifted the photo of the bouquet before dropping it to my desk. How could we both interpret the same moment so differently? I wandered out of my studio limp with exhaustion. Everything had gone wrong. I'd wanted so badly to make amends with Dan, yet instead, my temper made the situation even worse. Paul had returned to his chair in the living room to resume his reading. Leaning against the doorway, I watched him for a moment, still stunned by his defense of me.

"What happened in there?"

He lifted his head and looked at me. "He had no right to speak so rudely to you."

"He certainly did not, but still, he's a child."

"Dorothea, I will never stand for anyone to threaten you. I don't care who it is."

"Well, he's my son and he's dreadfully angry because of all the times I've left him behind to work. I need to make peace with him, not upset him even more."

"I'm sorry, I didn't mean to hurt or upset the boy. I'll do whatever I can to help you mend your relationship with him." He stood and opened his arms toward me.

I shivered, pulling my sweater close as I shuffled toward him and then buried my face into his neck, taking a deep inhalation of the lemony smell of starch from his shirt collar. Dan was fine. Paul had just been making a point. The quivering in my hands stilled. For so long, I'd been my own champion. I'd never felt the security of someone who would stand by me, no matter what. My father had left me. Maynard had failed me. But now I had Paul. He wrapped his arms around me, crushing me a little in the tightness of his grasp so I almost couldn't breathe. Almost. It felt good. I wanted to be crushed a little.

From my back pocket, a rustling of paper caught my attention. I reached around and pulled out an envelope. Dazed, I stared at it.

"What's that?" Paul asked.

"My job." I tossed Stryker's letter onto the floor with a sigh. "I was fired."

CHAPTER 32

Months passed. I hoped for a call or letter from Stryker but no word came. Meanwhile, Mr. Steinbeck's articles, along with my photos, were turned into a book, *Their Blood Is Strong*. It sold well. One of my images featured in the Steinbeck articles, a photo of a mother and her three children, continued to be requested for reproduction from news organizations. That particular photo, it was a funny thing—I hadn't planned the shot, yet it was the one everyone wanted.

I'd taken it a couple of years earlier, in the winter of 1936, at the end of a long assignment in Southern California. Rain had been falling steadily. With my foot anchoring the gas pedal to the floor of my station wagon, I sped along Highway 101 figuring I could be back in Berkeley by afternoon if I kept the speedometer at fifty. The roads were slick, the sky leaden, everything felt soggy and cold. I just wanted to be home. Around Nipomo, I passed a handwritten sign indicating a pea-picking camp. At first, I thought nothing of it. Similar signs dotted roadsides all over the state. But after a few miles, the sign started nagging at me. The rain was falling with such ferocity that I feared for anyone stuck outside. Whatever camp was back there couldn't have been in very good shape. Biting my lip, I drove a few miles more before finding a decent turnaround.

I backtracked, found the sign again, and veered off the highway onto a potholed muddy trail, my car bucking and spluttering in protest. When I pulled into a clearing, sagging tents and puddles the size of ponds greeted me. To the right of my car, a woman huddled under a drooping tarp with a mess of children. I pulled my black rain slicker from the passenger seat, and tugging the hood over my head, circled a large puddle to reach her. I introduced myself, but she just stared at me, unmoved. An infant lay in her arms, lethargic at her breast. Nuzzled next to her sat two shivering young children, a girl and boy, both purple-lipped and listless. Neither could have been more than eight years old. "May I take a few photos of you?" I asked. "It might lead to some help for you folks."

She gave a resigned heave of her shoulders in response.

The stormy sky made it a challenge to gauge if there was any direction to the light. Rainy day photography was not my forte. "Mind shifting a little that way?" I asked, trying to arrange the kids so they didn't block each other. The woman's exhausted, pensive expression was striking enough; the mournful-looking children added almost too much to the sense of desperation. "How about if you two look away from the camera?" They studied me balefully before burying their faces in the woman's neck.

I took several photos. Seven, to be precise.

Rattled by the hopelessness expressed by the woman and her children, I left as quickly as I came and sped home with a newfound urgency, eager to develop the images. Those people in that Nipomo camp, trapped in the rising waters and without food, were in danger. Once back in Berkeley, I left the car packed, ran to my basement, developed the images, and with the photography paper still damp, I took the ferry across the Bay and drove the photos to George West at the *San Francisco News* office. Without skipping a beat, he picked up his telephone and called the folks at the United Press. The story got onto the wires and prompted aid workers to descend upon Nipomo to help with food and shelter.

Each time that photo was reproduced in the weeks, months, and even years that followed, my name rarely appeared as a byline, but I cared little about getting credit for it. The fact that my photo had spurred action was enough. But at the same time, it was frustrating that while my work reached more and more people and fulfilled its purpose, I remained shut out of the RA.

Stryker's betrayal stung. Every time I saw that photo, the sting sharpened.

"WHAT IF WE create a book together?" I proposed to Paul one afternoon that spring. "We could tell the story of the new pioneer. These people no longer travel by covered wagon, but by station wagon and their old, dinged-up trucks."

Paul leaned back in his favorite chair in the living room to flip through the photographs I handed him. "These are good. This is a swell idea."

"There's a market for it. Look how well *Their Blood Is Strong* has done."

"I agree. If you come with me this summer to Nebraska, Arkansas, and Oklahoma, you can take photos while I work. You know, I need to go to Washington for the Social Security Board. You could always go visit Stryker at the RA."

I didn't want to think about Stryker, but agreed so we could keep planning our book. Paul and I had been traveling together for the last several years while we each worked on our individual assignments, but we hadn't collaborated on something since our early reports for SERA. Excitement bubbled within me at the prospect of our new plan.

As summer neared, Dan continued to skip more and more classes. It wasn't lost on me that I'd also been a truant during my high school years. I'd been bored by the classroom and curious about the world beyond Wadleigh High School for Girls. But Dan's defiance felt different. He skipped school to anger us and get attention. Maynard was no help and dodged any serious discussion about the boys. As soon as school let out, Paul and I sent Dan off to work and board on a sheep ranch in Nevada, hoping physical labor could solve his restless spirit. Ross, Paul's middle child, moved to New York to live with his mother for a spell. Paul's sister agreed to let Katherine, John, and Margot live with her for the summer. A tentative peace prevailed. Paul and I left to travel around the middle of the country, but before our departure, he insisted I write a letter to Stryker to arrange a meeting for when we were in Washington. We needed my salary from the RA. With a nervous feeling in my stomach, I wrote it. I wanted my job back but feared rejection.

I ARRIVED AT the Resettlement Administration's cramped Washington, D.C., offices and wistfully took in the frenetic scene. Stryker, his white hair sticking out in all directions, greeted me stonily from his desk. Three phones sat near his elbow. As one started to ring, followed by a second, he grunted, shook his head, and stood to greet me. We walked around the workroom, observing the photographs resting on light boxes. Gone was the elegant Walker Evans, fired a few months earlier for disappearing for long stretches of time unaccountably and often clashing with Stryker. Unfamiliar men scurried between the warren of desks.

"Where's Ben Shahn? Is he off on an assignment?" I asked. Paul had heard a rumor that Ben, one of the staff photographers, planned to quit to pursue his painting. If he and Evans were both gone, I figured my chances for getting hired again improved considerably. Surely, Stryker wanted one of his experienced photographers back.

Rather than answer, Stryker asked, "How was your trip?"

"You wouldn't believe conditions in the center of the country. Barren fields as far as the eye can see. Foreclosures everywhere. And now the corporations have moved in and it's just tractors that roam through the abandoned farms. The individual farmer is at the mercy of big business. They can't even vote since poll taxes are too high. It's like the small guy isn't even an American anymore."

Stryker shook his head and held up a strip of negatives and stared at them. After making a frustrated sound, he pulled a hole punch out of his pocket and clipped through each of the negatives. I grimaced at the thought of the ruined work. He saw my pained expression.

"Don't give me that look," he snapped. "If you had to deal with the flood of negatives and photographs that I'm drowning in, you'd want a quick system for identifying which ones were failures too."

"But now it's unusable," I protested.

"That's the point."

We were glaring at each other when a woman's voice floated through the office. I startled and turned. An attractive brunette headed toward us.

"Mr. Stryker? There you are. My goodness, you wouldn't believe those fellas back at the garage. I thought they were gonna keep me there all day while they gave me a detailed accounting of every single thing wrong with my car. As if I care about spark plugs! All I want is for it to be fixed."

"They probably just wanted to spend more time with a pretty gal," said a man reviewing a stack of photographs at a nearby desk.

"Well then, at least offer me a drink or something," she said with a wink and a smile. The man reddened and his head sank back down to his work, a goofy grin spreading across his face.

"Is the car fixed?" Stryker asked, avoiding my gaze.

"Yes, finally." By this point, she was standing right in front of us and looking at me curiously.

"Lange," I said, pushing my hand out toward her.

"Ah, yes, Dorothea! I'm Marion Post. I'm new here but I've heard all about your work. Why, everyone's always talking about you." She put her hand in mine. Up close, I guessed her to be about ten years younger than me. "What brings you all the way out here? You live in California, isn't that right?"

"Yes," I said, unnerved. What exactly was everyone saying? I pushed the thought from my mind and said, "My husband had some business to attend to here in the capital so I thought I'd stop in to see the latest."

We smiled at each other. A string of pearls glistened around her neck and cherry-red lipstick made her look like a film star. How did she look so crisp and peppy in the summer humidity? My sweaty light gray linen trousers stuck to me in awkward places while her fashionable navy-blue poplin dress accented the gentle curves of her slim figure.

"We were just on our way out," Stryker said to Marion. "I'll be back in a few minutes to go over the shot list I've prepared for you."

Marion nodded and wished me well, but I couldn't hear anything over the rush of blood pounding in my ears. He grasped my elbow to steer me toward the office door. Out in the hallway, I spun toward him. "I thought you were hiring *me*."

Stryker pressed his lips together and gestured toward the opening elevator door. We stepped into the elevator's stuffy interior without looking at each other. As the lift dropped, I tried to breathe through the fury building inside me. Once the door opened, we spilled out, a packed crowd swarming around us, pushing us through the lobby and outside onto the sidewalk, where the heat felt even more oppressive. Stryker pulled me over to the curb, out of the flow of pedestrians.

"So, what about my job?" I demanded, wiping a trickle of sweat from my temple.

"Listen, it's easier to have another staff photographer who's local. And now you're busy with your book," he said, lighting a cigarette and exhaling while watching me out of the corner of his eye.

"You heard your new girl: everyone's talking about *my* photographs." I raised my index finger at him. "I've been doing this type of work before your group even started; *it's what I do.* I've given everything I've got for this job. You need me back."

"The distance makes it impossible."

"The distance? How? I'm always responsive to your re-quests. I never complain when you change my trips. One week I'm preparing to go to the Pacific Northwest and then the day before I'm supposed to leave, you cancel it and tell me to sit tight. Do I ever complain? No. I always go wherever you ask."

"We've gone through this before. Your technical ability is not as good as these other guys'."

Beads of sweat rolled down my back as I shook my head in protest. "I'll bet my photos get the most reproduction requests." He looked away and I felt a swell of triumph knowing I was right. "And now that Ansel prints most of my negatives, I thought we'd stopped worrying about all of the development issues."

He took a drag on his cigarette. "You know my budget's always being slashed. Every penny, all of the postage and shipping—"

"Oh, come on, I keep my costs low and you know it. Why, you pay me less than all of those other photographers. I'm a bargain. My dedication to this project is greater than anyone else's you could possibly find. For crying out loud, I've crossed the damn country to come and tell you I want this job back." I leaned forward, aware that people passing us were glancing curiously. "I *need* this job back," I said in exasperation.

"Your husband needs to stop calling me insisting that I do this and that for you. And you must stop going over my head on things. This is *my* department. You don't know how it all works out here," he huffed. "I spend way too much time writing you letters about things you should just leave alone. It feels like I'm repeating myself all the time." He gave me the stink eye through the cloud of cigarette smoke enveloping him.

I paused to think about this. He'd never liked that I often demanded my photos of Negros be circulated to more newspapers. During my previous trips to the South, the miserable conditions of Negro sharecroppers and repressive segregation rules never failed to appall me. I'd written to Stryker over and over begging him to promote my photos of the sharecroppers more, but he'd responded that newspapers weren't interested in writing about race. I had no response for Stryker's complaint on this one, but he would get no apology from me. "Well then, just agree with me if you don't want to say no all of the time."

He grimaced. "And another thing: you've got to stop bossing my girls around."

"Oh for Pete's sake, sorry I don't have time to spritz my stationery with Chanel before sending them my supply lists. I tell them what I need. Bet they don't complain when your fellas do that."

We glowered at each other, but then he exhaled loudly and dropped the cigarette to the ground, rubbing it out with his toe. "Let's see what I can do when I get my new budget in September."

"September?" I narrowed my eyes and glared at him.

"I'll do everything I can to hire you back in the fall," he said more forcefully.

"Fine, but I'm not going away. I won't let you forget about this."

"If there's one thing I can count on in an uncertain world, it's that you're not going away. Just keep your husband off my back."

His sarcasm rankled, but I kept quiet. While I knew Paul made occasional phone calls on my behalf to Washington, I didn't realize he had made so many. I smiled to myself, pleased with his defense of me.

"All right," he said, interpreting my smile as acquiescence. He straightened his tie and glanced at the building. "Are we done here? Do we have an understanding?"

"Yes," I said, folding my arms across my chest.

He wished me a safe trip and marched back to the building's main door. If only I spent more time in Washington, I felt certain we wouldn't have all of these flare-ups over miscommunication. Walking to my station wagon, I pictured how Marion had captivated everyone in that office. I'd certainly never enjoyed that type of attention from the staff there, but I'd also never reduced myself to simpering and prancing about the way she had. Why, she might as well have offered to peel off her clothes down to her unmentionables and do the Lindy Hop. No, thank you. That kind of carrying on was not for me, but boy, it sure got results. I kicked the tire of my automobile before slumping into the driver's seat. Despondency over Stryker's betrayal stuck to me like spit-out bubble gum on the heel of my shoe. Could I trust his assurances?

CHAPTER 33

On our drive back to Berkeley, we stopped in Nevada to retrieve Dan. After a mere six weeks on the sheep ranch, he was already being sent home to us for being too disruptive. As soon as he collapsed into the backseat, he closed his eyes, uttering only occasional grunts when we tried to speak with him. Silence, brittle and oppressive, hung between the three of us on the final stretch to California. We arrived in Oakland exhausted and settled into home. A dull ache in my stomach had nagged at me since my divorce from Maynard, but a new pain, sharp and urgent, had taken its place during our drive back to California.

Paul took me to the hospital in Oakland, where a young doctor met with us. His clean-shaven cheeks were as smooth as the pages of a freshly opened book. Immediately, I regretted not driving farther to a hospital in San Francisco to find a doc with more mileage on him. After inspecting me, he announced I needed an appendectomy. When he left the examination room, I turned to Paul and whispered, "Did you see how excited he looked when he announced I needed surgery? Do you think I might be his first operation? Good heavens, let's go to the city."

Paul leaned over to kiss the top of my head. "No, I don't want to risk moving you. You'll be safe here." He left to consult with a nurse, fussing about more pillows for me. I kicked at my sheets in annoyance and groaned as new pain flashed through my abdomen. I was stuck.

Several days later, I lay in a narrow hospital bed, woozy from pain medication when I was told I had a telephone call. Paul wheeled me to the nurses' desk and handed the receiver to me. It was Stryker.

"Lange, why are you in the hospital?"

"Umm, I'm visiting a friend." Paul raised his eyes and shook his head at me crossly, but I ignored him.

"Huh, a kid back at your house told me to find you here. Well, at any rate, any interest in being a staff photographer for me again? I can even give you a raise this time. We're no longer a division of the RA. A little government reorganization has given us a new budget and a new name. We're now the Photography Unit of the Farm Security Administration, the FSA. More alphabet soup, brought to you courtesy of President Roosevelt."

I mustered a smile at Paul while working through the logistics of my return with Stryker. Though my surgeon insisted on me remaining in the hospital for several more days,

I plotted my escape. First, I urged Paul to attend a meeting on campus at the university. Once he was out the door, I called Imogen's house to find Rondal, telling him to meet me at the hospital immediately. I changed out of my hospital gown and got back into bed, pulling the sheet to my chin to cover my street clothes. Not more than fifteen minutes later, Rondal strolled through the door and plunked himself down on the chair next to my bed. His white teeth gleamed as he gave me a wide grin and ran a hand through his red hair.

"So, what now, boss?" he asked.

"Good heavens, that was fast. Did you fly here?"

"You'd be surprised how quickly I can get places when you're not hanging out the window with your camera telling me to slow down. Plus, Ma warned me you'd leave on your own if I didn't get here in time. Who knew where you'd end up? I think she couldn't bear the thought of Paul wasting away without you."

"Oh stop. He's the smartest man I've ever met."

"Well, I don't think he'd know what to do without you. Now, no more time for chatting. Let's get this jailbreak under way." He stood and held his arm out to me gallantly. "Our getaway vehicle's out front."

I smiled to myself, easing out of the bed to hobble outside on Rondal's arm. While he opened the car door, I closed my eyes and inhaled the dry smell of fallen leaves. The warm September sunshine on my shoulders felt heavenly after the antiseptic stifle of the hospital. After settling me into the passenger seat, he looked at me. "Where to?"

"Home. We're back in business. Stryker's hired me again and

wants us to make a trip down to the Salinas Valley. The newspapers are reporting labor unrest with the cotton pickers."

"Think you should rest longer? You can barely walk."

"We're not leaving today. Maybe two or three more days and then we'll hit the road."

He gave me a dubious look but then glanced over his shoulder as he backed out of the parking spot. "Paul will never agree."

"Don't worry about that, I'll take care of him. When we get to the house, I'll give you some cash. I need you to go pick up film for the Juwel, the Graflex, and the Rolleiflex."

"You're not going to bring the thirty-five-millimeter?"

"No, I don't like how I must lift it in front of my face. It makes it hard to talk to people."

"How long will we be gone? How much film should I get?"

As I tallied up the days in my head, storefronts slipped past outside the car's window. It felt good to be planning another field expedition. We continued discussing the trip until we arrived at the house. Rondal led me into the quiet foyer, lowered me onto the couch in the living room, and then brought me a notebook so I could start making lists while he disappeared to the back of the house to assemble supplies in my studio.

He returned, scratching his head. "Did you take the Rolleiflex to the shop to get it cleaned?"

"No, it's in fine shape. I polished all the lenses myself and put everything away in the usual places when Paul and I got back from Washington. Look again."

He shrugged and left, but was back after a few more minutes, empty-handed. "Dorothea, I swear that camera is not there. I've looked everywhere."

I groaned while he raised me to my feet and helped me back to the studio. But he was right. My camera was gone.

"Dorrie?" Paul appeared in the doorway, hands folded, expression stern. "What in the world are you doing? Dr. Englund was very clear about you remaining in the hospital for longer."

"I'm fine, but where on earth is my Rolleiflex?"

"Your camera?" Paul said, looking back and forth at Rondal and me in confusion. "Are you going back to work?"

"No, not immediately," I hedged, turning from Paul. "But where is it?"

My gaze swept across my studio. An empty spot on my desk stopped me. "Wait, and where's my typewriter?"

Footsteps echoed in the kitchen. Margot and Kathy popped their heads in next to Paul in the doorway to welcome me home. Their smiles fell as they saw our troubled expressions.

"Where's Dan?" I asked Kathy.

She shifted from foot to foot and lowered her eyes to the ground. "I'm not sure. He hasn't been around much."

"Where in the world has he been?" I demanded of everyone. No one could answer. Rondal returned to assembling the materials we would need for our upcoming trip. I returned to my spot on the couch, a sense of dread settling over me. From the coatrack by the front door, Paul snatched his hat and announced he was going to look for Dan. Berkeley was small, everyone knew everyone—someone would be able to help us find him. Or so I hoped.

Kathy brought me a grilled cheese sandwich on a tray that evening while I tried not to worry about the darkness outside the window beside me. My stomach ached with anxiety. I could barely touch my dinner. Why in the world had Dan taken my equipment? When the front door swung open shortly before nine o'clock, Dan skulked into the front hallway, followed by Paul. I fell back into the couch with relief. Paul nudged Dan forward to face me.

"I found him at the library," Paul said.

"The library?" I repeated, surprised.

Relief must have dawned across my face, because he shook his head. In a stern tone, he said, "Now tell your mother about her camera. And her typewriter."

MY TRIP TO the Salinas Valley was delayed by a week while Paul tracked down my equipment. While I'd been in the hospital, Dan had stolen my camera and typewriter and pawned them to a shop in Oakland. When Paul drove there to inquire about my possessions, both pieces of equipment rested in the storefront as if waiting for me. I was so angry with Dan, I could barely speak. The thought of him going into my studio and taking my Rolleiflex left me reeling. I'd had that camera for years. Why would my own son do such a thing? What had gotten into the boy's head? He blamed me for working too much, but when he saw my pictures of children covered in sores and flies, playing in tattered clothes, didn't he see what happened when parents couldn't support their families? Couldn't he see how other families suffered? We were lucky, damned lucky. Why couldn't Dan see that?

Finally, with everything back in place, Rondal and I started working again. We traveled around California for Stryker over that winter, but I shortened my trips to keep an eye on Dan. Still, it was no good. Increasingly, he stopped attending his high school classes and would disappear, sometimes for several nights at a time. When I tried to get Maynard involved, he remained unmoved, convinced the boy would grow out of these rebellions. But I could not stop worrying. I feared the direction in which Dan was heading.

IN APRIL 1939, John Steinbeck published *The Grapes of Wrath,* a novel about a migrant family in California, based on the research he had done for "The Harvest Gypsies." It became an overnight success. One morning, about a month after the book was released, I sat at the breakfast table across from Paul after the kids had left for school. The window next to me was open. A warm breeze blew through the room, riffling the pages of the *San Francisco Chronicle* opened on the table in front of me. I skimmed through a brief interview with the author.

"It appears 1939 will be the year of Steinbeck. Sales numbers for *The Grapes of Wrath* are through the roof. It bodes well for our book, don't you think?"

Paul leaned back from reading a report and stirred cream into his coffee. The liquid swirled, creating a pinwheel of white upon dark that vanished after an instant. "I spoke on the phone with Nelson yesterday."

"Our agent?" I asked absently, relieved to leave the business arrangements of the book to Paul.

"Yes. He's worried the market's saturated with these stories and thinks interest in our book is exhausted."

"Exhausted?" I repeated, snapping to attention. I tapped my finger against the newspaper. "But it says right here there's interest in the movie rights. People can't get enough of this."

"Apparently, they can," he said.

"Well, that's not right. It's important."

Paul pushed a plate of orange slices toward me. He had driven all the way to the city to my favorite store in Chinatown the previous day to surprise me with them. I didn't have the heart to confess how oranges aggravated my stomach pains. My appendectomy the previous fall had solved little. If anything, my stomach pains worsened. It had gotten to the point where I could barely eat.

"Nelson suggested seeing if Steinbeck would write a foreword for our book."

"That's a good idea. I can't imagine it will be a problem since my photos have been used so often to accompany his articles."

"Do it soon. I suspect our window of opportunity closes a little with every passing day."

"But that's crazy. People are consumed with this story." I scanned the rest of the newspaper. "Who do you think they'll cast as the lead in the movie? Let's hope it's a big name. Clark Gable? Spencer Tracy? Maybe Cary Grant?"

Paul chuckled. "Since when did you become such an expert on Hollywood?"

"I'm not, but honestly, I swear Kathy's obsessed with film stars. All she talks about is Olivia de Havilland, Hedy Lamarr, and Katharine Hepburn. If you ask me, the girl's head's been turned."

He nodded absentmindedly as he underlined a passage in the report lying next to his breakfast plate.

"Paul, listen to me: I don't think she takes anything seriously. Her biggest concern these days is making sure her hair is styled in the latest fashion. She doesn't think about anything larger than herself." I held back from saying she took after her mother and looked at him expectantly, but his eyes stayed on his report.

"I'll talk to her," he murmured after a moment.

I shook my head and nibbled on a piece of toast, scanning a headline about Adolf Hitler. "As if it wasn't enough to invade Czechoslovakia, now Germany's dividing it into two."

Paul's head shot up from his report. "That man. Someone needs to stop him."

He reached for the first section of the paper, and I handed it to him. Concerns about his daughter went right past him, but world events couldn't be missed. I sighed, eager to stop thinking about depressing events half a world away. We had enough to worry about in California. The fall elections had brought in a new crop of conservative politicians, and I feared for the FSA's future. I shifted the newspaper over a corner of my plate, hiding the remainder of my toast so Paul wouldn't notice my diminished appetite.

I WROTE MY letter to Steinbeck that afternoon but it did no good. He declined to write anything for me. I wrote another appeal, but he remained steadfast in his refusal. I said nothing to anyone, not even Paul, but it grieved me that the writer refused to cooperate. No doubt "The Harvest Gypsies" was fine journalism, but my photos enriched his work—of that, there was no doubt in my mind. And when the movie version of *Grapes of Wrath* was released a year later, it was practically an homage to my photography. Rumor had it that the film's director, John Ford, used my work to design and direct his scenes. Despite my hurt feelings, I complained to no one. Yet somehow, even without Steinbeck's coveted participation, a publishing house out of New York City bought our book, *American Exodus*, and scheduled its release for the end of 1939. We toasted the victory over two mugs of coffee one morning. While it was a thrill to have our work being published, the most satisfying part of it was that the book represented the strength of the relationship between Paul and me. We had spent hours sitting on the floor studying photos, grouping them in interesting combinations, discussing and debating the text that should accompany them. After years of working on my own, I couldn't get over my good fortune to have found him.

IN THE FALL, Paul secured Dan a spot at Black Mountain College, a new liberal arts college in North Carolina. The school's rural isolation, experimental nature, and commitment to the arts seemed to offer him the chance to start over. It would be a new setting, a way to do things differently. He had taken to spending much of his time lurking around our local library, where he cultivated a love for writing poetry. Perhaps a chance to study literature among some of the greatest artists of our time could be just the thing for him. I breathed a sigh of relief as he left Berkeley, but all sense of good fortune was short-lived.

He returned home a month later full of complaints about everything from the food to the muggy weather to the uppity professors. A haunted wildness lurked in his eyes. One afternoon I was working in the garden, splitting patches of lumpy white iris bulbs, when I paused to wipe my brow and looked to the house to see him watching me from the window of his bedroom. As our eyes met, he stepped backward, vanishing, a sad expression on his face. That night he disappeared and didn't come home for four days.

In the middle of October, Stryker called to fire me again. This time there was a finality in his voice that had never existed before. Although he assured me the office would still supply photos for my book, he told me in no uncertain terms that I was too difficult. My work with the FSA was over. I felt devastated, but I didn't have long to dwell on it. Dan was in crisis.

CHAPTER 34

I didn't pick up my camera for the next two years. With us all home, we bought a house, a rambler that sprawled down a steeply wooded hill on Euclid Avenue in Berkeley. I received notice that I'd won a coveted Guggenheim Award, but doubted I could complete the project. Poor health had been nagging at me on and off for several years. To further complicate matters, Dan had been circling in and out of our lives, disappearing and then reappearing only to fight with us and have scrapes with the law, but in the fall of 1941, he landed in his most disastrous situation yet.

I'd been in San Francisco with Imogen for an evening and missed the police delivering Dan to the house. By the time I'd gotten home, he was in bed. The next morning, he sat slumped in a chair at the kitchen table, his face drawn. He looked older than his sixteen years. Not knowing what to say, I set a small breakfast in front of us—a plate of sliced cantaloupe and two cups of coffee—then sat down. Dan reached for the coffee and pulled it close to his face as if he could use the cup to block himself from looking at me. His fingers, inflamed and bruised, wrapped around the handle. Scrapes etched his knuckles. I reached for his other hand resting at the edge of the table, but he flinched at my touch.

"Tell me what happened."

His expression darkened and he pulled his hand out from under mine.

I tried again. "Why did you take the car?"

"Are you accusing me of stealing it? It belongs to our family. I didn't steal anything."

At the aggression in his voice, all of the patience I'd been trying to keep close to my chest ebbed from me. "I own that station wagon. Paul and I earned the money for it. The automobile is not yours to use whenever you like. You must stop taking things that don't belong to you."

"So now you're going to bring up your old stupid camera and typewriter?" With this he sprang from his seat, tearing at his hair. "That was two years ago!"

I shook my head. "Dan, what happened? Why did you drive to Nevada?"

He started pacing the floor of the kitchen without looking at me. "Why are you making me repeat all of this? I told Paul. I know he told you." He sneered this last part.

I recrossed my legs, gathering myself to remain calm. "I'm trying to understand. I'm trying to see what happened."

Dan whirled around, jabbing his index finger at me. "You're trying to see?" He started laughing, but it almost sounded like sobbing. It was a horrible, searing sound that left him holding on to the counter, his back hunched, head down. "You have a famous eye, right? That's what everyone says. You can see people in all of their dignity, their humanity. Well then, why is it that you can't see me?"

I started to protest, but he cut me off.

"You've never been able to see me. *Never.*" His voice was hoarse and raw. He stopped speaking, and bolted from the room.

I managed to rise to my feet and stumble out of the kitchen door. Birds trilled from the leafy oak tree branches overhead. I slumped down onto a bench underneath my favorite oak and covered my eyes with my hands.

Paul had told me what had happened when I arrived home the previous night. Dan had met a girl at a five-cent-a-dance joint in Oakland. After his pockets were empty from buying dances, he and the girl rode the bus to our house and took our car from the garage, telling no one. They drove to Reno and married, only hours after meeting. Then they returned to California. Back in Oakland, the girl asked Dan to stop at a building where she lived with her mother so she could get a few things. She never reappeared.

"When the police brought him to the house, he was a wreck. His eyes were red and his hands bloody," Paul had said to me as I sat on the edge of our bed in shock.

I pictured Dan climbing the stairs in the building to look for the girl. Chipped paint in the stairwell, the burnt smell of frying oil hovering in the air. He would have started pounding on the doors, moving from one to the next, demanding to know where the girl was. Impatient neighbors wanted nothing to do with the lovers' squabble and called the police. I could only imagine how Dan must have felt in the back of the police car on the ride to our house. When the police officer asked Paul if he wanted to press charges for the theft of the vehicle, he had said no and brought Dan inside. Dan confessed to Paul what had happened and fled upstairs.

AT PAUL'S URGING, we took Dan to a psychiatrist later that afternoon. Before the appointment, I telephoned Maynard. When he answered the call, his voice sounded thin and raspy.

After I recounted the details of Dan's brief marriage, Maynard said, "Why can't he get his act together? When I was his age, I was making my own living."

"I was too, but he's different from us. He's very sensitive."

Maynard snorted. "That damned boy needs to toughen up. The world has no patience for sensitive types."

This was not helpful. Despite my entreaties to try talking to Dan, Maynard begged off. "Dorrie, you've been handling all of this so far. I can't get involved now."

"Well, clearly I've made a hash of raising him," I admitted, leaning my forehead against the wall.

A silence yawned between us and I thought our call had disconnected, but Maynard came back on the line, his voice softer. "You've done no such thing. None of this has been easy. Now I don't know what this fancy doc will tell you, but at some point, Dan will come around."

I needed that point to come soon.

Maynard's reassurances evaporated when Dan vanished beyond the frosted window of the doctor's office door a few hours later. I sat next to Paul, thumbing through the *San Francisco Chronicle*, a ball of worry coiling tighter and tighter in my stomach. After what felt like an interminable amount of time, Dan reemerged and slumped down on one of the wooden chairs. The doctor observed him for a moment before turning to us. A brief look of distaste flickered over his face, but it vanished before I could register what I'd seen with certainty. I frowned. I needed someone who could see my son with a clarity that I knew my own anger and fear were clouding. Despite my misgivings, Paul and I rose to speak with the psychiatrist. From behind his desk, the man pinched his nose and slid his glasses off his face, wiping them with a handkerchief he pulled from a pocket.

After hemming and hawing for several minutes about what he observed during his interview with Dan, the doctor leaned his elbows onto his desk and said, "I believe he's psychotic and should be institutionalized."

"Psychotic?" I repeated, incredulous. "What on earth makes you say that?"

"The anger he expresses when he describes you and Paul leads me to believe—"

Disbelief filled me. I stared at the man's lips moving as he spoke without hearing anything more. He finished talking and both Paul and Dr. Gilbert looked at me. I bent over to pull my pocketbook up off the floor and stood. "This appointment's over."

"Now, Dor—"

"No," I said, shaking my finger at both of them. "I do not think Dan needs institutionalization and I certainly don't believe him to be psychotic. Yes, he's angry. In fact, he's furious because he thinks I abandoned him when he was child. He needs someone to listen to him, to figure out what he needs to survive in the world, not institutionalization and medicine that will numb him to everything. Paul, we're leaving."

I crossed the room and threw the door open. I stood for a moment, waiting for Paul to catch up, and looked over at Dan. Absorbed in a magazine, he sat with his shoulders hunched to his ears, his legs crossed tightly. Everything about him radiated tense energy. Standing there, my heart ached. Though he was sixteen years old, suddenly he was seven again, and we were in San Anselmo, and he was sitting in the backseat of the car at the Tinleys', refusing to get out.

WHILE PAUL DROVE us home, I looked out the window without seeing anything, my thoughts spinning. *How could I have done things differently?* Dan sat in the backseat, saying nothing. When we arrived home and parked the car in the driveway, Dan opened his car door before we stopped moving, sprinted toward the house, and disappeared.

I followed. Inside our foyer, shirts, pants, and socks lay all over the living room floor, remnants of a pile of clean laundry I'd folded earlier that day. I pictured Dan kicking it apart before he climbed the stairs, but shook my head and left it all. I retreated to the garden and took my spot on my bench below my favorite oak.

When I thought back to my father leaving, it always seemed

obvious that he had chosen to go because I had not been worth staying for. My beloved father, the man who crawled into bed beside me and sang songs until I fell asleep, the man who lifted me onto his shoulders at *A Midsummer's Night Dream*, the man who always had a shiny nickel for me in his pocket— that same man had left me without so much as a look over his shoulder. There had been nothing apologetic in his straight-spine posture, nothing that spoke of regret, nothing that spoke of shame. And I never saw him again. Mother remained silent about his absence, leaving Martin and me to piece together an explanation in our own minds. What had I missed? Did I misinterpret his actions the way Dan was misinterpreting mine? I rubbed at my eyes as if I could erase the image of my father's swagger from my mind. I imagined Dan lying on his bed, believing I'd abandoned him when in fact I'd tried to save him. I'd tried to keep those boys safe, but all of my efforts had backfired.

Then I heard the gasp of a window opening and glanced toward the house. Above me, framed within his window, John sat on his bed and lifted his clarinet to his mouth. The gentle melody of "Moonlight Serenade" floated from his window. Tears blurred my vision. He continued playing, unaware of my presence below. He faltered several times with the wrong notes, paused and then proceeded. Sweet, steady John. How was it that one brother suffered so much while the other appeared more resilient?

Paul appeared in the kitchen doorway and stepped outside, clearing his throat. "Maybe you should get some rest. Did you even sleep last night?"

"I'm going to try again with Dan first. I need to fix things with him."

"Maybe you can't fix this. What if he needs to figure it out on his own?"

Paul sank to the bench beside me. In his large hands, my foot disappeared and I was tempted to slide over into his lap and allow my whole body to vanish into his. The tangle of emotions inside me felt too much to bear. Instead I inhaled and exhaled deeply, eased my foot out of Paul's grip, stood, and entered the house again, climbed the stairs, and knocked on Dan's door. No answer. I knocked again, tilting my ear for any sound within. I twisted the doorknob and opened the door. The room was empty.

I spun back into the hallway and hurried down the stairs. As I crossed the living room on my way to the garage to check on the cars, my gaze caught on a blank section of wall above the fireplace. Usually a painting of Maynard's hung in that spot. I stared before turning to pull myself upstairs again. In my bedroom, next to the mirror hanging over my dresser, another strip of blank wall. Normally three of Maynard's watercolors hung in that spot. With my body heavier and heavier with every passing step, I retraced my way down the stairs, across the living room, through the kitchen, and into my studio. I knew what I would find.

CHAPTER 35

I awoke the following morning and experienced a brief moment when everything that had happened with Dan felt like
a bad dream, but then it all rushed back to me. Maynard's
paintings and Dan had disappeared. I squeezed my eyes shut,
pulling the covers tight to my chin, and curled my body into
a fetal position, willing myself to fall back asleep. *Where was
Dan?* In his fragile state, the humiliation over the failed marriage, I feared for his safety. Next to me, Paul stirred and slid
himself across the mattress so my back leaned against him. I
tried to imagine that nothing would ever go wrong again.

"Don't worry," he whispered, "I'll find Maynard's paintings."
He sat upright, placing his glasses on his face. "I'll handle it."

What was I supposed to do? How would I find Dan? And
once I found him, then what? The dull discomfort always lurk-

ing in my stomach sharpened into a tight metallic pain. When I closed my eyes and breathed, the pain brightened the darkness behind my eyelids until I opened them again. I winced and Paul urged me to stay in bed, saying one of the girls would bring me breakfast. Exhausted, I complied, but I couldn't sleep. Instead I shut down into a strange state of inaction and unthinking for several more hours while Paul worked the telephone making inquiries into Dan's whereabouts.

Late in the afternoon, I opened my eyes to find Imogen sitting on the bed beside me. She stared out the nearby window, a private, solemn expression on her face. I stirred and she turned to me.

"I've made so many mistakes," I said.

"No one blames you for a thing."

"Dan does."

"He isn't thinking straight."

"I should call Maynard and tell him about his paintings."

"Paul already did. He needed ideas for where to find them. Oh boy, Maynard was blazing mad."

"At me?"

"God, no. At Dan. Why do you keep thinking this is your fault?"

I rolled to my back and stared at the ceiling. "I've failed him."

"Life is a complicated business. You've done the best you could." She paused. "Of course, Dan carries some pain, we all do. Now he has to make some choices about how he's going to move forward. So far, it's been a little rocky, but he'll figure it out."

"I'm going to postpone my Guggenheim Fellowship. My boy needs me."

Imogen nodded. "Now let's get you out of bed."

"Paul said I should rest."

"Since when did you ever do what Paul said? Rondal drove me here and he's downstairs with Kathy. She's talking his head off about some dance at school. We need to go rescue him," Imogen said, standing and pulling me gently from where I sat on the edge of the bed. She dressed me in a loose-fitting long skirt and blouse, smoothed down my short hair, and led me downstairs, my hand in hers.

JUST AS WHEN my camera and typewriter went missing, Paul searched through the area's local pawnshops. This time he was given leads to some dealers in illegal goods, and without providing me with many details about these meetings, he brought the paintings home. After hanging them back in their places, he came to find me in my studio, where I stood leaning against my worktable. "Do you have any idea where Dan is now?" I asked.

Paul straightened his tie. "No."

"So now what?" I said. "We just wait to hear what trouble he gets into next?"

"Dorothea." Paul pulled me into an embrace. "I think we've reached the point where we must let Dan do whatever it is that he needs to do."

I hated the idea of doing nothing, but what else was there? I stared past Paul's shoulder. He pulled away from me to look into my face, but I let my gaze drop. A crumpled brown bag sat on the floor next to the door.

"What's in there?" I asked, pointing at it.

Paul shrugged unconvincingly and moved to stand between the bag and me.

"No, really, what is it?"

He bent over and picked up the bag, shifting its weight back and forth in his arms. "I found a few copies of *American Exodus* at the bookstore on Telegraph Hill."

I crossed the room to peer in the bag, even though Paul tried to draw back. "A few! Why, there are at least a dozen copies in there. Why did you buy these?"

"They were marked down to one dollar each. I just couldn't bear to see them all . . ." He stopped and concerned himself with fussing over one of his cuff links.

I looked at the bag again. Of course it was disappointing that our book was so heavily discounted, but I didn't feel the same shame written across Paul's face. The process of making the book had saved me. The roads I'd driven, the fields I'd trod—I'd visited places I would never have gone to otherwise, seen things I'd never have known about, listened to people I would never have met. These experiences were no small thing. For me, the act of creation outweighed the final product. That our books sat in a dusty corner languishing unseen in a bookstore hurt, but I could understand how frustrating it felt for Paul. His activism, his message—his life's work was falling upon deaf ears. The country wasn't interested in the New Deal and agricultural reform anymore. Their time had passed. Our book had released to little fanfare two years earlier. Now all everyone spoke about was Hitler and his steady march across Europe. A new era was upon us.

I pulled a book out of the bag and opened it to a photo of

a woman shading her eyes with a tented hand while searching the distance as if she understood the country had already moved on to something else. I placed the book on the table and wrapped my arms around Paul. We had each other. Our partnership would have to be enough.

CHAPTER 36

On a Sunday morning in December 1941, the kind of day when the air is clear, colors vivid, and lines sharp and in focus, the Japanese bombed a port in Hawaii. Overnight we became a nation at war. Everything shifted: an urgency greased all of the gears grinding us along, and the speed of our lives increased. Two months later, Rondal arrived at our doorstep on a dry but cool February afternoon.

"Oh," I said by way of greeting as I took in his navy uniform. Its whiteness practically blinded me. In his hands, he held a bouquet of hyacinth. The small blue flowers were a shock of vivid color against the paleness of his freckled hand.

"I brought these for you, but don't worry, I asked Ma's permission before I picked them."

I took the flowers and looked down at the cluster, so he wouldn't see my troubled expression. "Thank you. When do you leave?"

"Tomorrow morning I'm to report to the recruiting office. Sounds like I'll be shipped to San Diego for basic training."

After all of the time I'd spent with Rondal over the years, hours in the car together as we crisscrossed the state, somehow there still managed to be an awkward silence as he waited for me to say something.

"Be careful. Shooting with a gun is mighty different from shooting with a camera."

The fluidity of how he threw back his head and laughed and his easy smile contrasted with everything inside me that remained tightly wound.

"Ma said the same thing."

"Well, that's something. It's not every day we agree."

"You two." He shook his head with a smile. "Your constant bickering doesn't fool anyone."

"Yes, well . . ." I put my fist on my hip, casting about for something to say, something to make him understand how much I would miss him. "Remember that time we were checking into a moldy little cabin down outside of Salinas and the manager fella at the front desk looked at us as if we were crazier than a box of frogs?"

"Yeah, and you signed us in as 'Dorothea Lange and fancy man.'"

I laughed, thinking of the manager's shocked expression when he reviewed the guest ledger. "Right, well, don't be a hero. You've done plenty of good already, all of our work with those folks in the fields. You were a big part of that, do you understand? Come back with your camera—there's still much to be done."

He smiled at me, softened by my obvious discomfort. "I know, Dorothea, I know. You take care too." His expression sobered. "Have you heard anything from Dan?"

"Last week a friend of mine called to say he's living in a shack on her building's rooftop in Oakland," I answered, trying to keep the weariness from my voice. "Paul has pulled a few strings with the draft board and gotten him a spot in the army despite his nearsightedness."

Rondal nodded, considering the idea. "Maybe some service will be just what he needs."

"Maybe." That was also Paul's reasoning and I couldn't argue. It was just a matter of time before Dan landed himself in some real trouble here at home, so while his shipping off to the military had its own obvious set of dangers, it also offered the opportunity to change. "He will be leaving for Fort Knox next week. He's not thrilled, but he's going to try it."

Rondal made a sound of agreement, but the way he averted his eyes and ran the toe of his shiny new shoe along the flagstone of the step revealed his doubts. "What are you going to do now?"

"I'm not sure yet, but really, I'm the last person you should be worrying about. Everything's going to be fine here."

We embraced and I called out goodbye, forcing a cheerfulness that belied the fear running through me. Pulling his car

away from the curb, he honked his horn in farewell. I continued waving until he turned a corner at the end of the block
and disappeared from view. Except for the buzz of a lawn
mower several houses away and the chirping of birds, it was
quiet. Given the peacefulness of the afternoon, the idea of war
felt very distant. That was all about to change.

CHAPTER 37

Two months later, I walked along the sidewalk toward the Oakland YMCA with Dave Tatsuno, one of Paul's former students. We moved slowly to accommodate the heavy suitcase he carried. A dry wind swirling down the block caused him to reach up with one hand to press his porkpie hat onto his head. At Woolworth's, a woman leaving the store pushed the door open and nearly collided with us. A package wrapped in brown paper slid from her arms, but in one fluid motion Dave caught it with his free hand. He straightened, handing it back to her.

"Dave?" the woman said, taking in the suitcase and looking back and forth at us. She tilted her head in bewilderment. The sun caught her golden curls peeking out from underneath her toque and she smiled. "Now, where are you going?"

He bowed his head. "I . . ." he started to say before stopping. He pointed at an evacuation notice pinned to the streetlight next to us.

ALL PERSONS OF JAPANESE ANCESTRY, BOTH
ALIEN AND NON-ALIEN, WILL BE EVACUATED
FROM THE AREA BY NOON, APRIL 9, 1942.

"Oh Dave, not you." Her eyes darted back and forth, traveling the length of the text on the poster before coming back to rest on him. She rubbed her lips together as if working out something to say, her lipstick leaving blurry red smudges beyond the edge of her mouth. "Not you."

"All of us, yes," Dave said.

"But . . . but what about the store?"

He shifted his suitcase to his other hand. "My father sold it. They're required to register here tomorrow. We don't know where we'll be taken."

The three of us remained planted on the sidewalk before she mumbled goodbye and hurried away, her eyes trained on the package clutched to her chest.

Not you, I thought. Exactly who did everyone think the evacuation signs were intended for? Did people even stop to think that it was their neighbors being forced to leave? Shopkeepers, teachers, college students, doctors, churchgoers, schoolchildren. These were not dangerous people, they were regular people, just like the rest of us. When Dave had come to the house two days ago to tell Paul and me of his upcoming evacuation, I asked if he and his family would consider hiding.

He stared at me. "Where would we go? There's no hiding that my parents came from Japan." Just thinking about that moment made my face burn in embarrassment. One-sixteenth Japanese ancestry; that's all it took to find your life turned upside down. I shifted my camera bag to my other shoulder. How many people of German and Italian ancestry were darting past us, keeping their eyes away from Dave's suitcase? My own German parentage smoldered in my chest as I walked alongside him. But at any moment I could walk away, head home, and do whatever I chose without fear of my neighbors eyeing me with suspicion.

We rounded the corner. The YMCA loomed in front of us, a line of dark heads snaking out the front door and down the sidewalk. Our gait slowed. Young mothers bounced infants on their hips, rocking back and forth. Clusters of teenage boys eyed the crowd, jeering each other, elbowing and jostling, their darting eyes contradicting the confidence their laughter projected. Old men and women sat on scuffed leather suitcases and dented steamer trunks. Dressed in dark, clean dresses and suits, everyone appeared to be in their Sunday best on their way to church.

I accompanied Dave to the end of the line. A young girl, perhaps four years old, turned to face us, her hand clutched in her mother's. She stared at me, eyeing my camera bag inquisitively until her mother gave a small tug on the girl's hand. Reluctantly, she turned away. I left Dave to check in with the officials running the site.

At the doors of the granite building, a soldier directed people to various lines, his expression as indifferent as if he were parking cars. After I showed him my credentials, he waved me inside where a War Relocation Authority official stood next to the check-in desk, a clipboard clasped in front of his chest. I introduced myself.

"See how peaceful this is?" he asked. "The Japs understand this is for their own safety."

I stared, shocked by the baldness of his lying. Then I did the only thing I could think of. I raised my camera and started photographing the long lines of old people waiting to enter the building, the limp American flag hanging next to the registration table, the troubled face of a woman as she fastened a newly issued identification tag to the baby in her arms. My photographs would have to tell the real story.

TWO WEEKS EARLIER, when the WRA offered me the job over the telephone, I took it without question. Paul and I thought the whole evacuation business smelled rotten, but taking the government's offer to document it gave me the chance to see what was happening; more important, I could show *others* what was happening. I figured I would shoot the whole event in narrative strands; follow a few individuals and families along their journey from preparation to registration to relocation. This felt logical and manageable. Unfortunately, things didn't go according to plan. Nothing prepared me for the job. I was like the lady on the street who saw Dave and said, *Oh no, not you.* I didn't think it through. What would it mean to photograph people being told they had to leave their homes? What would it mean to photograph people being told their loyalty was in doubt? These were questions I should have considered.

Instead I jumped in completely unprepared for what I would find. The government, the very institution intended to protect us and enable us to pursue our happiness and independence, was behind all of this. My work in the thirties had made me believe I could no longer be surprised by the cruelty of indifference, but I was wrong.

CHAPTER 38

Amid a swarm of schoolchildren, I walked toward Raphael Weill Public School in San Francisco's Japantown followed by Christina Page. With Rondal serving in the navy, I'd needed a new assistant and Christina's mother, Gert Clausen, one of my earliest clients and dearest friends, had been quick to suggest her daughter, a recent graduate of the University of California at Santa Barbara. Newly married to rising photographer Homer Page, Christina was eager to learn everything she could about my work.

Ahead of us, the cream-colored stucco school glowed against the bright blue sky. High voices chirped around us and playful shrieks and laughter surged from the playground, bouncing off the walls of the surrounding buildings. I searched the faces of the parents watching the procession, looking for some sign of concern, a sense of danger or worry, but their expressions gave nothing away. The mothers wrapped themselves tighter in their sweaters or buttoned up their lightweight wool jackets against the cool spring breeze—it was the middle of April— and drifted away from the school's entrance. Christina and I proceeded inside.

Within the space of two weeks, this school would become an assembly center to process the neighborhood's residents of Japanese ancestry and relocate them. Before everything turned upside down for these families, I wanted to see the children experiencing their regular school day. During morning announcements in the courtyard, all of the children gathered around a cluster of their peers, one of whom held a flag. Many of the students were clearly from Japanese families, but not all. Some were blond, some redheaded, some dark-skinned, some freckled and pale. No matter what their coloring, they all beamed with gap-toothed smiles. The students raised their right hands to their hearts and began reciting the Pledge of Allegiance. I raised my Rolleiflex and looked into the viewfinder as goose bumps rose on my arms as I heard all of the voices raised in unison to promise their allegiance to a nation that was questioning the loyalty of many of them.

I pledge allegiance to the Flag of the United States of America,
    And to the Republic for which it stands, one Nation under God
    Indivisible, with liberty and justice for all.

I'd heard the pledge thousands of times before, but it was there, listening to those children, that I truly listened and compared what they were saying to what was about to happen. That promise, so oft-repeated as to have become rote in my life, sounded different. It made me consider the magnitude of what we took for granted every day in our country. The government expected us to be loyal citizens, but didn't it owe its citizens loyalty in return?

Overhead, the flag snapped in the wind. I thought of the phone call we had received the previous week from Fort Knox. Dan was in the stocks for refusing to say the Pledge of Allegiance. I'd hung up the phone disgusted by his lack of patriotism, but in the courtyard of Raphael Weill Public School, I didn't know what to think. What did it mean to be loyal? Was doubting the government unpatriotic?

What had happened to the promise of our nation being indivisible?

CHRISTINA AND I spent most of April bouncing around the Bay Area, photographing the process of people's lives being taken apart. Job by job. Neighborhood by neighborhood. Home by home. Possession by possession. In Florin, we photographed a fifty-seven-year-old woman picking a final harvest of strawberries in the small field she leased. Her son had been furloughed from Camp Leonard Wood in Missouri so he could help her prepare to leave. I was glad to hide my face behind my Rolleiflex when I took a portrait of him in his smartly pressed army uniform standing next to his mother, a basket of strawberries in her hands. She had arrived in California from Japan in 1905 and was widowed seven years later. Although not an American citizen, her six children were. Two of her sons were serving voluntarily in the U.S. Army. She could lose both boys fighting for America yet she and her four daughters were scheduled to be evacuated in five days. How was her loyalty questionable?

AFTER A LONG day at a berry farm in Centerville, Christina offered me her arm as we trudged to the car. "Why did you take a photo of him?" she whispered, looking back at the white man in faded overalls leaning against the railing of the Tatanakes' front porch, watching us leave. Every time the man had nodded his head on the tour that Mr. Tatanake provided for the new owner, I felt ill. It left me cold to think of all the men I'd seen ten years earlier arriving beaten down from tough times in Texas and Kansas—these same men were now buying Japanese-owned farms and barely paying a dime for them. My, my, how times changed. As Paul said when I left that morning, "Now the oppressed joins with the oppressor."

I tightened my grip on Christina's arm. "He's getting pretty lucky from this whole thing. Why, I'll bet he's doing a little jig on the inside. All of these farmers taking over these places for a song—they sicken me."

In the car Christina tapped her thumbs together at the top of the steering wheel as she drove. "I think I have an appointment tomorrow in San Francisco. Maybe it would be good for you to spend the day reviewing negatives."

I glanced over at her in surprise. What was she talking about? We had already discussed going to Tanforan Assembly Center to photograph the arrival of the first evacuees.

"What time's your appointment? We could make the trip to San Bruno in the afternoon. It shouldn't take us too long to get there."

Christina paused and digested this, noncommittal.

I looked over at her. Indecision was unlike her. Aware that I was watching, she squared her shoulders. Her unblinking eyes remained on the road, her shoulders hunched. I thought of an image from this morning. Before we left, I had run upstairs to get my sun hat and left Paul and Christina talking in the kitchen. When I returned, the two had been huddled in quiet conversation. Both pulled back when I entered the room, neither one looking at me.

"Does this appointment have anything to do with a conversation you just had with Paul?"

A mottled flush blazed across her cheeks.

I pressed on. "He doesn't want me to go to Tanforan, does he?"

"Oh Dorothea," she said. "He's just worried about you. And I am too. I know you've been having more of those stomach pains. I can tell from the way your face gets so white, even though it's sweltering hot. We've been working such long days. A day off could be a good thing."

My back stiffened. It was true. Most days we left in the early hours before dawn and often arrived home long after dinner, but this was important. Each time I photographed the face of an evacuee, proud and unflinching, a little piece inside me dissolved. How could we let this happen?

"Paul should worry about something else. I'm fine."

"Don't be so stubborn. Why, he thinks the sun and moon revolve around you."

I shook my head. Dan had gone AWOL from Fort Knox the day before. I needed Tanforan to distract me. The last thing I wanted to do was sit around waiting at home for more news about him. The heat rose off the pavement in shimmering waves, making me dizzy and almost drowsy. I tucked a strand of hair under my bandanna and turned away from the windshield to rub my hand against the side of my stomach, trying to massage the ache throbbing inside. "Do you have an appointment tomorrow?"

"No."

"Then we're going to Tanforan."

PAIN AWAKENED ME early the following day. In the morning's gray light, I stretched to my right side, breathing in and out quietly, willing the wrenching in my gut to dissipate. Paul stirred but continued to sleep. After several minutes, the pain subsided enough that I could roll over to rise from the bed and creep to the bathroom to wash and dress. Minutes later I was in the kitchen fixing myself a plate of toast. After a few gulps of hot tea, I tossed the rest in the sink, resentful at being forced to give up coffee because of my stomach pains. I'd visited plenty of doctors over the last several years, but none of them had any answers to manage the ulcers that plagued me.

About thirty minutes later, I crossed the Bay Bridge and pulled alongside the pale pink Victorian façade of Christina's apartment in Cow Hollow to find her already outside waiting for me. She was dependable, that girl. I slid over to the passenger seat so she could drive us to San Bruno. We planned to arrive early, before the busloads of evacuees did, so we could get some establishing shots of the camp and its facilities.

"Today's light is good," Christina said.

I grunted in assent. Humidity, unusual for the Bay Area, gave the morning a golden-hued opaque haze. Already my blouse stuck to my back. A dull but steady headache started behind my eyes. The flash of telephone poles blurred by my window every few beats.

"Everything all right?" Christina asked.

"My lack of coffee is killing me."

She let out a sympathetic groan, but out of the corner of my eye, I could see her glancing at me.

"Really, it's nothing," I said. "The last thing I want to do is stop working and sit at home feeling sorry for myself."

She nodded and refocused her gaze on the highway. A chain-link fence topped with barbed wire appeared beside us, separating the road from the rolling brown landscape in the distance. It led us to Tanforan. Before its conversion to a resettlement center, it had been a horse racetrack. At one point, the place probably felt festive. Colorful pennants must have flapped in the breeze, people filled the place with their laughter, and the salty smell of popcorn would have hovered across the grounds. But now it looked lifeless, everything a dusty brown blur. We slowed before entering the main gate. Waved through by soldiers, we parked and entered the former clubhouse, where a harried-looking woman directed us to the office of the camp director.

A man with a grim expression nodded after our introduction. "I'm Colonel Beasley. Now, ladies, do you understand the rules for this job while you're under my command?" As he began to run through the litany of prohibited items and behavior, I stared at him. His square face nagged at my memory. I examined him, and his expression shifted into irritation. "Do you have any questions?"

"No, I'm well versed in what the censors will cut," I answered, waving off the question.

"If I find your work requires too much censoring, you will not be allowed to return."

"Now hold on. It's my understanding that I'm under command from the WRA, not the army. It's not within your command to prevent us from coming here."

A vein pulsed at the man's temple. "While you're on this site, you're under my jurisdiction. That means my rules. The rules are: no photos of guns, barbed wire, and fences." He spoke while coming around the desk to stand directly in front of me. I could smell the Juicy Fruit gum in his mouth and see the freckles dotting his skin like tiny splatters of mud. Both the gray stubble of his crew cut and his square bulldog jowls gave me the sense he was liable to bite if I disagreed with him again.

Looking into his pigeon-gray eyes without blinking, I gave my steadiest gaze. "All right."

"Good. I assume we will have no further disagreements."

"One can hope."

He gave me a severe stare, but then gesturing ahead, herded us from his office and disappeared down a hallway.

Christina, white-faced, clutched my arm. "Why did you have to rile him up?"

"A man like that? He was born riled up. Never mind him. He's just a big bully."

"I'll say, but still. He could make our lives mighty difficult."

I snorted. "I don't report to him." I paused for a moment, irritated, a sense of missed connection drifting just beyond my reach. "I swear, I know him from somewhere, but can't figure out where."

We left the administrative building through the back entrance. Above us, the American flag's red, white, and blue had been dulled to a sepia tone by dust. "Ugh, this is depressing," I said, looking beyond the paddock at the row of barracks spread out in lines within the middle of the horse track. We walked toward them. More appeared in the backstretch.

As we neared them, the stench of manure hit us.

"Good God, are they going to live in horse stalls?"

Christina gasped. "I promise, I'll never complain about the size of my apartment again," she murmured as we neared the row of squat wooden boxes.

I stepped through a doorway. Two tiny rooms took shape as my eyes adjusted to the dark. I had to pass through one to reach the deeper, tiny interior room. No windows, no lights. Dust lay thick as moss over everything and a fetid stink overcame me. "This is not right," I said, gagging. "How are people supposed to live here?"

She shook her head. I backed out of the stall, gulping fresh air from outside. Christina pulled a handkerchief out of her skirt pocket to wear around her face, covering her nose.

"No. Take that off. We cannot disrespect the people who will be living here by doing that," I said, walking the row of stalls. "Let's see . . ." I tried to determine the direction of the light in the haze overhead. "Set the tripod here." I scratched a line in the dirt with my heel.

While Christina set up the equipment, I explored until reaching another low building marked WOMEN. When I ducked my head to enter, a row of holes cut into a long board lined the far wall. A communal latrine. The whitewash stuck to my finger pad when I reached out to touch it, but even the smell of new paint couldn't cover the reek. The hastiness of the operation showed in the clumps of hay and dirt, dead spiders and flies, all stuck under the paint. I closed my eyes. The ache in my skull had increased from dull to pounding. The plank floor warped and bent in the putrid fug of the place. I staggered outside to join Christina. One look at my face, and she said nothing—simply handed me my camera. With every image I took, I gave thanks no one had arrived yet. How was I supposed to look people in the eyes in this place? My own presence made me complicit in their betrayal. Shame filled me.

After working in silence for a while, I glanced at my watch. Nine o'clock. We packed the equipment and hiked toward the main gate to set up for when the buses arrived. Within minutes, a convoy of trucks groaned into the yard. Exhaust and dust smudged the air. Soldiers pulled luggage off truck beds—trunks, suitcases, crates, duffel bags, a dented empty birdcage—and heaped everything into a pile next to the race-track. A brief interlude of quiet stilled the action before a low rumble echoed through the grounds.

"Was that thunder?" Christina asked.

One by one, plump raindrops splattered the dust surrounding us before turning into a downpour. Christina scooped up the camera bags and scurried to the cover offered by the empty grandstand. I trailed her and took a position beside her in front of a crudely hewn wooden bench. I shivered despite the heat. Beyond the shelter of the overhang, the rain pounded, transforming the ground into a churning sea of mud. And then, the rain ended.

"Oh," Christina gasped, pointing toward the racetrack. There lay the luggage, lumpy and wilting in the mud, surrounded by puddles, steaming in the sudden sun, soaked and possibly ruined. Over the last month, we had sat in people's living rooms, watching them sift through their households, vetting their possessions for their most important items. Family photographs of generations past. Gossamer silk kimonos. Fine linens. The few things they could bring into the unknown. The experience had been heartbreaking. Now it all lay in a sodden mess.

Christina and I picked our path through the puddles back to where more buses would be arriving. Colonel Beasley marched from the administrative building and moved toward a pair of soldiers at the roundabout. I hurried over to him.

"Colonel, all of the luggage. It's soaked."

"Although I run operations, I have no control over the weather," he said with a smug grin. Two nearby soldiers guffawed.

"I understand your limitations," I shot back, inwardly pleased to see his face redden. "Now are these people expected to lug everything to the horse stalls on their own? Have you not seen who is about to arrive? Women, children, and the elderly? Surely you don't intend for them to carry it all."

"They'll be fine."

"But your men could help."

"My soldiers are not bellhops."

I snorted. "No one will be mistaken into thinking this a fine hotel."

His nostrils flared. "The evacuees received instructions to bring only as much as they can carry." His voice was lost in the roar of buses pulling through the front gate and he turned away from me, yelling over his shoulder, "Now don't pester my soldiers. They're needed to maintain peace and order."

Did he believe a bunch of women and old people planned to stage an insurrection? I glared at the back of his head, disgusted by his indifference, and pushed some loose hairs out of my face. The glimmer of my silver bangle caught my eye. And that's when I remembered. Beasley. How could I not have connected that sickeningly sweet smell of Juicy Fruit chewing gum to him? Twenty years ago, I'd met him on a desolate stretch of yard outside the Tuba City Indian School in Arizona. My spine stiffened at the memory. The same man who'd cataloged the benefits of incarcerating Navajo children to civilize them had been promoted to imprisoning another innocent group of people.

Soldiers swarmed the buses. Evacuees trickled out, bewildered and stunned. Positioned beyond the buses, a row of soldiers stood, rifles out, bayonets at the ready. I got closer and angled my camera to follow a young mother past the soldiers. She carried a baby and led her two small children by the hand. I bent over to frame the shot, but my viewfinder darkened. Confused, I looked up from my camera. A soldier stood in my way, obscuring the shot. "No photographs of soldiers with weapons," he snarled, not yielding from his spot.

I clenched my teeth. More dazed evacuees filed past us, flimsy manila tags flapping from their jacket buttons. Each person wore an assigned number. A new identity. The numbers indicated which barracks to report to and which stall each family would live in. Soldiers grasped at the tags as they would a dog's collar, shouting instructions, pointing directions. Men were herded toward a makeshift infirmary located in the former ticket building. A soldier handed each woman a broom, bucket, and mop so she could clean her own living quarters. Everyone received a mattress tick bag and was directed toward a sodden pile of hay to fill it.

Women and children drifted toward the luggage, despair and pain registering on the faces of all who approached the waterlogged cargo. They gingerly lifted suitcases from the mud. Rivulets of water streamed off everything. A little boy raised a cardboard box from a puddle and the bottom gave way, spilling china bowls to the ground, yet each piece lodged into the mud and nothing smashed. A small blessing.

WEEKS PASSED. STOCKTON, Sacramento, Santa Anita, Turlock, San Bruno. Each relocation center provided its own definition of deprivation and tedium. The main activity for evacuees consisted of waiting in lines. People waited for the latrine, the laundry, the showers, the mail—everything. Meals were the worst. Each mess hall offered several mealtimes. The first serving of supper started as early as three o'clock in the afternoon. Inmates on mess duty ladled weenies, beans, potatoes, and a few leaves of wilted spinach out of dented garbage pails serving as large tureens. With the scramble to find seating a constant challenge, families rarely sat together at the long, narrow tables. Children roamed throughout the camps in packs. Men sat in doorways, eyes blank. Women spent their days washing and mending clothes, and sweeping dust and grime from the crowded stalls. Dull eyes and languid movement revealed loneliness, yet no one was ever alone.

Beyond the walls and barbed wire, life moved on. Outside of Tanforan, trucks rumbled up Highway 101. Former neighbors of the interned commuted to their jobs. A whole new industry sprang up in the shipyards of Richmond. Children packed into classrooms to learn the geography of battles in places like the Coral Sea, Wake Island, and Midway. A palpable sense of being abandoned permeated the camps, yet government officials had not forgotten about those interned there. Not yet.

CHAPTER 39

"We meet again," Colonel Beasley said when Christina and I entered the lobby at his new posting in Manzanar.

"Lucky us." I sighed, pulling a thermos out of one of my bags to take a long swill. The July heat was unbearable. Within minutes of arriving in the camp, my skin, eyes, and throat ached from dryness.

We had driven hours to the camp, located deep in the remote Owens Valley in the foothills of the Sierra Nevada. A sharp hot wind blew through the newly constructed wide avenues, sending tar paper flapping in the breeze off the sides of the barracks dotting the barren landscape. And wind wasn't the only discomfort. Dust rode along with it, covering surfaces, making hair gritty, even lodging its way in between teeth.

Beasley cleared his throat. Hopefully the dust pained him

too. "The old rules of Tanforan still apply, but now you will not take any photographs of the guard towers either. Absolutely no machine guns. Stay away from the edges of the camp. No photographs of any sort of resistance either."

The mention of resistance made me look up from my thermos. "Have you had any trouble?"

"Of course not. These Japs are very docile. You saw how easy assembly was."

I kept my face blank. It was true. Mostly true, at least. The interned understood there was nowhere to go. There was no escaping the army's lists of suspects.

"Don't take any photographs that make our soldiers resemble Gestapo or anything connected to the Nazis. And nothing that could send a message back to the Japs that they have people here lying in wait to aid them."

"The orphans in the Children's Village look particularly menacing," I murmured, bending over to glance through my camera bag on the floor.

Beasley folded his arms across his chest. "You've been looking quite peaked lately. I'm sure the WRA can send Mr. Albers back here to photograph if you're not up to the task."

"I'm fine. I'd like to get to work."

"I'm assigning Private Vance to watch over you today." A young man stepped forward, a small piece of tissue clinging to his neck from where he must have nicked himself shaving. When Beasley spotted it, his jaw tightened in annoyance. "Report back to me at sixteen hundred hours."

I turned to Christina, rolling my eyes, and didn't even glance at our new handler. We picked up our bags and marched out of the building, eager to be away from Beasley. Outside, wind swirled thick clouds of dust through the long straightaways between the buildings. We stopped in the shade of the mess hall to pull my Rolleiflex out of a bag.

"Here's a patriotic composition your boss will love," I said to Vance, raising my camera to focus the viewfinder toward the low-lying boxes of barracks. A flagpole stood in the middle of the buildings, a funnel of sandstorm blurring the background. The high Sierras reared up behind the barracks, jagged and imposing. This shot would follow all of the rules and find no objection with the censors. The image looked unassuming at first, but it showed the place as it really was: lonely and depressing, marked by extreme temperatures and misery. Prison-like. After snapping a few shots, I lowered my Rolleiflex and looked around. "Now, where's the new infirmary?"

Private Vance pointed down an avenue empty of people. Christina and I set off. The pain in my side had returned, pulsing sharply with every step. I took another drink from my thermos, hoping water would help. Christina watched me. The pain had started coming more often and lasting longer. I was almost certain Paul had said something to her about keeping an eye on me. I swallowed, putting the thermos away. With my bag fastened shut, I looked around. Several large rocks clustered around the entry of one of the barracks. Closer scrutiny revealed it to be a rock garden framing a small stone path leading to the steps into the building.

"Wait." I squatted with my camera to try to get a close-up of the succulents planted in the dust. An old man emerged from the doorway. "Your garden is beautiful," I said, nodding and smiling.

He bobbed his head in thanks and continued to watch us.

"Did you get a permit for this?" Private Vance demanded of the internee.

The old man frowned in response.

"You need a permit for all gardens." Vance spoke louder, but the old man looked at him without any change in expression. Vance tried again, "A permit." But the wind carried his voice away.

"Let's go, you can worry about his permit later. I want to get to that infirmary." I started walking again.

Vance let out an exasperated huff but followed us. "You can't take any photos of anyone ill. No one in bed either. Just portraits of healthy people."

The desire to hit him with my camera bag almost got the better of me, but I gripped my strap tighter and kept going.

AT THE END of the day, as Christina and I staggered toward my car parked behind the administrative building, a soldier called after us, ordering us to come back inside. In the stuffy warren of offices, we found Colonel Beasley, red-faced, pacing in front of his receptionist's desk. He gestured at a pile of negatives lying in a heap on the woman's desk. "You're supposed to turn in all of your negatives at the end of each day."

"I did. I gave today's film and plates to Private Vance to be inspected by the censors."

"Yes, well, I heard you visited the infirmary. Where are those images?"

"I only took a few, but they should be in there." I stepped closer to the pile and picked up the envelope of my negatives and tilted it upside down. Out slid several more. I tried to tamp down my triumph.

Beasley's face darkened to purple as he stared at the missing work. His secretary pulled back in her seat as if expecting him to combust on the spot. The three soldiers in the room lowered their eyes to the ground.

His left eye twitched. "Place them all in the order in which you took them."

I complied. When I finished, I stood up and nodded at him. "You're welcome. Now, may we leave for the day?"

Beasley nodded.

"Ladies, you will need this." The receptionist ducked her head toward a drawer of her desk, opened it, and handed us the distributor cap to my car. When I looked at her questioningly, she explained, "We remove these from all civilian automobiles so none of the evacuees may escape."

I stretched out my hand for it, staring at the piece of my car, and Christina pulled on my sleeve to hustle me out the door. Out in the parking lot, I pulled my arm from her hand and waved the distributor cap overhead. "Can you believe this nonsense? Can you believe some soldier came out here after we arrived and took this? Why, we were trapped there too, unable to go unless we had their permission. Just wait until I tell Paul about this. I'm going to make sure the press knows what's happening here."

Christina shook her head and opened the back door of my station wagon to place our equipment onto the backseat. "You know, you scare me sometimes. If you continue to push Beasley's buttons, who knows what's going to happen? You must be more careful." Her face, already red from heat, crumpled into tears. "I don't want to end up stuck here. And do you really think the press cares? Have any of your old friends from the *Chronicle* or the *Examiner* called you to hear what's happening here?"

I looked toward the wall of mountains, hazy in the distance.

"No one cares about this, Dorothea. Everyone thinks it's just as well to lock up the Japs. They're the enemy."

"Do you think that?"

She groaned. "Of course I don't, but what I think doesn't matter. We must be careful. Now," she looked both directions to assure we were not being overheard, "let's get out of here and find a room in Lone Pine."

She was right and I hated it.

About twenty long minutes later, we arrived at a dilapidated huddle of cabins and reserved a room. After lugging our bags inside and trying to ignore the lace of cobwebs covering the beams of the ceiling, we peeled off our sweaty layers and collapsed on the lumpy cot beds in only our undergarments, depleted. We fell asleep without dinner.

I dreamed of Maynard. We lay on a blanket outside in the dark, camping in a forest. Our arms linked together, my bare chest against his, we kissed. When I awoke, disoriented in the darkness, my heart hammered in my chest. The feeling of his smooth skin and the silkiness of his dark hair still tingled upon my fingertips. The sensation of the wool blanket still scratched at my bare shoulder blades. It felt so real, yet there I was alone with Christina. Propping myself up on one elbow, I pushed some hair plastered to my forehead off my face and exhaled. Silence pressed from every direction. The vivid sense of my body joined to Maynard's left me unnerved. My sleep had been plagued with strange visions ever since I began photographing the relocation camps.

I rose from the bed, fumbling my way to my bags, found my thermos, and gulped down mouthful after mouthful of warm water. It spilled from the opening, ran down my cheeks and neck, but I kept drinking until the bottle was empty. Only then, I limped back to the bed and slipped under the sheets, searching with my hands and feet for new, cooler spaces not yet heated from my body. Next to me, Christina sighed in her sleep and threw her arm overhead. A sour smell clung to the thin, pilled bed linens. I rearranged the pillow on my bed before lowering my head to it.

CHAPTER 40

July bled into August. Christina and I continued to photograph the evacuees arriving in Manzanar, but my interior shots of the camp left me dissatisfied. Inmates did their best to convert those miserable wooden boxes into homes by hanging school pennants on the walls and setting family photographs, potted plants, tea sets, and colorful textiles upon shelves and tabletops, but still, my photos of these cramped spaces never worked. After being developed, the compositions appeared flat, too dark, cramped, and uninteresting. I suppose they reflected the truth of the situation. These barracks lacked the filth of Tanforan, but they were shoddy and felt dangerously unsteady in the high winds buffeting them. Gaps in the walls and floorboards let in dust and wind. Women strung up sheets in an attempt at privacy and to create a semblance of hominess, but it was a lost cause. At first, frequent disagreements flared be-tween neighbors stressed by the close proximity of one another, but then many of the interned, especially the men, settled into a state of listless resignation.

I focused on the faces of the internees. Their resilience and stoicism broke my heart. At the end of each day, I left camp depleted from arguing with Beasley and chafing from the constant vigilance of the censors who trailed me throughout the camp, but most of all, the overwhelming sense of futility looming over us took a toll. No matter how many photos I took, the camp and its inhabitants remained trapped, unseen, and forgotten by the rest of America.

One afternoon after Christina and I loaded the camera bags and tripod into the backseat, I paused and leaned against the side of the car, brought up short by pain in my lower belly. Speckles of black dots shot across my vision like fireworks. I gasped. The steel of the car door burned against my back, but I didn't care.

"Come on, let's get you back to the cabin." The pleading tone in Christina's voice caught my attention and I lifted my gaze to meet hers. She gestured to the car. "Let's return to San Fran-cisco in the morning."

"I need one more day. We need to photograph those women we heard about earlier. If it's forced labor, it's illegal." In the camp's newspaper office we had visited that day, the internees had told us about a cadre of women who were making camou-flage netting for the army.

Christina's chin swung from side to side before I had even finished speaking. "No way. The censors will never allow it.

Beasley will lose his mind. As it is, he's mad about you even talking with the camp reporters."

"Well, if he didn't have anything to hide, he wouldn't have to worry about me talking to them."

"Do you want a list of all the stuff he's trying to hide here?"

"I know, that's my point. I want to document as much of it as I can."

My voice had risen and Christina's head swiveled around the dusty patch of parking lot, checking to make sure we were alone. "Please get in the car."

Sighing, I opened my door, grabbed a towel lying on the seat, and used it to wipe off the scrim of dust on the windshield. Seated next to Christina in the airless car, beads of sweat dripped down my spine. I winced with pain at each lurch as Christina shifted the station wagon into gear, backed up, and exited the parking lot, heading to the main gate. A brown expanse of wasteland rolled past. "Nothing's going to change in the next couple of days. Let's go home, rest, and then we can come back to do more work."

She slowed to a halt and nodded to the young guard who stepped toward the car, glancing at both of us with a bland expression before waving us on. After we passed him, I felt the pain in my side loosen slightly. The guards, the rifles, the constant scrutiny, the arguments—they exhausted me. But even worse than the sense of impending confrontation was the feeling of powerlessness I felt every time I looked at an internee. Shame filled me every time distaste flickered over a woman's face as she sat down to her meal in the mess hall; every time a young boy stood on the improvised basketball court and stared beyond the barbed wire toward the mountains; every time a seventeen-year-old girl tied a bandanna around her head in the futile hope of protecting her hairdo against dust. The whole place was wrong. Whenever I left the camp, I felt like a traitor. I could leave whenever I chose and my shame increased because I *wanted* to leave. I wanted to drive home and never return. But just by seeing these prisoners and witnessing what was happening, I had committed to something. I wasn't sure what exactly, but I knew I couldn't quit. If only people outside the camps could see my photographs, maybe they'd see how wrong this was.

I turned to say this to Christina but was silenced by the lovely glow of her face. Her skin, unlined and perfect, gleamed as afternoon faded into the magic hour of early evening. I said, "You must think me a terrible curmudgeon to keep you away from that handsome new husband of yours back at home."

Her face reddened. "No, no, I don't think that for one minute. If anything, I need to get you home to Paul. He worries about you all the time."

"Believe it or not, I remember what it's like to be young."

"You're not old."

"Maybe not yet, but I'm getting there. That's the thing about aging, you still can fool yourself into believing you're young. Every time I look into the mirror I'm shocked by the face looking back at me. I still see myself as the girl who somehow wrangled a fancy studio on Sutter." Actually that wasn't true; that naive girl had vanished long ago. So, who was I now? I was old enough to wear wrinkles and scars, but young enough to feel stronger and smarter because of them. I reached toward my hair to smooth it down. "You probably can't believe it now, but once upon a time I never needed to sleep . . ." My voice trailed off as I thought back to my old studio and the dancing that carried on all hours of the night. I sighed. "Before everyone was poor, before the war, we used to have the most wonderful times."

"I remember Mother's parties. My brother and I would creep down the stairs and watch you all through the bars of the railing. I still remember Mr. Klein and Mrs. Clark kissing on the landing one night." She giggled. "They almost caught us but were so consumed in each other they didn't even see us."

"My, my, did they?" I said, chuckling at the thought of Klein, the most buttoned-up lawyer I'd ever met, having a stolen moment with someone else's wife. "It's funny how it all feels like yesterday, but at the same time, it feels like a lifetime ago." A swirl of memories swept around me for a few moments before I clapped my hands together with conviction. "Tell you what, we will stay and work tomorrow, then drive home for a few days, but we must come back on Monday."

"All right."

"There's so much more here that I haven't even begun to capture."

Christina nodded as I described what I still wanted to photograph, but I could tell from the brightness of her eyes and the secret smile tugging at the corners of her lips—she was already back in San Francisco with her young husband, walking hand in hand along the seawall in the marina. I couldn't blame her. Someday she too would awaken during the night with the vivid sensation of someone else's body—maybe her husband's, maybe a long-lost love's—pressed upon her skin and realize with disappointment that it was only a dream. But at that moment, sitting beside me, humming to herself, she was young and I envied her.

CHAPTER 41

I sat in Colonel Beasley's office reminding myself not to squirm as I awaited a scolding over my latest offense. My left arm still stung from the grip of the guard who dragged me into the office, but I restrained myself from rubbing it and stared straight ahead, rigid with indignation over the young man's rough treatment of me. I closed my eyes and pictured the women I had just photographed, the work that led to me being yanked across camp to Beasley's office. The women had crouched in front of tall sheets of netting, weaving khaki- and olive-colored strips of burlap through the twine webbing to create camouflage nets for the War Department. Blooms of sweat darkened the backs of their stretch-knit cotton shirts. Mesmerized by the steady beat of breathing made visible from the rise and fall of their thin gauze face masks, I knelt down to capture the seriousness of the work. They leaned toward the nets without talking, weaving strips of fabric through the nets with surgical precision. When the MP accompanying us realized how bad the whole thing looked, he had pulled us out and dumped me in Beasley's office.

I opened my eyes, only to be stung by sweat trickling down my face, but I let it drip, my discomfort fueling my mounting fury. A thin layer of sand covered the colonel's desk. The damned sand, always the sand; it covered everything.

The door screeched open and the colonel strode in, trailing his ever-present scent of Juicy Fruit chewing gum. He stopped behind his desk but remained standing and barked, "Mrs. Taylor, how many times must we meet like this? You know the rules."

"Lange. My name is Lange."

A vein pulsed on Beasley's temple as he skimmed the contents of a manila folder opened on his desk and scribbled down a note of his own. "Your record of being difficult is going to be your undoing."

His tone needled with the same patronizing manner I'd encountered so many other times with men who, over the years, had treated me like a wayward child, a spoiled brat who asks for lollipops long after she's been told no. A nag. A broad. A bitch. It's always the same tone men reserve for difficult women, she who isn't compliant, who voices her opinion, who has ambitions. But I stayed still, resisting the urge to argue. If I was to have any hope of continuing my work, I could not fight back, and though I hated myself for staying quiet, I gave him nothing. He watched me, looking for any sign of anger, any sign of anything he could use against me to stop my work. I stilled my heel from jiggling and attempted to be motionless. When he saw he couldn't get a rise out of me, he shrugged. "Well, you're done for today. I've sent your film to the War Office in Los Angeles to be reviewed. My driver will escort you back to Lone Pine to await further instruction from my office."

"My car is here. We can drive ourselves."

"Your car will stay *here*. You're not going anywhere without my approval." He flicked his hand at me imperiously to indicate that I should leave. Despite the heat, a cold dread crept down my spine, raising the hairs on the nape of my neck and forearms. Had I finally been outplayed?

I stood and a sudden dizziness descended upon me, a burning pain shot through my belly, a thousand pinpricks of sweat rose all over my skin, but I blinked furiously to clear my swimming vision. *Give him nothing*, I commanded myself. *Nothing. One foot in front of the other. Aim toward the door*. The pimply faced guard moved from his post beside the entrance, took a sharp step forward, and pivoted to stand aside to let me pass into the outside hallway. There, Christina popped up from a bench against the wall and rushed toward me, her eyes wide.

"Are you all right?" She grasped my left hand, looking me up and down.

"I'm fine. We're being driven back to our room."

Christina frowned. "What about your car?"

"Apparently it will remain here."

A flicker of fear glimmered in Christina's eyes before she blinked a neutral expression into place and nodded. I bent over to retrieve my camera bag on the floor next to where she had been sitting but ended up clutching my side with shaking hands, trying to breathe through the pain ripping across my innards.

"It's that bad?" Christina whispered, huddled beside me.

Unable to speak, I nodded, trying to focus only on my breathing.

"Here, let me." Christina lifted the straps of my two camera bags and slid them up her arm. She then hoisted the tripod over her shoulder, before gesturing at me to follow. Once outside, a row of parked jeeps blurred in the heat waving skyward off the asphalt. Though the temperature neared the upper nineties, I was grateful the vehicle was covered. Grit hung in the air. Nearby, an internee sprayed water from a firehose onto the empty expanse of open ground in front of the administrative building in a futile attempt to tame the dust. Nothing else moved. Only the hiss of sand blowing in the wind could be heard.

Once we were moving, the jeep's jostling in the deep ruts of the camp's roads caused me to hold my breath against the pain tightening inside. Christina took my hand, and I focused on the contrast between our interlaced fingers: mine, wrinkled like peanut hulls; hers, smooth and lightly tanned. The vehicle lurched to a stop. I raised my gaze to a guard holding a rifle with a fixed bayonet. His blond hair and pale face, freckled in the desert sun, appeared haloed by the coils of barbed wire on the fence behind him. With a stifled yawn, he waved us through. *Now, there's a photo.* I framed the shot in my mind, but the moment slipped away as the engine growled with our acceleration through the camp's gate. Looking down, I noticed a small rent in the seam of the black leather seat next to my thigh. With my index finger, I worked the split into a gaping hole before stopping, satisfied with my small act of vandalism. Behind me, the low-lying cluster of Manzanar's buildings faded in the plumes of dust kicked up from the jeep.

CHAPTER 42

Back in Lone Pine, inside our cabin, the heat and the crunching sound of Beasley's guard pacing on the gravel path outside our door amplified our sense of imprisonment. I slumped down onto my bed, groaned, and clutched my side.

Christina peered out of the cabin's window, dropped the curtains, and crossed the small room to crouch next to the side of the bed where I lay. Her face hovered over mine in the dim light. "Is it that bad?"

I nodded.

She stood up and wagged her index finger at me. "That's it. I'm going outside and demanding to be allowed to drive you back to Oakland tonight. You're ill and need a doctor."

"Hold on. I don't want to go anywhere, not while Bozo's got all of my negatives. Who knows what he's going to do with them?"

Christina blew out her cheeks and sprawled onto the sagging twin bed next to mine. "Your health is more important."

"I'm fine. The work is important."

"No one doubts your commitment."

"No. We're staying. I've been dealing with these pains for the last seven years and have visited plenty of doctors. None of them help. They each have ideas, but nothing seems to work. I've had enough of their quackery. I'm not stopping this work. These people need our help."

Christina gave me a long look.

"Don't look at me like that. I know it sounds grandiose, but it's true. I refuse to leave until I've gotten the shots we need."

"Dorothea," Christina enunciated each syllable for emphasis, "who knows what Beasley's going to tell us tomorrow. Even if he lets us continue, someone else could take the photos. Didn't Ansel tell you he's gotten an offer to do this work too?"

"Ansel?" I snorted. "He can't think for himself. He's bought into the government's position hook, line, and sinker and won't listen to any of my suggestions. No, this is *my* project. I want to see it through. This work is important, dammit. I have a chance—*we have a chance*—to help these people." I smacked my palm against the rough pine wall next to my bed for emphasis, and for a moment, the stinging of my palm canceled out the pain in my stomach.

"All right. I won't do anything yet, but you have to take better care of yourself."

"Fine, I'll rest now," I grumbled, closing my eyes.

The sounds of twilight descended. The buzz of crickets. A whir of insects against the screen in the window. I imagined

Christina staring at me, annoyed and worried, but I refused to look at her. Instead I curled my knees into my chest to stretch my lower back. Finally, after a minute or so, the creak of a mattress spring released and the floorboards squeaked under her weight as she rustled around the cabin. The snap of the tin lid on our container of crackers reminded me we hadn't had dinner, but the thought of eating anything made my throat close. I rolled over onto my side and breathed through the hot pain wrapping around my gut. Tossing and turning in the heat of the cabin, I slept fitfully, replaying the angry confrontation with Beasley over and over in my mind. What was his next move?

When we awoke in the morning, Christina crept to the window next to our door to pull back the curtain. "Good Lord, he's still out there. We've been watched all night."

She handed me a cheese sandwich from our supplies bag. I almost said no, but knowing I had to eat something, I bit into it grudgingly and then couldn't stop myself from inhaling the rest. Christina rummaged through the bag and brought out crackers and a bruised pear. She set the paltry picnic at the foot of my bed. She then lay out a game of solitaire at the foot of her bed while I read through a draft of an article of Paul's. I couldn't focus on the words swimming on the page and gave up, letting the papers drop on my chest.

From the parking lot, a sudden rumble of motors cut through the quiet. We exchanged worried glances. An insistent knocking at the door prompted me to bolt upright. Christina hopped off the bed and moved across the cabin in three long strides to open the door.

"Colonel," she said, a warning in her voice.

I stumbled to my feet to join her at the door. The morning's brightness blinded me, but I blinked and brought myself to attention.

Beasley smirked, looking us up and down. Christina's hair remained pinned in curls, and her wrinkled clothes smelled of sleep. I tried not to wonder when I'd last seen my hairbrush. He cleared his throat before announcing, "You two could use some primping. Since your assignment has been terminated, you now have all the time in the world to make yourselves presentable."

I sniffed. "The War Relocation Authority hired me; you're in no position to fire me."

He raised his eyebrows and handed me an envelope. The return address stamped in the left-hand corner was from the WRA office in Los Angeles. Inside, typed on WRA letterhead, was a memo announcing my termination. He must have sent off one of his lackeys to Los Angeles the previous evening to retrieve this letter. Damn, he had outmaneuvered me.

He held up a handful of my negatives. "And these will remain with me."

Without understanding, I reached forward to take them, but he pulled back.

"No. See here?" He pointed at the edge of one of the negatives. *IMPOUNDED* was scrawled across the edges. "Your photos and negatives will remain with the army. The public will never see them."

Frozen, unable to breathe, I stood rooted to the lopsided step of our cabin, my brain unable to whir into action. The hairs on my arms rose despite the heat. If he had taken the pistol from his hip and aimed it at me, I doubt he could have stunned me more. I must have sagged under the shock of his announcement because suddenly Christina's arm was around my waist. I leaned into her.

"You can't do this," she spat at him.

He ignored her, squared his shoulders, and pointed at me. "*Your* work threatens to compromise the safety of America. You both must leave Lone Pine now."

"Is that a threat?" I croaked.

"Does it need to be?" He pointed to a jeep parked next to his own. "Sergeant Johnson is waiting for you in the jeep and will escort you back to your car and out of town," he said, turning to saunter back to the car waiting for him. "Godspeed," he added over his shoulder, the glee in his voice unmistakable.

I remained in the doorway. A deep exhaustion settled over me.

"I'll bet Paul can do something about this." The vehemence in Christina's voice surprised me.

I turned and reached for my suitcase on a stretcher next to the door. Holding it next to the small table between our beds, I swept everything—my travel clock, pill bottles, and a small notebook—into it. "This has never been his fight. Let's go home." The truth was that I could barely stand—barely even think—through the pain burning inside me. Despite all of my efforts, the government had betrayed me too many times. I'd made so many sacrifices but to what end? I needed my family.

CHAPTER 43

Once back in Berkeley, I worked the phones calling every-one I knew. Reporters, bureaucrats in Washington, local officials, board members from the university. I tried to get my impounded photos back. But no one could help. Instead I received new job offers from different government agencies, all eager to create images of how effective and strong the U.S. war machine was, but I committed myself to working near home so I could spend dinnertime with my family each evening.

The Office of War Information sent Ansel Adams and me to Richmond, an industrial town north of Oakland, to capture the factories churning out ships and war matériel around the clock. Men and women crowded into the boardinghouses, bunga-lows, and temporary housing, enticed by an endless supply of jobs. One afternoon I stood on a corner in the downtown area watching the flood of people pass me on the sidewalks. The smell of diesel filled the air. I studied facial expressions: how people stared at the ground; how they held their shoulders; how quickly they moved. Using the evidence of what I saw, I made up stories about them. *That gal's frown and the way she keeps touching her tightly curled hair—she's planning to break things off with her fella tonight. And that young man's hands balled into his pockets—he's just received a letter from home with news that his mama is ill.*

"You looking for just the right shot?"

I turned and found Ansel standing beside me, watching the crowds push past.

I shook my head. "The right shot is everywhere you look."

"Well then, where's your camera?"

"I'm just watching for now, trying to see."

He scratched the side of his neck. "I don't pretend to understand how you work."

I laughed. "You've got no imagination."

"If you say so," he said, smiling. "Anyway, I just packed up all my gear. Christina's waiting."

I followed him to where the car was parked in front of a row of boardinghouses, each with signs hanging in the windows advertising HOT BEDS in big red letters. With the factories running around the clock there was always someone who needed to sleep. Why not rent beds by the hour when you could fill them with different shifts of workers? A truck idled in the street, awaiting our parking spot, so I slid inside. Ansel revved the engine and we pulled away from the curb.

"Don't drive so fast!" I yelled.

He groaned, but it was six o'clock, shift-changing time, and the streets were clogged with workers leaving the factory from their day shifts as other workers headed to their night shifts. Never before had I seen so many different people—laborers, engineers, switchboard operators, clerks, and managers—packed into several city blocks. Such humanity! But the melee held no interest for Ansel. He liked the orderly process of photographing the industrial landscape of the port and factories—the cranes, the enormous ships, power lines, and the blocks of buildings. I liked contradictions, but even with the tensions that existed within this convergence of people and industry, my interest was waning. I'd been yanked around a few too many times by the government and my trust, my enthusiasm, had faded. I dared not throw my passion into this project, as I had so many others. Who knew when I'd be handed a pink slip?

After our stint in Richmond, the WRA hired Ansel to photograph Manzanar. And as I knew he would, his photographs highlighted the stark magnificence of the landscape and the beauty of the evacuees. Instead of photographing the guard tower, he managed to get inside one and photograph a sweeping view of the camp. At first, I'd been livid with him for being so compliant with the government's agenda. He faulted my criticism for being unpatriotic. At a stalemate, we proceeded as we always had: annoyed by each other's intent but respectful of each other's craft.

ON ONE OF my final trips for the Office of War Information, I reluctantly agreed to leave Berkeley and travel to North Carolina. There, in front of a filling station, I found a bunch of men, all white, wearing baseball uniforms for a local team. While I snapped several photos of the players, they mugged for the camera before heading off to play. In the background sat a Negro man, watching the shenanigans with a tense, unconvincing smile. After turning in my negatives, the OWI office transformed my photo into a propaganda poster by cropping the image. Only the white men grinned into the camera. Gone was the Negro. Gone was the stack of tires piled on the porch of the decrepit shop, the broken tools peppering the dusty yard, and the building's grubby and chipped clapboard siding. Ramshackle shops like it could be found along every road in the South, but the government edited this truth right out of the image. A message ran along the top of the poster: *This is America . . . Where a fellow can start on the home team and wind up in the big league.* My own caption, had I written one, would have said something far different, but I had fallen out of the times. No one cared about the small guy anymore. Everyone only wanted winners.

The war limped along toward its end. Newspapers described the daily deterioration in FDR's health. When he died in his beloved Warm Springs, both grief and relief coursed through me. And then my own health fell apart. Bleeding ulcers and a gallbladder disorder landed me in the hospital. I needed over twenty blood transfusions before my condition stabilized. Dan returned home only to vanish again. Five years passed. Hospitals, diagnoses, treatments. I couldn't register it all. Maynard died. Everything changed. Much of the world I'd known, explored, and loved vanished.

ONE EVENING ABOUT a year after Maynard's death, I opened the kitchen door to go out into the backyard and found Dan slumped against the side of the house, pale and gaunt, a feverish glint in his eyes. He smelled of sleepless nights, fear, and sickness. Kneeling next to him, I could feel the heat rising from his skin. I eased him to his feet, held his arm as he wobbled inside the house. Upstairs I helped him to undress and tucked him under the sheets of his bed, where he spent the next several weeks recuperating from fever.

One afternoon, he found me in the backyard on my knees, weeding some of the herb pots. Surprised to see him out of bed, I asked how he was feeling.

"Better," he said. He lowered himself to the ground next to me. "Thank you."

My hand, bulky in dirty cotton gardening gloves, stopped in midair. When was the last time he had thanked me for something?

Seeing he had my attention, he continued, "May I interview you? I have little to offer by way of gratitude, but I'd like to try."

I exhaled and dipped my hand deep into the loamy soil of the pot to ease a basil plant next to a clump of lemon verbena. When he had vanished over the years, we had often found him in the library, reading and writing. The idea of him exercising his creativity relieved me, but I feared for him too. He was so fragile, so sensitive to the opinions of others. I'd seen too many people wither and crumple under the pressures of producing art. Could he withstand the pains that creativity brought? Did he have the discipline? The tough skin? I was about to ask him all this, but stopped, inhaling the sharp tang of basil. It wasn't my place to ask. He had to try. "Of course," I said.

That moment marked the start of our tentative partnership. He earned five hundred dollars for writing the piece, the first honest money he had earned in his life. As he commenced on his new career, I resumed my own. At just past fifty years old, my ulcers still bothered me and my throat began hurting all of the time for reasons that perplexed my doctors. All of my weight loss from the last few years left me smaller and wizened, but somehow, I felt reinvigorated and ready for whatever came next.

Spring 1957
Berkeley, California

CHAPTER 44

Dorothea? Paul says you're leaving to teach your class soon, but I told him I'm sure you wouldn't mind seeing me."

I turned to find Imogen pushing open the screen door to my studio. She carried several bags and placed them on the floor while describing her bus ride over to the house. After arranging her possessions, she plunked down in a director's chair next to me, leaning forward to look at the photo I'd been examining. I attempted to block her view by sliding a nearby folder on top of it, but she stopped me.

"What are you working on?"

"Oh, an assignment for my students."

"Let me see."

I rolled my eyes at her, but let her take the photograph. "I've assigned my students to create a photo that they should title *Home.*"

Imogen said nothing and continued to study the photograph.

"I've been doing all of the assignments I give my students," I continue. "It keeps me fresh and makes things interesting."

Still, she said nothing. Just stared.

What would my students make of my photo? They were all so young. Smooth-skinned, thick-haired. Bright-eyed. They were clever and sure of themselves in the way of people who have never known real hunger, or worried about telegrams arriving with bad news, or feared that they could lose everything. They were a new generation and I envied them in many ways. But I was still unsure how much depth lay within them. They reminded me of white sugar, refined and sweet but without substance. Hopefully they would prove me wrong.

"This is home for you?" Imogen asked.

I nodded.

"You'll knock them sideways with this, you know. I expect they'll produce a slew of photos of windows and apartment doors. All predictable."

"I'm hoping they will surprise me." I'd taken to teaching this class at the California School of Fine Arts more than I expected. "Will it surprise you to know that I'm learning just as much as they do? And possibly even more."

"More than those rubes?"

"Well, the more I learn, I realize how little I know. I quite enjoy the feeling. Whoever said curiosity killed the cat had it all wrong. Curiosity is what gives that cat nine lives. Curiosity is the key to living creatively."

Imogen nodded slowly. "You never fail to impress me with everything you've got hidden away under the hood. I've said it once, I'll say it again: you're the toughest old lady I know."

"Well, then that makes two of us."

"We sure are." She laughed and raised her balding gray eyebrows. Her eyes twinkled behind the large circular lenses of her glasses. "Why, even my laugh is more of a cackle now. Maybe we're a pair of old witches. Our magic lies in conjuring images out of nothing. We could form a new camera club, make it more of a coven."

"A coven for creatives," I said, chuckling.

She placed the photo back on my work counter and we both settled into our chairs. Imogen's hair had gone almost completely white. Long wisps of it clouded around her face.

"I'm thinking of asking Dan to join me on a new assignment for *Life*."

"I thought Ireland was a debacle."

"It was no such thing." A couple years back, Dan and I had traveled together to Ireland's County Clare to complete a photo-essay for *Life*. I complained about how he drifted in and out of the project. He accused me of being too controlling. I threw up my hands and left him to spend his days sitting in pubs while I took photographs in the field. "Sure, we fought. Nearly every day, in fact. But we still met up every night for dinner. It was progress."

"Considering your history, I'd nominate you for a Nobel Peace Prize."

"Ha, I'd settle for sainthood."

"Wouldn't that be rich? The two of us, patron saints of nagging mothers." Imogen's raspy laughter ebbed and she placed one of her pale hands on my forearm. Veins fanned out underneath her thin skin like cobwebs. "But you know, you're doing well with him. You two have come a long way. For years, I worried you were going to lose him."

I rested my hand on hers. "Every day I still worry I may lose him."

We fell silent and our eyes traveled back to the photograph on my work counter. It showed my withered right foot, bending awkwardly to the side, pale, vulnerable, and imperfect. I wasn't one for self-portraits, but this one was different. All of these years I'd been looking for the gestures, the angles, the expressions that revealed a person. Well, here was my most telling feature in black and white. "I've had a recurring dream ever since I had polio. In it, I'd run, just run, faster and faster. It was the most joyous feeling, but then I'd awaken and it would all hit me. The grief, the anger, all of my sorrow over my foot."

"How often do you have the dream?"

"Once a month, maybe? More during times of stress."

Imogen clucked sympathetically.

"But here's the thing," I said, "I can't remember the last time I had it."

When I had contemplated this assignment, I'd mulled over what to produce for days. *Home.* What was home to me? I took the image of my foot one morning on a whim and realized its significance as I developed it. During all of my sixty-two years, I had never photographed my foot, never even thought about it. So, what changed?

I was tired of hiding it.

Dan and I sit at a table in a small room with a large, dusty file box in front of us.

"It's amazing this is still here. When I was in the army, I remember hearing about you going to Manzanar, but I'm not sure I really believed it," he says, shaking his head with a sadness that surprises me. He starts to remove the lid, but I place my hand on his forearm to stop him.

"There's something I didn't tell you."

Although it's only visible for a flash, Dan flinches as if to ward off a blow he thinks is coming.

"What?" It's the dejection in his voice that prompts me to take my hand off his arm and place it in my own lap while trying to steady myself. We're as fragile as we've ever been.

I freeze for a moment, unsure what to do next, but then I

reach into my pocketbook and take out the letter to hand it to him. The whiteness of the envelope is now scuffed. MoMA's return address now no longer glows. The edges are worn after three weeks of traveling inside my pockets and purse. "This arrived in the mail several weeks ago."

Puzzled, he frowns but takes the letter and reads it before looking at me, amazement bringing a boyish glow to his face. "Why didn't you say something? This is incredible. I can't believe you haven't told me yet."

I try to sound nonchalant, but my voice quivers as I say, "You're the first person who knows about it. Aside from the people at MoMA, of course."

"What? Why?" He looks at the letter again. "This is an honor—a retrospective show of your work. How many other photographers have had this? There can't be many." His voice is louder and he's shaking his head as he reviews the contents of the letter in disbelief. He puts it down and stares at me. "Wait, you haven't told Paul?"

"No." I can't explain how Paul's reaction will bring me little satisfaction. He's always believed in me. In fact, his confidence in me has been greater than my confidence in myself. If anything, he'll be annoyed it's taken this long for them to ask me.

"You'll do it, right?"

"Of course, but it's going to be a great deal of work. I'm going to need help. A lot of help."

He places the letter on the desk next to the file, folds his arms across his chest, and watches me. "Everyone will want to be a part of it."

I nod. "Dan, I asked you to come with me here because it's

your help that I want." I almost say it's his help that I want *most*, but I leave that off. I'm still cautious about putting too much out there.

"But Paul knows your work. Or Rondal . . . ? What about Imogen? They all know your art so much better than I do. They've been around you for years."

My heart hitches for a moment. *My art.* He says it so casually, so effortlessly that it brings tears to my eyes, but I blink them back. Having my work described as art still amazes me. After years of feeling on the outside of so many of my peers in photography, his words feel like a gift.

"Maybe if you get to know my art, you'll understand why I made the choices I made. Much of my work has been about starting a conversation. I'd like to think I've started conversations with many people over the years, but I need to have one with you. I know I've made choices that have hurt you, hurt all of you, I suppose, but you're the one who—" My throat feels raw from talking, and I stop and swallow, at a loss. Even though I've spent the last few weeks planning this conversation, I'm unsure how to proceed. "You and I have a complicated history. I don't regret my choices, but I'm sorry I hurt you."

His dark hair needs cutting and falls into his eyes. It blocks his expression from me, but I've learned to watch and wait. We steep in the silence of the room, and the warm smell of dry stale paper.

I point to the MoMA letter. "I want your help."

A thin, guarded smile creeps over his face, his expression reminiscent of Maynard. "Of course I'll work with you."

"You may change your mind once you see the piles and

piles of negatives, contact sheets, and prints to sort and inventory. It all may number in the tens of thousands. I've got some ideas of how I'll want to organize the work that's shown. And I'm sure the curator from MoMA who's in charge of the exhibit will have some ideas too. It may get difficult."

"I won't change my mind." He looks at his hands. "Thank you for asking me."

"Of course." Silence hangs between us, so I say briskly, "Now, should we see what's in here? I've been dreading seeing these photos. Everything during the war was so rushed. The files will be a mess."

While I catalog the many reasons I expect these photographs to disappoint me, Dan stands and lifts the cover off the file box, pulls out several smaller boxes, and sets one in front of us. I open it and feel a lump in my throat as photo by photo, Dan spreads them before me. The craggy mountains, the vast emptiness, the tense faces, confused and forlorn. Christina and I worked so quickly and under such stressful conditions, I was sure the photographs would be terrible.

But they're not.

"These will be important for the show," Dan says.

I shake my head. "No, the army still won't give me permission to make them public."

He opens his mouth and gestures wordlessly at the piles of photos in front of us. "But then why are we here?"

"I needed to see them once more."

He glances at me, alert to my use of *once more* but says nothing.

"When we get back, I have an appointment with a doctor

in the city. I've been losing weight. Look at me, I'm frailer than ever. There's something really wrong with me this time."

"Don't say that. You've been having health problems for the last twenty years."

"Exactly. That's how I know this time it's something different." I stop, trying to clear my throat, but my mouth is dry, every swallow a struggle. "The MoMA show offers me the opportunity to set the record straight on how I've viewed my career. No more government telling me what to do. This will be my vision of how the pieces of my career fit together. My evolution . . ."

"As an artist? Activist?"

"My evolution as a human with all of life's joys and sufferings. For me, it's been about finding connection through creativity." I bite my lip, thinking about all of the missed connections with the man who sits in front of me.

"Well, it's taken you long enough."

We both laugh and it feels good. Not good physically. A laugh can get my throat burning, I start coughing, and quickly, I'm a mess. But still, it's worth it. We haven't sat side by side and shared a genuine laugh over anything in so long that I want to stay in this little room forever. Instead we will leave soon, return to our hotel room in Georgetown. Then we will take the train up to New York City to meet with MoMA staff. I'll squeeze in a visit with my beloved Fronsie. Then, Dan and I will travel back to California to begin the long process of going through all of my negatives and prints. We'll throw many away, we'll gather others and begin curating this show. Imogen will weigh in with her many opinions. We will all argue over how the work should be organized and grouped. Everyone will believe this show represents the most important moments of my life, but it doesn't. The moments that profoundly shaped me happened when a camera was nowhere in sight: the feverish nights I spent fighting polio; the afternoon my father shut the front door behind him and left us forever; the morning Fronsie and I lost our life's savings to a pickpocket; the evening Maynard raised my foot to his lips and kissed it; the day I left Dan and John to be cared for by another family; the morning Paul first telephoned me.

This show is a collection of images, a view into the world as I've seen it. Although I'm quite certain I won't live to see it, Paul will. Dan and John will. My grandchildren will. My friends will. Each of them will look at these pictures and decide what they see. No one ever sees the same thing, and I've come to accept that and even hope for it. For me, art has never been recognition and what hangs on the walls of museums. Its significance lies in the act of creating it and letting it loose to find its own way in the world.

ACKNOWLEDGMENTS

Every day I'm amazed to be surrounded by such a wonderful group of supporters. Librarians, booksellers, book bloggers, bookstagrammers, and book club members—I'm grateful for all that you do to advocate reading. And thank you to the readers who find my books, take the time to read them, and encourage others to do so.

Thank you to my editor, Lucia Macro, for her enthusiasm and keen insight into this story. The entire team at William Morrow and HarperCollins worked tirelessly and patiently to bring this book into the world and I couldn't be more grateful for everyone's efforts. Thank you to Barbara Braun, my agent, who believed in this book from the first moment I mentioned Dorothea Lange's name. The rangers and librarians at FDR Presidential Library & Museum and the curatorial staff at the

Oakland Museum of California helped me to imagine Lange's world, and I'm indebted to them for their expertise and assistance. All errors are entirely my own.

Thank you to all of the early readers and supporters who helped in the making of this book: Jenny D. Williams, Renee Macalino Rutledge, Danya Kukafka, Devin Murphy, Chanel Cleeton, Ellen Dorr, Kelly Johnston, Kristie Berg, Kate Olson, Kourtney Dyson, Stacey Armand, Susanne Eckert, Paula Dowtin, Tamara Moats, Ray Wilson, Nancy Bowman, and my beloved colleagues and students at The Bush School. There's no better way to be held accountable for a deadline than to tell a room of high school students that you will do something.

I'm also always inspired and humbled by my community of friends who buoy me along with the stuff of daily life and then turn around and champion me as an author by coming out for my events, inviting me to book clubs, giving my books as gifts, and so much more. Thank you.

Finally, a heartfelt thank-you to my parents, brother, in-laws, and my daughters, Kate and Cookie. I couldn't have a more loving group of people in my corner. And a special thank-you to my husband, David, for always listening, laughing, and believing in me.

About the author

About the book

Insights,
Interviews
& More . . .

Meet Elise Hooper

Chris Landry Photography

A New Englander by birth, ELISE lives
with her husband and two young
daughters in Seattle, where she teaches
history and literature. *The Other Alcott*
was her first novel. ❧

A Note on Sources

Historical research was imperative to create a realistic portrayal of Dorothea Lange. First and foremost, I viewed the documentaries *Dorothea Lange: Grab a Hunk of Lightning; Child of Giants: My Journey with Maynard Dixon and Dorothea Lange; Maynard Dixon: Art and Spirit;* and *Maynard Dixon: To the Desert Again* many times to get a feel for Dorothea and the people closest to her. Suzanne Riess's oral histories with both Dorothea Lange and Paul Taylor were also critical for understanding how they viewed themselves and their work.

I relied upon Linda Gordon's excellent biography *Dorothea Lange: A Life Beyond Limits* for an assessment of this complicated woman that was both modern in its interpretation but grounded in careful research. Gordon was also kind enough to answer my questions over email. *Impounded: Dorothea Lange and the Censored Images of Japanese American Internment,* edited by Linda Gordon and Gary Y. Okihiro, was also essential to understanding Lange's artistic process and reaction to the evacuation and internment. My copy of Milton Meltzer's biography *Dorothea Lange: A Photographer's Life* proved to be invaluable toward creating a complete image of Lange and her world. Donald Hagerty's *Desert Dreams: The Art and Life of Maynard Dixon* allowed me to view beautiful color plates of Dixon's paintings and provided much-needed biographical information so I could better understand this man.

A Note on Sources *(continued)*

Some other important research sources include: *Group f.64* by Mary Street Alinder; *Everyone Had Cameras: Photography and Farmworkers in California, 1850–2000* by Richard Steven Street; *Restless Spirit* by Elizabeth Partridge; *Dorothea Lange: The Crucial Years* by Oliva María Rubio, Jack von Euw, and Sandra Phillips; *Dorothea Lange and the Documentary Tradition* by Karin Becker Ohrn; *California on the Breadlines* by Jan Goggans; *Imogen Cunningham: A Portrait* by Judy Dater; *Consuelo Kanaga: An American Photographer* by Barbara Head Millstein, William Maxwell, and Grace M. Mayer; and *The Worst Hard Time* by Timothy Egan. In addition, I found John Steinbeck's *The Grapes of Wrath* and his "Harvest Gypsies" articles important in providing evocative details and language of the era, as well as *Farewell to Manzanar* by Jeanne Wakatsuki Houston and James D. Houston for a primary account of life at Manzanar. Despite all of these resources, any mistakes I've made in this story belong entirely to me. ◞

A Conversation with Elise Hooper

Q: Why did you decide to write about Dorothea Lange?

A: After I finished writing *The Other Alcott*, I decided to be practical and find a new story set closer to home. I'd always found Oregon-born Imogen Cunningham's abstracted flower photographs to be beautiful and wanted to learn more about her. During my research, I discovered that her best friend, Dorothea Lange, had also been a pioneering photographer, although the women had very different views on the purpose of art and photography. When I learned Lange had photographed the internment of Japanese Americans and that these photos had been impounded due to their subversive points of view, I decided to shift my focus from Cunningham to her best friend, Lange. In the Pacific Northwest where I live, the internment's legacy is particularly relevant since many of Seattle's residents were forced to leave their homes and businesses after FDR issued Executive Order 9066. I wanted to know more about this woman who dared to believe the government was making an unconscionable mistake at a time when some Americans actively participated in discrimination against Japanese Americans or looked the other way.

Midway through writing this novel, the political climate of the United States shifted with the results of the 2016 presidential election. Women took to the streets in January 2017 to express many grievances over the direction of the nation's policies and values. This energy and rising political consciousness made me believe Dorothea Lange was more relevant than ever since she was a woman who had experienced a political awakening in her late thirties and acted on it. As a result of the worsening economic conditions in California and the breadlines threading down the sidewalk underneath her studio window in the 1930s, she became an activist for democratic values and social justice. Though she sometimes denied any political angle to her art, she often spoke about her desire for her work to prompt conversations about labor, social class, race, and the environment. Her awakening as an activist breathed new life into this project for me and made me more excited than ever to tell her story. ▶

A Conversation with Elise Hooper *(continued)*

Q: It's interesting that a woman who is best known for taking such poignant images of women and children had such a conflicted family life.

A: Dorothea's complex and seemingly contradictory feelings about motherhood fascinated me. Her own father abandoned her family when she was twelve, and this left her with a powerful sense of rejection. So deep was her hurt that she rarely spoke of it to anyone. In fact, it wasn't until after her death that Paul Taylor learned the truth of her father's absence in her life. Yet despite the anguish that her father's abandonment caused her, she fostered her own sons out during the Great Depression, a choice for which her children never forgave her.

No one faulted Maynard and Paul for not attending to their children, but people questioned Dorothea's choices and this criticism stung her. Her ambitions and talents put her at odds with many of the norms of the time when few women were the breadwinners in their families. So, although she sometimes felt guilty and selfish, she persevered with work she believed was necessary and important. This tension between ambition and parental duty drew me into her story. While I wrote this story, there were times when I struggled to make sense of Dorothea's choices to foster her children out to strangers, especially after she married Paul Taylor, but I had to remember that in the early 1900s commonly accepted ideas about child-rearing and child development differed from today. People tended to emphasize the resilience of children and overlook their emotional needs. In some ways Dorothea reminded me of another woman from the same era who is celebrated for her humanitarian work: Eleanor Roosevelt. Like Lange, Roosevelt had a fraught relationship with her children stemming largely from her active political career outside the home. The fact is that women who chose to pursue careers in the early 1900s lacked role models, mentors, affordable childcare options, and other supports that are now widely accepted to be critical to balancing motherhood with work outside the home.

Q: Given that Lange carried such psychic scars surrounding her own father's abandonment, how did she justify her choices?

A: To be clear, there were some major differences between Dorothea's father's departure and her decision to entrust her boys to someone else's care. She didn't fully understand the causes for her father's departure until years later when her mother provided more context. He had fled his wife and children in 1907 because he was in trouble with the law as a result of some unsavory business practices. Dorothea's mother hid it from her children, but she continued to meet with him in secret until they finalized their divorce on the grounds of abandonment in 1919.

Dorothea believed she was keeping her boys safe from a life of poverty that was unfolding around her on San Francisco's streets and beyond. The 1930s represent an era of hard times that almost defies comprehension to us today. People were desperate to feed their families. Orphanages were packed with children whose mothers and fathers couldn't support them. Families disintegrated. It was a period of vulnerability and danger for many children. So, while Dan and John never forgave Dorothea for leaving them with strangers, she felt she was doing the best she could to keep them cared for and safe.

Q: Why didn't Maynard or Paul do more to help with the care of their children?

A: The expectations of the time were that women tended to children. It was that simple. Regardless of social class, it never appears to have entered into people's consideration that men could have played a hands-on role with raising their sons and daughters. And this trickled down to the children of this generation. Interviews with Dan Dixon when he was an adult reflect that his hurt feelings were aimed mostly at his mother. He never seemed to hold Maynard accountable in the same way that he blamed his mother for leaving him. ▶

Q: What happened to Dorothea's two closest friends?

A: Fronsie's life is mostly fictionalized in this novel. After she helped to settle Dorothea in the photography studio on Sutter Street, she mostly disappears from Lange's biographies with the exception of reappearing as a guest at Dorothea's wedding to Maynard. Based on a note by Paul Taylor in the transcript of Dorothea's oral history with Suzanne Riess, it seems Fronsie ended up living in Los Angeles during the 1960s.

Imogen led a brilliant career as a photographer and lived until 1976, when she died at ninety-three years of age. She produced many books and mentored other photographers, and her work has been exhibited around the world.

Q: What happened to Dorothea Lange's impounded photos of the Japanese American internment?

A: The army impounded the images until after the war and then they were quietly placed in the National Archives. In 1972, Richard Conrat, one of Lange's assistants, published some of them when he produced *Executive Order 9066* for the UCLA Asian American Studies Center. It wasn't until 2006 when Linda Gordon and Gary Y. Okihiro published their book *Impounded* that the photos received widespread attention. In 2017, the Franklin D. Roosevelt Presidential Library and Museum produced an exhibit entitled *Images of Internment: The Incarceration of Japanese Americans During World War II* to commemorate the seventy-fifth anniversary of FDR's infamous Executive Order 9066. I visited the show and viewed photographs by Dorothea Lange, Ansel Adams, and others. Seventy-five years later these photos are still relevant and serve as a powerful reminder of the importance of maintaining civil liberties in our democracy.

Reading Group Guide

1. Dorothea Lange's photographs are recognized by many Americans, but few know much about the woman who created the images. How did your understanding of Lange and her art change as you were reading *Learning to See*?

2. In interviews Dorothea spoke about how profoundly polio changed her. During the course of her life, she viewed her right foot as both a curse and a gift. Discuss how you see her disability shaping her relationships, her career, and her view of the world.

3. During the early 1900s, laws to ensure safety, education, health, and care for children were still evolving into the many protections that exist now. Dorothea's decision to foster her children out to another family during the 1930s often stuns people today. It also caused a long-standing rift between her and Dan and John. Discuss her reasons for making this choice. Do you empathize with Dorothea's actions? How do you feel about Dan's reactions?

4. People who knew Dorothea well often describe her as difficult and controlling. Do you think that this is merited or an unfair characterization? What adjectives would you use to describe her?

5. Dorothea Lange was a trailblazing woman artist at a time when the art world was dominated by men. How did she navigate the complexities of these relationships and build a successful career? Are these challenges still relevant today?

6. Dorothea enjoys some important friendships with other women over the course of her life, including Fronsie Ahlstrom, Imogen Cunningham, Consuelo Kanaga, and Frida Kahlo. Reflect on how these relationships impacted her.

7. Before traveling with Paul Taylor, Dorothea had almost no experience with rural life. Discuss the many ways in which her exposure to farmers and agriculture caused her views to change.

8. Dorothea's relationships with Maynard and Paul reveal very different dynamics. In some ways both marriages reveal many gender role expectations of the 1920s and '30s, and in other ▶

ways the marriages defy conventions of the time. Discuss how the men she loved shaped how she viewed herself.

9. When Maynard and Dorothea end their marriage, he asks her if she thinks they would have stayed together if not for the Great Depression. How did the extreme economic downturn affect their relationship? Do you think their marriage would have survived during stabler, happier times?

10. Many of Dorothea's photographs are available to be viewed through the National Archives. After you spend some time looking at them, which of her photographs appeal to you the most? Why? Before reading this novel, do you think you would have selected a different one? ∾

Dorothea Lange Photos

Commonly referred to as *Migrant Mother*, this photo is Lange's most famous image. Her original caption reads: *Destitute Pea Pickers in California. Mother of Seven.* ca. 1936. Courtesy of the Franklin D. Roosevelt Library and Museum, Hyde Park, New York

Dorothea Lange in California, February 1936. Library of Congress, Prints & Photographs Division, FSA/OWI Collection, LC-USF34 -002392-E

Often referred to as *Ditched, Stalled, and Stranded*, this is another one of Lange's iconic photos of Dust Bowl migrants from 1936. The original captions reads: *Once a Missouri farmer, now a migratory farm laborer on the Pacific Coast. California.* Library of Congress, Prints & Photographs Division, FSA/OWI Collection, LC-USF347-002470-E

This photo of Lange's is not referenced in this novel, but it demonstrates Lange's keen eye for contradictions. *Towards Los Angeles, California* dates from March 1937. Library of Congress, Prints & Photographs Division, FSA/OWI Collection, LC-USF34 -016317-E

Dorothea Lange Photos *(continued)*

This photo is not referenced directly in this novel, but reflects Lange's ability to capture the racial and economic power dynamic between these figures through composition. Her original caption reads: *Plantation overseer. Mississippi Delta, near Clarksdale, Mississippi.* June 1936. Library of Congress, Prints & Photographs Division, FSA/OWI Collection, LC-USF34-009596-C

This is one of Lange's many portraits of migrant children. Her original caption does little to disguise her frustration with the poverty and helplessness she was witnessing. It reads: *On Arizona Highway 87, south of Chandler. Maricopa County, Arizona. Children in a democracy. A migratory family living in a trailer in an open field. No sanitation, no water. They came from Amarillo, Texas. Pulled bolls near Amarillo, picked cotton near Roswell, New Mexico, and in Arizona. Plan to return to Amarillo at close of cotton picking season for work on WPA.* 1940. National Archives Photo Number 83-G-44034

Dorothea's original caption reads: *San Francisco, California. Flag of allegiance pledge at Raphael Weill Public School, Geary and Buchanan Streets. Children in families of Japanese ancestry were evacuated with their parents and will be housed for the duration in War Relocation Authority centers where facilities will be provided for them to continue their education.* 1940–45. National Archives Photo Number 210-G-A78

Dorothea's original caption reads: *Florin, Sacramento County, California. A soldier and his mother in a strawberry field. The soldier, age 23, volunteered July 10, 1941, and is stationed at Camp Leonard Wood, Missouri. He was furloughed to help his mother and family prepare for their evacuation. He is the youngest of six children, two of them volunteers in United States Army. The mother, age 53, came from Japan 37 years ago. Her husband died 21 years ago, leaving her to raise six children.* She worked in a strawberry basket factory until last year when her children leased three acres of strawberries "so she wouldn't have to work for somebody else." The family is Buddhist. This is her youngest son. Her second son is in the army stationed at Fort Bliss. 453 families are to be evacuated from this area. 1942–45. National Archives Photo Number 210-G-A584

This is a portrait of Dave Tatsuno, one of Paul Taylor's former students from the University of California, and his father in front of the department store the family owned. According to an interview Lange did with Suzanne Riess for the Regional Oral History Office, one of Dave's children died of exposure while the family was incarcerated in the Topaz War Relocation Center in central Utah. The original caption reads: *San Francisco, California. Dave Tatsuno and his father, merchants of Japanese ancestry in San Francisco prior to evacuation.* 1942–45. National Archives Photo Number 210-G-C450

Dorothea's original caption reads: *San Bruno, California. Near view of horse-stall, left from the days when what is now Tanforan Assembly center, was the famous Tanforan Race Track. Most of these stalls have been converted into family living quarters for Japanese.* 1942–45. National Archives Photo Number 210-G-C630

Dorothea Lange Photos *(continued)*

Dorothea's original caption reads: *Manzanar Relocation Center, Manzanar, California. Street scene of barrack homes at this War Relocation Authority Center. The windstorm has subsided and the dust has settled.* 1942–45. National Archives Photo Number 210-G-C840

This photo is one of a series that Lange took of women producing camouflage nets for the army. To avoid running afoul of the Geneva Convention's laws against using prisoners of war in forced labor, the army claimed that the women were volunteers. The army also made sure these women were American citizens to avoid any conflicts over labeling the workers as POWs. Despite the army's efforts to claim the work was legal, Lange doubted this work was truly voluntary. Her original caption reads: *Manzanar Relocation Center, Manzanar, California. Making camouflage nets for the War Department. This is one of several War and Navy Department projects carried on by persons of Japanese ancestry in relocation centers.* 1942–45. National Archives Photo Number 210-G-C815